The Vision of a Mother's Heart

The Vision of a Mother's Heart

Katherine Hinchee Purdy

Vision of a Mother's Heart
by Kathy Hinchee Purdy
2nd Edition
© 2015 by Katherine Hinchee Purdy. All rights reserved.
K. H. Purdy Books

Unless otherwise noted, all Scriptures are taken from the *King James Version* of the Bible.

ISBN 13: 978-1-5152-9847-2
ISBN 10: 1-5152-9847-7
Library of Congress Catalog Card Number: 2010913525

I would like to dedicate this story in memory of my grandmother Isabel; her late siblings, Eugene, Curtis, Margaret, Sylvia, James Calvin, Avil, and Ralph; and their parents. I also would like to honor her brother Raymond.

Although I wrote this story as fiction, my grandmother's family experienced most of the events described in this novel. A special thanks to my mother, Barbara R. Hinchee, Dad Hinchee, and Aunt Sandra Baker for keeping the family stories alive.

I also would like to thank my husband, John Purdy, for his patience and support while helping me to "get out of the boat" and write the story the Lord impressed upon my heart.

In addition, I would like to thank my Dad, Charles McReynolds, for encouraging me and helping me get *The Vision of a Mother's Heart* published.

A special thanks to all of my friends and family who read the manuscript, critiqued it, and offered encouragement along the way.

The title of this book is from a song title. Thank you, Abigail Miller, for giving me permission to use your song title "The Vision of a Mother's Heart." To hear this song and other beautiful music, please go to www. abigailmiller.com.

Train up a child in the way he should go: and when he is old, he will not depart from it.

—Proverbs 22:6

Contents

Family Tree for William "Avil" Greene

Individual Facts:
Name: Greene, William ("Avil")
Birth: 1869 in Cave Spring, District of Roanoke Co. , VA

Shared Facts: Kelly, Martha Ann Elizabeth ("Lizzie")
Birth: 1887
Marriage: January 10, 1905

Children:
Greene, Eugene R.
Greene, William ("Curtis")
Greene, Katherine ("Isabel")
Greene, Margaret Louise ("Maggie")
Greene, Sylvia Mae (called "Sylvie" by her siblings)
Greene, James Calvin ("Jimmy")
Greene, Billy Jackson
Greene, Ralph M.
Greene, Raymond M.

Shared Facts: Thomas, Cora Lee
Marriage: 30 Dec 1886

Children:
Greene, Cleo
Greene, James ("Jim")
Greene, Frederick ("Fred")
Greene, Malinda ("Lindy") Elizabeth

Chapter 1

Home

ISABEL CLOSED HER eyes and pumped her feet to make the old, wooden swing reach high. She felt the warm breeze on her face as she soared higher. Butterflies fluttered in her tummy as the swing returned to the ground and then went up again. She loved that feeling—the scary sense of falling and exhilaration at the same time. Isabel had heard about rides at the fair that could produce the same sensation, but she could not imagine anything as wonderful as the old, wooden swing that hung from the limb of her favorite climbing tree. Besides, nothing could replace the musical quality of the squeak of the rope as she swung back and forth.

She breathed deeply, taking in the fresh air and smiling as the scent of freshly baked bread reached her nostrils. She remembered how she had made the last two loaves rising on the cupboard with her own hands, feeling pride in her newfound skill soar with the motion of the swing. Isabel closed her eyes as she raced higher from the earth so she could hear everything happening around her. She listened to her younger sisters, Maggie, 7, and Sylvia, 5, as they pretended to be grown ladies having a tea party. She listened as three-year-old Jimmy tried to convince the family's growing puppy, Sandy, to pull him around in his wagon. She heard ten-month-old Billy squeal with delight at some new discovery he had made in the dirt by the porch.

> Bringing in the sheaves, bringing in the sheaves,
> we shall come rejoicing, bringing in the sheaves.

Isabel smiled as Mama's rich voice drifted in the air as she finished hanging the last piece of laundry on the clothesline at the side of the house. Isabel loved hearing Mama sing.

Each familiar sound was like music to Isabel. She breathed deeply and pumped higher, as if she could reach the sky, humming Mama's song. Here, no one teased her about her old-fashioned clothes or called her "that poor girl from the Apple Tree Farm" as she had once heard Arlene Mason call her at school. At home, no one told her she was not trying because she could not understand fractions.

How well she remembered the day Mama helped her understand by demonstrating in the kitchen how to use fractions in cooking. Measuring the flour and sugar was fun, but it was dividing the portions among the plates in their very large family that helped her truly understand. Isabel smiled as she thought about the hot corn bread dripping with country butter as she followed Mama's instructions: "Cut the corn bread cake in half. Now cut in into quarters. Now let's cut each slice once more, and we will have just enough for Papa and each of my children."

"What about you, Mama, there will not be enough for you to have a slice," Isabel said.

Mama smiled and picked up her potholders and pulled out a second cast iron skillet from the oven. "Don't worry; I made two. Papa and your brothers will want seconds, as usual," Mama said with her gentle laugh that almost sounded melodious.

Isabel was not afraid Mama would scold her when she made a mistake; Mama encouraged her to try again until she got it right. When she was with Mama, Isabel even felt like she was just as smart and pretty as the other girls in their small community were.

"Hold your head high and speak clearly, Isabel," Mama would say. "You are a Greene; be proud of who you are."

Isabel's heart swelled with the rising of the swing as she remembered Mama telling her this very thing earlier in the day. School was to begin soon, and Isabel felt sick as she thought about the beginning of a new school year. She already knew many of the girls in her class were planning to wear store-bought clothes in the latest fashion. The only store-bought items Isabel had to wear were new shoes. Isabel closed her eyes tightly to shut out the memory of last year and focused instead on the three new dresses Mama had made by hand of fabric she'd bought from the remnant table. Isabel knew the other girls would snicker when she walked in, because it happened every year. They knew she wore handmade clothes.

She still could hear Arlene Mason's voice making fun of her last year. "Look at Isabel Greene," Arlene said when Isabel stepped inside for the first day of school. "Her dress is made from the same fabric as Mother's kitchen curtains. Wouldn't that make her a window?" The other girls snickered as Isabel walked past, and she could feel their eyes upon her the rest of the day.

The sound of an automobile pulling into the yard interrupted Isabel's thoughts and abruptly brought her back to the present. Suddenly the sun did not shine as brightly and Isabel's world did not feel as warm and cheerful. She opened her eyes in time to see Papa and her two older brothers getting out of Papa's "Tin Lizzie" as he called his Model T Ford. She watched as thirteen-year-old Eugene stepped out of the passenger side of the automobile. Isabel smiled as she thought how Eugene probably had tried to convince Papa to let him drive home, but obviously, Papa had refused. It had become a routine with father and son since Papa brought the car home two months ago. Eleven-year-old Curtis bolted out of the back seat and ran into the house in search of some treasure in his room.

Papa stepped slowly from the driver's side of the car, stretching his long legs as he ran his fingers through his full gray hair. As he did, their eyes met, and he said, "Isabel, why aren't you helping your mama?" Papa's deep bass voice called her to attention. "A girl your age should not be fritting the time away swinging when there's work to do. You are nine-years-old now; you are not a little child anymore." He reached out to slow the swing for his eldest daughter.

Isabel was in the habit of jumping out of the swing mid-air, and her mother often feared Isabel would injure herself. She shaded her eyes and looked up as far as her neck would allow, staring directly into Papa's piercing blue eyes before politely replying, "Yes, Papa." Isabel tried to hold back hot tears from her eyes. "Thank you, Papa. I'll go inside and help Mama now. She could have told Papa she had been helping Mama since daybreak, but she was sure Papa would consider her comment to be "sass," so she held her tongue as she headed for the cozy two-story house.

She met a surprised Mama at the back door.

"Isabel, I thought you were going to play until I called you for lunch." Then before Isabel could answer, Mama turned to Papa. "Isabel has been helping me all morning baking bread, and then she helped with the laundry after she made all the beds. If I don't insist that Isabel go outside to play, she will stay in the house and work all day," Mama added with a note of pride mixed with a hint of reproof, obviously for Isabel's benefit.

"What's wrong with that?" Papa said. "A child should work to earn her keep."

"Oh, Avil, you are a child only once and for such a short time." Mama added with conviction, "It's important to enjoy one's childhood in order to have a healthy adulthood. Besides, she needs fresh air and exercise."

"Horse feathers!" Papa said. "When I was a boy, childhood ended when you learned to walk and talk. Boys were expected to learn a trade, and girls were expected to learn how to keep house, cook, and sew. It has been that way for thousands of years, and I don't see any need for that to change now. Progress my eye! Hard work builds character; everyone knows that."

That kind of thinking makes for grumpy adults, but Isabel bite her lip to keep from speaking her mind. She picked up the corner of the cloth covering the rising dough; punched the soft, fragrant bread; and covered it to rise again. "This is the third batch of bread this morning. The one in the oven should be done soon," she whispered. "I wish we could afford to buy store bought bread like everybody else," but she knew better than to suggest this to Papa and Mama.

"If we cannot make it from the items we have in the pantry or grow it in the garden, we'll go without." That's what Papa always said when one of the children wanted something from the general store. Of course, living on a farm had its benefits. But Isabel often tired of churning butter and gathering eggs in chilly mornings; although, she had recently passed that chore to her sister Maggie, who seemed to enjoy the routine. Isabel was delighted to get rid of the black and blue marks on her arms that the cranky hens who did not want to let go of their eggs caused. For some reason, Maggie did not have a problem with the hens.

"Isabel, will you please see if the bread is ready to come out of the oven?" Mama asked. Then she continued her conversation with Papa while peeling vegetables to put in stew for dinner.

"Yes, Mama." Isabel wrapped dish towels around her hands and arms before opening the heavy, black oven door and pulling out the fragrant loaves.

Just as she sat the loaves on the windowsill to cool, the back screen door clapped and little Jimmy's voice announced his arrival. "I'm hungrier than a big ol' bear. Can I have sum thin' to eat?"

"*May I* have something to eat?" Mama corrected.

"Sure," Jimmy said. "You can have sum thin' too."

Mama smiled, dipped a napkin into water, washed Jimmy's face and hands, sliced and buttered a piece of freshly baked bread, and then placed it on a calico napkin. "Go and sit down on the back stoop with this cup of cold milk," she told him before she continued talking to Papa.

"Don't you see, Avil? It's just like little Jimmy here. He depends upon us for everything, and that is how God planned it," Mama said, her eyes shining and her voice becoming more excited as she continued. "I've never thought of this before, but have you ever wondered why God placed Adam and Eve in a beautiful garden with everything they needed already provided for them?"

"No," Papa said, "I've never thought about it."

"Maybe He wanted them to know His provision and mercy. He thought of them as His children, just as we provide for our children. When we knew our first child was on the way, remember how we fixed up his room with little lambs and farm animals on the freshly painted walls?"

"I remember," Papa said. "Of course, you started making baby clothes a month after we were married. Eugene did not make an appearance until four years later, so he was well set for clothes and blankets."

Isabel smiled as she lifted her ten-month-old brother, Billy, from his high chair and carried him to the sink to clean him up after his messy bread crust snack. Hoping her parents would not notice her presence, she moved quietly to hear more of this interesting conversation. She worked the pump handle and caught water in the white washbasin used for washing hands.

Mama looked at her, smiled, and then turned back to Papa. "Our children are to learn to trust God through us. They learn that God provides for them through Papa and Mama. He protects them through Papa and Mama. He loves them through Papa and Mama. Through us, they must learn security and love so that when they are old, they will trust Him to provide for them, trust Him enough to know right from wrong, and repent of their sin and turn to God."

Mama stopped long enough to take a deep breath and look at Papa for confirmation that what she was saying was true. "Perhaps I am not saying this right..." her voice faded, and she dropped her eyes as if to pray for the right words.

"I think what you are telling me is that God placed Adam and Eve in the garden for a time to have a secure place to learn to trust Him, to walk and talk with Him, and to just 'be' with Him," Papa said. "Is that correct?"

"Yes."

"So, in other words, children should be children and not little adults. They should play, trust their parents to provide for their needs, and spend time with us. They should enjoy their childhood. Is this how you wish to raise our children?"

"Yes," Mama said, without the confidence she held previously.

"Then how are we to teach our children responsibility? Are we to neglect to discipline our children? Should we allow them to do anything they wish?"

"Of course not," Mama said. "Discipline is important. Remember, God set boundaries in the Garden of Eden. He allowed them to eat from every tree except from the Tree of Knowledge of Good and Evil. Discipline is necessary because of Adam's sin. 'As in Adam, all have sinned and fall short of the glory of God.' Because of Adam's sin, we suffer. That is why Jesus died on the cross to pay the penalty. Part of Adam and Eve's punishment was that they had to leave the Garden of Eden. Adam would have to work hard from then on, Eve would suffer pain in childbearing, and we all bear the curse of their sin. They disobeyed God, and He punished them appropriately.

When children disobey their parents, we must discipline them so they will know how to obey those in authority. They must know how to behave. It's up to us to teach them; God gave us the responsibility.

Children should have chores appropriate to their size and age, but we should not expect them to work all day, and they shouldn't be expected to do the job of an adult. They are children. In the Garden of Eden, Adam was to name the animals and 'dress the garden' Both sound like pleasant chores, not 'sweat of the brow' kind of work. We should give children work meant for small hands and discipline them with love, keeping in mind the age and size of the child." Mama picked up the broom to sweep the kitchen.

Papa conceded, scratching his chin as he turned to walk outside. Before he opened the screen door, he turned to Isabel, "Listen to your mama, Isabel; you can learn a lot from her."

Mama won. However, she did not seem to bask in her glory. Isabel beamed a smile at Mama. She had never known Mama to speak so boldly to Papa, and Isabel was proud. "Thank you, Mama."

"You are welcome, Dear." Mama turned as if to go into the other room but changed her mind and stepped closer to Isabel, gently lifting her long, wavy, brown hair from her shoulder, smoothing it out, and letting it fall over one shoulder. Then Mama decided against the look and braided it slowly as she talked, pulling ribbons from her apron pocket. "Your hair is so beautiful, Dear. Have I ever told you that when you were born, you had tiny blonde ringlets?" Mama asked as she ran her fingers through Isabel's long hair. "It stayed blonde until you were about seven years old, and each year, it got darker."

"I know," Isabel said impatiently.

"Well," Mama said, "when you were outside on the swing and the sunlight your hair, it looked as red as Grandma Isabella's."

"It did?" Isabel asked as she reached for a strand of hair to examine it.

"Yes," Mama said with a chuckle. "The only color your hair hasn't turned is gray, and it will be a long time before you have to worry about that!"

"Isabel, did you know that your papa was raised by his elderly grandparents?" Mama deftly braided her daughter's thick tresses.

Isabel started to nod her head, but as she did, it pulled her hair in the process. "I think so. He talks about it sometimes, but I don't really listen," she said.

"Hmmm, I thought as much." Mama laughed. "I could have made the same confession about my father when I was your age. Anyway, your papa was born just a few years after the War Between the States, and things were not going well here in the South. Families who once were well to do suddenly found themselves without money, and some even lost their homes because of high taxes placed on houses and land. Of course, many loved ones died in the war. Did you know Papa's grandparents lost three sons in one month? Two of the boys died on the same day on the same battlefield. It was a dark time in our history. Anyway, your papa had to live with his grandparents, who apparently had forgotten what it was like to be a little boy. They treated him as if he were a little adult and expected him to work like a man. This is why he expects so much of his children. He didn't have a happy childhood. He did not get to play or even go to school."

"Papa didn't go to school?" Isabel asked as she twisted around to see Mama's face, pulling her hair again in the process.

"No, Dear," Mama answered as she patted Isabel's hair, "Papa did not go to school. Now be still while I finish your hair and the story."

"Yes, Mama," Isabel said. "Uncle Mitt went to school, didn't he? He is a preacher. Why didn't Papa get to go?"

"Well," Mama said, "your uncle was raised by his parents and Papa by their grandparents. You see, his parents could not take care of both children; their mama was not strong enough. I suppose his grandparents did not see the need to send him to school. He was taught to work on the farm, make barrels, and work as a blacksmith—like his grandfather and every generation of Greene men who stepped foot in America in the early 1700s. Can you imagine little Jimmy working in the field or trying to make a barrel like Papa?" Mama paused. "Will you remember this and try to be patient with your papa, Isabel? Can you do that?"

Isabel looked at Mama with tears in her blue eyes as she envisioned little Jimmy with his wavy blond hair plastered to his head with sweat and dirt and his little hands bruised, blistered, and bleeding as he tried to do the work of a grown man. It broke her heart to think of it. "I will try, Mama. I promise."

Chapter 2

Mystery

"IF PAPA DOESN'T show understanding to his family," Isabel muttered, "why should we try to understand him?"

Isabel's tirade had begun when Papa came in from the far fields early Monday morning just as she was hanging clothes on the clothesline.

"Hi, Papa," she said. She smiled at him and then fastened the wooden peg onto the line, securing a bright, white sheet.

"Go inside, Gal, and take the children with you," he said as he crept studied ground.

"But, Papa, I haven't finished hanging up the laundry yet," Isabel said.

"Do as I say, *now!*"

Isabel turned to pick up the basket, but Papa instructed her to leave it, so she picked up Billy and herded her younger siblings into the house. Isabel heard voices behind her and turned to see Eugene and Curtis coming out of the barn, where they had been cleaning the stalls.

"What's wrong, Papa?" Eugene asked as he neared the door where Papa was standing.

"Did you make these footprints, boy?" Papa asked.

"What footprints are those, Papa?"

Isabel watched Eugene through the open window as he stooped down to get a closer look and then pressed his foot into the ground as if matching his shoe against the print.

Eugene stood up. "I don't think so, Papa, my feet aren't that big yet. Besides, it looks like whoever made that print has a hole in his shoe. See the mark over there?"

Isabel watched Papa nod in agreement as he crept along the path down the hill to the road and back again. Curiosity almost got the best of her, and yet she couldn't get past the harsh way Papa had spoken to her for apparently no reason. Her heart was broken.

"What are we looking at?"

Isabel nearly jumped at the sound of Mama's voice and moved aside so she could see. "Papa sent us inside, and he's looking at something on the ground," Isabel said, excitement and fear mounting in her voice.

"Did he say why he wanted you inside?"

The children shook their heads and jumped away from the window as Papa looked their way.

"Well, don't you worry," Mama said. She reached down and picked up Billy, smoothing Jimmy's hair as she moved past him. "Go into the kitchen, and have a leftover biscuit with apple butter and milk. Isabel, will you see to that, Dear?"

"Yes, Mama," Isabel said. She took Jimmy by the hand and led him into the kitchen while straining to listen to any conversation that would explain Papa's peculiar behavior. She didn't have to wait for long, however, as Papa's voice boomed through the house when Mama opened the front room door.

"Lizzie, go inside and stay there," Papa said. "I do not want to see you or any of the children outside until I resolve this, so take these boys with you."

"Eugene, Curtis, come inside and have a biscuit in the kitchen with the rest," Mama said. Isabel could hear fear in her Mama's voice—fear and tears. And that suddenly chased away any thoughts of apple butter or buttermilk or anything she previously looked forward to sharing with her family.

Curtis and Eugene stomped into the kitchen, refusing to take a seat at the table when invited. They stood by the back door, looking out the window, instead.

"What's he looking for anyway?" Curtis asked as he pushed his hair out of his face and jerked open the back door, threatening to step outside.

"I'm not sure what he is looking *for*," Eugene said, "but what he is looking *at* are footprints in the path from the road to the door. He is trying to tell which prints are ours and which are not and to whom they belong," Eugene said. "It looks like someone with a hole in his shoes was here, but I did not see anyone. Did any of you?"

Isabel followed her brother's gaze around the room as everyone shook their heads and seemed surprised at the news. Then his gaze rested upon Curtis. Isabel realized he knew something he did not want to share by the way he avoided looking at Eugene. He looked past their older brother and even gazed above his head.

"What is it, Curtis?" Isabel asked. "Who was here, and why is Papa so upset?

"I don't know nothing," Curtis said and reached past her for an apple. Then he bolted for the steps leading to his bedroom, but Mama's voice stopped him in his tracks.

"Son, if you know what is happening," Mama said, "I wish you would tell me—now!"

"Ah, Mama," Curtis said, "I didn't do anything wrong. I promise."

"I did not think you did, Son. Just tell me what you know—why is Papa so upset?" Mama's voice quivered as she spoke, and Isabel noticed that all color had drained from Mama's face. She was not accustomed to Papa speaking to her so sharply, and Isabel's stomach constricted at the memory.

"Papa found footprints on the path from the road to the house that do not belong to us, and he is trying to figure who they belong to," Eugene said, "and I think Curtis knows."

"You snitch!" Curtis said to his brother with his hand drawn into a fist. His face turned deep red as he realized he had spoken in his mother's presence.

"Curtis Greene," Mama said, "I never want to hear you use words like that ever again. I have never had to wash your mouth out with soap, but I will if I hear you using the devil's language. We do not speak to each other that way in this house, or ever! Now, your reaction leads me to believe that you do indeed know about the stranger in our yard, and yet this does not explain why Papa is so upset.

"Now, Curtis, you have never lied to me, so do not start now. I want you to answer me truthfully. Did you see who was in our yard? If you promised not to tell us, you may nod," Mama said as she looked directly into her son's blue eyes.

Curtis nodded and then put his head into his hands as if he had betrayed a friend.

"OK, Mama said, "was this someone we know?"

Curtis shook his head.

"Was it a hobo in need of food?" Mama walked around the kitchen as she spoke, in anticipation of Curtis's answer. He merely nodded his head. "Good," Mama said, "I thought as much. Now, Son, I want you to tell me the truth. Did you give him something to eat?"

Curtis raised his head with a jerk, "How did you know?"

"I know you, Son. Ever since you were Jimmy's age, it broke your heart to see anyone or anything go hungry or cold. God has given you a heart of compassion, and there is nothing wrong with that, unless you lie to us about it. If you had asked, I would have fixed a nice plate of hot food for him to eat, you know."

The screen door slammed, and Maggie jumped. Papa's footsteps grew louder as he stepped closer to the kitchen. Isabel could not stop herself from giggling because Maggie had startled so easily.

"It is alright, Papa," Mama said as Papa entered the room. "The stranger was a hungry soul who was down on his luck. That is all. He is not here now, is he, Son?" She directed her question to Curtis, who stood rigid against the door frame, as if awaiting judgment.

"No," Papa said, "it is not alright. No one is to leave this house until I say so, and under no circumstances are you to open the door to anyone."

"But, Papa, what about the insurance man? He always collects premiums on the first Tuesday of every month," Mama said.

"Insurance man be hanged. Don't open the door to that crook or anyone…and I mean it," Papa said.

The three youngest children cried. Sylvia and Jimmy hid behind their Mama's skirts, and Maggie ran upstairs to her room.

"Now, where is that child going?" Papa took long strides across the room to the foot of the stairs, as if to call her back, and then turned, as if he had changed his mind, and looked to Mama for an answer.

"You are frightening the children, Papa. We have never seen you this way before. Please let them go to their rooms so you can tell me what our danger is."

Isabel followed her brothers up the steps with little Billy in her arms. She strained her ears to hear Papa's explanation, but they had moved into the front of the house, where the children would not be able to hear. Papa's strange behavior would remain a mystery.

Papa left in the Model T about thirty minutes later, instructing Eugene, "You are in charge as man of the house until I get back; keep a lookout."

Mama called the children to lunch, but she didn't talk about the earlier incident except to say they would be in the house for a while and must "behave accordingly."

Isabel tried to sleep that night, but she could not because of Papa's pacing. The night air seemed alive with excitement; every noise outside seemed to be footsteps and every movement of tree limbs convinced Isabel that someone was behind the tree just waiting to break in.

"Isabel," Maggie whispered, "are you awake?"

"Yeah."

"Do you hear that noise?" Maggie said.

"What noise?"

"*That* noise," Maggie said. She sat up in bed.

"Oh," Isabel said with feigned confidence, "that's just a tree limb brushing against the side of the house."

"Are you sure?" Maggie asked.

"Uh-huh."

"What if someone is trying to break into the house?" Maggie said. She was on the verge of tears.

"Why would anyone want to break into *our* house?" Isabel whispered.

"I don't know. Papa is afraid of something, isn't he?"

"I guess so." Isabel turned toward her sister, causing the springs in the bed to squeak loudly.

"I thought someone was going to kill us earlier," Maggie said.

Isabel could feel the mattress move as the springs squeaked again, indicating that Maggie was turning toward her in anticipation of a long conversation.

"Maybe," Isabel said. "He did seem very upset, and since we don't have anything worth stealing, I can't imagine why someone would want to break in.

The next two days were tense in the Greene household, especially since Papa did not allow the children outside except to go to the "necessary" and do chores. Even then, he insisted they not go out alone. Otherwise, Papa said everyone must stay inside the rest of the time.

Finally, Eugene reached his breaking point and strolled toward the back door.

"Eugene," Mama said, "where do you think you are going?"

"I'm going out to see why Papa is keeping us prisoner in our own home," he said. "Do you need anything from the general store?"

"No, Eugene," Mama said. "Obey your papa; he knows what is best."

"I'll be back," he said over his shoulder and stepped through the door. "Don't worry."

Mama and the children spent the next hour on their knees, praying for Eugene and Papa and about whatever had caused him to suddenly be fearful for their safety.

Eugene finally returned with newspapers under his arm. He pulled a sack of penny candy from his pocket and handed it to Maggie. "Here, Maggie, take the children into the front parlor, and give them each a piece of candy."

"Eugene," Mama said, "what is going on? What did you find out?"

"It is all right here in the Roanoke newspaper," Eugene said. He tossed the paper onto the kitchen table. The headline read, "Roanoke Woman Killed in Home by Unknown Intruder."

Three days ago, Miss Lottie Gorman was fatally stabbed in her home by an unknown intruder. A neighbor reported that she saw a strange man run out of the house and hop onto a train heading east at the tracks behind the murdered woman's house.

"So that is why your papa was worried," Mama said. "I am glad he didn't tell me. The intruder could have gotten off the train to find food, and since ours would have been the first house he came to, we could have been victims."

"That was the paper from two days ago," Eugene said. "This is yesterday's paper." He pulled the paper from under his coat. The headline screamed: "Man Arrested for the Stabbing of Roanoke Woman."

"He was almost in West Virginia when the police caught up with him," Eugene read.

"But I thought the paper said he was on a train heading east," Mama said.

"This article says the man heading east was the wrong man. He was just a man down on his luck who was trying to get to Lynchburg to find a job. He just happened to be in the wrong place at the wrong time. The man they caught had blood on his shirt and was driving an old truck that broke down along the side of the road near Bluefield. The paper said they are sure they caught the right man because he confessed."

"How terrible for something like this to happen so close to home," Mama said, "but I am glad they caught the murderer."

"We wouldn't have felt like prisoners if Papa had told us what had happened," Curtis said. He opened the door to allow fresh air and sunshine into the room.

"He didn't want to frighten us," Mama said. She shooed a fly away from the pie cooling on the table.

"If he would just learn to read, we could have gone outside yesterday," Eugene said. "The children have been frightened to death."

"How did Papa know about it anyway?" Isabel asked. She helped open the windows by the table, and a soft breeze filled the room.

"Papa heard the men talking about it at the store, but he hasn't been back since," Eugene answered. "Apparently, Mr. Meadows either did not know about it, or he did not think to tell Papa that the man had been caught. If Papa would let us get a newspaper, we would have known the danger had past," Eugene ran his fingers through his hair.

"Newspapers cost money," Mama said. She poured a glass of water from the pitcher and placed it in front of Eugene. "You are all out of breath. Drink this."

"I ran all the way home so that I could give you the news." Eugene picked up the glass of cool water and gulped it down. "At least we know it is safe."

"Who said so?" Papa asked as he entered the room and dumped an armful of firewood into the wood box.

"It says so right here in the newspaper, Papa," Eugene said as he pointed to the headline. "Would you like me to read it to you?" Papa nodded, and Eugene read the gruesome details.

Isabel covered her ears and left the room, wishing she had not heard the report. It was just too awful for words, but she felt comforted that Papa was looking out for his family, and she basked in the feeling of safety—even though they had suffered from fright and been penned in a whole day for nothing.

"Papa," Isabel said at supper that night, "I'm sorry I complained about staying inside. Thank you for watching out for us."

"That's what a papa is for," he said with a crooked smile.

Isabel wondered if he still was concerned or if he had heard Eugene's complaint that he could not read.

"Tonight in family altar," Mama said, "we must all thank the Lord for watching over us and for giving us a caring papa."

"Eugene," Papa said as he sopped up gravy with the last piece of biscuit on his plate, "maybe we can afford to buy a newspaper every now and then if you don't mind reading it to the family. We might be missing out on some important news we should know about."

"OK, Papa," Eugene said. "I'll be glad to."

"Me too," Curtis said as he helped himself to a large slice of pie.

Mama rushed to the stove to make sure the kettle had plenty of water for washing dishes. Isabel wondered if she did so to hide tears of joy.

Chapter 3

Honor Thy Father

—⚉—

EUGENE SWEPT THE kitchen as Isabel washed and Mama dried the dishes.

"Make sure you take the rag rugs outside," Mama said. "Shake them, and let them air out while you finish sweeping the entire floor, Son." She placed plates carefully into the cupboard.

Isabel smiled at her brother's sigh as he carried the rugs outside to shake them. He resumed sweeping near Isabel when he returned.

Isabel watched for Mama to cross the room before whispering to Eugene. "I told ya Mama would know if you sweep the dirt under the rugs."

Eugene swept the broom over Isabel's feet in response.

"Ouch." Isabel said and stuck her tongue out at her brother.

"What happened, Isabel?" Mama said with concern.

"Nothing, Mama…the water's too hot," she lied.

"I see," Mama said. "Add some cool water to lower the temperature—but not too much. The water must be hot in order to get the dishes completely clean."

"Yes, Mama."

"Eugene," Mama said as he swept the dirt onto the dustpan. "I wanted to talk to you about something you said this afternoon."

Eugene put the tools away and then pulled out a chair for Mama and one for himself as Isabel dried the dishpan.

"Earlier today," Mama started as she traced the design on the tablecloth before looking directly at her son, "you said that this incident wouldn't have happened if Papa would learn how to read."

"Yes, ma'am," Eugene said.

"Well, Son, even though things would be easier for your papa if he had learned to read, your words were dishonoring to him, and you need to make it right."

"But, Mama," Eugene said, "Papa didn't hear me."

"That doesn't matter, Son. You dishonored him with your words and in your heart," Mama said. "Do you remember what the Bible says?"

"It says to 'Honor thy father and thy mother,'" Eugene said. "But how do I do that?"

"Well, Son, you could apologize to him, but I am afraid that would cause him more pain and embarrassment, since he wasn't there to hear your remark. We don't want Papa to know you think less of him because of his inability to read. He already feels bad that he lacks the ability; though he would never mention it."

"Then what should I do?" Eugene asked, his voice rising.

"You could do something for Papa he doesn't expect. Pray about it, and I am sure you will think of something." Mama hung up her dishtowel and turned to leave the room. She stopped and turned to look Eugene in the eye. "You do still need to apologize to Papa for disobeying his order to stay in the house," she said as sternly as her soft voice would allow.

"What are you gonna do, Eugene?" Isabel asked after Mama left. Curtis entered the kitchen and took a cookie from the cookie jar.

Eugene shrugged his shoulders and then turned to his brother. "Curtis Greene, I just swept that floor for Mama, and if you drop one crumb on my clean floor, you're gonna sweep it up."

Curtis popped the entire cookie into his mouth with a grin and held his hands up to Eugene as if to show that there were no crumbs. "What are you gonna do about what?" Curtis asked as he reached for another cookie.

"Apologizing and honoring Papa," Eugene said. He stepped out to retrieve the rugs, but he returned holding a pair of muddy boots. "I know just what to do," he said. "Curtis, go upstairs and get the shoe shine kit, will ya?" he then turned to Isabel, "Where is the old scrub brush that Mama uses to clean the floor when we track mud inside?"

"It's in the pantry with the scrub bucket," Isabel said. "Why?"

"Well, you know how Papa prides himself on having a clean, starched shirt and shiny shoes every time he goes out?"

"Yeah," Isabel said. His plan became clear. "Shouldn't you wait to clean Papa's boots until after the mud dries? That way, you will only have to brush the mud away."

"I could, but I'm not. I think I can find a good, sturdy stick to use to get rid of the mud, and then I'll scrub them before I polish them to a spit shine. I might even shine the soles."

"I don't think I would do that," Isabel said. "He might track shoe polish into the house instead of mud."

"Where is Papa, anyway?"

"I saw him go upstairs to bed. You know what he always says, 'Early to bed, early to rise makes a man wealthy and wise.'" Isabel smiled at her brother. "If that saying is true, Papa should be a millionaire."

Just then, Curtis entered the room with the shoeshine kit in one hand and his arms filled with all of the family's shoes. "I know it isn't Saturday night, but Papa will be surprised if we polish all of the shoes tonight instead—without him asking first." He dumped the shoes in front of Eugene.

"Hey," Eugene said, "I was just gonna clean Papa's shoes."

"I'll help," Curtis said. He picked up a shoe and began working.

Isabel gazed at the star from her bedroom window and wondered what she could do to honor Mama and Papa. The answer came to her as she closed her eyes to sleep. "I will get up before Mama and go blueberry picking to fix blueberry pancakes for breakfast." Isabel whispered, "Boy, will Mama and Papa be surprised. But what if I oversleep and don't get up before Mama?"

Isabel counted every hour, according to the coo-coo clock in the front parlor. "Oh, be quiet you kooky bird," Isabel whispered. "Wow, 3:00 A.M., and I still haven't been to sleep yet." Her eyes finally closed, and she gave into sleep.

The rooster sounded the alarm outside of Isabel's window just before sunrise, and she jumped into her clothes, pulled the covers over her pillow, and then tiptoed downstairs and toward the back door.

"Good," she whispered as she passed the cold cook stove, "Mama and Papa aren't up yet."

She cringed as the back door squeaked, and then she closed the screen door gently as she stepped into the predawn light. Something bumped against her legs, causing her to jump and immediately put her hand over her mouth to stifle the scream that threatened to escape. "Sandy," she whispered to the friendly dog, whose tail wagged back and forth, "don't scare me like that. Come on, you may help pick blueberries. Besides, you'll scare away any snakes or bears that might be eating their breakfast in our berry patch." Isabel stopped by the barn and chose two buckets for her chore.

When Isabel returned forty-minutes later, the buckets were full, as was the bonnet Mama always insisted Isabel wear whenever she went outside. She smiled as she quoted Mama's words to Sandy, "You must take care of your skin, Isabel; we don't want your skin to get tough and tanned because it will cause wrinkles and dark spots when you are my age. If you take care and cover up, you will have a beautiful peaches-and-cream complexion." Isabel wrinkled her nose and popped a blueberry into her mouth as she headed back to the kitchen.

When she opened the kitchen door, Papa jumped. "What are you doing up at this hour, child?" He lit a match and placed it into the stove, blowing on it to make sure it caught on.

"I thought I would surprise Mama and make breakfast this morning." She smiled as she brought the buckets of berries into the house.

"Whoo-ee," Papa said as he lifted the buckets into the sink so she could wash them. "These look good." He snatched a couple and popped them into his mouth. "Boy, your mama will be surprised. Is this a special day?"

"Nope," Isabel smiled, revealing her blue teeth and tongue. "I just wanted to honor Mama, that's all."

"She'll be surprised alright." He grinned. "It looks like you have enough there to also make a cobbler and a jar of jam to boot."

Isabel beamed at Papa's exaggeration, as this was his way of giving praise.

Soon the fire in the stove was roaring and ready for cooking. Isabel washed the berries and set them in Mama's large colander to drain. She checked Mama's recipe card and pulled out the rest of the ingredients for her meal. Papa shaved at the kitchen mirror before heading outside to do his chores.

Isabel measured out the flour, baking powder, salt, and sugar without spilling too much on the worktable and the floor. In a larger bowl, she beat the eggs until they were light and fluffy and then added buttermilk and grease from the crock above the stove. Then she dropped in the dry ingredients one by one, until they were mixed well, being careful not to over stir as Mama had taught her—she wanted fluffy pancakes and not tough ones. Finally, she folded in a generous amount of berries as the skillet heated on the stove.

The first cake burned on the bottom. "The first one always burns." She carried the offending cake to the back door and fed it to the thankful dog.

By the time Mama came downstairs, Isabel had the coffee perking at the back of the stove, bacon frying in another skillet, and a platter of pancakes sitting in the warming oven as she poured the remaining batter into her skillet.

"I smelled something wonderful and thought I was dreaming," Mama said. She crossed the room and embraced Isabel, who was covered with pancake batter, splattered grease, and flour that was smudged across her cheek. "Oh, Isabel," Mama continued, "this is the most wonderful surprise I have ever had. Did you have anything to do with this, Papa?"

Papa splashed Old Spice on his face and wiped his hands on the white towel hanging by his mirror and shelf. "Nope," he said, "she came up with it all on her own. She went out before sunup, picked berries all by herself, and did everything except light the stove and lift the heavy skillets. You raised her right, Mama." He grinned as he picked up the shaving bowl and headed to the back door to pour the water on Mama's rosebush. "Well, I'll be," he said as he stopped short, "Mama, come out here, and look at this."

Mama and Isabel rushed to the screened-in porch and smiled at the long row of shiny shoes and boots, including Papa's work boots, which had been muddy the night before.

"Gal, did you do this too?"

"No, Papa," Isabel said. She heard footsteps on the back stairs. Eugene and Curtis entered the and stopped short, keeping their eyes on the toes of their boots.

"Boys, did you do this?" Both boys shuffled their feet and nodded their heads as they studied the floor with red faces. "I've never seen a better job of shining shoes; you even cleaned the mud off my old work boots." Papa rushed to the boys and ruffled their hair. "Why'd you do it?"

"Your boots were muddy," Eugene said. "You do things for us all the time...like keeping us safe. I'm sorry I disobeyed you, Papa."

"Yeah," Curtis said. "It feels good to see what a difference it makes when you clean something that is so dirty."

Everyone laughed, but Isabel noticed Papa and Mama had tears in their eyes.

"Hey," Sylvia said from the kitchen, "what's burning?"

"Oh no, my pancakes!" Isabel said. "Come on, everybody, breakfast is ready."

The room came alive with laughter as the family feasted on the meal intended to honor their parents.

"Thank you, Isabel," Mama said before she took her last bite of pancake. "This is the best surprise I have ever had—and it isn't even my birthday. Whatever possessed you to get up so early and fix breakfast?"

"You're welcome." Isabel smiled. "I just did it because I love you and you do so much for us." Isabel looked around the table at her siblings, who were devouring pancakes, and wondered if she should make more.

Then Billy, who spoke with his mouth full of food, answered her question. "Yummy Is'bel; more please."

"Me too," Jimmy said.

"Don't get up, Isabel," Mama said. She pushed her chair back, "I'll fix another batch; you sit still and eat."

"Yes, ma'am," Isabel said. She rubbed a piece of bacon into the sweet maple syrup before popping it into her mouth.

"Sylvie and I will clean up the kitchen, Mama," Maggie said. "We want to help too."

"My goodness," Mama said. "Papa, we have truly been blessed with wonderful children."

Papa nodded his agreement with a smile as he reached for the platter of breakfast meat and took his third helping of sausage and bacon. "Gal," he said as he turned to Isabel, "you're a right good cook."

"Thank you, Papa."

Chapter 4

The Singing

THERE WERE TIMES when Isabel found it easy to see the little boy in Papa. One such occasion was at the local church singing, in which the whole community seemed to be involved. Papa seemed particularly anxious for the singing to take place.

"Papa," Isabel said at breakfast the morning prior to the event, "you are acting just the way I feel on Christmas Eve."

Papa stood up and walked over to the stove, where Mama was stirring a large pot of grits for breakfast and gave Isabel a wink before speaking. "Well now, Gal, when I see your mama back up on that platform with that squeeze box in her hands, playing hymns to bless everybody's hearts, it will be Christmas, New Year's, birthdays, and our anniversary all rolled into one."

"Oh, Papa" Mama said with a shy smile, "sit down and eat your breakfast before it gets cold. You know grits are not good for anything but glue once they get cold. Besides, it may still be too soon for me to be away from little Billy, you know. He may need his Mama, and I am a Mama first; although, I am looking forward to playing music for the Lord again." She smiled.

The morning of the singing dawned bright and beautiful, and everything flowed smoothly. The evening finally arrived, and Papa ushered his family into the church in record time. He was wearing the biggest smile Isabel had ever seen under his handlebar mustache.

Isabel stopped in the middle of the aisle to listen to the cheerful gospel tune Mrs. Thomas was playing on the piano. Her brothers bumped into her, as she suddenly had stopped leading them to an empty pew.

"Mrs. Thomas makes that piano sing," she said. "Sorry, I just had to stop and listen."

"Well, don't do it again," Curtis said. Mama took the lead into the row and placed her Bible on the seat, shifting Billy in her arms as he waved at people in the room.

"Are ya' nervous Mama?" Isabel whispered. Her own tummy would be filled with fluttering butterflies if she were the one expected to sing and play in front of the gathering crowd.

"Well, not so much nervous playing for our friends and loved ones as I am that Billy will cry when he sees me up there. I am afraid it is too soon for me to be away from him. Besides, I don't know if my voice is in shape to sing in public yet either. I haven't practiced, really, and we must give the Lord our very best."

"You practice all the time, Mama. You sing when you hang up the laundry, wash dishes, sweep the floors, and especially when you rock Billy and Jimmy too. If that isn't practice, what is? Don't forget about our family Bible time; we sing then too."

Mama smiled and gave Isabel a hug before rushing up to the platform to meet with her brothers, who were beginning to play with Mrs. Thomas on the piano. Before stepping onto the steps to the platform, Mama turned to Isabel. "Thank you, Isabel, your words encouraged me. Keep an eye on your little brother, OK? Keep him at the back of the church until I come down. Perhaps he will not see me up on the platform."

Isabel nodded and put a protective hand on her brother's back. "You are getting heavy, Billy, but I'm holding you while Mama plays and sings, okay?" Then she turned so that he could see the group of children playing at the opposite side of the church and not be tempted to cry for Mama and ruin her opportunity to serve the Lord with her music.

It had been over a year since Mama had played, and she obviously missed it. Isabel smiled as she watched the toe tapping and hand clapping among even the most serious members. Smiles lighted every face, except the faces on the platform. Mama and her brothers, who were singing and playing their instruments, looked to Isabel as if their faces held no expressions at all. In fact, they were completely serious. Yet, they were singing and playing better and with more feeling than Isabel ever had witnessed. How could that be the case? She began to sway side to side with the music. As she did, Billy swayed with her.

"Mama! I want Mama!" Billy said.

The singing came to a sudden halt. Billy continued to scream with his arms outstretched towards the platform. For a terrible moment, Isabel thought he was going to jump out of her arms, and he probably would have if someone had not jumped up and pushed him back into her arms just in time. Papa came to the rescue, Aunt Jenny came to the rescue, and ten ladies came to Isabel's aid, but Billy would not be consoled; no one would do. No one would do but Mama. Isabel turned toward the door to take the child outside and across the yard to the Sunday school building, but she noticed the sky was dark and thunder rolled in the distance.

Now, to make matters worse, Jimmy chimed in and the two seemed to be having a contest to see who could cry the loudest, and all other babies in the house joined them.

Mama stopped playing immediately, and with a red face, she smiled weakly at the congregation to apologize. "I'm sorry, but as you see, my baby needs his mama."

"She's done spoiled that child," a woman whispered. Isabel wished to correct her, but with Billy screaming, she already had her hands full.

Uncle Ron tried to help by playing "Rock-A-Bye-Baby" and singing the lyrics gently to calm the little ones. Isabel thought it was working too, until he got to the part about the falling cradle and a little girl began crying and started the whole thing over again. At that point, the pastor finally called for a fifteen-minute cookie and punch break.

After the break, Mr. Webb, the song director, approached the pulpit. "Greater is He that is in you than he that is in the world," he quoted. "The enemy may have some power, but there is power, power, power, *power* in the blood of the Lamb. Let us stand together and sing with joy 'There Is Power in the Blood.' Make the rafters sing as we add four powers."

The crowd smiled, stood in one accord, and began to sing:

Would you be free from the burden of sin? There is power in the blood, power in the blood…"

During the break, Mama had put Jimmy and Billy into their pajamas, and now she let the small children lie on quilts on the church floor as she sat with them. They sat like little angels until they finally fell asleep, watching Mama's foot tap to the music.

Isabel thought the singing was the most glorious she ever had heard, even if Mama did not get to participate. Isabel's favorite group, the Criner/Thomas quartet, sang uplifting songs about heaven, and a little girl with long, red hair sang "Jesus Loves Me." There were at least ten people or groups who sang multiple songs, and then the pastor preached a powerful sermon on heaven. Isabel could almost see the streets of gold and the crystal sea.

"Just think," she told Maggie on the way home, "Grammy Isabella is there, and we will get to see her and spend all the time with her we want."

"Yes," Maggie said, "but the best part is that Jesus is there."

Isabel and Maggie snuggled under a quilt in the back of the hay wagon with Sylvia and their brothers while Mama shared the wooden seat behind the farm horses with Papa. Isabel sniffed the sweet hay and was about to drift off to sleep when she heard Papa chuckle.

"Well, Mama," he said, "I guess tonight was like Christmas after all. There you were looking beautiful, making beautiful music for everyone, when suddenly there was a lot of confusion with children all around the room screaming, and you are the only person in the building who could calm them down. It's just like our house at Christmas…and every day of the week, come to think of it."

Mama laughed, but Isabel noticed hers was not as hearty as Papa's was.

"Isn't it sad, though, Papa, that Satan will use the most precious to Jesus, the little children, to break the spirit of worship," Mama said. "Did you notice what we were singing when Billy began screaming? We were singing 'Nothing but the Blood of Jesus.' I couldn't help but wonder about that."

"What do you mean?" Papa asked.

"Well," Mama said, "if someone in the congregation was thinking about his sin and how he needs Jesus to wash it away, what better time for the devil to distract him?"

Curtis sat up in the wagon as if he had been stuck with a pin. "Mama, do ya really think it works that way? Is there really spiritual warfare like it talks about in the Bible?"

"Yes, Curtis," Mama said. "It really works that way, just as the Bible says."

"Mama, I want to ask Jesus to be my Savior. I believe Christ died on the cross for my sin and rose from the grave. Do you think the devil was trying to keep me from being saved?"

"Yes, Curtis," Mama said, "I think that is quite possible. Do you want to receive Christ as your Savior now?"

"Yes, ma'am. I didn't pray out loud, but I already asked Jesus to forgive me for my sin and asked Him to save me," Curtis said. "Does that count?"

"Oh, yes, Son," Mama said as she turned and caressed Curtis's hand. The Bible says to believe on the Lord Jesus Christ and you will be saved and no one or nothing can take you away from Him."

"It's what we've been praying for, Son," Papa said as he urged the horses forward. "Let's hurry home and give a prayer of thanksgiving!"

"That's swell!" Eugene said as he patted his brother on the shoulder. "Now we're brothers in Christ too!"

Isabel turned and looked toward the night sky, watching the clouds opening to reveal the moon and a few silvery stars. She began to wonder what lay beyond them. *Is heaven just beyond the stars? Is the street actually paved with gold and the walls jasper? What does jasper look like, anyway?* She fell asleep as she pondered these thoughts; yet the most important question of all remained unanswered for her: what about Jesus?

Chapter 5

Woman's Work

ISABEL SMILED AS she watched Mama trying to blow a long ringlet of hair out of her face. Isabel always had admired the way her mother's hair curled around her face when it was damp or humid. Today was both.

Isabel carefully removed the hot jars of tomatoes from the boiling water. "This is the last jar, Mama," she said. She carefully placed the sealed jar on the table.

"That's fine," Mama said. She pushed one more blanched tomato into a jar. "I think we have enough here for five more jars, and then we will be done."

Isabel looked around the room in disbelief. Everywhere she turned, she could see tomatoes or jars of tomatoes. "Fifty-five quarts of tomatoes," Isabel said. "What will we do with them all?"

Mama smiled and wiped her hands on her now soiled apron. "God certainly blessed us with an abundance of tomatoes this year, didn't He? We will store them in the cellar and give thanks to the Lord. Tomorrow we shall help Mrs. Meadows with her canning. As for our crop, we will share our harvest with unfortunate friends and family who will not have a good harvest this year. We still have kraut to make, and in a few weeks, we will have beans to string, snap, and can. We also planted many potatoes and yams, which will be ready to harvest in the fall. We will fill our bins to the brim. This winter we shall not have to worry about food for our family. We are truly blessed. Now, let's finish our canning so we can have supper on the table when Papa gets home."

"Is Papa going to market this Saturday?" Isabel asked.

"Yes, Dear, you know Papa goes to market every Saturday when we have produce to sell." Mama wiped off the newly canned jars of tomatoes and sat them in a box for Eugene to carry downstairs to the cellar.

"Do you think he would let me go with him this time?"

Mama blew hair out of her face. "You know Papa says the market is no place for little girls—he'll be much too busy to watch after you. With all those people hawking their wares; wagons, horses, automobiles, and the streetcar going back and forth; and the lure of the music coming from the American Legion building, it's just too tempting for you. Don't get me started on the muddy streets; you'd think they would pave that street."

"But, Mama, I'm not little anymore—Papa said so. I could help Papa sell the vegetables. Maybe we even could sell some of the tomatoes we just canned…"

"I don't think so," Mama said. "People will buy bushels of tomatoes to can for themselves…at least, we hope so."

"I know," Isabel said with excitement building in her voice, "I could tell them that for an extra twenty-five cents, they can have a quart of tomatoes to put into their stew for dinner *tonight*. Some people may have decided that they don't want to take the time to can tomatoes this year, but if they see how good they look, they might change their minds. Maybe we could even bake some pies to take with us. People get hungry when they're selling and shopping."

"People take their lunches in picnic baskets," Mama said.

"When they get a look at your blueberry pies, their mouths will water, and they'll just have to buy a piece."

"Just a slice?" Mama asked.

"A penny a slice or a pie for a dime," Isabel said. "I'll help ya bake the pies."

"Hmmm," Mama said. "That just might work. I'll talk to Papa about it later. However, you may want to reconsider the price. It will need to cover the ingredients, the pie pan, and a penny or two for profit. The pie pans cost at least two cents apiece at the thrift store."

Isabel and Mama worked silently the rest of the afternoon. Isabel hoped Mama was thinking of the pies they needed to bake for Saturday to sell at the market. *That's four days away.* Isabel thought of the excitement of going with Papa to the Roanoke City Market and then started wishing she could stay home with Mama in the fall and not go to school. Her thoughts were interrupted as the screen door squeaked on its hinges. Papa entered the room with a large, wooden object in his hands.

"Avil," Mama said, "you startled me. I didn't expect you home so early."

Papa grinned, removed his hat, and hung it on the rack by the kitchen door. "I finished early today. Besides, I have a surprise for you."

"Why, Papa, what is that?" Mama asked. She walked to the sink pump to wash her hands.

"This, my dear lady, is for you," Papa said. He placed the large box on the only empty spot on the floor. "Mrs. Ransom didn't have any cash and asked if she could pay me with this. We had an agreement from the beginning. I was to fix her roof for one used sewing machine."

"A sewing machine?" Mama said. She ran her hand over the smooth, brown wood of the case. Her blue eyes sparkled. Her cheeks flushed. And as Isabel looked at the curls framing Mama's round face, Isabel thought she had the loveliest mother in Virginia.

Mama cried. Isabel did too and wiped her eyes with the corner of her apron.

"How could Mrs. Ransom give away her wonderful sewing machine, with four daughters to sew for?" Mama asked. "Papa, you didn't talk her into this, did you?"

"No, Lizzie," Papa said, "'twas her idea. I asked her if she was sure she wanted to give it away, and she said she has never been surer of anything in her life. Don't know what she meant by that." He rubbed his chin. "I asked her if she got a new one, but she said she did not intend to do any more sewing, ever. I didn't press the issue any; I just thanked her and put the machine in the back of the wagon. She said she will come by mid-morning tomorrow to show you how to use it."

"Please open it for me, Papa," Mama said. Her eyes shined.

Isabel watched as Papa opened the wooden lid and pulled up the sewing machine. It was in a lovely cabinet, with a large, black, iron peddle underneath.

Mama ran her fingers along the sleek, black sewing machine and the elegant, gold letters spelling the name of the company that had manufactured it. "It's the most beautiful machine I have ever seen," Mama said. She pulled a handkerchief from her pocket.

"I hope it will make up for my buying the automobile last month instead of the new clothes you wanted for the children," Papa said. He hung his head low.

"I have already forgiven you for that," Mama said. She kissed Papa softly on his cheek. "Thank you, this is a wonderful surprise."

Papa grabbed Mama and waltzed her around, causing Isabel to giggle and blush at her parents' display of affection. Finally, Mama broke away and patted her hair into place before turning to Isabel.

"Just think of all the lovely garments I can make now. It will not take any time at all to make school clothes for all of you. I can make some new curtains for the kitchen too. And think of the hours of fun we will have sewing, Isabel. I will teach you and Maggie to sew. Sylvia is still too young, but I will teach her too when she gets older. Would you like that?"

It wasn't Isabel's idea of fun. She turned away to keep Mama from reading the expression on her face "Yes, Mama," Isabel lied. "I think I will like that." *Maybe sewing on a machine will be more fun than hand sewing,* she told herself. *If Mama wants me to sew, I'll do my best. Maybe learning to sew will be an adventure, and I know it will please Mama.*

"I will clean up the kitchen, Mama," Isabel said. "Why don't you wipe the dust off the new machine?"

"Thank you," Mama said. She set to work polishing her new toy and no doubt, dreaming of future projects she would complete. Mama hummed the tune to one of her favorite hymns as she worked.

"Only Mama can make work seem like fun," Isabel said to Eugene, who had followed Papa into the kitchen.

Mrs. Ransom arrived the following morning, bringing with her a beautiful hatbox filled with spools of thread, bobbins, ribbons, and other sewing notions she thought Mama would find useful. It was like every holiday on the calendar all rolled into one in the Greene household that morning. Everyone was interested in the contents of the hatbox and the workings of the marvelous machine.

Three-year-old Jimmy was especially fascinated with the foot pedal and the needle that bobbed up and down. Mama prevented a disaster many times by grabbing his hand just in time, before the needle pierced his skin.

"Jimmy Greene," Mama finally said, "go outside this instant, and do not come back into the house until I put the machine away. I'll call you when it is time to come back inside."

"But I want to see how it works," Jimmy said.

"Outside, *now*." Mama shooed the disappointed boy out of the house and locked the screen door.

He was devastated. Mama never had sent him outside as punishment before. Nor had she ever raised her voice.

"I'll go outside with Jimmy, Mama," Isabel said. She lifted the door hook from the eye on the door frame. She knew that Maggie would tell her all about the machine in minute detail later. *Maggie enjoys sewing.*

"Oh, just think of all the wonderful things we will make together, Maggie." Mama's voice drifted through the open window, and Isabel heard every word as she pulled Jimmy's wagon away from the house. "We will make dresses and skirts for you girls and pants and shirts for the boys. I will show you how to make buttonholes on the machine. It is much faster than doing it by hand…" Isabel never had heard Mama's voice so animated before, and it was comforting to know that Papa had done something to make her so happy.

After dinner, Mama sat at the machine, sewing and singing, which brought a smile to everyone's face except Jimmy's. He was still banned from the fascinating machine.

"Curtis," Mama said, looking up from her sewing, "would you please take your younger brothers outside and help them find lightning bugs? I would ask Eugene, but he's helping Papa in the barn. We have some old canning jars under the sink you may use. Be sure to add holes in the lid."

"Sure, Mama," he said as he laid his guitar aside to race with Jimmy and Billy into the kitchen.

After the screen door clapped shut, Mama turned to Isabel, Sylvia, and Maggie. "Now," she said, "we may get started on something to cheer up Jimmy. I thought we would use this wonderful brown fabric to make gingerbread men for him and Billy. I have already drawn the boys on the fabric. I need you to cut them out for me. I will sew them on the machine, and then you can stuff them for me. How does that sound?"

"It sounds like fun," Maggie said. "I'll get the scissors."

"Me too, Mama?" Sylvia said.

"Yes, Dear." Mama pushed Sylvia's hair from her face. "You may help with the stuffing."

Isabel watched as Maggie carefully cut around the pattern without a single mistake. "Maggie," she said, "why don't you cut out both of them, and I will stuff them. I'm afraid I will cut off his head or something. Mama, what about the gingerbread boys' faces?"

"I thought I would use a French knot for the eyes, and we can embroider the noses and mouths," Mama said. "We could use some bright fabric to make a necktie for each and embroider a 'J' on one and a 'B' on the other so Jimmy and Billy will not mix them up. We will embroider the faces before I sew them up, and then you can stuff them."

By the time the stuffed gingerbread men were finished, the boys were running inside with two glowing jars and smiles that reached from ear to ear. The excitement mounted when Mama presented them with their new toys.

"Oh boy," Jimmy said. He traced the crooked grin on his gingerbread boy. "I'm calling him Jay Boy," he said and stuck the toy into his pocket. Jay Boy became Jimmy's constant companion, always riding in the boy's pocket.

"This is my favorite kind of sewing," Mama said, "the kind that brings happiness."

Chapter 6

ALL WEEK, ISABEL pestered Papa to let her go with him and Curtis to market, giving her most persuasive sales pitch. The only response she could get out of Papa was, "We'll see."

"It's not fair," Isabel said. She swept the front porch Friday morning.

"What's not fair?" Curtis asked. "I'd much rather stay at home or go over to the American Legion Hall and play music than be tied to the fruit and vegetable stand all day."

"What if I help Papa sell the produce and you can go over to the music hall—after you help Papa unload the produce and set up?" Isabel asked. "Besides, I heard you always sneak over there anyway. Isn't that where you learned to play all of those new songs on your guitar?"

"OK," Curtis said. He moved the doormat for Isabel to sweep under it and turned to shake it over the rail. "But how will we convince Papa?"

"Maybe we could surprise him."

"Hmm," Curtis said. He wore a crooked grin. "You could hide under the canvas until we get there, and Papa will have to let you stay—he won't have time to take you home. After you finish breakfast in the morning, tell Mama you have to go outside, and then you can hide in the wagon. I'll cover you up with the canvas. Of course, we'll have to split the two bits."

"What two bits?" Isabel asked. "Do you mean to say that you and Eugene get paid to help Papa at the market?"

"Of course," Curtis said. "You don't think we just go for fun, do you?"

Isabel nodded and then placed the doormat back into place.

"Girls can be so dumb sometimes," Curtis said. He shook his head. "A fellow has to earn money somehow, you know."

"That's not fair," Isabel said. "I do a lot more around here without anyone asking me than you do, but no one ever pays me."

"That's because you're a girl," Curtis said. "Your payment is learning how to be a good wife and mother."

"It's still not fair. Besides, I'm never getting married. I'm gonna be a nurse and live in the city, where I can buy store-bought clothes; eat bread from the bakery; and get milk, butter, and cream delivered right to my back door." She stomped her foot before entering the house through the back door.

When she entered the kitchen, she pulled out the flour, sugar, lard, and rolling pin to start on the pie crusts. "I will earn my own money and spend it any way I want. I'll show Papa I can be more helpful than the boys. I'll even sell more, even if I have to beg people to buy the pies and cans of tomatoes." She muttered as she slapped the dough with the wooden rolling pin.

The next morning, Isabel arose at 4:00 A.M. and hurried to dress after she made her bed. Then she rushed downstairs into the kitchen to start breakfast. She smiled as she saw the crates of canned tomatoes and pies to be packed into the wagon with the produce the boys had packed after supper Friday evening. Curtis promised to save room for the crates and a corner big enough for her to hide in, if necessary, and he kept his promise.

"Well, aren't you the early bird this morning?" Papa said. He opened the stove and placed a match to the wood he'd banked before going to bed. "You don't usually get up to see us off on market days." He smiled.

"I worked hard on those pies and tomatoes; they should bring a lot of extra money," she said.

"Gal," Papa said, "the farmers market in the city is no place for little girls."

"I'm not a little girl anymore, Papa; you told me so—remember?"

"I remember telling you that you were too old to play instead of helping your mama," Papa said. He looked at the filled crates symbolizing her hard work and ingenuity. "I don't know, Gal, we'll see…"

Isabel rushed through breakfast and started on the dishes before Mama finished eating.

"Go ahead, Isabel—whatever it is you need to do," Mama said with a wink. "I'll finish up here."

"Thank you, Mama," Isabel said. She gave Mama a hug and then rushed to the back door."

"Isabel," Mama said, "don't forget to take some brown paper to serve the pie slices on…also a knife and the pie server."

"Yes, ma'am." Isabel hurried to accept the flour sack containing the necessary items and hurried to the wagon just as the sun was beginning to peek through the heavenly curtain.

"Hurry up," Curtis said.

She allowed him to lift her into the wagon. She slipped into the empty corner and tried to get comfortable in the tiny space Curtis had prepared for her and then bent down as he covered her with the heavy, white canvas. She could hear him pulling rope over the wagon in order to keep the contents covered.

She hoped she could breathe under the canvas. She noticed Curtis had raised the canvas a little so she had room to move slightly, and it allowed air to flow.

Isabel felt every rut in the road. One wheel dropped into a large hole in the road, propelling Isabel into the air and landing her again with a loud thump. *This would be fun if Maggie and Sylvie were with me, but without them, it is going to be a long, boring ride.*

"Are you sure you tied down that canvas?" Papa asked at one point.

Isabel held her breath, lest he should stop and adjust the roping. "Don't come back here. Don't come back here," she whispered and crossed her fingers.

Isabel envisioned herself small, afraid, and guilty, standing in front of the throne of God. "I defied Papa," she imagined herself saying to the Creator of the universe, "and I got my brother to help me disobey." Suddenly, she felt ashamed and sorry for her sin.

"Sure I did," Curtis said. He pulled out his harmonica and began to play it.

"Well, I hope so," Papa said. "We can't afford to arrive with damaged produce that nobody will buy."

Just as she decided to loosen the canvas in order to stretch a little, Isabel heard a light scratching sound coming from the other side of the wagon—where the pies were neatly stacked in the cart Papa had made for carrying multiple cakes and pies to family gatherings. Isabel leaned over to get a better look and came face-to-face with a little, gray mouse. Isabel bit her finger in order to keep from screaming as the little fellow wiggled his nose at her and then scampered toward the treats.

"Oh no you don't," she said to the cute critter. "You may not have those pies." Isabel looked around for something to scoop up the mouse in and crawled to the other side of the wagon in search of a shovel or even an empty jar. Just as she leaned over a bushel basket containing fresh vegetables, the wagon wheels hit a rut and sent Isabel flying. She landed face down, crushing several tomatoes in the process.

"What in blue blazes is going on back there?" Papa demanded.

Isabel could feel the wagon stopping and heard Papa walking around to the back. Just at that very moment, the mouse scurried across the baskets, and Isabel picked him up by his tail just as Papa opened the canvas.

"Look Papa," Isabel said. Tomato juice mingled with tears dripped from her face. "I caught a mouse."

"Well, if that don't beat all," Papa said. He took the mouse from Isabel's hand and placed it in the grass beside the road. "Gal, what were you doing back there anyway?"

"You didn't tell me I could go—you just said, 'we'll see,'" she said. Tears formed in her eyes, and Curtis jumped out of the wagon to join them.

"Hey, Sis," he said. "What happened to you?"

"She caught a mouse," Papa said. He helped Isabel out of the wagon.

"A mouse? What'd you do, try to eat it?" Curtis doubled over in laughter.

"It's not funny," Isabel said. "A mouse was in the wagon, and it tried to get into the pies, so I tried to catch him, lost my balance, and fell into a bushel of vegetables. Then as I righted myself, I fell smack-dab into a bushel of tomatoes." Her words turned into sobs as Papa joined in laughter with Curtis.

Isabel finally saw the humor when she fished out a small mirror from her apron pocket. "I guess I do look funny, don't I?" She accepted Papa's handkerchief and a jar of water to clean up.

"What I don't understand, Gal, is what were you doing hiding in the back of the wagon?" Papa helped her onto the wagon seat.

"You never answered when I asked if I could go with you," Isabel said. "You only said 'we'll see.'"

"That's because I was leaving it up to you," Papa said. "When you weren't in the wagon seat when it was time to pull out, I figured you didn't really want to go after all."

"You mean you were gonna let me come along?" Isabel asked with unbelief in her voice. "I didn't disobey you after all?"

"Nope," Papa said. "But I guess you did in your heart; we'll talk about that when we get home... Something tells me you didn't think of this alone—did she, Curtis?"

"It wasn't Curtis's idea, Papa. It was all mine, and I'm sorry. Will you forgive me?"

"I think you've learned your lesson," Papa said as he got onto the wagon seat, took the reins, and eased the horses and wagon back onto the road. "Disobedience or defiance always has consequences. Remember that, and you will be just fine."

The ride into town was quiet, but Isabel felt at peace after she asked Papa, and then Jesus, to forgive her. They did.

Isabel's eyes were wide with wonder as they reached the farmers market. The sights, sounds, and smells were even more exciting than she had imagined. The sounds of trucks honking their horns, horses and mules stomping, and the fragrances of the produce and perfumed ladies with pretty hats calling out orders to the merchants were almost overwhelming. "Oh, the rows of produce would make a beautiful painting with the reds, yellows, greens, and orange colors," she said with awe. Each produce stand was graced with a homemade sign, designed from cardboard boxes and crayons, that proclaimed the price of the wares.

By 9:00 A.M., the local band began practicing in the American Legion Hall across the street. The drums could be heard for several blocks. Isabel smiled as she watched Curtis tapping his feet. He was anxious to join them.

In the background, the streetcar clanked along the tracks as the conductor rang its bell. Excited voices filled the air as farmers and customers greeted each other, catching one another up on the latest gossip. Dodging the sawdust and mud puddles in the aisles of produce reminded Isabel of playing hopscotch. The experience delighted Isabel, who seldom had the opportunity to visit the famous Magic City, which had sprung up, as if by magic, around the railroad, practically overnight, about forty years earlier—or at least that is what she had been told.

Isabel helped Papa set up his produce stand on the back of the wagon, with a cardboard sign proudly displaying the prices in red crayon. Then they carefully placed a red and white tablecloth over the makeshift table Papa had set up for the pies and cans of tomatoes. Isabel hummed as she carefully set out the pies at one end of the table and Mama's canned tomatoes at the other end.

"How much for those pies, Miss?"

Isabel turned to her prospective customer with assurance, "Two bits per pie or five cents per slice."

"That's a bit steep, ain't it?" The man lifted his only arm and scratched his head. "I'll give you ten cents for the entire pie. After all, you don't want to cart all these pies back home again to spoil."

"I'll take my chances, sir," Isabel said. She smiled. "Lunch time is coming, and I'm sure people will be hungry by then."

"You drive a hard bargain," he said. Then he returned her grin. "I'll take two pies. Next time, though, you might want to consider fritters instead of pie slices—they're not as messy to eat without a fork."

Isabel looked at the pies and then back at the man—actually, at his empty sleeve, which was pinned up above the elbow. She wondered how he would manage to carry both pies with one hand.

The man turned and spoke to a young boy about the same age as Curtis. "Come over here, Son, and give me a hand with these pies. Won't your mama be surprised?"

"Yes, sir," the boy said. He obviously had a hard time looking Isabel in the eyes, but he managed to steal a glance or two. "I might just eat one of 'em before we get home."

Flustered by his actions, Isabel dropped the scissors she was using to cut twine to hold together the pies, which she had wrapped in brown paper. She could feel her face turning scarlet, and she ignored his comment, not knowing how to reply. She peeked at his face as she handed the package to him, and he rewarded her with a brilliant smile. His jet-black hair, worn short in the back, had one long strand that flopped across his face, covering one eye. A herringbone cap shaded his face, and Isabel wished she could ask him to remove it so that she could see his eyes. Then she blushed once more at the thought.

"Will you be here next week?" he asked as he took off his cap, dusted it off, and replaced it on his head.

"I don't know," she said. She glanced at Papa. "I hope so."

"Me too," he said with a wave as he walked away with his father. "I'll be looking for ya."

Isabel smiled all the way home as she held her box filled with coins from her pie sales. "I can't believe it," she said. "We sold everything. Next time, I think I'll make fritters; they're easier to eat without a fork. Besides, we can make bunches of them and sell them for a nickel apiece."

"We sold the canned tomatoes quickly too," Papa said. "And everyone who bought a jar bought at least a bushel of tomatoes. Who would've thought a sample of the finished product would nudge them to buy more? Those jars of tomatoes looked good enough to eat. I'll have to bring you with me every week."

Isabel basked in his praise.

"I forgot to mention one thing," Papa said. "Don't tell your mama we ate ice cream for lunch. Don't tell the other children either; it wouldn't seem fair."

"I won't, Papa," Isabel said as she tossed her braids over her shoulder. "It'll be our secret. Besides, I bought some penny candy for the others and flowers for Mama from Miss Pansy the flower lady."

"So," Papa said, "you met Miss Pansy. What did you think?"

"I think she's really nice," Isabel said. She turned to look at the potted geraniums and pansies that she had bartered for in exchange for a pie and two quarts of tomatoes. "She's really friendly, and I think she looks nice with flowers in her hair; although, I've never seen anyone older than Mama wear her long hair loose, especially since bobbed hair is in style now."

"Bobbed my eye," Papa said. He shook his head as if his words tasted bitter. "God never meant for women and little girls to cut their hair short like men. They even throw it in our faces by calling it a 'bob.' That should tell you something right there."

"But a bob isn't cut as short as men's hair, and it has more style with bangs cut straight and the sides a little longer and curled towards the face," Isabel said. "I think it looks nice. I saw a girl my age at the market today who had a bob, and she looked pretty."

"Maybe I spoke too hastily," Papa said. "Bringing you to the market may have been a mistake. You're getting too many bad ideas. Out of all the people you met today, you chose the wrong people to befriend."

"Papa," Isabel said, hoping to divert his attention, "who was the gentleman with only one arm? He seemed really nice."

"He is nice," Papa said. He urged the horses forward.

"What happened to his arm?"

"I hope you didn't stare at it, Gal," Papa said. "It's rude to stare at people, you know."

"I just noticed it; that's all," Isabel said.

"I think he was born that way, but he doesn't let it stop him," Papa said. "No sirree. He's the most industrious person I think I have ever met. Fallon—that's his name, James Fallon. He moved here from Kentucky around 1890, about the time thousands of people were moving here from all over, hoping to get jobs with the railroad or to set up businesses to make money off the workers. Mr. Fallon is an educated man. He can read, write, do sums in his head, and he even went to college, but nobody would give him a chance to prove himself because he only had one arm. He eventually took the job as street cleaner. "Nobody wanted that job since most people around here rode horses or mules and the street cleaner had to scoop up after em'. You'd think he would be bitter or discouraged, but he whistled while he worked." Papa shook his head at the memory. "I once asked him why he was so happy when he had a job nobody wanted. He just smiled and said, 'Praise the good Lord for giving me work to feed my family."

"What does he do now?" Isabel asked.

"He collects scrap from all over Virginia. Guess he sells it to Roanoke Scrap Iron & Metal or the Virginia Scrap Iron & Metal, depending upon who has the better offer. Sometimes people cleaning out their attics or barns want to get rid of stuff, and Mr. Fallon buys it from them, cleans up the 'good stuff' to sell, and then the rest goes to the scrap yard. Yep, he's a fine Christian man. Goes to First Presbyterian Church whenever he is in town; takes his boy with him too."

"Is the boy he called to carry the pies his son?"

"Yup," Papa said. He urged the horses forward.

"His name's Lee," Curtis said. He pulled his harmonica from his pocket. "We learned a dilly of a tune today. Want to hear it?"

"Maybe later," Isabel said. "Does he go to church every Sunday?"

"Who?"

"Lee."

"Sure, he goes," Curtis said. "But they must be mighty strict—they make the kids memorize a whole book about the Bible. He called it cati-something. Lee said he has to answer all the questions in the book in order to become a member. He said the only way he can memorize all of that is by putting it to music. He said he thinks better if he turns the words into a song." Curtis seemed to admire Lee.

"That's keen," Isabel said. "Is that how he learns his school work too?"

"He dropped out of school in the third grade," Curtis said. "His Mama told him he had to go out and earn money, so he works most of the time. When he isn't selling newspapers, he's shining shoes or mucking the stalls at the livery."

"Oh," Isabel said, "that's sad."

"Yeah," Curtis said. He began to play his harmonica.

"What's so sad about that?" Papa said. "The lad shows initiative. Don't know how he gets away with it, though; the government's getting strict about children in school these days. Though, I didn't go to school, and it never hurt me none. I was Grandpa's apprentice. Learned how to be a farmer and blacksmith and made barrels to sell. At least I could make a living. Look at Mr. Fallon. He has an education and can't find a decent job—just because nobody wants to hire someone whose body isn't perfect. It just don't make sense."

Curtis wiped his harmonica on his sleeve and then began to play as Isabel's thoughts turned to the people she had met at the market. Mr. Fallon was nice, and Lee was *really* nice, but she wished she could have seen his eyes. She felt her face blush with the thought. She started looking upward toward the clouds, in hopes that neither Papa nor Curtis noticed. Miss Pansy was funny and nice. "Papa," she said. She turned back to the flowers in the wagon. "Why isn't Miss Pansy married? She's really nice and smiles all the time. She knows all about flowers and even wears them in her hair."

"Miss Pansy is what we call a spinster," Papa said. "She has had more than one opportunity to marry, but she chose to stay at home and take care of her elderly parents. When they passed away, she put all of her energy into her flowers. She even had a glass house built just for growing things. She knows just about everybody in town, and they know her, but I guess she is just too busy with her flowers to think about getting married. Being a wife is a full-time job, you know; she wouldn't be able to take care of a husband and her flower business too."

"She must get awfully lonely," Isabel said.

"Probably so," Papa said. He urged the horses to turn onto the dirt road leading to Apple Tree Farm. "Home, sweet home."

Isabel jumped from the seat with a little help from her brother and then ran into house with flowers in her hands and a box of money under her arm. "Mama, Mama," she said as she entered the house, allowing the screen to bang shut behind her, "I had so much fun at the market. I'll tell you all about it…"

"Oh, Isabel," Mama said. She handed Isabel a clean dish to dry and put away. "I'm disappointed you deceived Papa and also involved your brother. Your stubbornness concerns me. It can cause problems the rest of your life, unless you nip it in the bud now. You must be willing to trust Papa and me to make decisions for your good."

"But Papa and Jesus forgave me, Mama," Isabel said. Tears welled up in her eyes. "Papa said that it's OK."

"Isabel, my dear, if we did not truly love you, we would let it go and just laugh it off as a silly antic. It is more than that, Dear. You were disobedient and deceitful."

"But, Mama!" Isabel said. Her face grew red. "Papa wouldn't give me a real reason for not allowing me to go with him."

"When Papa says, 'We'll see,' it is his way of saying that if everything works out as it should and if you are prepared to go, you may. He doesn't like to make promises he cannot keep."

"I know that now," Isabel said. "I won't do it again."

Mama smiled and pushed Isabel's hair away from her face before speaking. "I hope so, Dear. Just to be sure, you will help your papa muck out the stalls this week. You also will go to your room every night directly after our family altar time."

Isabel started to protest, but she noticed Mama's nostrils begin to flare and changed her mind.

"Now," Mama said, "let's go to your room and settle your finances."

"What?" Isabel said. She placed the last dish in the cupboard. "I've already counted it."

"We need to give ten percent back to the Lord and give an offering; after all, He provided it for you."

Isabel's enormous eyes began to tear, and her nostrils flared.

"And then there are ingredients to pay for. I am not charging you for the use of the kitchen, stove, or for my time baking. We'll call it my contribution. Lets go upstairs and go through the money you have, and we will separate the cash into envelopes that I have marked for you. You should save at least ten percent, and the rest is your profit."

"But that's not fair!" Isabel said. She pulled her apron off and tossed it on the wall hook. "It was my idea. I helped with the baking, and I did all of the selling." "Yes, Dear," Mama said, "with the family flour, eggs, fruit, and other ingredients. I am not doing this to be mean; you must learn to handle your money now, while you are young. Many adults never learned this lesson, and they end up living in the poor house. You must pay your creditors, always spend less than you earn, add to your savings, and never spend it unless there is a real emergency. Most of all, give to the Lord first."

Disappointment filled Isabel as she stuffed each envelope, watching her coins literally slip through her fingers, until finally, Mama said, "Isabel, you have eighty-five cents profit. Perhaps next week you will have even more. I'm sure people will be watching for your delicious treats. Soon word will get around, and you will double your profit; just watch and see."

"Mama," Isabel said, "do you really think we can double the amount next time?"

"One does not become rich by being lazy. Your efforts will pay off if you are diligent and fair," Mama said. She accepted the ingredients envelope and slipped it into her pocket. "We will take this to the store and buy more flour, salt, and sugar for your baking."

Isabel sighed as she hid the envelopes in her dresser drawer under her hankies. She took ten cents out of her "keep" envelope and placed it proudly into her change purse, just to know that she had her own money to carry. If Papa allowed her to take her baking to market every week, she could save enough to buy a Christmas present for everyone in the family. She fell asleep dreaming of things she would buy.

Chapter 7

Isabel's Special Day

ISABEL COULD FEEL excitement in the air, even before she opened her eyes. She had waited for this day for so long. "August 24, 1924—Ten years old," she whispered to herself as she breathed deeply, appreciating the moment.

With little money to work with, Mama always found little ways to make birthdays special. This bright Sunday was to be a very special day for the entire extended family. Isabel knew that after church, the entire Greene and Kelly clans would picnic together to celebrate. She also knew there would be a large birthday cake *and* lemon meringue pie, her favorite, and that alone was enough to cause excitement.

Her belly grumbled as she smelled bacon frying in the kitchen and the fragrance of coffee brewing on the black cook stove. Mama always fixed a good "farm" breakfast, but today would include Isabel's favorite—blueberry pancakes. And since it was her birthday, Isabel did not have to help. She got to sleep until 7:00 A.M., just like a princess. Isabel threw aside her covers and reached for her robe. She was surprised that her sisters were already up and she was in the room alone.

Suddenly, the door opened and her entire family greeted her with a birthday song.

"Hurry up and get dressed, Isabel" Sylvia said. "Today's your special day, and it's time to get started." Sylvia danced around the room, singing a silly song while Maggie placed a paper crown on her sister's head.

"Maggie, where did this come from?" Isabel asked.

"She got up really early this morning and worked over an hour fashioning this masterpiece out of newspaper and tinsel she had found in the Christmas box," Curtis said. He leaned against the doorframe.

"Oh, Maggie, that's the prettiest crown I've ever seen," Isabel said. She ran to the mirror, adjusting it on her head. As she did, Maggie blushed at the compliment.

"I helped," Sylvia said. "I helped glue on the tinsel."

"You both did a wonderful job. I love my birthday gift," Isabel said. Isabel shooed her brothers and Papa out of the room and quickly dressed.

When the girls entered the kitchen, the table was set for breakfast. Eugene set a small jar of flowers in the center of the table.

"Oh, thank you, Eugene. Did you pick these flowers for my birthday?" Isabel asked.

Eugene nodded before taking his seat across the table.

Curtis, not missing an opportunity to tease their older brother, spoke up. "He's just modest, Isabel, he went out over an hour ago just to pick flowers for your birthday."

Isabel's eyes lit up as Mama placed a plate of pancakes in front of her. Her serving had blueberry eyes, a nose, and a long smile. Everyone laughed and tried to make a "pancake face" of their own.

After breakfast, each of the other children gave Isabel a homemade gift or card. Papa presented her with a lovely hand-carved wooden pencil box. She smiled as she opened the box and found two brand-new pencils. She could hardly believe her good fortune. She felt like a queen dressed in the cornflower blue, drop-waist dress with a wide, white sash bow she had helped Mama make just for today. She turned around in circles just to watch the skirt flare out, just as she had done when she was a small child, and smiled with pleasure. She looked up to see Mama returning her smile.

After church, the family met for a picnic with a lovely view of the Blue Ridge Mountains. Isabel looked at the smoky blue and green mountains as she listened to the happy voices surrounding her and suddenly felt wrapped in a quilt of love.

Just then, her older half-sister, Cleo, handed Isabel a small gift and hugged her tightly. She said, "Well, how does it feel to be ten years old, Isabel? Do you feel any older?"

"Oh, yes," Isabel said. "I'm in double digits now, you know."

"You will not want to admit that for long, Dear," Cleo said.

Isabel didn't mind her teasing. It just added to the fun.

Isabel hugged Sandy, the family dog and held him tightly. "This is my best birthday ever."

"It isn't over yet, my dear," Mama said. She sat down beside her. "Tomorrow we will go shopping together, just the two of us."

Isabel could not imagine a more wonderful birthday.

Chapter 8

Shopping

"CAN YOU BELIEVE it?" asked the lady with the small, sassy hat. "I heard she has seven children. That old man she married certainly keeps her busy. I still can't believe she married a man old enough to be her father."

"I know," said the plump lady eating an ice cream sundae.

"They are as poor as church mice. I hear he's a tenant farmer east of Roanoke, at the foot of one of the mountains."

Isabel slowly sipped her soda as she listened to the ladies gossiping at the table behind her. They were talking about Mama. She just knew it. She scooted her chair back to let the gossiping former friends of her mother know just what she thought about them. *The problem is, Mama doesn't approve of eavesdropping, especially on her old friends.* Isabel took another sip of her soda. *I wish those ol' gossips would go away before Mama comes to the table with a napkin.*

The conversation continued. "They might be poor, but there is a lot of love in that family. She is a wonderful mother. Lizzie was always a mother hen to us when we were in school," said the lady with bobbed hair. "Esther," she said, "do you remember the time you fell and tore your skirt? Lizzie pulled out the threaded needle she always kept tucked in her shirtwaist and mended it for you to spare you embarrassment. Amy, do you remember the time the school bully ate your lunch? Lizzie gave you hers. I think we should discuss good things about people. Let's not gossip about our old friend."

Isabel sighed with relief and turned her attention to her mother, who had just returned to the table after asking the waiter for another napkin. It had been a wonderful day shopping with Mama, and Isabel would not allow idle gossip to ruin their day. Each of the ladies greeted Mama as if she were a long lost friend, and each told her how much they missed her and wanted to get together sometime just to talk and make up for lost time. Isabel looked at Mama to see if she had heard their ugly words. Her countenance did not show she had. Indeed, Mama was almost giddy.

This was the first time Isabel and Mama had gone for a shopping day together without the rest of the family. Isabel had learned much about buying clothing and fabric for such a large family. Mama had taught her things such as buying material with more threads per inch to ensure the item would last longer and be softer. She also noticed that Mama chose heavier fabrics that would be appropriate for fall, winter, and early spring.

"It's important to spend your money wisely, Isabel. Make every penny count. If you can buy one nice article of clothing that will last two years, it is wiser than buying two dresses for the same amount of money that will only last one season. It's always wise to think ahead. Ask yourself if this dress will be out of style next year. If so, don't buy it. Choose something classic and sturdy; you may need to pass it down to your sisters, who will not want to wear something they consider out of fashion. Besides, you will need to make wise purchases for a family of your own someday."

Isabel smiled and blushed at the thought of herself as a Mama, and then she returned to the present. "Mama, is that why you like to make our dresses instead of buying them?" Isabel asked. "I noticed a lot of the dresses in the window are so thin you can almost see through them." She scooped out the last of her soda with a spoon. "Did you see the pretty blue sailor dress? I really like that."

"Making most of your clothes at home is less expensive, and we can make them exactly the way you want them. Some store-bought dresses don't fit properly. Plus, I add a large hem because you are growing so fast. I would love to be able to buy the most expensive fabric in the store, but you know we must make do with the money we have. Right now, we must buy from the remnant table. The fabrics are perfectly respectable and reasonable."

Isabel wondered whom Mama was trying to convince— Isabel or herself.

The fact that Mama made most of Isabel's dresses by hand had never bothered Isabel until last year when some girls made fun of her. This year she dreaded the thought of walking into school in a handmade dress. It was not that the dresses and skirts were not well made. Mama was known throughout the area for her lovely stitching. The problem was that the girls at school recognized the fabric from the remnant table and made fun of Isabel. She didn't like the feeling that she was wearing someone's kitchen curtain, but she could not summon the courage to tell Mama so.

"Isabel, what's bothering you? Now that you have seen the fashionable clothing available in the stores, you probably don't want the clothes your mama makes for you; is that it?" Mama asked.

"Oh, no, Mama," Isabel said. She quickly swallowed her last bite of ice cream before answering. "It's just that…well, some of the girls at school laugh at us because we…" Isabel looked down at her shoes, adjusted her socks, twisted in her seat, and took a sip of water.

"Yes, Isabel?" Mama said. "Why do the girls at school laugh at you—do they laugh at your clothes?"

"Yes, ma'am," Isabel said. "It's not the way that you sew, Mama; everyone knows you do a wonderful job sewing."

"If that is true, Dear, why are they laughing?"

"Because we are wearing Mrs. Mason's kitchen curtains," Isabel said. Tears streamed down her cheeks. "But that's OK, Mama; Mrs. Mason made curtains out of dress fabric."

"Oh, Isabel, why didn't you tell me last year? I could have at least dyed the fabric, and the children would have never known what bolt of fabric your dress was made from. I could have saved you some pain if I had just thought it through. I should have known. Will you forgive me?"

"Of course, Mama."

"Good, then this is what we will do. We will buy our fabric from the store here in Roanoke instead of the local store, so the chance of repeating last year's problem is slim. Then we will dye last year's clothes any color you wish, as long as it covers the yellow flowers. Does that sound like a good plan to you?" Mama smiled as Isabel nodded profusely. Then she hugged her daughter protectively. "Now, the main reason we came out today is to buy you a store-bought dress. Let's find something that will make those girls want to go shopping with you."

Isabel followed Mama into a shop on Campbell Avenue that was known for selling bargains. Isabel blinked back tears as Mama walked to the dress counter and found a blue sailor dress identical to the one at the more expensive store.

"At this price, Isabel," Mama said, "we can buy a white straw hat with a blue ribbon to match. Would you like that?"

"Oh, yes, Mama," Isabel said. Excitement mounted within her. "That would be wonderful."

"Now," Mama said, "let's see if we can find some fabric that your friends will approve of, shall we?"

"Oh, yes," Isabel said. She walked through the store with her head held high.

"Children, wake up." Papa's voice boomed from the foot of the stairs.

"What time is it?" Maggie mumbled.

Isabel turned to see the clock in the darkness. "It is still dark outside," she moaned. She pushed the covers from her and swung her legs over the side of the bed.

"Why does Papa make us get up in the middle of the night just to go shopping for shoes?" mumbled Sylvia as she pulled the covers over her head.

Isabel gently shook her to wake her up. "Because he knows that Mr. Pugh will do anything to make the first sale of the morning—even if that means dropping the price until the customer says, 'I'll take it,'" Isabel said.

"Last year, we got Jimmy's shoes for free," Maggie said admiration in her voice.

"But why would he give us a free pair of shoes?" Sylvia asked. She tried to button her dress and then backed up to Isabel for help.

"Because," Isabel said, "Papa says that Mr. Pugh is superstitious and thinks if he sells shoes to the first customer of the day, he will make a sale to every customer who comes in that day. If he doesn't make a sale, he thinks he will not make a sale to anyone. So Papa pretends he is not interested and threatens to leave so that he can buy our shoes cheap. It works every time."

Breakfast was a rushed affair, with everyone eating sausage biscuits and fruit on the road to Roanoke.

"The streets are empty," Curtis said. They turned onto Jefferson street. "What time does the shoe store open?"

"In a while," Papa said. "What time is it?"

"It is 6:00 A.M." Mama sighed.

"Good," Papa said, "we should be the first customers indeed." Nearly two hours passed before Mr. Pugh walked up to the small shop and unlocked the door.

"Hurry up now," Papa said. He ushered the children and Mama out of the Model T. "Now, line up in order, with Billy first and Eugene last." Excitement mounted in his voice as he opened the shop door. A bell over the door signaled their arrival.

"Good morning," Mr. Pugh said as he entered from the back room, and then he frowned when Papa stepped through the threshold. "Oh, hello, Mr. Greene. I haven't seen you in a while. A year ago, wasn't it?"

"Yep," Papa said with a grin. "School starts in two weeks, and all of the children have outgrown and worn out their shoes. I will need seven pair this morning; that is, if the price is right."

"Of course," Mr. Pugh said. He pulled out his handkerchief and wiped his forehead. "Who is first?"

"Papa," Sylvia said, pulling on his jacket coat, "may I have a pair of Mary Jane's?"

Papa took the small, leather shoe from her outstretched hand, turned it over, and placed it firmly back on the shelf. "Those things will not last six months. Pick something sensible."

"Yes, Papa," she said. Isabel wished with all her heart that she could get them.

By the time the Greene family left the store, shoeboxes strewn all over the floor, and the poor merchant declared he had practically given the shoes away for less than he paid for them. However, he smiled and welcomed them to come again, believing that because his first customer of the day left happy, he would have good luck at selling that day.

Papa left the store with a smile on his face and coins jingling in his pocket.

"Poor man," Mama said. She stepped up into the automobile. "He probably wishes he had chosen bad luck and not reduced his prices to get our business."

"Yep," Papa said. He tipped his hat as Mr. Pugh stood watching them from the window. "Ah, don't worry Mama… that man could give away two dozen pairs of top-quality shoes and not put a dent in his wallet."

Chapter 9

Trust an Old Maid

LATER THAT EVENING, after Isabel put the last dish away and Maggie finished sweeping the kitchen, Mama called the children into the parlor to gather around Papa and her for family altar. As she picked up her Bible, she smiled at the children and said, "Do you have a favorite song that you would like us to sing before Bible reading?"

"Let's sing 'Jesus Lover Of My Soul,'" Isabel said. She had just learned to play that song by ear on Aunt Jenny's piano last week, and the excitement of having played it all by herself made her almost giddy.

"That's a lovely choice, Isabel," Mama said. "I am looking forward to hearing you play it on the piano again. Are there any more requests?"

"I like 'Onward Christian Soldiers,'" Curtis said. Everyone smiled because they expected this request. It was his favorite.

The request that surprised the entire family came from four-year-old Jimmy. "I want to sing 'Trust an Old Maid,'" he said.

"You wish to sing...what?" Mama said as if she did not trust her ears.

"'Trust an Old Maid,'" Jimmy said. The confidence in his voice caused the room to explode with laughter.

"You know," Jimmy said, "an old maid, like Miss Smith, my Sunday school teacher." He finished with a stomp of his little foot, and his little hand balled up into a fist. "Why is everybody laughing? That's not nice." He began to cry.

Isabel poked Curtis, who was holding his side and rolling on the floor laughing. "It's not *that* funny, is it, Maggie?" Isabel said as she turned to her kind-hearted sister for support. However, Maggie and Sylvia were hiding smiles behind their hands—at least, they were trying to. Both girls' shoulders were shaking from laughter. Isabel looked to her older brother for support, but he was just as bad as Curtis. He also was literally rolling in the floor, tears streaming down his cheeks. Isabel looked to Mama, who was shaking her head at Papa, who was slapping his hand on his knee.

"Best laugh I've had all week," Papa said.

Isabel could contain her composure no longer. She swept Jimmy up in her arms and swung him around the room until he too was laughing. Before she put him down, she whispered in his ears, "The song is 'Trust and Obey,' not 'Trust an Old Maid.'"

The following week was "Sunday go to Meeting," as church services were held only once a month, for the preacher was in the area only that often. Although, Sunday school was held weekly.

Isabel looked forward to church with the rest of the community, as it was an all-day event, which included special music and a picnic on the grounds after the services. Baptisms might even be included. Those who'd had a birthday had to come down the aisle and drop a penny for every year of their life into a bank that looked like a white church with a tall steeple. The children looked forward to this…the adults seemed to dread it. It was a day to prepare for, and all knew it would be long remembered, at least until next month. The sermon was the topic of discussion for weeks in the more spiritual circles. The socialites discussed who sat with whom and knew just what everyone had said and worn. This was why Isabel would never forget the Sunday the song director asked for requests.

Isabel helped Mama gather the children after Sunday School, which was located in a small building behind the church. Jimmy was helping Miss Smith push the tiny chairs under the small table and gathering crayons that had fallen onto the floor.

"Thank you, Jimmy," she said. "You are my best helper." She smiled and patted him on the head.

Isabel noticed him blush. He could not seem to look away from the toe of his shoes. It seemed odd to her too that he didn't say anything. Isabel had never known her little brother to be at a loss for words, but she did not waste any time wondering about it. She needed to pick up Billy and meet Mama back in the church. She wondered, however, why Jimmy thought Miss Smith was an "old maid." Isabel did not think she looked that old—maybe twenty-two or twenty-three. "Guess little boys think differently," she said to herself.

The Greene family finally settled in their pew, with Mama at one end and Papa at the other. Isabel sat in the middle to help control her younger siblings and to relay quiet messages between her parents. The service finally began.

"This is the day that the Lord hath made; let us rejoice and be glad in it." The song leader quoted from Psalms as he reached the pulpit and opened his hymnal. "Everyone open your songbook to page twenty-three and lift your voices unto the Lord."

Isabel found the page and helped Sylvia and little Jimmy, who were sitting on either side of her, to find the song in their books. She smiled as they sang loudly with the rest of the congregation. Thankfully, everyone knew the song. The following song was not quite as familiar, but Jimmy did not let that stop him from joining in.

After the pastor gave announcements and lifted up prayer for those in need, the song leader once more approached the pulpit and surprised the congregation by allowing them to choose a favorite hymn. To everyone's amazement, four-year-old Jimmy Greene stood up on the pew and shouted out his favorite, "Let's sing Miss Smith's song."

An amused song leader turned to a perplexed Sunday school teacher for the answer. "Well, Miss Smith," he said, "what are we singing?"

"I'm afraid Jimmy will have to enlighten us," Miss Smith said. She obviously was becoming quite amused, for she could see the activity on the Greene pew, which was quite comical.

Isabel tried to catch Jimmy before he could make his request, but he was determined and quite serious. Mama on the far end of the pew nearly dropped Billy in order to get to Jimmy, stepping on Curtis, who yelled out in pain. Papa who was sitting at the opposite end of the pew with Eugene also tried to divert the problem, but the humor was not lost on him—a fit of coughing hampered his progress.

Just as Mama reached for Jimmy, Sylvia stood up and explained in her sweetest voice, "He meant to say 'Trust an Old Maid'...I mean, 'Trust and Obey.'"

Isabel reached up and pulled her down, and a very red-faced Sylvia buried her face in her sister's shoulder as the congregation exploded with laughter.

"Well," Director Webb said, "we don't have any old maids that I know of, but that sounds like sage advice coming from one so young. Open your hymnals to page 285. There's no other way to be happy in Jesus but to *trust and obey*."

At the end of a very moving service, everyone was surprised when Mrs. Eleanor Sheffield, the eldest and most respected

Sunday school teacher, tearfully walked down the aisle and asked the pastor if she could address the congregation.

"Sometimes it takes a small child to show you the sin in your life," she said. With tears still coming down her face, she looked at Jimmy and Sylvia and smiled before continuing. "The Greene children made me realize that I have been guilty of the sin of jealousy and also of the sin of gossip, and the children must have heard me. You see, I was jealous because my grandchildren are learning more in their Sunday school class with Miss Smith as their teacher than their parents or any child I have ever taught has learned from me. They quote scriptures and ask each other questions about the Bible, just like it is a fun game, and they make decisions based on God's Word. Three weeks ago, when I asked my Bud where he learned to do that, he said, 'Miss Smith taught me.' Bud is only four years old.

"So, I started listening through the wall to Miss Smith as she was teaching. That is easy to do because I do not allow my students to make any noise, you know. I make them sit very still and listen to *me*. Anyway, she seemed to make the lesson come alive for the little ones. She even allowed them to participate. Before, I would have said that she did not have control of her classroom. Now I know the Lord Jesus Christ has control of that classroom, and He is so much better. However, it took me a while to admit that fact; until just now, actually.

"You see, last Sunday after Sunday school, I complained to two of my friends in the hallway that the children were making too much noise and disrupting my class. Little Jimmy Greene, there, overheard me say, 'Trust an old maid to think of something ridiculous for the children to do in Sunday school and call it learning; she doesn't know anything about children because she doesn't have any.' Well, that was wrong." Mrs. Sheffield stopped to dab at her eyes with her hankie and wiped her nose before continuing. "Miss Smith," she said, "will you and the two Greene children please join me?"

Isabel helped Sylvia and Jimmy up the aisle and sat on the first pew to wait for them as they stood nervously before the stately woman. When Miss Smith joined the children, Mrs. Sheffield continued.

"Miss Smith," she said as she turned toward the younger woman, "you obviously love the children in your class, and they are happy to learn from you. You do not talk down to them, but to them, I have never done that. I have taught with rigid rules and cared more about 'my lesson,' and I was jealous because the children loved you back. Would you please forgive me for my horrible words and for my jealousy?"

"Of course, Mrs. Sheffield," Miss Smith said. Her eyes were bright with unshed tears as she gave her sister in Christ a hug of forgiveness.

"Now," Mrs. Sheffield said as she placed a hand on Jimmy's shoulder and the other on Sylvia's, "I want to thank both of you for bringing my sin to my attention; even though you did not realize that was what you were doing. You were very brave to stand up and request your song, and I thank you."

"You're welcome," Jimmy said with a grin. He motioned for Mrs. Sheffield to bend down, and he planted a kiss on her cheek and hugged her neck until Isabel thought the woman would protest, but she did not. She smiled instead and thanked him for his forgiveness.

"And, Sylvia, don't worry about messing up the words; God used your words to convict my heart. If you had not spoken up for your little brother, I would have ignored God's call to repentance once again. Thank you, Dear."

"You're welcome, Mrs. Sheffield," Sylvia said. She scrunched her shoulders bashfully before turning and practically sprinting down the aisle to the safety of Mama's arms.

"Thank you for listening and for your patience," Mrs. Sheffield said. "I felt the Lord was leading me to make my restitutions public, for I do not know who may have heard me, so I am asking you all to forgive me and to pray that He will have control of my tongue from now on."

Director Webb had an announcement of his own at the end of the service, which brought much rejoicing to everyone except little Jimmy.

"Miss Smith and I are to be married here next month, after the morning service, and you are all welcome to attend. So you see, Miss Smith will not be an 'old maid,' but we can all trust her with the children of the church."

"Papa," Sylvia said on the ride home, "was Mama an old maid?"

"No, ma'am," Papa said with a chuckle, "your mama was just a young filly when I married her. The prettiest filly in Virginia."

"Really?" Sylvia said as she gazed at her mother.

"That does not mean much, Dear, when you are compared to a horse." Mama directed her words to Sylvia but kept her gaze on Papa as she spoke. Then she turned toward Sylvia. "I borrowed a hymnal from the song leader so that every evening this month we can copy the words of the hymns so that we will not have any more misunderstandings."

"The prettiest filly in Virginia, with the heart of a cruel taskmaster—otherwise known as a teacher," Papa said.

Sylvia did not appreciate his joke, but Mama seemed to.

 School Days

ISABEL PULLED THE covers over her shoulders tightly as the sun peeked through the window and the first wind of "school days" crept through the crack of Isabel's otherwise happy existence.

"Wake up, Isabel," Mama said. "You must get up now, or we will be late for school, and that will not look good. Besides, Papa will be angry if you do not get your chores done before school; you know how Papa is."

Maggie cajoled, bribed, and pleaded with her older sister to get out of bed and prepare for the first day of school.

Just as Isabel was convinced, Sylvia bounced into the room with much enthusiasm for school to begin, causing Isabel to bury herself deep under the covers. Finally, Maggie went in search of Jimmy and returned carrying little Billy, who was almost bigger than Maggie, with Jimmy in tow. The boys seemed to know instinctively that baby kisses and tickling were exactly what their big sister needed in order to come out of her cocoon, and come out she did. It seemed little Billy needed a diaper change, and now her bed did too.

"Good morn', Is'bel. I luv you," little Billy said. He planted a wet baby kiss on her nose, and Isabel cried at the thought of going to school and leaving the baby at home.

Isabel took a deep breath and smoothed the invisible wrinkles in her new dress before entering the classroom. She felt several pairs of critical eyes surveying her and wished she had not let Mama french braid her hair after all. "My hair is all wrong. I really look like a farm girl," she whispered to Eugene, who pushed her through the threshold and into the room.

"Good morning, Isabel. Don't you look nice this morning," Sally Anne said. She waved at Isabel to sit in the desk next to her.

Isabel felt warmth of gratitude for the compliment and sat with uncertainty as Arlene Mason gave her a look that could have frozen an erupting volcano. The cold stare played havoc with Isabel's nerves, and she seemed to drop everything she touched. Her new carved pencil box opened and dumped pencils all over the floor while Miss Catron was talking. When the textbooks were passed out, the history book, which seemed to have a mind of its own, jumped out of her arms and landed on the floor with a loud thud, making everyone in the room jump and then giggle. That is, everyone except Isabel, who merely wished for the floor to open up and swallow her so she could sprint home, where she did not have to worry about what other people thought. Isabel reached down to pick up her book, but someone else had beaten her to it.

Ernie Mason picked up the history book, wiped it off, and smiled before returning the book to Isabel. She was not sure, but it almost looked like he winked at her...almost, or was just it her imagination?

"Isabel, Ernie Mason just winked at you," Sally Anne whispered from across the aisle. "I thought he liked you last year, and now I know it."

"Who, me?" Isabel said. "Nobody likes me."

"Oh, yes they do, Isabel," Sally Anne said. She watched the teacher, who was gathering information from a new student. "Everybody likes you; only you just don't know it."

Isabel turned her attention to the teacher, but her thoughts kept returning to Sally Anne's remark. Could it be true? Had she misjudged her classmates because one or two were unkind? She determined to talk it over with Mama later.

Isabel pulled her lunch pail out of her desk at lunchtime and ran to greet the rest of her siblings under the oak tree for lunch. As she sat down on the ground, she saw Sally Anne eating and laughing with Arlene Mason and two of the most stuck up girls in school. "Rich girls stick together," she said as storm clouds passed by overhead.

Chapter 11

Unkind Words

"SHE IS SO stuck up, she probably has never even seen the ground," Isabel said to Maggie as they walked home from school, and to Sylvia, who was almost running to keep up.

"Oh, Isabel," Maggie said, "that isn't very kind. Besides, I don't think Sally Anne is stuck up at all. She seems kind of lonely to me."

"You always take up for people, Maggie. Don't you remember when Sally Anne and her friends made fun of our dresses?" Isabel stopped in the middle of the road to confront her sister. In Isabel's mind, for Maggie to take up for Sally Anne was tantamount to treason against the Greene clan. Maggie seldom spoke her mind to Isabel, and when she did, she was usually right. This time, however, Isabel, felt betrayed and did not know how to react, so she counted to ten as Mama had taught her, then turned and calmly continued walking towards home.

"I think she's nice," said Sylvia, who finally had caught up, breathless from her run. "She tied my hair ribbons last week, and she smiled at me."

"She did? I don't see how she even noticed your ribbons were untied," Isabel said with a hint of resentment in her voice. "She holds her nose so high in the air that it's a wonder she doesn't drown when it rains."

Her sisters could not help but giggle at the mental image, but Maggie gave Isabel "Mama's look" to remind her that the words she had spoken were unkind. Then, at that moment, they were all surprised to hear a voice from the woods beside the road.

"Who's gonna drown, Is'bel?" Isabel turned to see her young brother and their dog, Sandy, digging in the dirt, covered from head to toe in Virginia soil.

"Jimmy Greene, what are you doing here? Does Mama know where you are?" Isabel said, knowing her mother did not allow him out of sight of the house.

"I'm looking for buried treasure. Sandy and I followed a squirrel. She stopped here and buried something, then scurried away. I think it was gold. Sandy thinks it was a bone. So, we got to work digging it up, and you walked by."

"It's just a plain ol' nut, Jimmy," Sylvia said with the authority of a first grader. "Squirrels store away nuts for winter like Mama cans fruit and vegetables to store in the cellar. If you dig up his winter supply, he will starve, so you should just leave them alone."

"Oh, alright," Jimmy said, "but I still think he has some gold hidden back here. If he does, you'll be sorry." Jimmy picked up a rock, looked at it, and slipped it into his pants pocket.

"If that squirrel turns up with some gold in his mouth, you can dig all you want, Jimmy," Isabel said. She took him by the hand to lead him home, and Sandy led the way, tail wagging happily. Isabel forgot about Sally Anne for the rest of the day.

Jimmy's treasure hunt was the topic of conversation at the supper table that evening. Eugene and Curtis encouraged their brother's imagination by telling him about the elusive Beale treasure of Bedford County, Virginia. "People search for that buried treasure to this very day," Curtis said. "And that treasure was buried over a hundred years ago."

"Maybe Papa will find a treasure one day when he is till-in' the garden or planting apple trees for Mr. Meadows," Jimmy said. Then he tried to stuff an entire muffin in his mouth before Mama could stop him.

"Don't stuff your face, Son, mind your manners," Papa said. "The treasure your brothers are speaking of is miles away in Bedford County, not Botetourt County, which is where we reside. Besides, if I did happen upon a treasure, it might be exciting, but the money would belong to Mr. Meadows. This is his land, so everything on it belongs to him," Papa said. "Treasure hunting is for little boys to dream about, but strive to work hard and earn an honest living. That will make your papa and Mama proud. Do you understand, Son? Jimmy nodded, for he seemed to have trouble talking or even in swallowing his muffin, which was a little dry. His cheeks were red and puffed out. His eyes began to water.

"I think he's choking," Isabel said.

Suddenly the room was alive with activity. Mama and Papa rushed to his aide. Each pulled his arms over his head, patting him on the back, scolding everyone about the dangers of gulping your food. Finally, Mama ordered him to spit everything out into his napkin, then Papa patted his back hard, and Jimmy finally started coughing. Mama made him drink water and fussed over him during the rest of the meal. When he stood up to leave the table, Isabel noticed he swiped a muffin and stuffed it into his pocket and then ran out of the room.

Isabel forgot all earlier conversations of the day as she considered the brevity of life and the necessity of taking small bites of food and chewing each bite thoroughly. She almost forgot that Sally Anne had asked Miss Catron for Isabel to be her partner in the history project; the problem was that Isabel could not understand why.

Chapter 12

The Project

THE NEXT MORNING as Isabel got dressed for school, she tried to figure out why Sally Anne Albright would want her for a history project partner. They were so different.

"Sally Anne is rich and lives in a mansion. I live in a little house on somebody else's farm and share my bedroom with two sisters. She wears beautiful clothes and is popular. I wear homemade clothes, *and I ain't popular*," Isabel said. So why would Sally Anne choose me?" Isabel asked Maggie as they prepared for school. "Is this a trick to make fun of me?" Sally Anne had never actually mocked Isabel, but her group of friends had, many times. For as long as Isabel could remember, this certain circle of friends had been unkind to many unfortunate girls and boys. Isabel had often wondered what Sally Anne saw in them. All Isabel could see was silliness and meanness, though, this did not really seem to apply to Sally Anne.

When they were very small children, Isabel and Sally Anne had been playmates, but that was before they were aware of class distinctions. Isabel smiled as she remembered how they had once had a tea party with their dolls on a tree stump under the shade of the old oak tree. Mama had let them drink real tea with lots of cream and sugar and had served tiny sandwiches in the shape of triangles and cookies for dessert. They had dressed up in Mama's finest dresses and hats from her old trunk and even managed to put a dress on Isabel's kitten, Pearlie. It had been great fun until Pearlie decided to chase the girl's long hair ribbons and jumped from girl to screaming girl and then landed in a cup of tea, much to Pearlie's delight. She drank the cream and then climbed the oak tree to clean every drop of cream from her pearly white coat, ripping her lovely dress in the process. The girls had laughed and cried and then laughed again before they realized they would have to explain the broken teacups, spilled cream, and a ruined baby dress to Isabel's Mama. The worry was unfounded. Mama had been watching with amusement from the kitchen window and consoled the girls immediately.

Isabel smiled at the memory and then sighed when she remembered that she and Sally Anne were no longer small children crying over spilled milk. They were in the fifth grade now, and they were not even friends any more, so what could she want from Isabel? She supposed she would find out soon enough. Mama's voice called her back to the present as she reminded her daughter she would be late for school if she didn't get moving.

The day dragged for Isabel, and it seemed that every time she turned around, Sally Anne was beside her, behind her, or waving to her. Isabel became quite unnerved. Not knowing the girl's motive was getting a lion's share of Isabel's attention, and the teacher had to call her to attention twice, which made things even worse.

Isabel urged her siblings to hurry home after school, and that made Eugene suspicious.

"What's eating you, Isabel?" Eugene asked. "You have been grumpy all day, and you know Sylvia can't keep up if you run home."

"Oh, it's that dumb ol' history project. I have to hurry up and get my chores done and then get to Sally Anne's house. I told you that." She ran on ahead, determined to meet her unpleasant task head on. Besides, curiosity was taking its toll…on everyone.

Isabel held her breath as she neared the large, white colonial house on the hill overlooking the valley. The view was breathtaking, but she hesitated because she felt nervous about entering the portal of such a structure. Compared to the humble Greene home, Sally Anne's house seemed like a mansion to Isabel, and she did not know how to act. In fact, Isabel had never known how to behave around Sally Anne—especially after they grew up. When they started school and Isabel realized the differences in their lives, there seemed to be a wall she could not scale.

"Why did she choose me to be her partner in the school project?" she said to herself. She smoothed her homemade dress and pushed her wavy, brown hair away from her face before knocking on the ornate door. She looked around at the neatly trimmed rose bushes in the garden and the gravel paths divided by more neatly trimmed bushes and thought how Mama would enjoy such a garden and then decided it was a bit too structured for Mama, who liked things to look more natural and graceful—not forced and stoic. Suddenly her thoughts returned to the present as she heard footsteps approaching the door. Isabel expected to see her classmate. She was surprised, however, to see a thin, bantam woman wearing a gray uniform and a white apron open the door.

"I'm here to see Sally Anne," Isabel said, not really knowing what to say to this scary-looking woman.

"Miss Sally Anne's expecting you," the woman said. She didn't show any emotion, and Isabel nearly shivered over the women's cold salutation. "You are to go directly up to her room." Then she turned and walked away from the door and disappeared into another room, leaving poor Isabel to find her own way.

Isabel looked around the room and gasped as she realized that she almost had stepped on light blue plush carpeting before wiping her feet. She stepped back outside the door and wiped her feet several times on the doormat, checked the bottom of her shoes, and then stepped back inside, tiptoeing carefully on the rug. There were two large rooms on either side of the foyer. One seemed to be a sitting room and the other a library. Clanging of pots and pans was coming from the kitchen beyond the sitting room and behind the steps. Isabel took a step forward, thinking Sally Anne's room must be upstairs and she must climb the grand staircase to get there. She marveled at the highly polished wood and smiled when she thought of her brothers sliding down such a banister. Jimmy would be beside himself if he saw this banister…so would her young sister Sylvia. They would be in a race to see who could slide down the fastest. Her sister would probably win.

"Isabel," Sally Anne's voice rang out in pleasure. Isabel turned to see her classmate coming through a door behind the steps with a plate covered in her hands, as if she was hiding it. "Upstairs, first door on the right. Run." Both girls took off, taking two steps at a time, running into the first bedroom, closing the door, and landing on the bed in a pile of giggles.

"Why are we running?" Isabel asked. She held her side, which was aching from laughing so much.

"Because of this," Sally Anne said. She pulled back a napkin from the plate she was holding, revealing a plate of divinity fudge. "And this." She pulled two green bottles of Coca Cola from under her sweater. "Cookie would skin me alive if she knew I took these from the kitchen, but I don't care. I don't get to have special guests very often, and I wanted today to be special."

"But Carolyn and Arlene talk about coming over here with you all the time," Isabel said. She was unable to hide the surprise in her voice.

"Oh, they do. Lots of girls come over, but they come over because they want something. You came because I asked you to. You are my friend, Isabel. The other girls are not. Do you remember how we used to play dolls together when we were little?"

Sally Anne continued talking, but Isabel did not hear a word. She could not get past the word "friend." Shame and confusion enveloped her. Why would she consider Isabel her friend and not the girls she always hung around with? It didn't make sense. Isabel would have continued this line of thinking, but the offering of refreshments diverted her attention, and she began to relax and survey her surroundings.

"Your room is beautiful, Sally Anne. Do you play with all of those lovely dolls?" Isabel admired a display of twenty or more porcelain dolls on a shelf extending around the perimeter of the room. Each doll was dressed in an exquisite outfit with a parasol or basket or some other prop to make her appear more interesting. One was a mother-daughter combination. Isabel thought it was the loveliest of all.

"I see you have spied my favorite. They look so happy, don't they? I wish my mother looked at me like that," Sally Anne said. "It reminds me of you and your mother, Isabel."

Isabel swallowed a lump in her throat. "It does?"

"Oh, yes. That is why I asked for that one last Christmas. When I saw it in the window at the toy store in Richmond, it almost made me cry. Yet, it rather gives me hope. You know."

Isabel nodded as if she understood, but she did not. She was confused. Feeling confused and sad for the girl of whom she always had been jealous. She did not know what to say, so she quickly finished her Coca Cola with a smile and wiped her mouth with the white linen napkin lying on her lap.

"Now," Sally Anne said, "what shall we do for our history project? I was thinking about the War Between the States. Wouldn't it be fun to dress up in antebellum dresses? We could wear our hair in ringlets and carry parasols and talk real southern."

"Yes," Isabel said. She giggled. "That would be fun. You know, Papa was born not too long after the war. He was born in 1869. He has many stories his Papa told about the war. We even have some confederate money. Of course, it isn't any good." She rolled her eyes. "Where would we get the dresses?"

"Mother has a trunk upstairs. She told me all about it. It has old dresses, pantaloons, bustles, parasols, hats, and *everything*. I already asked her if we could use them, and she said we could as long as we don't make a lot of noise or make a mess. Sally Anne stopped for a breath after talking continuously. Isabel had never heard anyone talk so fast or use so many words in such a short period. "We will have to air the clothes out though. Mama said they are quite dusty and smell like mothballs." Sally Anne pinched her nose for effect. "We will have to be very quiet and sneak up to the attic. Follow me."

"Why do we need to sneak upstairs if we have your mother's permission?"

"Oh," Sally said, "the household staff doesn't like me very much because they say I cause them too much work. So I try to be as quiet as possible. I want to be friends with them, but I don't think they want to be my friend. They live up on the third floor, and we have to go on their floor in order to get to the attic. Why don't we make a game out of it—pretend we are southern belles and hiding from the Yankee soldiers during the war? They were in this area, you know."

"OK," Isabel said.

They quietly opened her door and checked the hallway for intruders. Carefully, they tiptoed from door to door, to the end of the hall, to the back stairs, straining to listen for sounds of footsteps behind them. Tiptoeing all the way, they avoided squeaky boards. Isabel felt strange about sneaking around someone's home, especially with the homeowner's permission. Yet, it was an exciting game, albeit confusing.

The girls ascended the stairs to a narrow hallway with white walls and doors. "This is the servant's quarters," Sally Anne whispered, as if it were normal to have a servant's quarters in one's home. "We will go upstairs to the attic at the end of this hall. Shhhh." She held her finger over her lips and tiptoed past the last door. "This is our gardener's room. He suffers from severe headaches, so we must be very quiet."

Isabel felt her muscles tense up as she tiptoed past the gardener's room. She breathed a sigh of relief as they reached the end of the hallway and then turned the corner and started up a narrow, dark stairway. About halfway up the steps, Isabel noticed the sweet, yet pungent odor of old wood.

Suddenly, the steps began to creak loudly, and Sally Anne froze in place, as if she did not know whether to continue up or turn back and run to the comfort of her own room.

"What's wrong?" Isabel whispered.

"I don't know. It seems spooky up here." The blood seemed to drain from her face.

"Do you come up here often?" Isabel asked.

"No, I have never been up here, not ever."

"Land sakes, why not?" Isabel knew she should not pry, but could not stop herself.

Sally Anne held onto Isabel's hand, as if to gain courage, took a deep breath, and then began her story. "When I was a little girl, my nanny told me when I was naughty that she was going to lock me in the attic with all the ghosts and spiders and not let me out until I could always be good. I have not liked the attic since."

"What did you do that was so bad?" Isabel whispered.

"I cried."

"You cried? All children cry," Isabel said with a slight raise in her voice for emphasis. "What were you crying about?"

"I wanted my mother, but the nanny told me to be quiet and go to sleep, but I couldn't. The more she fussed and told me to be quiet, the harder I cried. So, she threatened to put me into the attic. In fact, every night she told me if I didn't go to sleep, she would put me up here."

"I've never heard of anything so mean!" Isabel's nostrils flared. "How could anybody be so cruel? I hope your mother fired her when she found out."

"She never knew. I've never told anyone before."

"We can go back downstairs if you want to and find another project to do," Isabel said. She patted her friend on the back as if she were comforting a small child.

"No," Sally Anne said, "I must face this old attic sometime, and I would rather face it with you than anyone." The girls traversed the narrow stairs together, and the brave child reached out and turned the tarnished knob on the dark door at the top of the narrow stairs. The door creaked as if it resented the intrusion.

Isabel stepped inside and looked around at the dusty, cluttered attic. Slowly, her eyes became accustomed to the light filtering through the filthy windows, and she was delighted with the array of treasures she saw. She turned to see Sally Anne's response and was surprised to see her still clinging to the door. "Come on in, Sally Anne," she said. "It's just a dusty, old room filled with great stuff. If there were such a thing as ghosts, I'll bet they are happy ones with this much stuff to play with."

That comment brought a smile to her friend's lips, and finally Sally Anne slipped into the room. "It is a bit like a treasure room, isn't it, Isabel?" Her voice quivered. "Oh, look over there. There is an old teddy bear. Isn't it sweet? Maybe I will take him downstairs and fix him up. It looks like he could use a friend." She picked up the soft, fuzzy, brown bear with stuffing coming out of one paw and one eye dangling precariously. She laughed at his silly grin and adjusted his dark green bowtie. "It looks like we were meant for each other, pal," she said to the little bear.

She carried him to Isabel for her inspection. Isabel called him a "dandy fellow," and thus, he became known as Dandy Teddy. The girls were suddenly in the mood to work on their school project.

The trunk containing items from the War Between the States was not difficult to locate. It was the oldest and dustiest trunk in the room. It also held center stage and was covered with an old confederate flag.

"Where did the trunk come from, Sally Anne? Did it belong to one of your grandparents?" Isabel asked. They began to dig through yards of silk, satin, and velvet ball gowns.

"I don't know. Mother just said there's a trunk of old Civil War clothes that we may use. She was too busy to tell me anymore. She was on her way to play bridge in Roanoke."

"Oh," Isabel said, as if she understood. She could not imagine Mama ever brushing her off like that. She couldn't even imagine Mama playing cards at all.

Sally Anne's voice interrupted Isabel's thoughts. "Just look at these dresses, Isabel. Whoever wore them must have been tiny. See how small they are?" Sally Anne held up a petite white dress. Which dress do you want to wear, Isabel? I think this blue would look lovely with your hair and eyes."

"Really?" Isabel said. "It's so fancy. It even has pearls on it. What if something happens to it?"

"What could happen to it? Besides, it has been locked away in a dusty, stinky ol' trunk for a bazillion years. It is time for someone to wear it. It needs to be brought back to life."

"That's a funny way to think of it. I've never thought of clothes as being alive before."

"Well, maybe the dress is not alive, but it's time it is worn by a live person. I mean, to show the world the beautiful design and stitches. Whoever made this dress created a work of art. It is a shame to hide it in mothballs."

"You mean like a fashion show or a fancy museum?" Isabel said.

"Both. Do you think Miss Catron would allow us to put on a real fashion show? We have enough dresses for every girl in the class. These dresses look quite small, so maybe the dressmakers or mothers won't have to alter them too much. I love to sew. I could work on one or two of them myself. Then perhaps we could keep the dresses on dress forms somewhere in the classroom for the rest of the year. We could even add other Civil War items. I know the boys have bullets and belt buckles and things like that."

"You sew?" Isabel said. She fingered the fancy stitching on the dress she was holding.

"Oh, yes. I used to love watching the dressmaker when she came, and one day she asked me if I would like to learn to sew. I couldn't believe she would teach me, but she did. Now I love going into the sewing room and taking a flat piece of fabric, folding it, placing a pattern on it, cutting it out, and then sewing it. It's almost like magic, Isabel. Just think, a simple piece of material can become anything you want."

"I've never thought of it like that before," Isabel said. "Where would we get the dress forms?"

"Mama has a few in the sewing room. She has the dressmaker come all the way from Richmond to make clothes for us. Sometimes Hannah stays a month, until everything is perfect." She looked around the attic. "I'll bet there are some old ones up here, and if not, I'm sure mother would furnish some for the school."

"That would be wonderful," Isabel said. "And don't forget about the Confederate States of America Currency. Papa said we have relatives in Floyd County who actually used theirs as wallpaper to keep the wind out of their cabin. Can you imagine? Money wallpaper."

Sally Anne shook her head. "It must have been sad, Isabel. They lost everything they had. To have all that money, and suddenly, it is worthless. Just think what things would be like if that happened today. Imagine taking a dollar to the store to buy food for your mama, and the storekeeper said your money is no good. It was good just last week, but not now. What would you do? Unless you had Union currency, you would go hungry. However, losing their money and having their things stolen by the Yankee soldiers was only part of it. So many men and boys lost their lives. Women and children were left alone, unprotected, and without anyone to work in the fields. They had to do whatever they could themselves. They may have been able to plant gardens and milk the cows, but if soldiers happened by, they confiscated the food for the war effort, and the families starved. It was a terrible time."

"Land sakes!" Isabel said. "You sound just like the teacher. How do you know all of this?"

"Oh, I read a lot. Father loves history and has a lot of books in the library downstairs. There is a lot of history in our area, you know. Battles took place in Bedford, Hanging Rock, Hollins College, and you know, the Shenandoah Valley was very important. That is where Stonewall Jackson and his men were from. Many men from Virginia fought in the war. Don't forget that Richmond was our Confederate capital. It is our heritage, even if we do not agree with every issue of the day."

Suddenly, the afternoon began to seem like a history lesson, and Isabel noticed it was getting late. "I need to get home and help Mama with supper," Isabel said. She gently folded the blue dress and placed it back into the trunk. "Which dress are you wearing?"

"I haven't decided yet. What do you think?"

"Well, I think either the deep green velvet or the deep burgundy will look beautiful with your long, blonde hair. You will be the belle of the ball. They both look like they are made for you. With all that velvet and silk, you will look like a princess."

"Isabel, will you come back Friday and spend the night? We can try the dresses on, fix our hair like they wore it in the old days, and everything," Sally Anne said, excitement mounting in her voice. "I already asked mother, and she agreed that you will be an excellent influence on me. She even said we could eat in the dining room."

Isabel was taken aback by the offer, but even more so by the shine in Sally Anne's eyes at the prospect of eating in her own dining room. "Where do you usually eat?"

"I usually eat in my room, at that little, round table by the window. Cookie says it is too much trouble to set the table just for me. She just brings a tray of food to my room. My parents are seldom home for dinner."

Suddenly, the silence in Sally Anne's enormous house became overwhelming to Isabel, and she wondered how this young girl managed to survive. Indeed, how could she manage to be so cheerful all the time? Isabel thought she understood now why Sally Anne always had a crowd of kids around her. She was lonely and was trying to fill the need for "family."

Isabel's eyes filled with tears on her way home. She was never more thankful to hear the laughter of her brothers and sisters as she neared the yard. She waved a quick hello and went directly into the kitchen, where Mama was kneading biscuit dough at her worktable. There was a streak of flour across her forehead where she had tried to push her hair out of her face. She looked up to greet her eldest daughter and gave her a brilliant smile. Isabel's heart warmed with love for Mama and broke for poor Sally Anne.

"There you are, child," Mama said. "I was beginning to worry. Pour yourself a glass of milk and have an oatmeal cookie before you set the table and tell me all about your afternoon."

Isabel started for the icebox to get the pitcher of milk and then turned and rushed to her Mama, giving her the biggest bear hug she could manage.

Mama hugged back, careful not to get flour all over her daughter. "Sweetie pie, what's this all about?"

"You're the best Mama in the whole world," Isabel said. Tears streamed down her face.

"Well, I am glad you think so, but I don't know about that. Perhaps in this house, maybe." She chuckled. "Why don't you pour your milk and tell me all about it? Perhaps we can help. At the very least, we can pray about it. God will give us wisdom if we ask Him and seek His face."

Mother and daughter sought wisdom and blessing from above for the lonely and previously misunderstood Sally Anne.

Chapter 13

Lead on, O' Sandy Turtle

ISABEL RETURNED HOME Saturday afternoon from her overnight stay with Sally Anne and was thankful for her cozy, little home and cheerful family. She felt the loneliness Sally Anne must feel every day. The Albrights were not a close family. Indeed, they did not seem to realize they had an obligation to their daughter at all. It seemed to Isabel that the girl she perceived as a stuck-up rich kid with everything she ever wanted was really a sad little girl who was treated by her mother as a mere porcelain doll. She was like a fancy toy that her mother could display at parties; yet, when it was not convenient, she could merely put Sally Anne on a shelf and forget about her. At least that is what Sally Anne told Isabel as the large grandfather clock struck midnight and the delinquent parents had not returned home from a dinner party they were attending in Roanoke.

Breakfast had been a quiet affair, and Isabel felt sorry to leave her new friend as she headed for the comfort of home and Mama's welcoming arms. Even the thought of chores sounded good to Isabel, who could not imagine what it must be like to have someone assigned to make your bed for you. As she left, she looked back to see Sally Anne watching from her bedroom window. Isabel was thankful her new friend had their school project to work on, for she was almost beside herself with excitement over their assignment. She already had altered their two dresses and was planning which dresses to put on Maggie and Sylvia. This thought comforted Isabel, who felt guilty leaving Sally Anne behind. She could not help but think about her first reaction at being partners with the richest girl in school and feel ashamed. She could not wait to get home to talk it over with Mama.

"Mama will know what to do to help Sally Anne," Isabel whispered to herself. "Mama always knows how to help." She walked along the dusty road that led to the small, white cottage with green trim, that was surrounded by a white picket fence. As she approached it, she said, "Ah, this is more like it. Our house may be small, but it is cozy and filled with love."

So deep in thought was Isabel that she walked right past her brothers, who were giving Sandy a bath in the yard, against the poor dog's will. In fact, Sandy, seeing Isabel enter the yard, appealed to her good graces for help. Alas, the poor dog, after receiving no help, broke away from her captors and ran past Isabel, covered in soap lather, followed closely by three screaming brothers. Isabel did not pay attention to the parade.

The commotion continued as Sandy ran toward Maggie, who was standing on a chair hanging sheets on the clothesline, assisted by Sylvia, who was handing Maggie a clean, white sheet from Mama's wicker basket. Sandy and the parade of soap-covered boys pushed through, knocking over Maggie's chair (with the startled sister landing in the basket of wet sheets), pulling down the clothesline of clean clothes, and dragging the clean laundry behind them. Sandy continued running, with Mama's white sheet draped over her head. She ran headlong into a vat of green dye, in which Mama was dying flour sacking for quilting.

"Mama's sheet is green!" Maggie said.

"Sandy looks like a turtle," Jimmy said as he ran after her. Sylvia joined the chase and sang, "Lead on, O' Sandy Turtle," with enthusiasm. She sang loudly, and her brothers followed her example, making quite a noisy parade. Little Billy stood on the porch steps laughing and clapping at the sight as Isabel remained oblivious to it all. She walked straight past him toward the kitchen door.

Just as she reached for the screen door handle, Mama rushed to open the door. Her eyebrows were raised, and her hands were grasping her face. Isabel began speaking without greeting her mother, as if they had been working together all morning and as though nothing unusual was happening outside. She did not even notice the confused look on Mama's face.

"I always wondered what it would be like to be an only child," Isabel said to Mama.

Mama opened the screen door for Isabel and reached out to her, but just as Isabel stepped inside, something wet and green brushed past Isabel, almost knocking her down, followed by a parade of Greene children singing, "Lead on, O' Sandy Turtle," and laughing as if they were having a wonderful time…until they realized they were standing on Mama's formerly clean kitchen floor.

Isabel looked around and saw to her horror that the floor was covered in mud and green dye and soapsuds. The terrible smell of wet dog was the worst of the mess, especially since Mama never allowed even clean dogs into her kitchen.

"I'll bet ya being an only child sounds pretty good right now, doesn't it?" Papa said from the corner of the room, where he was enjoying a cup of coffee.

Isabel felt ashamed and hid her face behind her hands as she realized how selfish she had sounded a moment ago, especially when so much was happening in the yard and she had just walked past without paying attention to a thing.

"I'll clean this up, Mama," Isabel said. "You take care of the bread, and I'll take care of the rest of this mess." She reached for the broom, mop, and bucket to restore order.

"Thank you, child," Mama said. "That would be helpful. We have a lot of work to do. Oh, my sheet! It's green. Oh well, it looks like someone will have to live with a green bed sheet from now on.

"Eugene, Curtis, take Sandy to the creek with some soap and a pitcher to pour the water over her to get the suds out," Mama said. "She will be more receptive to playing in the creek than in a tub of bubbles. I just hope you can get the green out of her lovely red coat.

"Maggie and Sylvia, you will need to rewash the sheets, and then I want you to give your little brothers a bath. Jimmy stomped in the dye, and little Billy is outside playing in the mud as we speak, and no one is watching him."

"Yes, Mama," they said in unison.

"And Sylvia, dear," Mama said, "we need to talk about changing the words to church songs and making them silly. I do not think this pleases the Lord, do you?"

"No, Mama," Sylvia said. "I guess not."

"Your song was very clever, Dear, you thought of it very quickly," Mama said with a smile.

Sylvia turned and ran to Mama, giving her a bear hug and staining her starched, white apron in the process.

"Well, Mama, I'd love to stay and help you clean up this mess," Papa said. He reached for his hat from the hook near the door. "But I promised the boss that I'd check on that farm equipment at the farm store in Roanoke. We ordered it two months ago, and it should be here by now. The clerk promised it would be there today."

"That's alright, Papa," Mama said. "I think we can handle this. Besides, now Maggie and Sylvia will have two laundry lessons in one day."

After Isabel put the kitchen back in order, Mama turned to her with a smile, "Now, when you came home, you said you always wanted to be an only child. I didn't know you felt that way, child," Mama said. She wiped her hands on her apron and walked over to embrace her.

"Oh," Isabel said. "I don't, not really. I just always wondered what it would be like to have a room of my own...or even a bed to myself—to have a closet of beautiful clothes and shoes to choose from when I wake up each morning and not to have to share Mama and Papa all of the time."

"And you discovered this was not as wonderful as you dreamed?" Mama asked. She gathered the vegetables and placed them in the stewing pot to boil and then returned to making biscuits for dinner. She looked to Isabel, who was putting the potato peelings into the scrap bucket for the pigs.

Tears were threatening to spill over as she looked up at Mama. "It's much better to have a Mama and Papa with brothers and sisters who love you and to be poor than it is to be rich and to not feel loved. Oh, Mama, I never knew how lonely Sally Anne is. Her mother never pays attention to her. The housekeeper takes care of her, and she eats at the table alone. Her parents go to grand parties at the Hotel Roanoke. Sometimes they go to Richmond or Washington for a week or more, and they leave Sally Anne all alone, with only the household staff."

"Was it as you expected?" Mama asked.

"Yes and no," Isabel said. She reached across the table for an oatmeal cookie to dunk into the glass of cold milk Mama was pouring for her. She dunked her cookie, took a bite, smiled appreciatively, and then continued the conversation. "Sally Anne's house is so fancy. I was afraid to walk on the floors. Thought I might scuff them up with my shoes. The furniture looks nice too, but the servants look at us as if they are afraid we might sit on it and get the upholstery dirty or something. They even give Sally Anne funny looks, and it is her home. There are fancy pillows everywhere, even propped against windows. Sally Anne said they are called window seats. I did like the window seat in her bedroom. We could see the Blue Ridge Mountains during the day, and at night, watching the stars from the window seat was like being at the picture show. We even saw a shooting star." She finished her milk and washed her glass before finishing her story. Mama seemed to sense Isabel's need to sort out her feelings about her discovery of class distinctions. "The thing I noticed the most, Mama, was the silence."

"Silence?" Mama said.

"Yes, when we first opened the door, the only sound that greeted us was the ticking of a clock in the hallway, a great big grandfather clock that has a face and everything," Isabel said.

"Did anyone greet you and Sally Anne at the door?" Mama asked.

"No, that seemed strange to me; no one ever did. The first time I was in her house, a maid answered the door, and Cookie was somewhere in the back of the house, but we did not even hear them or see them when we came home from school.

"Sally Anne said her Mother was in her room, but we did not even see her at all. She did not say 'hello' to Sally Anne, and she did not even tell her 'good night' at bedtime."

"Didn't her parents tuck her in at night or at least check on you when they got home from their dinner engagement?" asked Mama as she stepped closer to Isabel and patted her hand.

Isabel shook her head as she studied the pattern of the linoleum on the floor in order to hold back the tears threatening to race down her cheeks. "I asked Sally Anne if her mother was ill, if I should go home, but she said her mother was OK and that she seldom talked to her. She was surprised I was concerned. Mama, I know Sally Anne is lonely. All this time I thought she was just stuck up, but maybe she does not know how to be friends."

"I think you're right. You may invite her over sometime for supper, if you wish. Monday after school would be fine, if it is all right with her mother. In fact, I will speak to her mother after church tomorrow. I'll get permission so you may ask Sally Anne at school."

"Thank you, Mama," Isabel said. She hugged Mama tightly. "I'll ask her Monday morning."

Just at that moment, there was a commotion outside as little Billy opened the screen door and allowed poor, dripping Sandy into the safety of the house. By now, however, instead of soap bubbles, she was covered with a combination of soap, mud, dirt, and mama's once bright white sheet, which had turned an ugly brown in spots. The other children followed nosily behind, with their own version of the events leading to the demise of Mama's sheet.

"Oh, Sandy, not again," Isabel said. She looked at the mess around her, and to her utter surprise, Mama started laughing. "Mama, are you alright?"

"I was just trying to imagine poor little Sally Anne in her quiet tomb on the hill and envisioning her face when this gang entered the room just now, and the look was priceless. We must have her over often. She needs us…and I have a feeling we may need her too."

Chapter 14

The Lesson

AFTER SHE FINISHED laughing, Mama said, "I think the Lord must want us to learn a lesson from this. Let's all go outside and see what lesson the Lord has for us as we rewash this filthy sheet."

Isabel followed Mama and the children outside, helped her dump muddy water, and refilled the tubs with clean water for washing as Eugene built a fire under the wash water.

"This dirty, filthy sheet reminds me of something," Mama said.

"Mama," Maggie said. "I don't think it's just dirt and mud… this one stinks."

"Oh, Sandy," Mama said. She picked up the corner of the sheet and held it up for the children to see. Do you know what this reminds me of?"

"Sandy?" Curtis said. He had a wide grin on his face.

"Doing laundry?" Eugene said.

"Sin," Maggie said.

"Yes," Mama said. "It does remind me of sin, especially since we continue to sin again and again, but Jesus has washed us clean in His precious blood so that all the Father sees when He looks at us is the precious blood of His Son…and not our dirty, stinky sin. However, that is not the lesson I came outside to teach you today."

"It isn't?" the children asked.

She showed the sheet to each child, making sure each one got a good whiff as she passed by. "This sheet reminds me of my good works."

Isabel could hear gasps, her own among them.

"Isabel," Mama said, "I have heard you often say lately that you are 'doing a good deed today,' and I want to make sure that my children are not counting on good deeds to get them to heaven." Mama stopped and looked seriously at each of her children before she finished her thought. "You see," Mama said, "the Bible says that all our good works are as filthy rags to the Lord[1]. There is absolutely nothing that we can do to earn our way to heaven[2]. God is so holy, so good, that in comparison, the very best we can do is…well, like this filthy sheet."

"Ugh, that's really bad."

Isabel turned to see which brother had spoken, but she could not see for the tears in her eyes. She wondered about Mama's good works. *If they are as nasty as that sheet, what about mine?* The thought cut to her heart. She always had been told that she was a good girl—certainly not a sinner. *Of course,* everyone *is a sinner,* Isabel admitted to herself. Isabel thought about the unkind words she had said about Sally Anne before she really knew her, and suddenly, she remembered talking back to Papa in her heart. She then thought of all the times her pride was hurt by the other girls at school, and she knew without a doubt that Isabel Greene was indeed a sinner. Her heart pounded, and her stomach churned as she remembered Romans 3:23 and silently quoted it to herself. *"For all have sinned, and come short of the glory of God"…that means me. Romans 6:23 then there's which says that "the wages of sin is death," and that means separation from God—we learned that in Sunday school. What was the rest of that verse? Oh yeah, "But the gift of God is eternal life through Jesus Christ our Lord."*

Isabel returned her focus to Mama, who was just about to dip the sheet into the wash water, which Isabel knew contained Clorox˚ bleach, for she had noticed Mama pouring liquid from the brown bottle into the water while the children were talking amongst themselves. Isabel listened carefully as Mama continued to speak.

"Our good works will not get us to heaven. We cannot work our way to heaven or buy our way. There is nothing we can do. Going to church does not save us either. There is only one way to heaven. Jesus said, 'I am the way, the truth and the life, no man cometh to the Father but by me.'[3]

"Jesus died on the cross and shed His blood for our sin.[4]" Mama put the sheet into the soapy water, sloshing it around with her hands and rubbing it on the scrubbing board as she talked. "The Bible says, 'Though your sins be as scarlet, they shall be as snow; though they be red like crimson, they shall be as wool.[5]'"

When she pulled the sheet out of the water, it was clean and white.

Mama whispered something to Eugene, who disappeared and quickly returned carrying Mama's goody tin. Mama opened the tin as she spoke. "Salvation is a gift. A gift is free, you cannot earn it, or it would not be a gift; nor can you purchase it. Do you understand what I am saying?" Mama looked at her children.

Isabel looked around to see if everyone understood and was surprised to see Sally Anne and some neighborhood children sitting in the grass with them. Isabel smiled and returned her attention to Mama and the important gift of salvation. Everyone was leaning forward, as if listening to every word. Isabel noticed Maggie nodding her head and Sally Anne wiping her eyes with a handkerchief. Eugene and Curtis had their heads bowed. It looked as if they were praying.

"Good," Mama said, "I'm glad you understand and accept the truth of the Word of God, but you have not yet *received* the free gift, have you? All that is left for you to do is to receive God's gift of salvation, just as I have this little gift for you." Mama reached into her tin, pulled out a peppermint stick, and offered it to Sally Anne, who reached out and took it with a polite "thank you."

"Now," Mama said, "that gift is yours to keep, and no one can take it from you; it belongs to you. Salvation is just as simple. You trusted me to give you a good gift and opened your hand to receive it; we call this faith. Trusting the Lord Jesus Christ for salvation is faith. John 1:12 says, 'But as many as received Him, to them He gave the power to become the sons of God, even to them that believe on His name.'

"When you receive Christ as your Savior, you become a brand-new creation.[6] This is part of His gift...new life." Mama gave a "gift" to everyone before continuing. "Part of receiving the gift of salvation, my dear children, is repentance. This means to be truly sorry for your sin, ask Jesus to forgive you, and leave that sin with Him. Some preachers say it this way: 'take your sin to the cross, lay it at the feet of Jesus, and then turn and go the other way.' In other words, don't go back to your old, sinful way; remember, Jesus washed your filthy sins away—see the dirty water?"

The children stood up, looked into the tub of muddy water, and nodded.

"Mama," Isabel said. "I want my sins cleaned away so that I will be white as snow."

"Me too," Maggie said. Tears ran down her rosy cheeks.

"Let's pray together," Mama said. She hugged each daughter close to her heart and then directed them to the back porch steps, where they tearfully laid their sinful selves at the cross, asking and receiving the forgiveness that Jesus extended to us all on the cross of Calvary. They opened their eyes as new creations in Christ.

"Mama," Maggie said with a trembling voice, "should we be baptized now?"

"Yes, Dear," Mama said. "It is an act of obedience to show the world that you are now a new creation in Christ—a believer."

"But, Mama," Isabel said. "Jesus has already washed my sin away. Why do I need to be baptized? You know I don't like to go under the water."

"Baptism doesn't save us, Dear. It is a picture to the world that you have died to yourself, are buried with Him in baptism, and are raised to walk in newness of life; at least that is the words our pastor always uses. Do you remember when we had a baptism service down by the creek?"

Isabel nodded because she vaguely remembered the service, but she was embarrassed that she had not paid attention to her pastor's words because she had been was too busy making faces at Arlene Mason, who had just walked past Isabel in her fancy dress that she had bought in Richmond and had told Isabel that she looked nice in her homemade dress. The memory made Isabel blush, and immediately she felt guilty for her unkind thoughts toward Arlene. She felt something that she had never felt before: a desire to share Christ with Arlene.

"Mama," Isabel said, "what happens when you sin after you become a Christian? Do I have to get saved all over again?"

"That is a very good question, Dear. One that God's Word is very clear on. Let me ask you a question. How many times did Jesus die?"

"Once," Isabel said. A smile spread across her face as she remembered the passages of Scripture verses she had learned in Sunday school. "He died once, and He arose from the dead."[7]

"That's right," Mama said, "and remember when He was hanging on the cross, His last words were, 'It is finished.' His work was complete…it did not need to be repeated. Therefore, you do not need to be saved again. You see, He loves us so much that no one or nothing can take us away from Him. His

Word, the Bible, actually says that nothing can pluck us out of His hands. He is holding us mighty tight in His strong hands." Mama pushed Isabel's hair away from her face and took a clean handkerchief out of her apron pocket and wiped Maggie's tears that began streaming down her face again as she listened to Mama and Isabel's conversation.

"As for our sin," Mama said, addressing all of her children, who were still sitting around the wash water and listening, "we simply go to our heavenly Father in prayer in Jesus' name and ask forgiveness for our sin. First John 1:9 says, 'If we confess our sin, He is faithful and just to forgive our sin and to cleanse us from all unrighteousness.' His forgiveness is like a never-ending fountain. Agree with God that whatever we did was sin…don't try to sugar coat it, now. Remember, God is Holy, and He sees you as you really are. We cannot lie or pretend with Him; to do so is sin. Anything that we think, say, or do that displeases God is sin."

"You mean like killing somebody?"

"Yes, Curtis, murder is sin."

"Telling a lie?"

"Yes, Sylvia, telling a lie is a sin."

"What about being proud that you have the prettiest colt in the class? Is that a sin, Mama?"

"Well, Eugene, do you think it pleases the heavenly Father that you are so proud of your colt that it occupies your mind so much that you forget to do your Sunday school lesson or that you prize your colt above everything else and possibly taunt the other boys at school because their horses may not be as nice?"

"Yes, Mama, it is sin. I'll pray about it right after we dump the wash water," Eugene said. He hung his head low as he reached for the washtub.

Sally Anne rushed up to Mama and hugged her tightly. "Thank you, Mama Greene," she said and then turned and ran down the road toward her home.

Just as they were cleaning up, Isabel heard the Model T pulling into the yard, and she ran to meet it.

"Papa, you won't believe what happened." Isabel stopped to catch her breath as Papa stepped out of the automobile and closed the door behind him.

"What's this big news that I won't believe?"

"Maggie and I received Christ as our Savior this afternoon, and it's all Sandy's fault."

Papa looked from Isabel to Maggie's smiling faces and then to Mama.

"It is just like Isabel said, Papa. God used the antics of our dog to lead our little girls to Christ. Come inside, and I'll tell you all about it…and then perhaps we can discuss tethering Sandy on laundry day," Mama said with a smile at Sandy, who was resting demurely under the porch swing.

Isabel looked around the yard with new eyes and with a heart filled with love and compassion toward her brothers, sisters, and neighbors, who had all scampered back to their own homes.

Chapter 15

The Dinner Guest

MONDAY MORNING ARRIVED too quickly—as it always did during school months for Isabel. However, this particular Monday held special significance for the family. They were having a dinner guest, and apparently, Isabel was not the only family member looking forward to the visit.

Sally Anne was so excited at the invitation to dinner at the Greene household that she squealed in anticipation. Isabel could hardly believe her ears. "You mean you wouldn't mind eating farm style?"

"I would love it. Do you think your mama would let me help in the kitchen? I have always wanted to help, but Cookie always chases me out of the kitchen and says I just get in the way."

"Oh, I think you can count on helping in the kitchen," Isabel said with a laugh. "We all pitch in at our house. At least, the girls do. The boys do too when they aren't outside helping Papa. Mama always says that every girl and boy should know his or her way around the kitchen. Eugene and Curtis at least know how to fry bacon and eggs and know how to make Mama's famous stew. At least they will not starve if they live alone when

107

they grow up. She even makes sure they wash the dishes every once in a while and sweep the floors, and they are required to make their own beds every morning."

"Mother insists that our housekeeper takes care of those things. I am afraid I will never learn how to do anything," Sally Anne said.

"Well, if Mama has anything to say about it, you will learn at our house," Isabel said.

"I hope so," Sally Anne said. "It would be a dream come true."

Isabel kept her thoughts to herself concerning Sally Anne's dream. It seemed a lowly one, but she had been wrong about so much lately. She wondered if God might be up to something by allowing her to have Sally Anne over to her house on a regular basis.

The school day progressed as normal. The day seemed especially long for Isabel, who just wanted the day to be finished. Sally Anne seemed quite excited and could not wait for the day to end. She attracted Isabel's attention several times throughout the day, motioned toward the clock, and rolled her eyes in a comical fashion to indicate time was not moving quickly enough for her. The teacher seemed to talk on forever.

At lunch, Sally Anne ignored her usual entourage and joined Isabel, Maggie, and Sylvia for lunch. "I'm so excited about having supper at your house tonight, Isabel, I could just…burst," she said. "What are we having? Should I bring anything?"

"Oh, no. Just bring yourself," Isabel said, trying to match her newfound friend's enthusiasm. "We're just having chicken and dumplings tonight."

"Chicken and dumplings—really?" she squealed. "I have always wanted to try chicken and dumplings. They sound delicious. I went past a house where a family was eating outside at a picnic table and I heard someone say 'pass the chicken and dumplings' and the dish smelled so delicious, it made my mouth water. I went home and asked Cookie if she would please make some, but she said absolutely not and don't ask such a ridiculous question again. I never did, but I have always longed to taste them."

"Well, you will have your chance tonight. Mama makes it at least once a month. When we have chicken for Sunday, she saves the leftovers for Monday dumplings."

"You mean you actually have leftovers? With a family of so many boys, I did not think that was possible," Sally Anne said.

"She always makes extra chicken on purpose so we can have dumplings on Monday," Sylvia said, as if she were divulging a great secret. The girls laughed with her as they picked up their books.

When the girls arrived home after school and opened the back door, the familiar, sweet fragrances of stewed chicken and dumplings, green beans, homemade bread, and apple pie wafted through the house.

"Oh, I believe I have died and gone to culinary heaven," Sally Anne said.

Everyone laughed as Mama accepted her praise humbly with a curtsy, as if receiving praise from a queen. Isabel looked at Sally Anne nervously, for fear that she had been offended, but she was laughing good-naturedly. She returned Mama's curtsy with a regal nod of her head.

"Mrs. Greene, thank you for inviting me to supper. Everything smells wonderful. I have always wanted to try chicken and dumplings, so I have been waiting a long time for today," Sally Anne said. "I hope you will allow me to help. I must warn you, though, I do not know anything at all about cooking. Though, Cookie has gone nearly mad with my constant pleadings to teach me how to cook and clean and do those household things, but especially cooking."

Mama offered Sally Anne a taste of the entrée from her large, wooden spoon.

"Oh, Mrs. Greene," she said, "this is so delicious." Sally Anne grinned and licked her lips. "I want to learn how to make this so that I can have some every day!"

Mama smiled at the girl's exaggeration. "We will have to remedy that, won't we, Isabel?" Mama said.

"Yes, Mama," Isabel said. She was hoping for an excuse to get out of chores for the afternoon since she had company. However, when she saw the stars in her friend's eyes at the prospect of helping in the kitchen, the task suddenly became a privilege rather than a chore.

"I have lettuce and red cabbage soaking in cold salt water," Mama said. "Will you please show Sally Anne how to rinse the vegetables well, remove the outer leaves and core, and then tear them into bite size pieces for salad? Then we will see if she is interested in peeling and chopping carrots and celery." Mama gave the girls a large bowl and paring knife. "Don't forget to wash your hands first." She tied an apron around each girl and pulled their hair back and deftly braided it, securing each braid with a ribbon conveniently placed in her pocket.

Isabel rolled her eyes and started for the door to do as bidden.

"Thank you, Mrs. Greene. This is the best day of my life."

It was obvious to Isabel that Sally Anne had never prepared food before, but she was a willing and quick student. She also had an eye for detail. She delighted in the colors of the vegetables and arranged them in such a way that even Isabel saw the beauty.

Supper went well, and everyone declared that the salad was the best they had ever eaten. Sally Anne beamed at their compliments. She glowed as the family included her in their conversation, especially Papa and Mama. Eugene and Curtis seemed to take pleasure in teasing their guest as if she were their sister—at least, that is what Isabel thought at first.

"Have some more chicken n' dumplings, Sally Anne," Eugene said. He spooned a serving onto her plate. Before he finished speaking, Curtis chimed in with an offer for more buttered biscuits and proceeded to give her two. Not to be outdone by his big brothers, Jimmy crawled out of his seat and ran around the table to be near their honored guest in order to offer her a bite of his special concoction—apple butter, grape jelly, and strawberry preserves on a biscuit.

Isabel was mortified. Sally Anne seemed to be charmed by the little guy, and Isabel looked at her little brother again. He did look appealing with jelly smeared on his face while grinning from ear to ear with sincerity shining in his sky blue eyes.

"Have some, Sally Anne, it's delicious," he said. He cocked his head to one side.

Everyone held their collective breath as they waited for their guest to give a polite decline. Mama began to intervene on her behalf, but Papa caught her eye and shook his head slightly. Sally Anne surprised them all by pinching off a generous portion and popping it into her mouth. Isabel cringed as her friend chewed the disgusting combination, admiring the acting scene she was playing on behalf of the little boy.

Sally Anne chewed and finally swallowed the interesting treat. "It has a sweet, yet tangy flavor, doesn't it, Jimmy? Did you think of it all by yourself?"

"Yup."

"Then I shall have to try it again sometime, but not tonight, because I am saving room for your mama's famous apple pie," she said.

Jimmy wore her compliment like a badge as he strode back to his seat, grinning at his amazed older brothers en route. Isabel's heart swelled with love for her small brother. She wanted to pick him up and hold him tightly in order to keep him a baby. At that moment, she glanced up and met Mama's eyes, which seemed to reflect Isabel's very thoughts. She knew Mama must have been thinking that Jimmy was to start school in the fall and Billy would be her only baby at home. Isabel sensed her sadness at the thought. Isabel could not imagine what Mama would do with so much time on her hands.

#

Chapter 16

THE GREENE FAMILY gathered around the fireplace in the front room after dinner. Papa sat in his old mahogany and leather rocker on one side of the hearth and Mama in her old gooseneck rocker on the other. The children scattered on the floor at her feet, with one-year-old Billy snuggled in Mama's lap. Papa quieted his family as Mama opened her Bible.

Mama always had read the Word to her family, but recently she had been including the older children by having one child read the text each evening.

"Tonight is Eugene's turn," Mama said. "Will you please read John 14 for us?"

"Yes, ma'am," he said as he reached for the book. Eugene began to read aloud, softly at first, and then with more excitement as he realized the text Mama asked him to read was talking about heaven. "In my father's house are many mansions…"

After the reading of the Word, Curtis asked his brother for the Bible so that he could see the passage. "Does it really say that there are mansions?" he said. "Rich people houses?"

Before Mama could answer, Isabel spoke up. "Will we live together in the mansion like we do in this little house now?"

"Well, we will be together in heaven. The Bible is very clear about that. As long as you have received Christ as your Savior, you will be in heaven. There is no other way. Do you remember the verse Eugene read? 'I am the way, the truth and the life. No man cometh to the father but by Me.'

"However, we only know that He is preparing a place for us, and I think He means one for each of us since He usually takes his children home to heaven one at a time. I am so glad you asked about this, Curtis."

"Mama," Sylvia said, "do you think if we asked Jesus nicely He would let us all live together in the same house? I want to live with you and Papa always."

Mama smiled and lifted Sylvia up on her lap. "We shall see, Dear. I think we will be happy as long as we are with Him, but we can certainly ask Him."

"Good," Sylvia said. "Thank you, Mama."

Chapter 17

Sally Anne and the School Project

ISABEL HURRIED TO school early on Monday, a first for her, since she preferred to stay at home with Mama. However, today was the day for announcing the history projects, and Sally Anne had Isabel almost as excited about their project as she was. Isabel had talked about the project so much at home that the entire Greene family had swelled with enthusiasm and chosen The War Between The States projects as well. Maggie and Sylvia glowed with pleasure at the thought of modeling dresses from the "olden days" as they called them. Isabel sincerely hoped there was clothing small enough to fit the girls. She did not want to disappoint her sisters.

Papa seemed to come alive with stories told to him by his papa and grandpa. He told stories of uncles and cousins who fought on both sides of the conflict. "It was a sad time indeed," he said. "Families were torn apart in more ways than one, and bitterness still exists today because of it." He eased himself out of the rocking chair and stretched. "I think I'll turn in early tonight. Guess this jaunt down memory lane makes an old man tired. I'll see ya in the morning."

The following morning, Curtis, Maggie, and Sylvia rushed ahead as they walked to school in order to discuss their projects with their friends. Isabel and Eugene lagged behind.

"How could anyone hold a grudge so long?" Isabel said to Eugene. "Those people are not even alive today."

He shook his head. "I don't know, Isabel. I guess they were so deeply hurt that they passed that hurt onto their children. Doesn't the Bible say something about that? The sins of the fathers passed onto the sons for generations—or something like that?"

"I think I remember reading that, now that you mention it," she said. "I guess it's sin, huh?"

"Yes."

"Do you suppose that could be why we lost the war?" she asked.

"What do you mean?" Eugene stopped in his tracks and faced Isabel.

"Well, we always talk about the pride of the South, and pride is a sin. Like our Bible verse: 'pride goeth before destruction; and a haughty spirit before a fall.' Papa says we are to have pride in our appearance, though, so I don't understand," Isabel said.

"That's a different kind of pride, silly," he said as he took off his cap, scratched his head, and then continued with the thought. "The kind of pride we are talking about here means arrogance. It means to cherish yourself and your things or your land above everyone else. As if yours is the best and everyone else is inferior to you."

"Oh," Isabel said as she swung her lunch pail and continued walking. "I see what you mean. We were so arrogant that we thought we could…" Isabel stopped walking, watching a Blue Jay chasing a sparrow from an apple tree before continuing. "Well, not *us*, but many people in the South treated human beings as slaves because they did not look like us or have the same ad, ad, what's that big word, Eugene?"

"Advantages?" Eugene asked as he turned to face his little sister with a smile. "Yeah, but many were kind too. Folks around here treated their slaves like family." He picked up a stone and threw it at the noisy Blue Jay and then continued speaking. "Some slaves or servants chose to stay with the families when President Lincoln granted them their freedom. Doesn't that mean something?"

"How do you know that?" Isabel asked as she swung around to face her brother.

Eugene grinned and pointed to his ears. "I listen," he said. "I've read a couple of books about it too. It helps to actually pay attention to the teacher, you know."

Isabel scrunched her face and then rolled her eyes. "Yes, I suppose so, but they were still legally owned by someone else, as if they were a workhorse or oxen. I can't understand how anyone can see a person that way. Can you?"

"No," Eugene said, "but our family was not involved in that, remember? We were fighting for our rights, also to be our own Confederate government. We did not want the federal government coming down here, telling us what to do and how to do it and bringing factories, destroying our land; and most of all, we were protecting our wives, sisters, mothers, and property. It was more than just having good manners, Isabel. People from the north seem to think of southerners as either genteel," he raised his pinkie as if he were sipping tea, "or they think we are dumb country hicks with one tooth in our head and a gun slung across our shoulder as we go hunting barefoot."

Isabel giggled at his word picture and wondered which they would think of her. The thought made her uncomfortable. "Do you really think people think of us that way?"

"You have been to the picture show. You know how they portray country folks—especially those of us from south of the Mason-Dixon Line. Some people seem to think our location precludes any manners and knowledge. People are people made in God's image, regardless of our location. I have to remind myself of that sometimes. I have to remind myself that people north of the Mason-Dixon Line are people with different opinions and styles and are unique too.

Brother and sister walked the rest of the way in silence, each deep in his or her own thoughts.

Miss Catron was just opening the door as the children reached the little, red brick school building. "Good morning! It's nice to see you so early," she said.

"Good Morning, Miss Catron," they said in unison.

"We thought we would come early today," Isabel said. "Is Sally Anne here yet?"

"As a matter of a fact, she arrived about ten minutes ago, and she is wearing the same glow that you have on today. Go on inside; you have a lot to talk about," she said. "How are you on this beautiful morning, Eugene?"

Isabel heard her teacher talking to Eugene, but she did not stay to hear her brother's response. She was too anxious to meet with her friend.

"Isabel, you're here!" Sally Anne said with outstretched arms. "I have so much to tell you. Did you know that our mothers talked after church yesterday? I think they are planning to help with our project. Can you believe it? *My mother* is going to be part of our project. I can hardly believe it. It's like a dream come true."

"She is? I didn't know that. Mama has not said a word," Isabel said. Tears gathered in her cornflower blue eyes. "What are they planning?"

"Well, Mother said we can have the fashion show in our garden. Father even said he will have the gardener plant some fresh flowers and put up a large, white tent to hold tables for refreshments."

"Refreshments too?" Isabel said. "It sounds like a grand party."

"Isn't it wonderful? Mother and Father have had many parties, but they have never had a party for me. I am so excited."

Children began filing into the classroom. "Alright class, everyone take your seat," Miss Catron said. "We have much to talk about this morning before we have our Scripture reading. Now, I know everyone is excited about your history projects, and you may be even more so after you hear my announcement. Mr. and Mrs. Albright have consented to hosting a Civil War Memorial Day in their beautiful garden. Sally Anne and Isabel Greene will organize a fashion show for the girls featuring antebellum clothing."

Cheers erupted from the classroom. Oohs and aahs were so loud from the girls that Sally Anne and Isabel blushed.

Miss Catron smiled and allowed a short time for celebration and then held up her hand for silence. "We will also have a tent set up with tables for refreshments...please, no more applause. Now, how many of you have items of clothing, diaries, weapons, or any kind of family heirlooms from the Civil War?"

Isabel turned to see many hands raised. She was surprised to see that almost every family was represented.

"Very well," said Miss Catron, "how many of you could bring something to display at the Civil War Memorial? You will need your parents' permission, of course. You may have it back at the end of the day." Isabel heard a few sighs—as if they were afraid the teacher might keep them. "One other thing, if you know a Civil War veteran relative still living who is willing to speak to us or if you have written journals from that time that someone could read from as a dramatic reading, I will give you extra credit for the year. This will take place in the spring, so you will have plenty of time to prepare."

"Oh boy, I'm pass in' history," a red-haired, freckled-faced boy said. He always sat on the back row and never spoke up in class.

The class exploded in laughter.

Chapter 18

Misunderstanding

ISABEL AND THE family managed to find excuses to invite Sally Anne to their home as often as possible. Mama included her in the housekeeping activities in order to ensure proper instruction for the "poor child," and Sally Anne seemed to love every minute of it. She found reasons of her own to come by the Greene home just to be near their family and was welcomed with open arms.

Several months had passed since Sally Anne's first visit, and she was quickly becoming a contributing member of the family, as she came home with the children after school at least three days a week and joined in doing chores; learning housework; cooking; and doing farming chores, such as milking the cows, feeding the chickens, and tending the gardens. Her place at the table seemed empty to every member of the family on the days she did not join them.

One Thursday afternoon, gray clouds rolled in, and Mama told Isabel to bring in the rag rugs before it started to rain. Mama carefully placed a cake pan into the hot oven. "I want them to air out, but we do not want them to get wet. It looks like we are in for a bad storm."

"Yes, Mama," Isabel said. She hastened to do her Mama's bidding just as rain began to bounce happily along the tin roof, playing a merry little tune. Isabel returned with the rugs in her arms just as the tune stepped up in intensity and lightning streaked across the sky, causing everyone to jump in fright. Nervous laughter filled the room to cover embarrassment of being startled by a little lightning.

"Mother Greene, may I read to the children for a while?" Sally Anne asked as she gathered Sylvia, Jimmy, and Billy around her, reminding Isabel of a mother hen gathering her baby chicks.

"Certainly, Dear. Isabel and Maggie can help me finish up here in the kitchen. Why don't you read to the children by the stove, where it is warm. Then we can also enjoy the story."

Isabel listened with interest as her friend turned common story tales into exciting stories by the rise and fall of her voice. Jimmy lay on the floor with his face on his elbows, his eyes shining with excitement. Billy clapped at the most happy moments and cried in fear when Sally Anne became the wolf that was ready to blow the little piggie's house down, and the entire family exploded in laughter. Isabel was so engrossed in the children's stories that she did not notice the storm had passed, leaving only a gentle rain tapping lightly upon the tin roof.

"And they all lived happily ever after," Sally Anne said. She gently closed the book amid protests from Billy and Jimmy. "I must go home, boys, it is getting late."

"But you can't go home now, Sally Anne; it's raining," Jimmy said.

"That's alright, Jimmy. I have an umbrella. I will be fine," she said.

"Oh, no, Sally Anne," he said. He rushed to her, hugging her tightly. "If you go out in the rain and look up, you'll drown."

Isabel felt her throat constrict and her stomach churn as she remembered her unkind words on the road home from school so many weeks ago, before she and Sally Anne had become friends, and she wished with all her heart that she could take them back. Instead, Jimmy was bringing them out again to their beloved new friend, and Isabel felt helpless to stop him. She opened her mouth, but she was speechless. She tried to move, but she was paralyzed. Her friendship seemed to crumble before her eyes.

"I'll drown? Why will I dro… She stopped and looked at Isabel with tears in her eyes.

"I know, Jimmy. You don't have to answer. It's because I am stuck up with my nose in the air—is that what you have heard Isabel say?"

Jimmy nodded his head slowly, and his voice quivered as he watched a single tear on Sally Anne's cheek. "Why are you crying, Sally Anne?"

"It's OK, Jimmy," Sally Anne said. She patted the boy on his head. "It is not your fault."

A pale-faced Isabel stepped in front of her friend to stop her from leaving so she could somehow find the words to explain. However, the words did not come, and Isabel just stood there with tears running down her white cheeks. Finally, after what seemed an eternity, both girls started to speak.

"Go ahead," Sally Anne said. "I thought you were my friend."

"You are my friend, Sally Anne. You are the best friend I have ever had." Isabel twisted her apron in her hands as she tried to come up with an explanation or an apology, but words just did not seem to be good enough.

Finally, she and Sally Anne spat out words at the same time, one not listening to the other. Jumbled thoughts and troubled emotions made them appear senseless until Mama began laughing.

"Mama?" Isabel said. Both girls turned to Mama as if she had lost her senses.

"Silly girls," Mama said. "You are both saying essentially the same thing. Just listen to each other. Now, I want you both to go into the front parlor and close the door. Tell each other what you are feeling, and do not come out of that room until you are friends again."

"I'm sorry, Sally Anne. I said that a long time ago, before we were friends," Isabel said.

"Before we were friends?" Sally Anne began to cry again, and Isabel rushed to her side with a fresh handkerchief. "Thank you," Sally Anne said as she unfolded the embroidered square. "But, I thought we were always friends."

"We were friends when we were little," Isabel said, "but then you became friends with those mean, rich girls, and you forgot all about me."

"What girls are you talking about?" Sally Anne walked to the window and waited for thunder to sound after lightning flashed across the sad sky. "Do you mean Arlene and Mavis?"

"Yes," Isabel said, "among others."

"Those girls are not my friends and never have been." Sally Anne raised her voice to be heard above the thunder. "They insist on following me everywhere, and Papa insists that I invite them over because he has business connections with their fathers, but they are not my friends."

"What about last year, when school started? I heard what you said to them about me."

"What I said?" Sally Anne had a blank look on her face.

Isabel almost changed her mind about the incident, but she quickly returned to the insult. "You know good and well what you said, Sally Anne Albright. You made fun of my clothes and you told those girls that my mama makes my dresses and they all laughed."

"Oh, Isabel," Sally Anne said, "you heard it all wrong. I wasn't making fun of you… I was taking up for you. I always took up for you. Don't you know that?"

Isabel shook her head slowly, and Sally Anne continued.

"They were making fun of your dress, and I said it was lovely. I told them that your mother makes your clothes by hand and that she is the best seamstress in town."

"You did?" Isabel asked.

"You bet I did, and I told them in no uncertain terms that you were the best friend I had ever had—that friendship is about the person and not about the clothes they wear or the houses they live in."

"You really said that?" Isabel began to sob as she realized how she had misjudged the girl and wished she could take the words back. "I'm so sorry Sally Anne. Can you ever forgive me?" Isabel asked through her tears.

"Of course, but when did Jimmy hear you say that?"

"Before we started working on the school project," Isabel said. "I thought you were like the other girls and were only being nice when they were not around in order to find something to laugh about later with them."

"I wouldn't do that," Sally said. She rushed to her friend. "I'm sorry you felt that way. If I had known you felt that way, I would have defied my father and not associated with those ridiculous girls at all. You know, they don't really like me; they like my father's money and social standing in the community. I guess they think if they stick with me, people will think they are wealthy or something, but it isn't true, not one word of it."

"You mean to tell me that their fathers do not have a lot of money?" Isabel said. Sally Anne shook her head. "What about all those pretty clothes they wear?"

"That's what happened to their father's money…the girls and their mothers spend it all on frivolous things, and I heard Father say that if they don't learn to budget their money, they will lose everything. So, it's kind of sad if you really think about it."

"That is sad," Isabel said. "Do you think all those fancy clothes make them feel like they are rich?"

"Yes, but it is a false feeling, and they couldn't possibly feel good about themselves, could they?"

"No, I guess they don't. Do you think we should pray for them?"

"Yes," Sally Anne said. "Let's pray for them to come to know the Lord like you and I did after your mama told us about Him, and He will give them the same joy He has given us."

The girls got on their knees together to pray. Isabel asked for forgiveness for her cruel words, for saying something unkind in front of her sisters and brother, and for harboring bitterness against Sally Anne and the other girls. "Help me, Lord," she prayed, "to use my tongue to say good and kind words and not hurtful ones." They both prayed for the insecure girls to come to Christ and that He would let them be a good example and witness.

By the time Mama had supper on the table, Isabel and Sally Anne were fast friends with a mission. They both agreed that what could have been a destroyed friendship became a restored one because of Mama's wisdom, and they each gave her bear hugs to show their appreciation.

The girls did not share their conversation about the "mean, rich girls" with anyone, knowing to do so would be gossip. They did continue to pray for them, however.

Chapter 19

Brighten a Corner

CURTIS ENTERED THE kitchen, slamming the door behind him, much to Isabel's surprise.

"Curtis, what's eating you," she said. She turned to offer him a taste of the stew she was stirring and then changed her mind when she saw the look on his face. He seemed as if he could explode or cry at the least provocation, and she decided not to be the one to provide it. Curtis was about to answer when Mama entered the room.

"Why, Curtis dear, what is bothering you?" she asked. She rushed across the room, "Tell Mama all about it."

To Isabel's surprise and dismay, her twelve-year-old brother began to sob. "It's not fair, Mama. It's just not."

"What's not fair, Son?"

"Mrs. Flora and her children down by Tinker Creek—they are starving... I know they are. I saw it for myself. Apparently, the only food she had to give them was gravy. Nothing else, just a pan of gravy on the stove, so she had the children all sitting down, and they ate gravy from their plates with a spoon. She gave every bit she had to them. There was nothing left for herself, and she looks like she just has skin pulled over her bones." He stopped to take a breath and blow his nose in the handkerchief from his pocket.

Isabel searched for her own hankie in her apron pocket as her eyes began to water. "Mrs. Flora gave me a cookie one time," Isabel said. "Remember when Papa took us fishing and I wandered off? Mrs. Flora found me wandering around in the woods. She gave me a drink of cold water from her well and a cookie to eat, and then she had her eldest girl walk me over to the creek to find Papa."

"Your papa never told me that," Mama said. "What happened?"

"Well," Isabel said, "I was watching Papa and the boys fishing—they were pulling in a big one—and then a beautiful butterfly landed on the flowers in front of me, so I decided to catch him, but he fluttered away, and I chased him. Suddenly, there were trees all around me. Nothing looked familiar, and I started to cry. There was a clearing, and I saw a house; a woman was hanging up clothes. She saw me and asked my name and how I got there, but all I could say was I wanted to go home. Mrs. Flora told me her name and introduced me to her children and she gave me a cookie and a glass of milk before telling her eldest girl to take me back to the creek to find Papa. I had almost forgotten about it until Curtis said her name."

Mama embraced her tightly. "Curtis," she said, "what were you doing at Tinker Creek when you were supposed to be doing your chores?"

"I'm sorry, Mama," he said. "I got hot and decided to go for a quick swim and did not think anyone would notice that I was missing. I thought I would be able to clear the field before Papa returned from the farmers market."

"We will discuss that later. We must get busy," Mama said. She stood in the middle of the kitchen with her face resting on her arm in her thinking position. "Now, Curtis, where was Mr. Flora?"

"He was slumped over a jug on the porch," Curtis said. "I think he'll be out for a while."

"Alright, Curtis, go downstairs, and get two bushel baskets. Fill one with fresh vegetables from the bins. Bring up some quarts of tomatoes, relish, pickles, and preserves; everyone deserves something sweet, you know. Then go up into the attic, and bring down a sack of flour. I am glad Papa had our wheat finely ground at the mill so we have enough to share this year." Then she turned to Isabel, who was awaiting instructions. "Isabel, look in the drawer, and pull out two flour sacks. Put three loaves of bread in one sack, and the apple turnovers will go into the other sack. We will make biscuits for our dinner and bake more bread tomorrow. It is more important to get fresh bread to the family in need as soon as possible." She filled a basket with food as she spoke. Suddenly she looked up, apparently noticing the hesitation in Isabel's eyes. "Isabel, why aren't you obeying me?"

"I'm sorry, Mama. It's just…what about Papa? He said Mr. Flora is not, well, he…" she stuttered to find the right words.

"Yes, Isabel," Mama said, "Mr. Flora throws his money away on moonshine, and his family suffers. You just heard what Curtis said. They are starving, and it is our responsibility to provide food for them. There are five small children, at least four children older than you are, and they are trying to live on *gravy*. I do not know if they even have a cow, so the gravy may just be made from a little bit of fatback or bacon grease, water, and flour, or corn meal. The children need vegetables and meat, or they will get sick and die. Do you want that on your conscience?"

"No. ma'am," Isabel said.

"Do you suppose your papa would want that on his conscience?" she said. "Besides, Jesus said to feed the hungry, and we are doing just that. Now, my child, brighten a corner for the Flora family." She began to tap her foot and sing:

Brighten the corner where you are! Brighten the corner where you are! Someone far from harbor you may guide across the bar. Brighten the corner where you are!

"The Lord loveth a cheerful giver," Maggie, who had been quietly listening, said as they worked together, preparing food for a starving family.

"Curtis and I will take the food to the family," Mama said. "So, Isabel, will you please watch the children?" She took off her apron and headed for the door.

"Yes, Mama," Isabel said. She handed Mama a sack of apples to take with her.

When Mama and Curtis returned an hour later, the entire family gathered around the table to hear about the mission.

"I couldn't believe it," Curtis said. He used his hands for emphasis. "Just as we drove up to their property, Mama and I saw someone bent down against a fallen log. Mama called out, 'Are you ill?' and the woman looked up. It was Mrs. Flora. She was crying and praying for the Lord to feed her children. Mama got down from the wagon, put her arms around her, and cried too.

"Mrs. Flora," she said, "about five years ago, you did something kind for my little girl, Isabel. Her father was fishing and Isabel wandered off. He never would have found her if it had not been for you. Apparently, the child wandered into your yard, and you gave her a cookie and had your older child take Isabel back to the lake to her papa. I just learned about this today. Isabel told me. I suppose her Papa didn't want me to know that he had lost her."

"Yes, I remember her," Mrs. Flora said. She dabbed at her eyes with the corner of her apron. "She was a cute little thing, with crocodile tears streaming down her face. All she could say was 'I want my mama.' I'm amazed that she remembered."

"Well," Mama said, "that is how the Lord is. He is never too early or too late, you know. Here you are praying for food, and the Lord had placed on our hearts the need to bring you some—to thank you for your act of kindness to Isabel."

"You should have seen the look on Mrs. Flora's face," Curtis said to his family. She kept saying, 'You've brought food? You brought food to us?' She could not quite understand it. Mama convinced her that the Lord sent the food, and she accepted it after she cried on Mama's shoulder. And then she hugged me." Curtis pulled out a handkerchief and blew his nose.

"What have you learned from this experience, Son?" Mama asked gently.

"I learned that when God speaks to your heart, you must obey right away, and someone will be blessed. And if you don't obey right away, someone may suffer."

"Son," Mama said as she turned to Curtis, "I pray you will always listen to the still, small voice of the Lord and obey Him as you did today."

"Now," Mama said, "let's see what we can scramble up for our dinner."

Chapter 20

Christmas

ISABEL LISTENED TO Miss Catron in school as she watched red, orange, and amber leaves falling and swirling before gracefully landing on the wide windowsill. Fall had faded into winter, and suddenly, the air seemed alive with excitement as Christmas became the focus of discussion.

"Isabel, won't it be fun to dress up like Mary in the Christmas program?" Maggie asked as she skipped along beside her sister on the way home from school. "Do you think Miss Catron will pick you?"

"I don't know," Isabel said. "I think Arlene is trying out for the part, and you know she gets everything she wants."

"I don't think so. Miss Catron asked you to read the part *twice*."

"Yeah, but I don't have a costume," Isabel said. "You know Mama and Papa can't afford to buy something for me to wear for some silly program."

"Well, Curtis is going to be a shepherd, and Sylvie is an angel…"

"That's different," Isabel said. She kicked a rock with the toe of her shiny shoe. "Curtis just has to wear a bathrobe with a towel on his head, and Miss Catron already has the angel costume for Sylvie to wear."

"Mama can make something…"

"Oh no she can't," Isabel said. "Mama is already too busy. Besides, we can't afford the fabric to make a costume. Anyway, I think Sally Anne wants to be Mary, but she won't say so."

The following morning, Miss Catron announced that Isabel Greene would play the part of Mary as she handed her a brown package tied with string.

"This is your costume, Isabel. I wore it when I was your age and think it will fit you perfectly."

"This is the best Christmas we have ever had," Isabel whispered to Maggie. They climbed aboard the hay wagon with the rest of their classmates.

"I know," Maggie said. "You get to be Mary in the Christmas program. Plus, Papa hid a bundle of packages in the barn last night when he came home from town. Now we get to go Christmas caroling, and it's *snowing*. I heard Miss Catron say we are stopping at Sally Anne's house for refreshments; hope they have hot chocolate and donuts."

Isabel smiled at her little sister and nodded. She happened to know that there would be many treats prepared for each of them, but Sally Anne had made her swear to secrecy. The horses pulled against the reins, causing the children to sway into each other with peals of laughter.

"Dashing through the snow…" they sang, their voices bouncing oddly as the wagon wheels hit potholes in the road. The children didn't mind; it only added to the fun.

The children serenaded every house within ten miles with Christmas carols, and the inhabitants seemed delighted—with the exception of one person.

"Why is Widow Barker so grumpy?" Sylvia said. They pulled away from her home at her request. "She wouldn't even let us sing 'Away in a Manger.'"

"She wouldn't even keep the pretty star we made for her," Maggie said.

"I guess she doesn't know Jesus," Curtis said. "We'll have to pray for her."

Caroling on Christmas Eve was only eclipsed by the festive tree and gifts that seemed to appear overnight for Christmas morning. Jimmy and Billy were beside themselves with excitement as they pulled goodies from their socks that hung on the mantel. Isabel felt the thrill of having purchased small gifts for everyone in the family with the money she had earned at the market. Toys and warm clothing for each child were handmade by Papa and Mama, but to Isabel, they were beyond compare.

For the rest of the winter, Isabel thought of Mama every time she buttoned her new coat with brass buttons and put on the matching blue, knitted scarf, hat, and gloves. Wearing such finery almost made it worth going to school on cold mornings.

A Grand Occasion

SPRING FINALLY ARRIVED, and the day for the school project dawned bright and clear. Isabel arose before the rooster had a chance to crow, for she had been awake all night in anticipation of this grand event.

After breakfast, Mama and the girls washed the dishes, put them away, and swept the floor. Isabel dressed in the antebellum dress that Sally Anne had altered for her. She surveyed herself in the mirror and then ran into Mama's room for help with her hair, which was wound tightly in rag curlers.

"Oh, Isabel," Mama said, "you look lovely. Come and sit down in front of the mirror, and we will see what we can do with those lovely locks of yours." Mama gently removed the short rags.

Isabel shook her head in order to see the spiral curls bounce. "It feels like I have a cat on my head that does not want to get down," Isabel said with a laugh. "It sure does feel funny."

"It might take you a while to get used to the curls," Mama said, "but they look wonderful. You look as if you stepped out from the pages of *Little Women*."

At that moment, Maggie and Sylvia burst into the room amid gales of laughter.

"Mama," Sylvia said, "there are too many buttons, and my fingers got tired trying to fasten them all."

"Come in girls," Mama said. "Isabel and I will help you."

Soon the girls were dressed in their bright costumes, complete with bustles, and the boys entered the room wearing Confederate Kepis. Eugene carried an unloaded rifle, which had belonged to his grandfather, and Curtis carried a sword belonging to the same grandfather. Jimmy trailed behind, waving a small Confederate flag.

"Why are you carrying that?" Sylvia asked as Jimmy waved the piece of fabric under her nose. "You don't even go to school yet."

"I know," Jimmy said. "Eugene said I could be the flag holder, and I'm doing a great job."

"Yes, you are," Isabel said. She ruffled her small brother's hair.

"Hey," he said, "you cannot do that because I am a soldier."

Everyone laughed as he stomped his foot for emphasis.

Isabel attempted to sit on the bed to watch Mama fix her sisters' hair, but her dress rose up in front, revealing ruffled pantaloons. She decided to stand instead.

When the wagon pulled into the Albright yard, Isabel was amazed at the transformation. There were white tables and chairs everywhere that were covered in white linen, with a bouquet of flowers on each table. Mr. Albright had built benches around the trees, and there was a very long table laden with food and another with desserts. Mama took her basket of confections to add to the display. Isabel was just about to sneak an oatmeal cookie when Sally Anne's voice rang out.

"Isabel, you're here." Sally Anne rushed to Isabel's side to welcome her. "Oh, you look wonderful. I'm glad you are wearing the blue dress. It matches your eyes."

"Thank you," Isabel said. "And you look beautiful in that dark green. It is perfect for you. Is Miss Catron here yet? When do we start?"

Sally Anne giggled as Isabel peppered her with questions. Sally Anne waved her fan towards the side yard. "Miss Catron is setting up the display of artifacts."

"The…what kind of art?" Isabel asked.

"Artifacts are things from the Civil War era," Sally Anne said. "You know—things like belt buckles, Kepis, bullets, and stuff like that. There are also some journals and letters from soldiers and their wives. There is even a letter from General Stonewall Jackson. He had written it to the mother of a soldier who had died on the battlefield. Do you want to see it?"

"Yes," Isabel said. They ran to the artifacts table. As they reached it, Isabel heard the song "When Johnny Comes Marching Home" from the backyard. "Who's playing that music?"

"Didn't you know?" Sally Anne said, walking to the backyard. "Some men in the community have set up camp and are singing around the campfire, just like the soldiers did between battles. Your papa or brothers didn't tell you?"

"No," Isabel said. She watched as Papa played the banjo, Curtis played on a mandolin, Eugene played the harmonica, and her older half-brother, Jim, played a juice harp. Other men had penny whistles and even a small drum. Still other men stood up shaving in front of mirrors that were hanging on trees.

One man was kneeling under a large oak tree, praying.

"General Thomas Jonathan 'Stonewall' Jackson used to get up early before his men to pray," Sally Anne whispered as they tiptoed past him and led Isabel away from the camp.

"The big surprise comes later." Sally Anne said. She jumped up and down with excitement.

"What kind of surprise?" Isabel asked.

"The kind only Father would think of," Sally Anne said. "Now come on; there's so much to see." Sally Anne took Isabel's hand, and they ran as quickly as their costumes would allow, past the flower garden, to a fenced-in area, where sheep were gracing—seemingly oblivious to the activity around them.

"Oh," Isabel said, "when did your Father buy sheep? Are you raising sheep now?"

"No, Father rented them for the day. Come into the tent on the other side of the fence. You won't believe your eyes."

The girls raced to the tent that had a colorfully painted sign in front, signifying the activity inside was "For Our Boys." Isabel couldn't believe her eyes as she stepped into the tent, where baskets of fleece were stacked by the door. "Look," Isabel said. "Arlene Mason is spinning wool. I didn't know she could do that."

"Neither did I," Sally Anne said. "Her grandmother taught her how. She never told us that she could spin because she thought we would laugh at her. Can you imagine that?"

"No," Isabel said. "I thought she was too *modern* to do something so old fashioned."

"Her little sisters are carding the wool—cleaning it with large, sharp combs that pull out all the briars and stuff. Her mother and aunts are knitting scarves, mittens, and socks with the wool Arlene just spun."

"It's called 'homespun,'" Arlene said. "And Grandma has a loom set up out back and is working on a blanket like the ones made for the soldiers. Fabric for their uniforms were also made on looms, you know."

"Oh," Isabel said, "I didn't know all that. Couldn't the army just give them everything they needed?"

"Perhaps the officers had what they needed, but the regular boys couldn't afford to buy uniforms—especially later in the war," Mrs. Mason said. "The North made it impossible for necessities to get through, so we took care of our own—as best we could." She continued working on the sock she was knitting. "Come back later, and we will let you have a turn, if you wish."

"Oh, I don't know how to spin or weave," Isabel said. "Mama tries to teach me to knit and crochet, but I just can't get it. I start thinking about other things and get all messed up and have to pull out all the stitches and start over." Isabel wrinkled up her nose.

"Well," Mrs. Mason said with a smile, "it takes practice, patience, and a willingness to learn."

"Yes, ma'am, thank you. I'll try harder next time."

Isabel and Sally Anne wandered outside to watch with fascination as Arlene's grandmother wove the shuttle through the threads; pulled a wooden plank down as she pressed a foot petal, adding a new line of thread to the fabric; and then started all over again.

"Look at the beautiful fabric she's making," Sally Anne whispered to Isabel.

"I don't know how she works so fast," Isabel whispered back. She smiled at the woman as she and Sally Anne headed back to the front lawn, which was beginning to fill with people. Suddenly, a bugle rang out, and everyone wandered over to a temporary stage decorated with red, white, and blue bunting. Two dozen chairs were lined up at the back of the stage, and a runway decorated with plants and flowers was obviously meant for the girls' fashion show.

"May I have everyone's attention?" A gray-haired gentleman, with a gray beard, wearing a confederate uniform, walked up a set of steps leading to the stage and signaled for the bugler to sound once more. "Your attention please," he said. "We would like to open our program with a word of prayer, and then Miss Catron will explain the events for the day."

Isabel closed her eyes as the man in general's clothing asked for God's blessing on the festive day and asked for wisdom, understanding, and cooperation today, and always.

When Miss Catron stepped on the stage, dressed in a light gray antebellum dress with white lace trim, with her hair neatly pinned up under a matching hat, the crowd applauded and cheered.

"Thank you for coming today," she said. The noise subsided. "What began as a school project has turned into a community event to be proud of. Your children have obviously put a lot of work into this history project, and you have made it a day to remember always. We will begin with our fashion show at 9:30 A.M., and then we will have a refreshment break at 10:00. Chaplain Farley will then conduct a service for us, just as the chaplains would have preached to the men during the war. We will have several groups sing gospel music as well." The crowd erupted in applause once more.

"After the church service, luncheon will be served on the front lawn. I would like to thank all of you mothers and fathers for the wonderful food. As you know by that wonderful aroma, several of the men have been up most of the night preparing slow-cooked pork, beef, and lamb for your enjoyment. We have tried to prepare food in the old-fashioned way, and I am sure we will all have an old-fashioned appetite by lunchtime. I noticed there are at least two long tables laden with desserts, and there are plenty of vegetables, so no one should go hungry, as our soldiers experienced." People murmured and nodded their heads in agreement.

"After luncheon, you will be free to walk around and visit the various tents set up around the property. The first tent will house artifacts, and you will be able to meet a true Civil War soldier and listen as he recounts his story."

A man with a long, white beard stood up and waved. "Sorry I'm not in uniform folks," he said with a grin, "but it don't fit me no more."

"Thank you, Mr. Minnix," Miss Catron said. "We are all looking forward to hearing your account of the war. The other tents are well marked, and you will be delighted with each one, so don't waste too much time playing around, boys." She looked at the group of schoolboys standing near the coffee and punch table. Isabel was amazed at the amount of things placed on the table. And by the end of the day, she had modeled her dress, listened to an elderly man tell of his experiences as a young soldier in 'Lee's Army,' joined in a sing-along, sampled many foods, and enjoyed her first taste of punch.

As they were cleaning up after the event, Miss Catron said, "Girls, our Civil War day was a huge success, and we owe it all to you. You should be proud of your accomplishment."

"Oh," Sally Anne said, with stars in her eyes, "we didn't do much; everybody contributed."

"Yes," Isabel said, "we just had fun."

"Indeed," Miss Catron said, "it is a day we shall all remember for a long time. I hope everyone learned something they did not know before today."

"I learned that when we all work together," Sally Anne said, "wonderful things happen. It is too bad our country did not know that. Of course, if they had, there would not have been a Civil War, and we would not have had such a spectacular day."

"I didn't know that learning could be so much fun," Isabel said. "May we do this again sometime?"

"I certainly hope so," Miss Catron said.

"Me too," Isabel said. She observed Mr. and Mrs. Albright smiling at Sally Anne, just as they had done all day. They had bragged to everyone that it was "our Sally Anne's idea," and she beamed in their compliments.

Chapter 22

Shampoo and Rain Water

"WELL," MAMA SAID as she placed the last loaf of bread into the oven, "tomorrow is Sunday, so we need to wash your hair, girls."

"Can't we wash our hair in the rain?" Isabel asked. She looked outside at the cool, steady rain from the kitchen window. "You always say that rain water smells so good…and we won't have to use up the well water for our hair." Isabel smiled as she made the last comment, knowing Papa was worried that the well would go dry before the end of the summer.

"Well," Mama said, "I suppose it would be alright as long as you agree to come back inside at the first sound of thunder. Go upstairs, and put on your bathing clothes so you will not mess up your work clothes."

"Yes, Mama," Isabel said. She headed for the back steps to her room. Maggie and Sylvia followed and passed her on the steps.

"Oh boy," Sylvia said as she raced to their room. "I love playing in the rain."

"Well," Isabel said, "we are not playing in the rain; we are washing our hair."

"We will still be standing in the rain getting wet, won't we?" Sylvia said as she quickly got dressed.

"I guess you are right," Isabel said. She pulled out her bathing suit and shuddered. "I wish Mama and Papa would allow us to wear the new style like everyone else. These old things are heavier than our regular dresses. Besides, they look ugly, and they are no good for swimming. The last time we went swimming, I nearly drowned because my clothes were full of water and dragging me down."

"I remember," Maggie said. She giggled and watched Isabel make funny faces at the offending fabric.

"Ye gads," Isabel said. She attempted to button the dress portion of her swimsuit.

"Isabel," Maggie said, "you just used God's name in vain."

"No I didn't," Isabel said. "I just said the same thing everybody says today."

"Not everybody, Isabel," Maggie said. "Mama would not like it, and neither does God."

"Oh, Maggie," Isabel said to her sister, who was also struggling with her suit, "you are such a goody-goody sometimes. Besides, I said g-*a*-ds and with a little g…like the Roman gods, you know."

"That does not make it right, Isabel. It is still using God's name in vain," Maggie said.

Isabel decided to drop the issue.

"I'm telling Mama that you're swearing, Isabel," Sylvia said. She headed for the bedroom door.

"No, Sylvie," Isabel said, "don't tell her. It will only upset her, and I promise never to say that again. Sylvia twisted the doorknob, and Isabel spoke up once more. "I will give you a nickel if you promise never to tell Mama what I just said."

"Alright," Sylvia said. She took the coin from Isabel and headed to her side of the room to hide it. "Now shut your eyes, and no peeking." She wanted to be sure her sisters were not looking.

Even with her eyes closed, Isabel could hear Sylvia placing the coin under her mattress for safekeeping. Next, Isabel could hear a soft thud as Sylvia removed her hand from under the mattress and a trashing sound as her hands were smoothing out wrinkles from the covers.

"As if we did not know where she keeps things she doesn't want us to see," Maggie said as Sylvia exited the room.

"What do you mean?" Isabel questioned with suspicion.

"Sylvie always puts her money and other secret treasures there," Maggie said. "Didn't you know?"

"No," Isabel said.

"I know where you hide your things too," Maggie said. "You keep your diary in that old hatbox in the far right corner of the closet, and the key to unlock it is on a string hanging behind the picture on the wall."

"Maggie Greene," Isabel said, "you've been snooping."

"Who, me?" Maggie said sweetly as she walked to the window and pulled back the curtain, revealing the old climbing tree a few feet from the house. "If you want to hide something in our room, you should close the curtain or make sure no one is sitting in the tree reading."

"You were not 'reading' if you were watching me," Isabel said. She finished buttoning her elaborate bathing suit. "Besides, it is impolite to spy on people; you should have let me know you were there."

"If I had," Maggie said as she reached for the doorknob, "I would not know that you have a boyfriend."

"Margaret Louise Greene, I do not have a boyfriend."

"Isabel and Arnie sitting in a tree…" Maggie chanted as she took off down the steps with Isabel close behind.

"No running in the house, girls," Mama said as they entered the kitchen. They changed their pace to a quick walk as they stepped outside into the pouring rain.

"Now, girls," Mama said as she stepped onto the back porch with a jar of her special egg shampoo concoction. "Lather your hair twice, and be sure to get the suds out. I will mix up the rinse and be back in a few minutes."

The three girls twirled around in the rain until their hair was completely wet and then stepped back onto the porch.

"Here," Isabel said. She picked up the jar of shampoo. "I'll pour some on your hair, and then you can pour some on mine." She poured the yellow liquid onto Maggie's hair and massaged it into her sister's hair. Next, Isabel turned and repeated the same for Sylvia. Then Maggie poured the slimy liquid onto Isabel's head.

"Be sure to work up a good lather," Isabel said as she worked the shampoo through her own long hair. "Sylvie, it looks you're wearing a crown on your head. Maggie, let's see how high we can pile the suds on your head." The girls giggled as they made funny figurines on their heads. "We'd better rinse it off, or our heads will get itchy," Isabel quoted Mama, who warned them each time they washed their hair.

"We know that," Maggie said. Then she raced off the porch to rinse the suds from her hair and was followed by her sisters.

The girls danced around in the rain again as they attempted to rinse out the offensive lather.

"Oh no," Isabel said, "the rain is slacking off."

"Let's do the second lather before it stops altogether," Maggie said. They ran back to the porch and repeated the procedure. Just as they stepped off the porch, the sky seemed to open up with the heaviest rain they had seen all year.

"This is fun," Sylvia said. She twirled around, allowing the rain to wash her face as well as whisk away the shampoo.

"My hair feels softer already and smells good too," Isabel said.

Mama stepped onto the porch with a tray containing three jars. "Here, Isabel," Mama said. She handed her the jar with an amber colored liquid. "Apple cider vinegar to rinse your pretty brown tresses."

Isabel wrinkled her nose as she drenched her hair with the pungent rinse. "It stinks," she said.

"It will make your hair nice and shiny, and it will wash away the suds. Lemon juice for you two," Mama said. She handed the jar to Maggie and then poured the liquid from the remaining jar onto Sylvia's head and worked it through her hair.

"Why do we have to use lemon juice?" Sylvia asked.

"Because you have blonde hair; it will make it shine and keep it nice and light," Mama said. "Now, run back into the rain and rinse."

The girls obeyed their mother and stepped back on then the porch to squeeze all of the water out of their hair. Isabel ran her fingers through her hair as she pushed the water out and then squeezed. "Do you hear that?" she said. "Squeaky clean."

"Perfect," Mama said. She handed each daughter a dry towel. "Now squeeze the water out of your suits, and go inside to change before you catch pneumonia."

After changing from their wet clothes, Isabel and her sisters returned to the kitchen to sit by the stove to dry their hair as they enjoyed freshly baked cookies and hot chocolate.

"I love washing my hair in the rain," Isabel said.

"Me too," the younger girls agreed. The earlier argument with Maggie was lost in the suds under the raindrops.

"Yes," Mama said, "if only we had more rain this summer to help the crops grow."

Chapter 23

Fried Foods and Chocolate

ISABEL RUSHED THROUGH the kitchen door and grabbed her apron in one motion as her nose sniffed the air. "Mama, what are we having for dinner tonight?" She was hoping Mama's mood had improved since this morning.

Mama's answer was not as comforting as Isabel hoped, especially since she'd had butterflies in her tummy lately, warning her that something was definitely not right.

"We are having fried pork chops, fried eggs, fried link sausages, fried potatoes, bacon, fried okra, fried squash with onions, and fried apple pies for dessert," Mama said as if she were reciting a normal menu.

"Yummy," Isabel said with forced enthusiasm.

"What's wrong with dinner?" Mama asked. She turned to face her daughter, and as she did, Isabel noticed Mama looked more pale than usual. Her face looked taunt and drained.

"Oh, it's just that you do not usually allow us to eat so much fried foods, you know."

"Squash is a vegetable and so is okra," Mama said.

"I know, but you always remind me that okra is covered in cornmeal and fried in lard; therefore, it hardly counts. At least, that is what you usually say…" As Isabel whispered her last words, she could see Mama's neck was turning red and her nostrils were beginning to flare, which was something that never had been directed at her daughter, and Isabel did not want to break that record. "Would you like me to boil some peas and carrots? I could mix a batch of biscuits too."

"Oh no," Mama said. Her complexion turned a shade of pale green. "Just the thought of smelling vegetables boiling and bread baking makes me feel nauseated."

"Lizzie."

Isabel and Mama both turned as Papa entered the room.

"Martha Elizabeth Anne Kelly Greene, is there something you need to tell me?"

Mama reached for the back of a chair as if stunned. "I don't think so, Avil. Why do you think I have something to tell you?"

"Well," Papa said slowly as he rubbed the whiskers on his chin, "you have been awfully emotional lately. Why, just this morning you were upset about putting little Billy into big boy pants and would not hear of letting me cut his hair."

"Yes, I know," Mama said. She pulled a hankie from her apron pocket and wiped her eyes. "He is growing up too fast. You wanted to make him grow up overnight, that is all."

"And then last week," Papa said, "you were crying because Isabel said that she is too old to play with dolls. Now you must admit that crying over a ten-year-old giving up toys is pretty emotional for someone who does not have anything to tell…" Papa tilted his head and let his sentence hang in the air for Mama to grasp.

Isabel turned to Mama to see her response.

Mama gave Papa a shy smile, as if she were ready to concede. Yet she stubbornly continued her line of thinking. "Surely not, I just thought, well, Mama's sister went through the change early,

I just thought…besides, I'm just a little off my feed, that's all, probably.

"Well, maybe so for your Aunt Bessie," Papa said. He scratched his chin. "But I think it's another youngin for us," he continued with a wink and a grin. "Let's see," he said as he turned to Isabel, "the last time it was a boy, and your mama craved fried foods, just as she is now. When she has girls, its peas and carrots she wants. And chocolate, lots of chocolate. I'll wager your mama's giving you a little brother in, oh, seven or eight months or so—wouldn't you say, Mama?"

"Yes, Papa, you are probably right," she said. "However, I will make one correction." She turned to her daughter and smiled as she spoke, "Isabel, would you and your sisters like to help me make fudge after dinner? I have been craving chocolate all day."

Papa reached for his hat and scratched his head before putting it on, muttering as he reached for the door, "She's craving fried foods *and* chocolate? Now *that* is a new one on me."

Chapter 24

Speculations

"IT'S GONNA BE a boy."

"No it ain't; it's a girl."

The shouting match began around the supper table that night when Papa made the blessed announcement. First came shouts of joy, and then everyone had an opinion of who the little one would be.

Isabel smiled at Mama, who smiled back weakly as she obediently drank the three glasses of milk Papa insisted she drink instead of her usual cup of coffee. Isabel was surprised at the amount of food Mama ate. She had taken a second portion of everything, including dessert, which was unusual for her since she normally was hard pressed to finish her first serving. Isabel dropped her napkin and pulled at Maggie's sleeve to help her find it.

"No wonder ladies who are having babies get so fat," Isabel whispered under the table. "I've never seen Mama eat so much in my life." The two girls giggled as they returned to a sitting position in time to join in the conversation at the table.

"We need another girl so it will be even," Sylvia said. "Besides, if I had a little sister, I could braid *her* hair, right Mama?" She turned to Mama for support.

"That's right, Sylvia, my girl. When we are all lined up brushing and braiding hair, you would no longer be at the end of the line. You would have a little sister to braid."

"Ah, that's sissy stuff," Curtis said. "We need to think ahead to the future. Eugene and I are older and will be off on our own—either married and working or maybe even in the service of our country, and Mama and Papa will need help around here. They need another son, not a silly ol' girl."

"Besides," Eugene said, "Papa isn't as young as he used to be—sorry, Papa—and if anything happened to him, who would look after Mama?"

"We would," Isabel said before she could think to control her voice. "We all would work together to take care of Mama, and you know it. Besides, that is why Papa has Mama pay money to that horrible Mr. Lyon, the life insurance man, right, Papa?"

"That's right, my gal. If anything should happen and I kick the bucket, my grave, coffin, and funeral will be paid for, and Mama will be given money each month to live on, but it will not be much, especially for a large family. Mr. Meadows has agreed to allow your mama to continue to live here as long as she wishes in exchange for help around the farm. She would help Mrs. Meadows with gardening and canning as usual, and he will need you boys to work on the farm. They will need help from the girls from time to time too and will pay each of you for your work. He said he would expect you to negotiate each year as you grow older and stronger. Of course, your financial needs will grow as well. He understands that. So you see, negotiating among yourselves for a brother instead of a sister for financial reasons is not necessary," said Papa with a chuckle.

Then he turned to little Billy, who was feasting on his fried apple pie and milk in his high chair, which was now pulled to the table without the tray. "What do you want, Billy, a baby brother or a baby sister?"

"Billy want a puppy."

"That's silly, Billy. Mama can't have a puppy; she's having a boy or a girl," Jimmy said. He shook his head and rolled his eyes at his little brother, which brought laughter all around the room.

"Which do you want, Jimmy?" asked Papa.

"I want a little sister," he said. That surprised everybody.

"A little sister, why in tarnation would you want another girl in the house?" Curtis said. "You already have three sisters."

"I don't have a little one."

"You have Sylvia."

"She's my big sister, not my little sister. She picks on me, and she looks after me. I don't have a little sister to look after."

"You have Billy," Eugene said.

"Billy takes my toys and follows me around and gets me into trouble sometimes."

"Oh," Mama said, "but a little sister wouldn't do that?"

"Nope." Jimmy shook his head. "A little sister is cute too. Especially if she has curly hair. I saw one at church." Jimmy put the last piece of fried apple pie in his mouth, washed it down with milk, and got down from the table as if he had settled the argument. As far as he was concerned, Mama would have a little girl with curly hair.

Chapter 25

Papa's Birthday

THE FOLLOWING MORNING after breakfast, the kitchen filled up with family members who began to roll in for Papa's birthday celebration. They just happened to show up in time for Saturday morning cinnamon rolls and coffee.

"I always enjoy cooking for all of Papa's children and grandchildren," Mama said when cars and trucks pulled into the yard. "You know, I went to school with them, and I know what they love to eat!" Mama knew they were coming early, so she made extra batches of cinnamon rolls for the adults and oatmeal raisin cookies for Papa's grandchildren, some of whom were older than Isabel. (This fact always had fascinated Isabel, especially when she remembered she had two aunts who were younger.)

"What is that delicious odor wafting on the air?" Papa's firstborn son, Fred, said. "It seems to be coming from Papa's house, and we could smell it all the way from Roanoke."

"Good morning, Fred," Mama said. "You smell homemade cinnamon rolls, and you know it. Pour yourself a cup of coffee, and help yourself to a roll or two." She smiled as she wiped jelly from Billy's face and allowed him down to play with the other children who had just arrived. "Billy, ya'll go on outside and see the new calf, but stay away from the pen now, you hear? Isabel, keep an eye on the little ones, will you?"

"I'll do it, Grandma Lizzie. I love looking after the children," said fourteen-year-old Suzy as she took Billy and her small brother by the hand and led them outside.

"Suzy will make a fine mama someday," Mama said.

"Hold your tongue, Lizzie," said Suzy's mother with mock horror in her voice, "I hope that will be a long time from now." Everyone laughed as the adults settled at the table with coffee and refreshments while Isabel, Maggie, and Jim's eight-year-old Gracie started on the dishes in able to listen covertly to the adult's conversation.

Besides, being with the adults always made Isabel feel more grown up. Oh how she wished to be a mature young lady. She often found herself teetering between childhood and adulthood and chose maturity, much to the chagrin of her family.

"Lizzie, there is something different about you lately," Lena said. She helped herself to another cup of coffee as the last husband left the room and Aunt Jenny arrived simultaneously.

"Different?" Mama said as she poured a glass of milk for herself instead of coffee before taking a second cinnamon bun.

"Yes, different," Lena said. "I cannot put my finger on it exactly. Well, maybe I can. The other day when I saw you at the store, I thought you looked positively radiant. Lizzie, are you with child?"

Isabel turned in time to see the reaction on each of the faces in the room. There was an array of expressions, ranging from shock to sheer happiness. Aunt Jenny seemed to register something completely different from anyone in the room, and Isabel could not read her face. She recovered too quickly, and then she immediately burst into action as she, Lena, Lindy, Cleo, and Mary gathered around Lizzie in a group hug.

"Alright, don't crush her or the baby even before it is born," Aunt Jenny said as she stood up and pumped water into the teakettle and set out Mama's favorite china teacup. "Lizzie, sit there and have a cup of chamomile tea. You need to do a little less around here now."

"Goodness, Aunt Jenny, that is a lot easier said than done, especially with this brood." Mama laughed and gave her sister a good-hearted hug, which Aunt Jenny quickly shrugged off as unnecessary.

"I suppose *he* is strutting around here proud as a rooster in a henhouse," Aunt Jenny muttered. She placed the teakettle on the stove a little too hard.

"What does Papa think about all of this?"

Isabel turned to see who had asked the question, for her older sisters sounded so much alike, their voices were indistinguishable. Lindy had made the inquiry, but everyone waited with equal interest for the answer.

"Well," Mama said slowly, "you know your papa. He loves his children, every one of you. However, he is concerned that the crops may not do as well this year as they have in the past. He is a bit nervous at the prospect of becoming a Papa again at this stage of our lives. He is fifty-five years old today, and for some reason, he seems uncharacteristically, how can I say this?" Mama wrung her cloth napkin in her hand, and she appeared to struggle for her words. "He is somewhat cautious."

"What do you mean by cautious?" Lindy asked. She reached for Mama's hand to assure her.

"Well, he's concerned about money, of course, and clothing for the baby," Mama said.

"Oh, is that all?" Someone laughed in the background, and everyone joined in, offering words of encouragement. "All husbands are like that."

Just as Mama was about to speak, Lena walked toward the sink with her empty cup. "Ahem," she said as she motioned towards the girls with her head. "Little pitchers have big ears. Isabel, why don't you girls pour yourself a glass of milk and take your snack outside?"

Isabel bristled at the remark but quickly obeyed as she led the girls to the back porch and sat down near the door, where she still could hear the conversation.

"It's not just that," Mama said. "It seems as if his confidence has left him. He has not been strutting around here *like a rooster*; it is more as if he has been hiding away, trying to find more work. I know it's because the baby is coming, but it just is not like him. Something is different, and he will not talk about it. Nor will he pray with me about it. He just pretends nothing is wrong." Mama stopped as if she had said too much, or perhaps she could not go on. Isabel did not know which.

Just as Isabel was about to join the other children playing in the yard, Lena spoke up and said, "Why don't *we* pray about it?"

The rest of the day was a wonderful celebration, and Isabel was beside herself with the excitement of it all.

Papa received numerous gifts he wanted, namely a new shaving mug, shaving brush, razor strop, and store-bought soap. Sally Anne even stopped by with a bottle of after-shave lotion. "Why, that's top shelf merchandise. I feel like a millionaire," Papa said. "Mama, you will have to press my best collar for Sunday morning and wear your best dress. I might even take you to the diner for lunch."

Mama's smile lit up the room as she looked deeply into Papa's eyes. "I would like nothing better, Papa, than to accompany such a handsome gentleman for lunch."

"Well," said Jim, who had been listening by the door, "that settles it. The children can come home with us Sunday after church so Papa and his lovely bride can have some time together."

"Best birthday gift of all, Son," Papa said with a chuckle. "Now, maybe my 'bride' will play some of her good music on the squeeze box. How about it, Mama?"

"Only if you join me on the banjo." Mama smiled and lifted the instrument from its case and began playing a lively tune as the children danced. Papa grabbed his banjo, Curtis picked up his guitar, and soon the little cottage rang with music and laughter and the inhabitants' love for each other.

"Papa," Lindy said. Papa sat his banjo aside. "Please sing your song before we go home."

"Now, you know I don't sing."

"Oh, yes you do," Lindy, Cleo, and Jim said in unison.

"Sing the song you sang for Lizzie when you were courting her," Lindy said.

"That was nearly twenty years ago," Papa said. Mama and Papa gazed at each other as if they were the only two people in the room. Mama lifted the squeezebox and played an intro, and Papa began to sing quietly at first and then with more volume and conviction as he looked deeply into his wife's eyes: "Beautiful dreamer…"

Isabel watched her parents, first with embarrassment, and then with awe, for she had never heard Papa sing so beautifully. She observed Mama, whose face turned a lovely shade of pink as a single tear dropped on her flaming cheeks. Mama seemed transfixed as she looked deeply into Papa's eyes.

Applause and good-natured teasing broke the spell.

"I didn't know Papa could sing like that," Isabel whispered to Maggie.

"Me either," Maggie whispered back.

Jim picked up his guitar and played the introduction to "Let Me Call You Sweetheart," and everyone serenaded Mama and Papa.

When the last note faded and the singing was done, Isabel felt that something wonderful was ending and wished to sing all night.

"This is the best birthday I ever had," Papa said as everyone headed home for the night.

Chapter 26

The Long Wait

THE FOLLOWING MONTHS were difficult for Mama and for the children as her time to deliver drew near. "Mama just does not act like herself," Isabel said on the way to school.

"I know," Maggie said. "She actually raised her voice this morning when you were outside milking the cow."

"She did?" Isabel said. She kicked a rock out of the way to vent her frustration. "What happened?"

"Well," Maggie said, "Billy did not want to eat his oatmeal, and Jimmy played with his. He pretended it was quicksand and his piece of bacon was a little boy who thought it was just a muddy pond and jumped in, getting pulled under, and the toast came to the rescue."

Isabel smiled as she envisioned her animated brother's imaginative play with his food.

Maggie smiled briefly before continuing the story. "Mama turned from the stove and shouted, 'Jimmy Greene, you stop playing with your food this instant and eat.' She fussed at Billy too. Then, she turned around and pulled a pan of almost burnt toast from the oven and set the pan down hard on the stovetop and said, 'Oh, horse feathers.'"

"She didn't," Isabel said. "Mama does not use words like that, and she doesn't even like Papa to use that word."

"Oh, yes, she did," Curtis said. He was walking a few paces behind the girls. "Even Papa was reprimanded for taking too long shaving at the mirror in the kitchen because he was in her way."

"But Papa always shaves there," Isabel said. "His shelf with his shaving mug and razor are under the mirror, with the razor strop nailed to the wall. Where did she want him to shave?"

"I don't know," Curtis said. "I think she just wanted him out of the way."

"Oh boy," Isabel said. "How long before the baby comes?"

"I heard her tell Papa that the baby should arrive in January," Eugene said, "but she is already bigger than she was when Billy was born, and he was late."

"January," Isabel said. "It's only the beginning of November. I guess we have a long wait ahead of us. We need to help her more…beyond just doing chores, because Mama seems tired all the time. Maybe that is why she is so grumpy lately."

"I guess so," Eugene said. "Let's all try to do better, especially in the mornings. Isabel, I will milk the cows so you can stay inside and help Mama prepare breakfast. Maggie, you are in charge of getting Billy dressed and fed, and Sylvia can help Jimmy to get dressed and encourage him to behave. Make eating his breakfast a game or a race or something—can you do that?"

"Yes," Sylvia said. "I think so, but who will braid my hair? Mama said she didn't have time and 'for goodness sakes, run a comb through that unruly hair.'"

"I can help you with your hair, Sylvie," Isabel said. "Besides, your hair looks real nice combed out with a ribbon holding it back. You should wear it like that more often."

With a plan in place, the children determined in their hearts to help Mama through her difficult days by being pleasant and helpful—even if it killed them.

That night, Isabel had a difficult time getting to sleep, so she tiptoed down the back stairs to the kitchen with a cup of hot cocoa on her mind. She was surprised to see a light already illuminating the room. She was even more surprised to see Mama sitting at the table crying.

"Mama, what's the matter?" Isabel said. She rushed to her mother's side.

"Oh, Isabel, what are you doing up? It's almost 10:30."

"I couldn't get to sleep, Mama, so I thought I would fix some hot milk with cocoa like you do when we cannot sleep."

Mama smiled as she dabbed at her eyes with a large handkerchief. "I'll fix it for you, child."

"That's OK, Mama. I know how to do it," Isabel said. "Would you like some too?"

"Yes, Dear," Mama said, "that would be wonderful. I probably should have fixed hot milk instead of hot coffee."

Isabel hurried around the kitchen, preparing the warm beverage. She also sliced a piece of pound cake for each of them. "It was a beautiful day today, wasn't it, Mama?"

"Yes, Dear, it was a remarkable day. The sky was so blue I felt as though I could reach out and touch it, just as I would if it were a body of water," Mama said. She gave Isabel what appeared to be a forced smile.

"Mama, what's wrong?" Isabel asked. She placed the tray of goodies on the table and smiled as Mama picked up her fork and started on the pound cake.

"Oops," Mama said as she dropped her fork onto the plate with a clang. "I cannot believe I just started on that cake without giving thanks first."

Isabel smiled at her mother, who had never behaved this way as long as Isabel could remember. "That's alright, Mama.

Jesus knows how delicious that cake is." Isabel's smile widened as Mama began to laugh. When they both were able to stop laughing, Isabel gave thanks for the gorgeous day and for the food. She also asked for strength and energy for Mama.

"I know this has been a difficult time for you children and Papa," Mama said. "It seems as if I do not have control over my mouth lately…"

"That's alright, Mama," Isabel said as she stirred her cocoa. "It must be hard to do all the work and to carry a baby around in your tummy all of the time."

Mama laughed. "Yes, you could say that, but there is more to having a baby besides gaining weight. It affects many areas of your life. You suddenly want to eat strange foods you would have never before considered eating, while normal foods that you eat every day suddenly make you sick, even to think about them. Smelling certain foods can send you running for the little house or a bush, whichever you reach first. Yet it seems that you are always hungry. You can't go into a room without accidentally bumping into something, and it makes you tired all the time, so you need a nap in the middle of the day; therefore, you end up getting behind in your work."

"My goodness," Isabel said. She tried to imagine what it must be like. "I can help you more, Mama. I promise."

"Do you know what the worst part is, Isabel?" Mama took a sip of cocoa and smiled before continuing. "I think the worst part for me is the swollen, achy feet and legs. It is difficult to stand at the stove to cook and wash dishes, and to think, I have two more months of this. Maybe it is my age, but it has never been this bad before, and I have never been this big…not even in my last month."

"Maybe we're having twins," Isabel said. She loved babies and thought two babies would bring as much joy as a couple of puppies.

"Oh, Isabel," Mama said. "Don't even think such a thing." After a few moments of silence, she spoke again; yet it seemed as if she were talking to herself. "Twins run in the family; they surely do. I had not allowed myself to consider the possibility."

Mother and daughter sat in silence as they finished their cocoa. Finally, Isabel cleaned up the dishes and kissed Mama good night. As she took a step up, she heard her Mama say "twins" under her breath.

The following night, just as Isabel was about to fall asleep, she heard soft footsteps outside her door. Suddenly, the door opened slightly, and light from the hallway filled the room.

"Isabel, are you awake?" Isabel sat up and saw Mama standing in the doorway.

"Yes, Mama, is everything alright?" Isabel whispered so she would not awaken her sisters.

Mama came into the room and stood by her bed. "Put on your robe, and come downstairs. I want to show you something."

Isabel donned her robe and slippers as Mama gently covered Sylvia and kissed her forehead and then pushed hair from Maggie's face before leaving the room. Together, they maneuvered the narrow stairway, walked through the kitchen, and front room, and went outside to the front porch.

"Just look at that beautiful sight, Isabel," Mama said with conviction. "Just imagine, the One who created that gorgeous sky with millions of sparkling diamonds cares for you and me." Mama quoted softly, "The heavens declare the glory of God; and the firmament sheweth His handiwork. Day unto day uttereth speech and night unto night sheweth knowledge. There is no speech nor language where their voice is not heard."[8]

She paused. "It's hard to imagine people thousands of miles away are looking at the same moon and stars that were spoken into existence," Mama said. "Do you ever think about this too?" Mama turned toward Isabel.

"Sometimes I do," Isabel said, "but mostly I just think they are pretty."

Mama smiled and turned her gaze back to the sky. "The same One who created all this," Mama raised her hand toward the heavens, "is with this little one…or perhaps I should say with these little ones," Mama added with a silvery laugh. "And He has a plan for their lives, just as He does for you. I hope I didn't frighten you last night with my selfish speech."

"No, Mama, you didn't. You were tired; it was a long, busy day."

"Yes, it was, but that's no excuse." Mama pointed to the sky and continued speaking. "Some nights it seems as though there are no stars in the sky because of fog, clouds, or rain. We cannot see beyond the clouds and realize God's grand display is still there. We just cannot see it *at that moment*. Sometimes the tears in our eyes make it difficult to see the wonderful provision, well, *miracle* He has provided. Do you understand, Dear?"

Isabel nodded her head and then shook it from side to side. "I think so, Mama, but I'm not sure what you are trying to tell me."

"You see," Mama said, "last night I had tears in my heart's eyes and could not see the glorious blessing He has provided for us."

"Oh, do you mean the baby—err—babies?" Isabel smiled at her stumble, not knowing which word to use.

"Yes, that is exactly what I mean," Mama said. "And it is two babies, for I felt them kick at the same time in very different directions," Mama added with a soft laugh.

Isabel noticed Mama rubbing her tummy in a circular motion and wondered if they were kicking again. "Oh boy," Isabel said, "I hope they're girls or one of each. Two boys would fine too, I guess."

"You are becoming a young lady, Isabel, and I just wanted you to know that even though becoming a mother can be uncomfortable and cumbersome, it is the most glorious thing that can happen to a woman. In just a few short years, you will meet the young man God planned for you to marry, and I pray He will bless you with many beautiful children."

"You pray about that, Mama?" Isabel asked in wonder.

"Oh, yes. I pray for each of my children and for the person you will marry. I pray that you will allow the Lord to have first place in your life and in your home. I even pray for your children and grandchildren—that they will come to know the Lord at an early age and will follow Him," Mama said softly.

"You mean we can pray for people who haven't been born yet?" Isabel asked.

"Oh, yes, Dear, our heavenly Father already knows them and has a purpose for each one. He loved us from the very beginning, you see."

"I never thought about it that way," Isabel said. "Do you think it would be alright if I start praying for my future husband and children?"

"I think that would be very wise, Dear," Mama said. "Now, I think we should go back inside. It is getting cold."

As they stepped back into the house, Isabel noticed that Mama had set the tea table with tea and cookies on Mama's favorite crochet tablecloth.

"I enjoyed our time together so much last night," Mama said, "I thought we could have a little tea party tonight."

Isabel sat down with stars shining in her eyes and carefully fingered the gold encircling her teacup, which had once belonged to her great grandmother Permelia.

"Now," Mama said, "tell me all about everything that has been happening in your life over the past few weeks. How is school?"

"School is alright, Mama," Isabel said. "Did I tell you we have a new boy at school?"

"No," Mama said. "Tell me about him."

Isabel grinned and took a sip of her tea before answering. "Oh, Mama," she said, "he's the bee's knees."

Chapter 27

Special Time with Mama

ISABEL AND MAMA continued their late-night tea times twice a week until the birth of the babies, and Isabel looked forward to their special time, planning ahead the things she wanted to ask Mama.

"Mama knows everything," Isabel told Sally Anne as they walked the lane to Sally Anne's house one cool afternoon.

"I know," Sally Anne said. "That's why I love coming to your house. I always learn something important."

Isabel laughed and nodded. "I feel the same way; though, I didn't last year. Last year I just nodded my head when she talked, but I didn't really hear what she was telling me. I guess I have you to thank for some of the change. Thank you for showing me what a special mother I have."

"How did I do that?" Sally Anne asked.

"Well," Isabel said, "first you showed me what your life was like, and then you told me how special my mother is. And you actually listened when she talked to you. Then you started to learn how to cook and keep house from her, and I realized that all mothers are not like that."

"I'm glad I could help," Sally Anne said. "She has helped my mother too, you know."

"She has? How did she do that?"

"Mama said that she showed her what it means to be a mother," Sally Anne said. "You know, Mother did not know her own mother. Grandmother Sally Anne died when Mother was just a baby. That's when Cookie came to cook for the family. Mother loves her. Grandfather wouldn't allow Mother to associate with the help except to give orders. So when I came along, Mama did not know what to do, so she let the nanny take care of me."

"I'm sorry, Sally Anne," Isabel said. "I didn't realize it was that bad."

"But things are different now, and because she has been spending afternoons with your mama, things will be different for the new baby."

"Your mama has been spending afternoons with my mama?" Isabel had not known about this. Then the full impact of Sally Anne's words hit her. "Baby? What baby?"

"My mama is having a baby too," Sally Anne said as she clapped her hands and jumped. "It should be born in the spring. Mother is so excited; I have never seen her so happy."

"Oh, Sally Anne," Isabel said, "that's wonderful. You won't be a 'lonely only' anymore."

"Do you think your mama will let me learn how to take care of babies when hers is born?"

"You mean the twins," Isabel said.

"Twins?" squealed her friend. "Oh, you must be about to burst with excitement. Do you think your mama will let us give them a bottle or change diapers sometimes?"

"Well," Isabel said, "Mama is the only one who will be able to feed them for a while, you know, but I am sure she will let us help with the diapers and maybe even rock them to sleep and when they are bigger, give them a bath and spoon-feed them their mushy food."

"It sounds like a dream come true," Sally Anne said. They reached her front gate. "Having babies in both of our houses will be wonderful. Maybe we could even take them for a stroll. I guess your mama will need a large carriage, won't she?"

Later that evening, Isabel shared her conversation with Mama, complete with Sally Anne's squeal at the news that Isabel was to have twins joining the family.

"I'm glad Sally Anne is so happy. A baby brother or sister will be good for her," Mama said. "She can come over any time, and I can teach you both some important things about baby care. Of course, you already know the basics. You have always been a mother hen to your sisters and brothers." Mama poured hot chocolate into Isabel's teacup and offered her a cookie.

Isabel smiled and dunked her cookie. "Mama, how old were you when you first met Papa?"

"Oh, let me see," Mama said. She stirred sugar into her cup of tea. "I wasn't much older than you when I first met your papa. I knew him as Mr. Greene, my classmates' father."

Isabel smiled as Mama looked straight ahead with a far-away look in her eyes, and Isabel knew that a good story was in store.

"Mr. and Mrs. Greene came to our Christmas play at school; Jim and Lindy were in it, you know."

"You knew Papa's first wife?" Isabel said.

"Oh, yes. Of course, I didn't know her very well—just as Lindy's mama, you know."

Isabel nodded, and Mama continued her story.

"Then one day, Mrs. Greene, Cora, became very ill and died a few weeks later. Lindy and Jim were devastated. So was their Papa. He did not take her death very well. By this time, Fred and Cleo had met their beloved ones and had married. Soon after, Jim and Lena pledged to be man and wife before everyone in a lovely ceremony at the church. That's when I first really noticed your papa. By this time, I had finished school and was playing the organ at church. This is why I was at Jim's wedding, you know. Anyway, Mr. Greene seemed so sad and lonely."

"Did Lindy still live at home with Papa?" Isabel asked.

"Oh, yes, but by this time, she was quite a young lady and already had suitors coming by to take her for rides in the newfangled horseless carriage. She cooked for Papa and kept the house neat as a pin, but he still was lonely. As I said before, when I saw him at Jim's wedding, he seemed like a different man than I had known as a child. He no longer laughed, joked, or sang. He was just… there. So, I started praying for him. Oh, not because I had eyes for him, but because he seemed to need a friend to cheer him up, and that is just what I prayed for. I didn't know that when you pray for someone, God brings that person into your life, but I soon found out.

"Lindy met the man she thought was her intended, and against Papa's wishes, she soon announced she was getting married. Well, that meant that your papa would soon be all alone, and the thought saddened me. I decided to cheer him by baking cookies and leaving them on his porch—anonymously, of course. Then I asked Pa to invite him to dinner, and I did the cooking. My parents found him to be delightful but too old for me, so I started praying for them to see what a good man he was and that he needed me. You see, I had fallen in love with this funny, sensitive, caring man. He often came to our home for dinner, and I volunteered to mend his clothes, as his daughters were now busy with families of their own. When I was twenty years old, he asked me to be his wife; I thought he would never ask."

"Oh, how keen," Isabel said. She tried to imagine Papa and Mama so long ago. "Did you have a big fancy wedding with a beautiful gown and everything?"

"Oh, no," Mama said. "We had a small ceremony in my parents' front parlor. We just had family and a few friends over. Of course, we had such large families, it probably seemed like a big wedding to some. We wanted our loved ones to share our special day with us."

"I'll bet Lindy was happy. You must have been like sisters."

"Lindy did not approve of our relationship. I think she thought I was taking her papa away and trying to replace her mother. Of course, I never intended to do either. In time, she understood, and our friendship became stronger than ever."

"I didn't know that," Isabel said.

"We don't talk about it, Dear," Mama said. "As you know, she is very dear to me."

"What did you wear for your wedding?" Isabel asked.

"I wore a long, white skirt and shirtwaist that I had made just for our ceremony. It had lace on the bodice and sleeves, which were billowy with big cuffs. I must have set in those sleeves ten times before I got them just right. There was a white, embroidered belt that tied it all together nicely and white high top shoes."

"Did you wear a veil and carry flowers?" Isabel wanted to know all the details.

"I wore a hat that I decked with fabric flowers and netting. As for flowers, I covered my small, white Bible with white ribbon and flowers to show that Christ would be the center of our home."

"That sounds beautiful," Isabel said. "How come I've never seen it? You must have been the most beautiful bride in Roanoke."

Mama waved her hand at Isabel's last comment and turned the conversation back to the wedding attire. "It is put away in a trunk in Pa's attic, I think. Perhaps we will find it for you some day. Who knows what we will need to move to get to it. That attic is cluttered to the beams. If you or your sisters would like to wear it for your wedding someday, I would be delighted. However, if you want your own things, I will be just as happy."

"Could I really wear your wedding dress, Mama?" Isabel whispered.

"Of course, Dear, I couldn't think of anything that would make me happier—as long as you are marrying the man God has chosen for you. Only if he loves the Lord and you with all his heart and can support you."

Isabel went to bed that night dreaming of wedding gowns and that special someone she had yet to meet. She saw in the shadows of her dream, a boy with a bright smile and hair falling into his face, covering his eyes.

Isabel noticed over the next few days that Mama was spending special time with each of her children. She and Maggie were making special quilts for the babies, she was teaching Sylvia the fine art of somersaults and cartwheels, she took a special interest in rock collecting with Jimmy, she set aside special cuddle/story time with little Billy every afternoon, she was engaged in music lessons with Curtis, and she was helping Eugene, who was making eyes at the new girl at church.

Papa also noticed the extra time Mama was giving to each child, and Isabel overheard him caution her to take it easy. "Lizzie," he said, "you should be resting."

"Oh, Papa," Mama answered softly, "this is the only chance I will have to be part of their lives like this for a long time… at least until the babies are Billy's age. Eugene could find a girl and get married by then."

"Horse feathers," Papa said. "You should be resting and not working. Mark my words, Mama; if you don't take care of yourself now, you may have a hard time of it when those little ones arrive. Now, drink a glass of milk, and take a nap. Isabel will prepare dinner tonight."

Mama laughed softly and accepted defeat. "Alright, Papa, I will take an afternoon nap if it will make you feel better—as long as Isabel and Maggie can look after Jimmy and Billy."

"Maggie," Isabel whispered to her sister, who was listening from the kitchen, "we need to help Mama more. We can't let anything happen to Mama."

Cool weather accompanied the coming of December, making tasks harder for Mama, who was having a difficult time maneuvering around the cottage.

"Isabel," Mama said as she sliced bread for dinner, "since we were not able to can as many vegetables and fruits this year due to the drought and my condition, we must plan our meals carefully and not use up our supply before our garden produces more for us in the spring."

"Yes, ma'am," Isabel said. She already had thought about the pitiful amount of produce they had canned over the summer and fall. "Mama," Isabel said as she placed the last fork on the table, "we don't have enough to share."

"Yes, Dear," Mama said. "We do not have much, but there may be others who have nothing. We will share with others in need until we have depleted our supply. God expects us to, you know. He did not give it to us to keep it to ourselves. We are blessed to help others."

"But are we blessed, Mama?" Isabel asked. She remembered how much her brothers enjoyed eating.

"Oh, yes, Dear," Mama said. "We are abundantly blessed in many ways."

Chapter 28

A Sparse Christmas

ISABEL REACHED FOR her coat and then pulled her scarf and mittens from the sleeve before putting it on. "Mama made these for each of us last year," Isabel said to Sally Anne, who was buttoning her stylish coat. "I don't think she had time to make anything for our Christmas this year. She has been busy making things for the babies, you know. Besides, she has been spending a lot of time with each of us; so that's sort of like a present, isn't it?"

"Oh, yes," Sally Anne said. "I wish Mother would spend extra time with me like your mama does."

Silence filled the air as the Greene children and Sally Anne walked down the lane in the crisp winter air.

"Maybe it will snow this year," Maggie said hopefully.

"Isabel," Sylvia said, "does this mean we won't have Christmas this year?"

"Of course we'll have Christmas. It's Jesus' birthday. Just because it's Jesus' birthday doesn't mean we have to get presents every year, does it?"

"I guess not," Sylvia said. "But we always have before."

"I know," Isabel said. "But this year, we don't have much money, and Mama can't do as much as she usually does because two babies are coming at once."

"Can't we put up a tree anyway and hang our stockings?"

"I hope so," Isabel sighed. "It's a lot of work for Mama, though."

"Why don't we do it?" Maggie said. "Eugene and Curtis could cut a tree and set it up for us, and we could decorate it with popcorn and make paper ornaments."

"I could bake cookies," Isabel said. "And we could make cards for Mama and Papa too."

"I made a scarf for Mama," Maggie said. "I can make one for Papa too, and they can be from all of us."

"That could be from you and Sylvie, since she helped you hold the yarn," Isabel said. "I still have some money in my savings envelope from last summer. What better way to spend it than Christmas?"

Suddenly, Sylvia stopped in her tracks. "Santa will still bring us something, won't he?"

Isabel turned and looked at her sisters, who were anxiously awaiting an answer. "I hope so, Sylvie, but don't get your hopes up. I don't think Santa has much money this year either."

"He doesn't?" the two stricken sisters asked in unison.

"Oh, I wouldn't worry about that," Sally Anne said. "He has been working all year, you know. He *couldn't* forget about you and your brothers."

Isabel's stomach churned as she thought of the disappointment Christmas morning might bring. "Even if he doesn't stop by our house," Isabel said, "we still get to hear the Christmas story from the Bible—since that is what Christmas is all about anyway. God gave His only Son, for us. Mama always bakes a birthday cake for Jesus, and we love cake!"

"We can still sing Christmas carols," Sylvia said. She jumped up and down with excitement. "Do you think Papa will take us Christmas caroling this year in the hay wagon?"

"Maybe," Isabel said. "It doesn't cost a thing to do that."

"And people invite us inside for cookies and hot chocolate," Maggie said.

"If you do, may I come with you?" Sally Anne asked.

"Yes," they said together.

Isabel carefully set the table as she thought about how to ask Mama about Christmas. She watched as Mama spooned watery stew into a serving bowl and then pulled a plate of biscuits out of the warming oven.

"Mama," Isabel said, "are we poor?"

Mama sat the biscuits on the table beside a dish of hand-churned butter. "I suppose if you compare us to some people who live in fine houses with beautiful furnishings, one could say we are poor. However, I don't see it that way."

"You don't?"

"God has given us so much. We have a house with a roof that does not leak and wood to keep our home warm. We have food on the table and love in our hearts. The biggest blessing of all is that we have each other. When you stop to count your blessings, you may realize that we are rich in mercy and grace."

"But what about Christmas?" Isabel asked with tears threatening to spill over.

"Christmas is about Christ," Mama said.

"I know, but Sylvie is expecting Santa to come."

"We have never made *Santa* the center of Christmas. In fact, we have never given credit to anyone but the Lord for the things we have." Mama poured milk into each glass at the table.

"I know, but the other children at school do," Isabel said. "We always hang our stockings on the mantle on Christmas Eve, and they always have goodies in them on Christmas morning."

"Yes, I know you do, Dear," Mama said softly, "but I'm afraid this year will be different. Now please ring the dinner bell before supper gets cold."

Later that night, when everyone in the house was asleep, Isabel quietly slipped out of bed and stood by the window, gazing at the sky. "Please, Lord," she prayed, "help us make this a good Christmas for Mama, Papa, and the children too."

When she awoke the next morning, snow was swirling outside of her window, and the grass and trees were already covered with the sparkly white blanket. She could hear Papa stomping snow off his boots as he came inside after milking the cows. Isabel dressed quickly and hurried downstairs to start breakfast.

After breakfast and chores were completed, everyone scattered to work on secret projects for Christmas. Eugene and Curtis disappeared for several hours and returned at lunchtime, pulling a beautiful tree behind them. The children were beside themselves with excitement as Papa placed the tree on a stand and set it up in the corner of the parlor. There were a few ornaments from previous years, and the girls filled in blank spots with popcorn strings, paper chains, and ornaments Eugene fashioned out of tin.

Mama's eyes misted as she entered the parlor after a long nap.

"Surprise!" the children said. They pulled her to the tree to see what they had made. Mama and Papa exchanged glances over the children's heads, and Isabel noticed concern in their eyes.

"Don't worry, Mama," Isabel said. She poured a cup of hot chocolate for Mama. "This year, we're doing Christmas for you and Papa. Eugene will even read the Christmas story tonight, and I will bake a chicken for our dinner on Christmas Day. I guess we'll just have soup for Christmas Eve. Merry Christmas, Mama! Do you like the tree?"

"The tree is lovely, and you all are wonderful," Mama said. She dabbed her eyes with a hankie.

Just as the family sat down for their Christmas Eve soup, there was a knock at the door.

"Mrs. Meadows," Eugene said, "come in."

"I didn't come to stay. I just wanted to thank you for all that you have done this year." She handed Eugene a large basket filled with goodies, confectionaries, and jars of vegetables and fruit. "We wanted you to have this too." She reached outside the door and presented them with a large turkey. "We know it has been a difficult year and wanted you all to have a Merry Christmas."

Later that night, Papa heard a noise outside after all the younger children had been put to bed. He went outside to investigate and came back inside with a large box filled with toys and a basket of candy and baked goods. Isabel ran to the porch and looked around, but she saw no one—not even footprints in the snow.

"This is a Christmas we will never forget," Mama said with wonder. "And to think that we didn't have enough to fill stockings this year except for a piece of fruit, some nuts, and a candy stick. The Lord is good."

Chapter 29

The Arrival

IT HAPPENED EARLY that snowy January morning. Mama was up before sunrise preparing breakfast when the first labor pains began.

"Isabel," Mama said. She placed bacon into the cast iron skillet. "You must stay home from school today to help me."

"OK, Mama," Isabel said, "is everything alright?"

"No, Dear, it's time."

"Time," Isabel said. Then the full impact of that single word dawned upon her. "What do we do? Shall I call Papa from the barn now?"

"Yes, Dear," Mama said. "Please ask him to use Mrs. Meadow's telephone to call the doctor and then to call your Aunt Jenny to come *now*."

"OK, Mama," Isabel said. She ran for the door and then remembered that Mama was still standing at the stove and went back to help her to her room.

"I will be alright here for now," Mama said. "Now go and find Papa. Hurry!"

Papa jumped on the white horse and set his course for his employer's house. "Don't know why Jenny needs to be here; she puts her nose in our business enough as it is."

Doctor Barkley arrived at the Greene home forty-five minutes later, just as Aunt Jenny's Dodge pulled into the yard. Little Ralph made an appearance two hours later.

"Isabel," Aunt Jenny said, just as the baby let out his first cry, "come in here, and help with the baby."

Isabel held her breath and nervously entered the room. Mama's hair was plastered to her head. Dr. Barkley nodded his greeting as Aunt Jenny placed the small bundle wrapped in a towel into Isabel's arms. She looked down at the small, pink cherub with golden strands of hair that almost curled on top of his head. She could hardly breathe lest he break.

"Oh," she said, "he is so cute. Look at his button nose, and his mouth is so tiny."

"Yes, he is beautiful," Aunt Jenny said. "Please take him into the kitchen, where it is nice and warm. Open the oven door, and put the baby in your mama's laundry basket near the stove to keep him warm. It is important that you do not let him get cold. Can you do that?"

"Oh, yes," Isabel said. She slowly walked to the door and turned sideways as she passed through the threshold in order to avoid hitting the baby's head on the doorframe, just as Mama had taught her.

"Isabel," Mama said from her bed, "thank you for taking care of your little baby brother. You are such a good girl."

"Thank you, Mama," Isabel said. She pulled the door closed. Then she heard Mama moan and knew that it may be a while before the other baby made an appearance."

"Look, Papa," Isabel said as she entered the kitchen, "isn't he beautiful?"

Papa nodded and headed back into the front parlor to await the arrival of the second child. Isabel noticed he looked tired and worried, but she turned her thoughts to the new life in her arms as tears slowly slid down her cheeks.

"I'm your big sister," she whispered. She laid the baby into the prepared basket in the kitchen and placed the basket on a wide chair in front of the oven. "I love you." She placed a kiss on the baby's head.

Suddenly, there was a knock at the front door, and Papa hastened to open it.

"Is Dr. Barkley here?" asked an excited boy. "There has been an accident, and he is needed right now."

"Yes, he is here," Papa said. "But he cannot come now; my wife is having a baby. It shouldn't be long now. She has delivered one, and the other one is on the way. Just tell me where Doc is needed, and I will give him the message. He will be there as soon as possible."

Isabel heard the front door close, and Papa began pacing the floor again.

Finally, she heard a scream and then a baby's cry. "I hope it's our *sister*," Isabel whispered to her newborn brother. She wanted to rush into Mama's room, but she knew that she must not leave the baby alone.

"It's another boy," Papa said. He rushed back out to be with Mama.

The doctor stepped into the kitchen to look at the baby and then left quickly, without saying a word. Isabel supposed he was rushing to the accident victim, just as Papa had promised the boy at the door.

#

Chapter 30

"JIMMY CRACK CORN and I don't care, Jimmy crack corn and I don't care…" Isabel sang as she hung up the last sheet on the clothesline.

"Isabel," Mama called from the house. "Are you finished hanging the laundry yet? I need your help for a minute."

"Yes, Mama," Isabel said and skipped into the house, allowing the screen door to clap behind her. She squinted as she entered the dark room, allowing her eyes to focus after being out in the bright sunlight. She smiled at little Margaret and Sylvia, who were quietly playing with the rag dolls Mama had made for them. Jimmy was helping his little brother Billy build a town with blocks. Mama was trying to prepare dinner, but the twins were crying, demanding their own dinner that only Mama could provide.

"I'll hold Ralph while you feed Raymond, Mama," Isabel said as she picked up her screaming brother. "You have a good set of lungs for a little baby." Her soft voice soothed the crying child. He reached up and touched her face with his pudgy, little hands.

Mama sat down in the rocker with Raymond and began to nurse her hungry baby. She smiled and gently brushed blonde curls away from his face. "You know, Isabel, God designed us not only to give life to little ones, but also to sustain them. You will find when you are married that sometimes the best time of the day will be when you are holding this God-given person in your arms and providing the care that only a mother can give. Always remember that children are gifts from God and never a burden. Always love them as your heavenly Father loves you."

The rest of the afternoon ran smoothly after the twins were fed and put down for their naps.

"Papa will be home soon, Isabel. Will you set the table, please?"

"Of course, Mama." Isabel reached for the plates and cutlery.

Voices soon filled the house as Papa, Eugene, and Curtis came inside. They stopped at the sink and washed their hands in the cold pump water, drying their hands on Mama's soft towel. Mama worked quickly and quietly as all of the family sat down together at the table.

"Pinto beans and corn bread again?" Eugene said. He generously buttered his corn bread with the butter he had helped churn.

"Yummy. Fried potatoes." Jimmy said. "Isabel fixed them."

"They're the best fried potatoes I've ever tasted," Curtis said, making Isabel blush from the compliment, especially since she had almost burned them.

"Yep," Eugene said. "I like them best when they're good and crispy like this. They taste better than ol' soggy potatoes." Everyone laughed, and Mama gave Isabel a wink and a smile.

"Don't let them know you almost burned them, Isabel. They'll never know," Mama had said before they got home, and she was right.

Mama's always right. Isabel carefully wiped the dishes and put them away in the cupboard, handing a few items back to

Maggie to rewash. Sylvia sat on the red kitchen stool, supervising as Mama swept the floor.

"Why can't I help with the dishes?" Sylvia asked. "I'll get them clean. I promise."

"You can't wash the dishes because you're too small," Maggie said. "Right, Mama?"

"Dear Sylvia," Mama said in her most soothing voice, "you will soon be big enough to help with the dishes, and then you will wish you were too small again. Besides, you have a very important job."

"I do? What is it?"

"Choosing a cleanup song, of course, and keeping us on key. What shall we sing tonight?"

Sylvia smiled brightly, showing the space where two teeth should be. "How about 'Bringing in the Theets?'" The smile quickly faded as her two older sisters snickered at the song and the way her tongue stuck out between her teeth when she tried to say sheets.

"That's sheaves, Sylvie, not sheets," Isabel said. "It means the harvest."

"I wondered why we sing about the laundry in church," Sylvia said.

Isabel started singing, and her sisters joined in, with Mama harmonizing in her rich alto. This was Isabel's favorite time of the day. She loved cleaning the kitchen with Mama because they always ended up singing.

Curtis stood in the doorway and listened as if enraptured. He obviously loved listening to Mama sing; he always said so. He loved evenings filled with music, especially when Mama got the squeezebox out of its box and began playing happy tunes and singing. Isabel knew he hoped she would entertain them tonight, and he was not disappointed.

Everyone loved those times, especially Papa. His wife was beautiful and talented too. He often said his children were going to be just like her, and anyone could see that this thought made his heart swell with pride. It showed on his face as he watched Mama play her music and sing with the children. Isabel observed her parents as they quietly communicated this unspoken love to each other. Then she quickly looked away, as if she had witnessed something too precious for her eyes to see. She turned her thoughts to her siblings instead.

All of the children displayed some talent; those who could not sing or play an instrument displayed a wonderful sense of humor and spent hours teasing one another, in playful way, and laughing. They sang song after song, until they could not think of another song to sing.

"Now that our hearts are filled with music," Mama said, "let's gather around God's Word for our family devotions."

Chapter 31

To Grandpa's House We Go

TWO DAYS LATER, Mama was in an especially good mood and rewarded the children for their exceptional behavior. After breakfast and morning Bible reading, she was almost giddy as she announced, "We are going on an adventure today. Papa said we could take the horse and wagon and go into Roanoke to see your grandparents."

"Hooray!" cheered the older children. The younger children held hands and danced around in a circle. The twins opened their eyes and smiled at the jubilee.

Mama quickly established some order to the happy chaos. "Eugene, why don't you and Curtis get the horses and wagon ready while Isabel and I pack a lunch? Margaret, do you think you can bundle your little brothers in their coats and hats?"

"Yes, Mama." She was happy to help.

"What can I do, Mommy?" Sylvia asked.

"You may do the most important thing of all," Mama whispered. "Please remind your brothers and sisters to visit the little building out back before we leave."

"Oh, Mama." Sylvia giggled and then skipped through the house, with her blonde braids bouncing behind her, to do her mother's bidding.

Soon the lunch was packed and the children sufficiently bundled against the cold and ready for the journey to Roanoke.

"Mama," Maggie said, "why doesn't Papa take us in the TinLizzie?"

"Papa is working the farm today and can't get away," Mama said. She carefully placed the baby into a box filled with hay and quilts and then turned to Eugene, who passed her the other twin. Mama placed a light blanket over the box cradle to keep air off the babies. "Besides, we will not all fit into the automobile, you know. We were already crowded, but with the new babies, diapers, changes of clothes, and our box lunch to eat along the way, there is absolutely no room for us. Now, find a seat, and stay put." She passed out old quilts to each child. "Put this over you, and you'll be nice and cozy."

Isabel stationed herself by the hay-filled boxes, which served as cribs for little Ralph and Raymond. She sang happy songs to keep them entertained. The other children chimed in, and soon, they heard Mama's lovely alto voice harmonizing with them.

"We are going to have a lovely visit with your grandpa and Grandma Betty," Mama said. They pulled into her father's yard. Grandpa was there to greet them and to care for the horses.

"Go right inside with those little ones," Grandpa said. "Grandma Betty has been beside herself preparing for your visit. She thinks you are frozen and half starved."

"Thanks, Pa," Mama said. She gave Grandpa a peck on the cheek. "I always look forward to visiting you."

"Me too, honey," he said. "Me too."

Grandma Betty met the chilled family at the door and quickly ushered them into the nice, warm kitchen. Delicious fragrances emanated from the old, green cookstove.

"Give me that precious baby," she said. She took Raymond from Isabel's arms. "I have been itching to hold the twins all week. I've been after your pa to visit you, but he just hasn't been able to get away." She removed layers of blankets from the little one in her arms.

"Lizzie, I couldn't believe you would actually bring these little ones out—they're not even a month old," she said.

"Well," Mama said as she took baby Ralph from Eugene, "today is unseasonably warm, and I had them bundled and covered well. They have been cooped up in the house too long. I am planning to take them to church on Sunday, so today is our first official outing." Ralph looked up at her.

"Well, ya'll come on and sit down. Lunch is ready, and your pa has been sneaking food from the cooking pots all morning." Grandma Betty placed steaming bowls of food on the table. "If you children eat all of your vegetables, we have fresh donuts for dessert."

"Yummy," the children said. They eagerly sat at the table with their two young aunts, Gina and Tina.

"I brought some food along with us," Mama said. She motioned to Curtis to retrieve the box from the wagon.

"Oh, just hold on to that. I made plenty. Besides, those boys might get hungry on the trip home," said Grandma Betty.

Isabel enjoyed the day with her mother's family and wished they could stay longer in the warmth of her grandparents' home.

Chapter 32

Mama's Bad Day

TWO DAYS LATER, Isabel hurried home after school in order to help Mama with the twins and to get dinner on the table before Papa came in from doing chores. She could hear the babies crying before she reached the first step, and her stomach lurched with guilt at having left Mama alone with all the work while she went to school all day.

Mama sat in the rocker with a white shawl modestly draped over her nursing baby, and his twin lay in the handmade cradle at her feet. He was screaming. Jimmy tried to divert his attention from his hunger by shaking rattles and trying to touch his nose with his tongue as he implored his tiny brother to stop crying. "You're screaming louder than a banshee, and I don't even know what that is," he declared in frustration. "All I know is, it hurts my ears."

The doctor had told Mama that the twins needed to gain weight, and she was feeding them almost constantly; yet they still seemed hungry. By the time she finished feeding one baby, the other was ready to nurse again. Meanwhile, Billy clung to Mama's skirt, crying while attempting to crawl up her leg to sit upon her lap, even though the chair was too crowded for him to join them.

"Jimmy dear," Mama said, "Isabel will take over now. You may run and play."

Isabel picked up the crying baby and waited until Mama had finished feeding and burping baby Ralph. They then exchanged babies so Mama could feed Raymond.

"Oh oh," Isabel said, "somebody needs a diaper change. May I change him, Mama? I promise not to gag this time…honest." Just as she was speaking, the front door opened. Maggie and Sylvia entered the house like a herd of cattle.

"There you are, girls," Mama said. "I was beginning to worry. Go to your room, and change into your chore clothes. Then you may have a snack before you help Isabel; she will tell you what you need to do. Hurry now; it is getting late."

Isabel carefully carried her brother into the next room.

"Hold the back of his head," Mama reminded, "and be careful walking through the doorway. You do not want to hit his head on the doorframe. Walk sideways. Better safe than sorry."

Isabel turned and slowly walked through the doorway, holding her breath the whole time. She almost closed her eyes and then reminded herself that closing her eyes would not be a good idea. She finally made it into Mama and Papa's room and gently laid the baby on a square of canvas that Mama kept on the bed to protect the bedclothes. Little Ralph looked up at his sister and smiled, and then he opened his heart-shaped mouth as if he wanted to speak. Isabel felt her heart swell with love and pride for her little brother.

Isabel folded the white, square cloth into a triangle and realized it was too big. Then she folded it over again into a smaller triangle. "This should fit nicely," she said. She unfastened Ralph's soiled diaper. "Ew, it's green." She held her breath as she tried not to gag. At that very moment, she looked up and saw that the baby was watching her, and she suddenly stopped gagging and smiled. "You did a good job filling up your diaper this time, Ralphie." She dropped the diaper into the pail, for Mama to clean later, all the while keeping the baby covered with a handkerchief to prevent an unpleasant incident. Mama had taught her this trick when Billy was a baby. Ralphie smiled back and started to coo as if he were telling her all about his day with Mama. Then she reached into the bowl of soapy water on the bed stand for a warm washcloth to clean the baby as her Mama had taught her; dried him carefully with a soft, white towel; and reached for the yellow box of cornstarch.

"Mama," Isabel said from Mama's bedroom, "how much cornstarch do I sprinkle on, just a tiny bit or a whole bunch?"

"Only sprinkle enough to keep his little bottom dry, Isabel. We want to keep his skin from getting irritated, so you need just enough to do the job, but not too much," said Mama with a hint of weariness in her voice.

Isabel heard her siblings enter the room, but she was so busy she did not pay attention to their activities until she heard a thud and realized she should have been watching them more closely.

"Ma-Ma," Sylvia said, "can Isabel sweep the half of box of cornstarch off the floor and put it back into the box and reuse it?"

"How did the cornstarch get on the floor?"

"I'd rather not say," Sylvia said. She sauntered through the bedroom door into the front room, her voice hinting at a smile.

"It's OK, Sylvie. It landed on Jimmy," Isabel said. "Don't you move, Jimmy." Isabel returned to diapering the baby. She carefully pinned the diaper on the baby, carefully positioning her hand so that if anything got stuck by the diaper pin, it would not be the baby. Then she placed him on a folded quilt in the middle of Mama's bed and positioned pillows around him to prevent him from falling off.

Isabel took a clean canvas, laid it on the floor beside Jimmy, and then put a clean diaper on it. "Now, Jimmy, I want you to roll over and shake your shirt onto the diaper." The three sisters watched breathlessly as Jimmy shook out the cornstarch onto the diaper. Except for a few cookie crumbs, her plan worked just as Isabel hoped it would. "Now we are all set for the next two or three diaper changes, and all we have to do is shake the yellow powder into the diaper instead of on the baby."

"You are so smart, Isabel." Maggie looked up to her sister with admiration, and Isabel beamed. She was quite proud of her new and improved way of diapering the babies and was sure Mama would be delighted.

Mama, however, was not delighted. "I am sorry, Dear, I appreciate your effort, but we cannot use this cornstarch because it has been contaminated. Do you see the little bits of cookie crumbs? They will irritate the baby's tender skin and ultimately cause him pain. I know you tried to help, but we need to throw this away." Mama picked up the diaper filled with cornstarch and cookie crumbs and headed for the backdoor. A disappointed Isabel followed her through the hall into the kitchen. Isabel saw that the breakfast dishes were still on the kitchen table and the pans still lay unwashed in the sink.

"Mama, what happened today?" Isabel asked. Mama always cleaned her kitchen immediately after a meal's completion.

"What happened today?" Mama repeated in a comical tone. "Let's see, Raymond apparently had colic, and Ralph was a good brother and cried sympathetically...all day. Jimmy stuffed a frog into his pocket yesterday, and it hopped onto the table after you children left for school. I made him set the poor thing free outside. Then Jimmy decided to build a fort in the parlor with my good sheets and quilts—you can see that it is still there—then he proceeded to go in search for Indians, which were unwillingly played by Billy. Meanwhile, Billy has formed an attachment to me today and for some reason will not let me out of his sight for even a minute. He wants me to hold him all the time and cannot seem to understand that I must feed the babies. When I am not holding him, he sits on the floor at my feet crying, just as you found him when you came home from school. I don't know what is going on with him. I thought perhaps he was jealous of the twins, but now I am beginning to wonder if he is coming down with something. He is usually too cheerful to act this way." Mama took a deep breath and then continued her story. "When Papa came home for lunch, I had a bawling twin in each arm, Billy in my lap, and Jimmy had gotten a splinter in his finger, so he was crying too. I'll tell you what, Isabel; I was close to tears myself."

"What did you do, Mama?" Isabel asked.

"Well, I did not have a nice lunch ready for your papa as he expected, so he decided to have lunch with the hired hands at the Meadows' place, just this once. He took Jimmy and Billy with him, and it was much easier to get the little ones quiet and down for a nap. By the time Papa brought the boys home, I had the breakfast pots and pans soaking and was able to meet my men with a smile." The sound of breaking glass from the front room preceded a chorus of "Ma-Ma" from Mama and Papa's room.

"This is how it has been all day," Mama said with a sigh. She turned toward the front of the house. "Will you find out what happened in the front room, please? I need to see to the babies." As they reached the end of the hallway, Mama touched Isabel on the shoulder. "Isabel, I'm glad you're home. You are the best helper a mother can have."

"Thank you, Mama," Isabel said. She practically floated through the room.

Chapter 33

ISABEL SCOURED THE last of the breakfast dishes and sighed as she watched her weary mother making simple preparations for dinner. She finally had gotten the twins down for their late afternoon nap, and Maggie was trying to keep Billy occupied until dinner time.

"Papa and the boys will be in any minute, Isabel. Please set the table and put the biscuits in the oven so we can eat as soon as they come in," Mama said.

Isabel turned and looked at Mama, who did not seem like herself. "Mama, are you OK?"

"Yes," Mama said. She pushed her hair out of her face and shoved another piece of wood into the stove. "I'm just tired, that's all; it has been a long day."

"Mama, if you want me to, I'll stay home from school tomorrow to help you. Sally Anne can bring my school work by after school."

"That won't be necessary, child," Mama said, "but thank you."

Isabel already had been envisioning herself spending the day playing with the twins. Her musing was interrupted as footsteps stomped on the back steps, as if dislodging mud or snow, and Isabel knew that Papa and her brothers were home for dinner. She rushed to complete her task of setting the table so they would have an inviting table to greet them after their busy day of farm work.

"Something smells mighty good," Papa said. He sauntered over to the stove to peek into the cooking pots.

"It's nothing fancy," Mama said. She took light, fluffy biscuits from the oven and placed them into a napkin-lined basket.

"Who needs fancy when you can have good food like this," Papa said. He grinned and winked. The boys followed Papa's example and agreed wholeheartedly, making Mama blush.

"Isabel," she said, "call the children to supper before the food gets cold."

Just as Isabel stepped into the front room to gather the rest of the family, Billy began to cry once more for Mama. By the time he reached the kitchen, he was inconsolable and became so upset that no one could understand what he really wanted.

"Billy, eat your dinner," Papa said. He tried to console him, but Billy would not listen to Papa.

"Billy, let me feed you so Mama can eat," Isabel said. She tried to tempt her small brother to eat his mashed potatoes, but he closed his mouth tightly and shook his head as he struggled to get out of his chair in order to get to his mother. "Look, Billy, I'm adding more butter to your boiled potatoes, just the way you like them." Billy cried all the harder, reaching for Mama.

"Mama, rock ages," Billy said continually through his sobs, making him difficult to understand.

"What is it, Billy?" Mama said. She placed the last dish of steaming vegetables on the table and rushed to the side of her distraught child. "Why, Papa," she said, "the child is burning up. He has a fever. No wonder he is so fussy. I knew he was coming down with something. He just does not act like this unless something is wrong. Besides, his coloring is all wrong today, and his eyes look awfully weak." She gently lifted Billy from his chair and carried him to the sink, pumping cool water into the dishpan and dipping a cloth into the water. She began wiping Billy's face. "Look at his mouth, Papa. It has a bluish tint, and he sounds a little congested."

"Rock ages, Mama, rock ages," Billy said. He laid his head on Mama's shoulder.

"What do you mean, Dear? What is 'rock ages'?" Mama said. "Do you want Mama to rock you?"

Billy nodded.

"Then this can mean only one thing," Mama said to the rest of the family, who were watching from the kitchen table. "We must go to the Rock of Ages as we rock in that old rocker in the front room."

Isabel finished her dinner and put a plate in the warming oven for Mama before cleaning up the kitchen with the help of Maggie, Eugene, and Curtis. After every dish was washed and put away and the floor was swept, Isabel stepped into the front room to offer to hold Billy so Mama could eat. Mama was holding Billy as if he were a baby again, softly singing, "Rock of ages, cleft for me; let me hide myself in Thee…"

"Mama," whispered Isabel, "the dishes are done and the floor swept. Can I do anything else?"

"Thank you, child. Bring me Billy's blanket and a bowl of cool water and a cloth and put it on the table beside me. We need to get his fever down. It looks like it is going to be a long night."

"Alright, Mama," Isabel said. "Shall I bring your supper now?"

"Thank you, Dear, no. It looks like I won't be eating tonight." She repositioned Billy so she could move her arm, and he started to cry again.

"Sing rock ages, Mama, rock ages," Billy said. He started to cough—a dry, hacking cough, and Isabel knew it indeed would be a long night.

Mama continued singing "Rock of Ages" throughout the night, for whenever she changed the song, Billy started to cry. His cough continued to get worse. Mama instructed Isabel to put pots of water on the stove to boil. She recognized the cough as croup. Billy had suffered it more than once. Each episode had been worse than the last.

Mama sent Eugene and Curtis to the cellar for a few onions, and she instructed them to cut the strong vegetable. Isabel cooked them, put the translucent onions into a folded piece of cheesecloth, and placed it into a piece of flannel to put on Billy's chest in order to break up the congestion. Papa moved the rocker from the front room into the kitchen so Billy would get the full effect of the onions and the steam. By morning, the congestion had abated, and his breathing was easier.

"Now, if only his fever would break, we could all breathe easier, knowing that he will be OK," whispered Mama to Papa and Isabel, who had entered the kitchen after bottle-feeding Ralph and Raymond and putting them down to nap so she could start breakfast.

By afternoon, Billy was playing quietly and asking for cookies.

"Well," Mama said, "one thing I know for sure is, when we call upon the Rock of Ages, He answers.

Chapter 34

Tragedy

"WAKE UP, GAL," Papa's voice interrupted a perfectly lovely dream, and Isabel tried to understand if his voice was part of the dream. "Isabel, wake up. Your mama needs you; she's burning up with fever."

Isabel sat up immediately, as if struck by a bolt of electricity. She was wide awake. She threw back the bed covers and rushed across the room, vaguely aware of the cold beneath her bare feet as she reached for the door. Papa stood outside in the hallway, looking pale and holding a lamp. Isabel realized it was still dark outside.

Mama had stayed up with her sick boy for three days, for the fever had returned each night, along with a raspy cough. She had begun to look tired and worn. Isabel remembered that Mama was coughing a lot, but she had insisted that she was merely clearing her throat. She finally had gone to bed on time for the first time in days, Isabel recalled as she dressed hurriedly, knowing she would not have time to dress later, for it would prove to be a busy day.

"You're to fix breakfast, Isabel," Papa said as she entered the kitchen that was just beginning to warm up. Papa added another piece of wood to the fire Mama had banked the night before. "And take care of the children. Your mama needs to rest. I'll be back in to check in on her as soon as I finish." He headed outside to start on his chores.

Isabel set the table, made coffee, and gathered ingredients for breakfast. She looked at the clock and realized she was a little early, so she tiptoed into her parents' room to check on Mama and the twins, who were sleeping soundly. Mama looked ghostly to Isabel, for she was as white as her sheet, except for the pink flush in her cheeks. As she turned to leave the room, Mama's hoarse voice startled her.

"Isabel, will you bring me a glass of water, please? I am so thirsty."

"Yes, Mama, I'll be right back," Isabel said, She hurried to comply. She returned with a pitcher full of cool water and was surprised when Mama drank three full glasses. "Would you like some more, Mama, or shall I fix a pot of tea and toast?"

"Maybe later," Mama said. "I think I will get some sleep now, before the babies wake up."

By the time the rest of the house awoke with the sunrise, Isabel had breakfast on the table, the twins diapered, one twin bottle-fed, and the other waiting patiently in his kitchen cradle.

"Where's Mama?" Maggie asked as she rubbed sleep from her eyes.

"Mama is sick, so we need to be very good today and help her."

Isabel answered each inquiry with a gentle warning in her voice, especially to her brothers.

After breakfast, the boys hurried through their chores; Maggie gathered up the dishes and filled the dishpan with hot water from the large, whistling teakettle; and Sylvia picked up a dishtowel to dry. After feeding and diapering the babies, Isabel swept the floor. Each child above the age of three found something helpful to do. Even two-year-old Billy, who had made a remarkable recovery, tried to help his brothers carry wood. He had the privilege of pulling a wagonload of kindling wood into the kitchen to fuel the fire in the big, black iron stove. Soon all of the chores were completed, and everyone except Isabel went to school. She stayed home to take care of Mama and the babies.

The children had just returned from school and were eating apples and drinking a glass of milk before starting on their chores when they heard loud, clicking footsteps on the front porch steps. Then, there was a loud knock on the glass door.

"Who could that be?" Isabel wondered aloud. She watched Curtis sprint to the door. Raymond had just fallen asleep, and Isabel was rocking Ralph in hopes he would join his brother for his late afternoon nap. "Nobody we know knocks like that. Now I will have to wash hand prints from the glass."

"Oh no," Curtis said as he peeked behind the parlor curtain, "it's ol' Widow Barker."

"Widow Barker," the children said. "What does she want?"

"We'll never find out if you don't open the door," Isabel said. "Besides, she'll just keep knocking until we do, and the noise will wake up Raymond."

Curtis took a deep breath and opened the door with trepidation, greeting their visitor with his best manners. "Good afternoon, Mrs. Barker. Won't you come in?"

"It took long enough for you to answer the door. Are you all deaf?" The woman stepped inside, obviously surveying the room with scrutiny. "Well, are you?"

Curtis's face turned red. He made a fist by his side and then relaxed his hand as he answered the grumpy woman. "No, ma'am, we just were not expecting company with Mama sick and all. She does not allow us to open the door without first checking to see who is here."

"Humph. You did not need to check this time, seeing it was I who was at the door, and you know me."

"Yes, ma'am," he said. "What can we do for you?"

"You can take me to your mama; that's what you can do for me."

"Mama is sleeping now, but we will be glad to tell her that you called," Curtis said.

"Sleeping or not, take me to her," the woman raised her voice as she pushed past Curtis and headed toward the bedroom. She rapped on the door with an umbrella and then turned and handed Curtis a package before entering the room.

"Lizzie Greene," she said, "I heard that you had taken to your bed, but I told those gossips that you were not the lazy type…" She walked in and then shut the door. The children strained to hear the conversation, but they could only hear her muffled voice, and occasionally, Mama coughing.

"The ol' bag," Curtis said. "If she upsets Mama, I'm gonna…" he stopped as if trying to think of something to do to, but he could not find anything fitting.

"What did she bring us, Curtis?" Sylvia asked.

"I don't know," he said. "Let's look and see." He opened the bag and pulled out a dark loaf of bread.

"It's burnt," Sylvia said.

Just at that moment, Mama's door swung open and the unwelcome guest stepped into the parlor. "It's not burned; it is pumpernickel. Haven't you children ever eaten pumpernickel bread before?" The children shook their heads. "It is better for you than white bread, don't you know that? That woman is not only lazy but also delinquent."

Curtis was fit to be tied. "Our Mama is not lazy or delinquent." He stepped toward her and then put his hands behind his back and clasped them together as Mama had taught him to do whenever he was tempted to use his hands in a way not pleasing to the Lord or to Mama. "She is in bed because she is very sick, and you had better not upset her. Besides, your old bread is black and feels heavy as a brick. You probably just burned it and tried to pawn it off on us." He picked up the bread and threw it at her. "You can keep it!"

"Well, I've never been treated so shabbily in all my life. Your father will hear about this." She rushed across the room and opened the door.

"Good," Curtis said. "I hope you do. We will tell him that you upset Mama."

The children rushed to the window and watched the woman rush down the path to the dirt road. Suddenly, they started laughing in spite of their shaking hands and knocking knees. None of them had ever been spoken to that way before, with the exception of Curtis, who had been the object of Widow Barker's scorn since he was four years old and had the misfortune of wandering into her yard unsupervised. Since then, it seemed as though she had picked on him every chance she got.

Isabel heard a gasp and turned to see Mama standing in the doorway, holding the frame for support. She looked so frail to Isabel, who rushed to Mama's side. But she waved Isabel aside.

"Oh, Curtis," Mama said. "You were rude and unkind. I did not raise you to behave that way."

"But Mama," Curtis said as the color drained from his face, "she deserved it; she was mean to you."

"You are not responsible for her actions Son," Mama said. "You are responsible for your own. Go and get the stationery box, and take out a piece of paper and a pencil. You are going to write a letter of apology to Mrs. Barker. Isabel, I want you to bake a batch of oatmeal cookies, and Curtis will deliver them to Mrs. Barker along with his note."

Isabel hurried into the kitchen and gathered ingredients to bake cookies for the unkind neighbor, quoting the scripture Mama had taught her long ago. "Love thy neighbor..."

"Mama," Isabel said when she took a tray of food to her mother for dinner, "why is Mrs. Barker so mean? It seems like she hates us sometimes."

"Her husband died a long time ago, leaving her with three young boys to raise alone. Then she met a kind, handsome widower who had just lost his wife. She made eyes at him, brought him food, and asked him to help her with small emergencies in her home, but he did not show an interest in her other than as a neighbor. Then he married a woman much younger than he was, and Mrs. Barker was furious. She has been bitter toward us ever since."

"You mean she wanted to marry...Papa?" Isabel almost giggled at the thought.

"Oh, yes," Mama said, "your papa was quite a catch, you know. He was so handsome and charming too; still is, as a matter of fact. I guess she has never forgiven us."

"Did you say she had three sons?" Isabel said. "I didn't know that. Where are they?"

"Well, Dear," Mama said, "that is probably why she is so bitter. Her boys needed a father. Since they did not have one, they ran wild and eventually got into serious trouble. I understand they will be in prison for many years."

"That is why she does not like boys," Isabel said. She thought of all the times Widow Barker had complained about her brothers.

"Yes, Dear," Mama said, "I am sure that is why. She probably thinks of her own boys when she sees ours. This is why we need to be patient and understanding of her. We must pray for her."

"Yes, Mama," Isabel said. She picked up Mama's tray. She had not been able to eat more than three spoonfuls of soup.

People came to visit Mama with home remedies in hand or chicken soup, but nothing seemed to help. It seemed to Isabel that instead of helping Mama, they just made matters worse.

Sally Anne stopped by every day after school to drop off Isabel's homework and to explain the assignments to her.

"Mama seems to grow weaker and weaker every day, Sally Anne," Isabel said. She poured her friend a glass of milk. "She tried to get up this morning to take care of the twins, but she was too weak and fell back on the bed, coughing so hard it shook her entire slender frame. She has lost weight, you know. The fever comes and goes, but it is worse at night. I've tried every home remedy Mama has taught me, but nothing seems to help."

"Has the doctor seen her yet?" Sally Anne asked.

"No," Isabel said. "Papa says we cannot afford to get the doctor—that we are still paying him for delivering the twins. Besides, he thinks if we use the right remedy, Mama will be good as new."

Papa had his own ideas about how to make Mama well, but she vetoed his plan.

"Lizzie," Papa said, "you must drink this to get rid of that cough. It is for medicinal purposes."

"William Avil Greene," Mama said, "I have never touched a drop of alcohol, and I do not intend to now. Drinking alcohol is sin, and you know it. What kind of an example would I be to our children if I were to partake of that horrible stuff?" She pushed the bottle away, almost knocking it out of Papa's hands. "Whisky is the devil's brew; it drives men mad, causing them to do horrible things. It destroys families, causes poverty, and takes food out of the mouth of babes, and you expect me to drink *that?* Where did it come from anyway?" Mama lay back in a fit of coughing. "It is illegal anyway; don't you remember prohibition?"

"This is for medicinal purposes. Please drink it so that you will get over this cold," Papa said.

Isabel watched Papa as he shuffled his feet and then ran his fingers through his hair before continuing in a steady voice. "Old Barney heard that you were sick and gave this to me for you. He said 'it will knock the cold right out of ya.'" Papa grinned.

Mama was not amused. "Old Barney," Mama said, "is a prime example of my point. He has not eaten or drank anything but that poison for the past ten years, and he has lost everything, including his family, his job, and his health. He is alone and just sits alone on his porch facing the alley behind the store with his jug. I am surprised at you for even talking to him, much less accepting a bottle of poison from him."

"I accepted it from him because he was concerned about the lady who brings him food every week and tells him that God loves him," Papa said. "He said you are the only person in town who loves him, and he wanted to do something for you."

"Oh, that poor, poor man," Mama said.

"Then you will take your 'medicine'?"

"Absolutely not," Mama said. "However, you can thank Barney for his kindness and take a basket of food to him this afternoon when you take Isabel shopping.

Papa and Isabel found a proper bottle of cough medicine at the store and followed the directions perfectly. But despite their best efforts, Mama's condition did not improve; it seemed to get worse with each passing day.

"Isabel," Eugene said, "I'm worried about Mama. She should have gotten better by now. I think we should call the doctor."

"I think so too," Isabel said. She carefully poured canned milk into the freshly sterilized baby bottle. "I have been asking

Papa for days, but he said Mama is strong, and besides, we don't have the money to pay for a doctor."

"Well, we have to do something."

"I know, but what can we do?"

"I know what I am going to do," Eugene said. He reached for his coat. "I'm calling Aunt Jenny; she will know what to do. I'll use Mrs. Meadows' phone." He ran out the door and across the yard toward their landlord's home.

When Aunt Jenny arrived at her sister's house, she gasped. "Lizzie," she said, "you must have lost at least ten pounds since I saw you two weeks ago. I should have been called sooner."

Mama could barely talk.

"We can't get her warm enough, Aunt Jenny," Isabel said. They stepped away from the bed to talk. "We put all of the extra quilts on her bed. She is wearing Maggie's woolens under her nightgown and Papa's nice wool socks. We put hot bricks at the foot of the bed to keep her feet warm. I was just about to refill the hot water bottles, and look, she is still shivering." Aunt Jenny shook her head in disbelief. "I have tried to feed her some broth, but Mama can barely swallow. She just shakes her head and pushes the spoon away."

Aunt Jenny stepped closer to the bed. "Isabel, take the children, and go upstairs. I do not want any of you to come back into your mama's room. Do you understand? She may be contagious."

Isabel took the children into the kitchen. "Contagious, that's bad," whispered Isabel as she ushered her siblings from Mama's room.

Aunt Jenny sent Eugene to get their Papa to call for the doctor.

"I'm afraid, Isabel," Sylvia said. She clutched her rag doll tightly. "What if Mama dies?"

"Shh, Sylvia," Isabel whispered. "It will be OK. The doctor is coming, and he will make Mama well again." Isabel hoped she had spoken the truth to her little sister.

Soon after Doctor Barkley arrived, he sent for the ambulance. "No wonder she has a high fever," he said. "With all these blankets piled on her, it's just making her worse."

Isabel felt her knees buckle under her. "I made Mama worse?" she whispered.

"It's pneumonia, Mr. Greene," said the doctor. "We will admit her at Roanoke Hospital. You can come see her, but the children must not come, you understand; the hospital has rules."

"Yes, of course," Papa said. His Lizzie was sick, and he could do nothing to help. He already had buried one wife. To think of losing his beautiful, young wife was almost more than he could handle. What would they ever do without her? No, he would not even think of such a terrible thing happening. She would be home soon. She must. They just could not go on without her.

Isabel and Eugene sat on the steps, listening as the doctor spoke to Papa, hearing every word. They entered the room and hid behind the open door, hoping the adults would not notice them. The doctor's words floated in the air like a dark mist clouding their senses. *Pneumonia. Hospital.* A cold fear gripped Isabel's soul and formed ice around her heart, making it difficult to breathe. *What if something terrible does happen to Mama and she never comes home?*

"Is Mama going to die?" Isabel heard the words uttered by her siblings, but she could not respond. She looked up to see Curtis standing in the doorway.

Papa rushed to Mama's side after the doctor spoke to him. He did not want to let her go. As he held tightly to her hand, telling her that everything would be OK, she kept repeating the same thing. She was so hoarse that her words were difficult to understand. Finally, it registered with everyone. She was pleading with Papa never to let them put the children in an orphanage. "Please, Avil, promise me. Do not let them go to an orphanage. I couldn't stand it if I knew our children were in an orphanage. Promise me, *please!*" she said.

Mama's eyes were bright with fear and pleading, and Isabel had the horrible feeling that Mama knew she would never come home again, the same way that Mama knew when Billy was sick before he showed symptoms and the way she knew if her children were up to something they should not do. She always knew, and she was always right.

"Mama's afraid she will never see us again until we join her in heaven," Maggie said. She sobbed quietly behind Isabel.

"You'll get better and come home soon, Lizzie. You are coming home; you must." Papa was trying to conceal his tears, but he couldn't hold them back.

"Please, Avil."

"I promise, Lizzie," he said. "We will stay a family. I'll never put them in an orphanage, never!"

Mama seemed relieved. She laid back, and Isabel saw her mouth the words, "Thank you, Lord." Then apparently a new thought struck her, and she began to panic again and reached for Papa once more. "Papa, don't let anyone talk you into putting your mark on any papers either; they may try to trick you and take the children away."

"Who would do such a thing, Mama?" Papa said.

"The state may try to take the children from you, Avil. You are fifty-five years old, without a wife, and have nine children to raise. It will be hard, Avil, and the state will take the children if you are not careful."

"Now, Lizzie," Papa said, "we do not have to worry about anything like that because you will be home in a couple of days, feeling as fresh as a daisy."

Isabel felt a new fear welling up inside of her, beyond the thought of losing Mama. She could lose her entire family, but she closed her eyes and recited Romans 8:28 and wondered how this could possibly work together for good unless Mama got well. She quickly looked behind her to make sure Maggie had not heard Mama's last plea and was thankful Eugene had sent her upstairs to watch the younger children.

"Eugene," Isabel whispered, "do you suppose that could ever happen—that the state could just come in and take us away from Papa?"

"I don't know," Eugene said. "I've heard stories..." his voice was interrupted by the sound of Mama's hoarse voice.

"Trust the Lord, Avil," she whispered. "He will help you if you just trust Him."

The children came downstairs and stood by Isabel and Eugene. "We want to kiss Mama good-bye," Maggie said. Isabel saw that even Billy looked frightened as he waited for his turn to kiss Mama. Papa looked to the doctor for his approval, and he nodded that it would be OK.

The attendants placed Mama on a stretcher and wrapped white blankets around her. As they carried her through the front room, she asked them to stop so she could tell her children "good-bye" again. She whispered something special into the ear of each child.

"I will, Mama," they said through their tears. "Yes, Mama, I love you too."

"Mama, I want Mama," Billy said. He tried to jump out of Isabel's arms, and Aunt Jenny rushed up and took him from Isabel. She carried him into the bedroom, and Isabel could still hear him screaming.

With tears in her eyes, Isabel stepped close to Mama and took her hand. "I love you, Mama," she said. "We will be praying for you so you can come home soon."

Mama gripped Isabel's hand tightly. "Isabel, always be a good girl. You know what I mean, Isabel. Promise Mama you will always be a good girl, and remember what I have taught you. And remember, I will always love you."

"Yes, Mama, I promise. Don't worry about us; just come home soon. Please get well. I love you, Mama."

Isabel watched as the attendants carefully placed Mama in the ambulance. Eugene jumped in beside her while tightly holding onto her hand. She could hear Mama pleading with Eugene. "Son, promise me you will look after your brothers and sisters and help your papa. No matter what, help Papa keep the family together."

"Yes, Mama," Eugene said.

Isabel could tell he was trying not to cry. *Boys are not supposed to cry, but he might as well try to pluck a star out of the sky. It is impossible not to cry. Mama is sick and thinks she is going to die and leave us forever.*

"Eugene, I feel so alone," Isabel said. She stood in the doorway, watching the ambulance drive out of sight, leaving behind a devastated family.

"Let's pray," Eugene said. He gathered the children into the front room after Papa jumped into his auto and followed the ambulance, leaving them behind with Aunt Jenny. They knelt on the oval rug and surrounded Mama's rocker. "Please, Lord, heal Mama and bring her home soon. We need her," Eugene prayed.

"Please do not let Mama die," Maggie and Sylvia prayed.

"Make those bad men bring my mama back home," Jimmy said. How could he possibly understand what was going on? But God knew.

"Dear Father," Isabel prayed, "I know You have the power to heal Mama so that she can come home to us. You know how much we all need her, and we love her so much. We would not know what to do if we did not have Mama. Please heal her."

Isabel felt a hand on her shoulder and was surprised when Aunt Jenny started to pray with them. When they stood up, the clock chimed 4:00. They had been praying for an hour.

No one slept much that night or the night after. Aunt Jenny insisted upon their regular bedtime, but there were too many tears.

"We can't just go to sleep as if nothing has happened," Isabel said. Aunt Jenny threw up her hands in exasperation. "We are all thinking about Mama and wondering if she is alright. The children need comfort now, not someone fussing at them," she continued as Aunt Jenny's face turned red and her nostrils began to flair, just as Mama's did whenever she was upset. "Why don't you let Jimmy and Billy sleep in here with us, and I will read them a bedtime story." Isabel tried to smooth over her disrespectful words.

Aunt Jenny smoothed her hair, picked up a piece of clothing lying on a chair, and then turned to face the children. "Alright," Aunt Jenny said with a forced smile, "just this once."

Billy fell asleep in Isabel's arms and Jimmy with his head on Isabel's shoulder as she sang them to sleep after their third bedtime story. Maggie and Sylvia lay across the foot of the bed, with Eugene and Curtis sleeping across the room in the girls' bed.

"Now, what's this?" Aunt Jenny asked as she came to the door and was clearly not happy with the sleeping arrangements.

Isabel could see that she was about to wake the boys and send them to their room, but she stopped her. "Please let them sleep in here tonight; we all need to be together," said Isabel as she protectively put her arm around Billy and pulled the covers over Jimmy. "Just put the comforter over the girls, and they will be fine; they have plenty of room," Isabel pleaded.

"It's against my better senses, but I suppose they can stay there—for a little while anyway." Aunt Jenny picked up Mama's old comforter from the quilt holder and spread it over Maggie and Sylvia, pushing their hair out of their faces before turning to leave the room.

"Aunt Jenny," Isabel called to her aunt just as she was exiting the room, "thank you for coming and taking care of Mama. We didn't know what else to do. I tried steam, onion plasters, and mustard plasters, but nothing worked, and Papa said that we could not afford to call the doctor because we are still paying for the twins being born."

"It's OK, child," said Aunt Jenny as she re-entered the room, pulled up a chair next to Isabel's bed, and sat down. "You did everything I would have done. You did a very good job, especially for a child!"

"But she got worse and had to go to the hospital," Isabel said through her tears. "I made her fever go up by trying to get her warm—the doctor said so."

"Doctors don't know as much as they want you to think. Your mama had the shivers, and everyone knows that when someone is shivering, you try to get them warm," Aunt Jenny said with a sniff.

"But the doctor said…" Isabel began to cry.

"Isabel," said Aunt Jenny with finality, "that was not your fault! Her cold got worse, and she ended up with pneumonia because she wasn't properly cared for before. She was just too weak."

"It wasn't…before what, Aunt Jenny?" Isabel asked as she received a hankie from her Aunt and blew her nose noisily.

"It wasn't," Aunt Jenny confirmed. "No, your mama hasn't been the same since the twins were born. I think something went wrong and we just didn't realize it. Two weeks ago, when I visited your mama, she was still experiencing pain, and she shouldn't have. Those babies are two months old. I know, since I am a midwife. I deliver babies all the time, and I think…" Aunt Jenny did not finish her thought. Instead, she stood up and patted Isabel on the head. "Well, that's just my opinion, and you are too young to hear it. Try to get some sleep. I'll be on the sofa if you need anything."

"Good night, Aunt Jenny," Isabel said.

Chapter 35

A Long Night

PAPA CAME HOME the next morning to wash up and to pack some clothes.

"It looks like your mama is going to be in the hospital for a few days," he said. He pushed his starched white shirts into a valise. "Eugene, I'm leaving you in charge of the house, and Isabel, I want you to look after the youngins while I'm gone."

"Who will stay with us at night?" Curtis asked. He looked around the room at his younger brothers and sisters. "Isabel cannot take care of the twins and the boys and cook and everything."

"What about Aunt Jenny?" Eugene said. He watched Aunt Jenny in the kitchen. She was preparing lunch for the children.

"Aunt Jenny has to go home," Papa said. "She has women who need her to deliver their babies, so she can't stay here. I'll see what I can do about getting someone to come and look after you." He headed for the door. "You children obey your brother and sister and help with the youngins. I'll be back when I can. Don't you worry now, your mama's gonna be fine." And then he was gone.

The hours passed, and no one came. Isabel discovered Aunt Jenny had stayed up all night caring for the twins and baking for the family.

When Isabel opened the breadbox, she found it full where it had been empty. She also found two apple pies, two chocolate pies, and an enormous cake in the pantry. She also discovered there was a roast in the icebox, and Aunt Jenny had left a large chicken roasting in the oven with vegetables and biscuits cut out and resting on a pan in the icebox. Isabel merely needed to take out the chicken when it was done and put the biscuits into the oven for dinner.

"Well," she said to Maggie, who came into the kitchen to help, "it looks like we don't have to worry about dinner tonight or lunch tomorrow. Aunt Jenny thought of everything."

"I'm not hungry," Jimmy said. He stood beside Isabel, peering into the full icebox.

"Not hungry?" Isabel said as she picked up her brother, who was growing at an alarming rate. "Jimmy, are you feeling alright?"

Isabel felt his arms tighten around her neck and felt a cool, wet droplet on her neck as he answered, "I miss Mama."

"I know, Jimmy," Isabel said. "We all do. She's at the hospital, where the doctors and nurses can help her get well so she can come home soon. Would you like to draw a pretty picture to send Mama?"

"Yes," Jimmy said. He ran to his room for the box of crayons he had received on his last birthday.

"Is Mama going to die?" Maggie asked.

"I hope not, Maggie," Isabel said. "Let's pray for her again." The two girls knelt together on the rag rug Isabel had helped Mama make for the kitchen and prayed together for Mama to get well.

Isabel felt a small hand on her shoulder. Jimmy was standing by her, sucking his thumb. It had taken a long time for Mama to convince Jimmy to stop putting his thumb in his mouth, but if he needed to act like a baby today to ease the pain of missing Mama, it was understandable. In fact, Isabel thought she might suck her thumb too if it would really help ease the pain.

Isabel gave Jimmy a drink of water and offered him a cookie. Suddenly, a cry rang out, "The twins are up," Sylvia said, "Who's gonna feed 'em?"

"Oh dear," Isabel said. "I guess one of you will have to help me feed one of the twins." She rummaged through the cabinet for canned milk. "Here it is. Now, Maggie, will you open a can of milk, please? I will put the bottle and nipple in some boiling water to kill the germs."

After the bottles were sufficiently sterilized, Isabel filled each bottle with canned milk and added a little brown sugar so the little ones would drink it."

"How did you know to do that?" Maggie asked. Her eyes were round with wonder.

"Mama taught me, and she said that when they are just a little bit older, we will add some cereal to the milk so they'll sleep all night. Of course, we'll need to make the hole in the rubber nipple larger so they can get the cereal out." She held the small nipple up to the light to examine it before securing it on the skinny bottle.

"Did she teach you that when Billy was sick and wouldn't let her put him down?" Maggie asked as she surveyed the rich, canned milk in the clean bottles.

"Why can't we just give them cow's milk, like we drink," asked Sylvia.

"Because, little sister, it doesn't have all the nutrients the babies need," sighed Isabel impatiently as the cries from the crib grew louder. "At least, that is what Mama said."

Isabel put the filled bottles in a pan of warm water and showed her sisters how to test the milk on their wrists. Isabel and Maggie carried the bottles to Papa and Mama's room, where the twins slept. Isabel placed Raymond on Maggie's lap with the baby resting his head on Maggie's arm on Mama's pillow. He seemed a little uneasy in his small sister's arm. Isabel scooped up Ralph with his head resting in the crook of her arm which rested on Papa's pillow. He smiled at Isabel who had fed him when Mama was sick. Both babies soon settled into a rhythmic routine, drinking the sweet milk, stopping only to smile their appreciation. The girls gently raised the babies to their shoulder and were awarded with loud burp. Soon the bottles drained with a squeak as the last drop was consumed. Isabel attempted to make the squeak sound; "all gone," she whispered." Both babies had fallen into milk induced comatose. The sisters giggled as the babies' eyes seemed to roll back into their heads. They had contented looks on their faces.

"They're so sweet!" Maggie said. "No wonder Mama loves babies so much."

Just as the babies were finishing their bottles, Billy awoke from his nap crying for Mama, and Isabel silently prayed for strength and wisdom to take care of the little ones alone.

"Billy, if you behave and stop crying," Isabel said, "I promise to read you a book when the twins go to sleep."

Billy sniffed, wiped his eyes with his sleeve, and sat down at Isabel's feet. Isabel was silently thanking the Lord when there was a knock at the door. Isabel heard Eugene open the door and Sally Anne enter the room.

"Where have you been?" Sally Anne said to Isabel. "You missed the arithmetic test, and Miss Catron was concerned that none of you have been to school. What happened?"

Isabel took a deep breath and wondered if she would be able to explain to her friend without crying like a baby. She told her about Mama, and the tears spilled down her cheeks and her shoulders. She shook as sobs overtook her.

"Oh, Isabel," Sally Anne said, "I'm so sorry. Which hospital did they take her to?"

Isabel looked to Eugene, who answered so softly that she wondered if Sally Anne would be able to hear the answer.

"They took her to Roanoke Hospital," he said. He picked up a piece of wood and shoved it into the stove.

"Then she should be in good hands. She should be home in a few days, feeling chipper as a robin in the spring."

Isabel smiled at her friend's effort to cheer her up, but then more sobs overtook her. Sally Anne rushed to her side with a sisterly hug. Isabel noticed Sally Anne was crying also.

"Who's staying with you?" she asked. She looked around the room.

"Nobody," Eugene said.

"Papa said he would send someone," Maggie said.

"Does it look like Papa sent anyone?" Eugene said. "He has been gone since 10:00 this morning. If someone were coming, they would be here by now."

"Maybe they're coming after supper," Sally Anne said. She picked up Billy and sat him on her lap.

"I hope so," Isabel said.

"It's scary at night without Mama and Papa," Sylvia said from the rug in front of the blazing fireplace. "We all slept with Isabel last night, and Aunt Jenny was here." Her voice quivered as if she were about to cry.

"Do you want me to telephone anyone?" Sally Anne asked. "I'm sure Mama or Cookie would love to come and stay with you tonight. I could come too."

"Nah," Eugene said, "we will be OK by ourselves. After all, I'm practically a grown-up, and Isabel can cook and knows how to take care of the babies. We'll be fine."

"Alright," Sally Anne said. "I'll tell Mama and Papa, though. They will want to help."

When Sally Anne left, the house seemed empty again—empty and scary, as the wind had picked up and was blowing sleet against the windowpane. Isabel shivered, even though the house was toasty warm.

Sally Anne returned later with a basket of food, followed by her parents, who were covered in snow.

"I thought you might need some extra blankets," Mrs. Albright said. She knocked snow from her boots before entering the house. She handed Isabel a large bag containing diapers, woolen baby stockings, and sweaters for the babies. "I have been meaning to come by to bring some things I bought for the twins last week. They were on sale, and I just could not resist such a bargain. When Sally Anne told us about your mother, I had to do *something*."

"Thank you, Mrs. Albright," Isabel said. "I was almost out of diapers; it seems like we have to wash them every day."

Mr. Albright stepped forward with a box of emergency supplies, "just in case," and walked across the room, deep in conversation with Eugene and Curtis.

"Are you sure you don't want to come home with us? We can leave a note for your papa so he will not worry," Mr. Albright said. "Or we would be glad to stay here with you until he comes home."

"Thank you, sir," Eugene said, "but we will be alright. I can look after them. It was real thoughtful of you to invite us—and for the supplies too. We want to be here when Papa and Mama get home."

"Well, that's fine," Mr. Albright said. "If you need anything—anything at all, send Curtis or telephone us from the Meadows' house. We stopped by there first, and they promised to keep an eye on you. Mr. Meadows said if anything happens and you need them, just go outside and ring the dinner bell. They should be able to hear it and get here quickly."

Tears formed on Isabel's cheeks, and she quickly wiped them away as she watched her friends climb into their automobile and drive away. She sighed as they drove out of sight.

"Well, one thing's for sure," Curtis said, "with all the food Aunt Jenny made and with this dinner and goodies from the Albrights, we won't starve."

That night, after the chores were completed and Eugene read the Scriptures, the children decided to sleep in Mama and Papa's bedroom so Isabel could take care of the twins.

The children knelt at Mama and Papa's bed and prayed Mama would return home soon, and they prayed for their safety. Eugene and Curtis checked the doors and windows one last time before turning in and banked the stove for breakfast.

Eugene and Curtis camped on bedrolls on the floor, and the other children crowded into the bed together. Jimmy and Billy held tightly to the gingerbread boys Mama had made for them.

Isabel breathed deeply into Mama's pillow. "It still smells like Mama, even though Aunt Jenny changed the bedding," she said. Each child sniffed Mama's pillow before going to sleep.

All night they listened to the howling wind and thought of Mama. She loved the snow. However, the fierceness of this storm matched their emotions. One by one, the children fell asleep with tears on their cheeks, catching their breath in their sleep as if they were still sobbing.

Isabel would reach over and pat them gently to comfort them until sleep finally overtook her.

Family members and neighbors came the next day, bringing food and clean diapers for the twins. Some even brought candy to cheer up the sad little ones, but nothing helped. Candy could not lift the veil of gloom that filled the room. They wanted their Mama; nothing else would do. Nothing else could do. Papa's older children volunteered to stay with the children, but they would not hear of it. They had survived the night alone and knew they would survive another night. They wanted to be alone to cry, to long for their mother, to pray, and to hope. Surviving the night alone had somehow given them the confidence to take care of themselves. Besides, they felt that the presence of someone else would be disloyal to their mother, and they would not have that.

"Isabel," said her older half-sister Cleo, "you children cannot stay alone. At least let my Caroline stay with you at night. She is almost seventeen years old and knows all about housekeeping and taking care of children. You need an adult to stay with you, you know."

"Thank you, Cleo," Isabel said, "but we're fine. It just wouldn't seem right to have someone else to take Mama's place, except me, you know."

Cleo finally gave up. "It doesn't seem right to let you children stay here alone. Aren't you afraid?"

"No, Jesus watches over us. Besides, Eugene is fourteen now."

"What will you do if a stranger knocks on the door and wants to come in?" Cleo said as she reached for the doorknob.

"We will ask, 'Who is it?' and if we do not know them, we will say that we cannot open the door," Isabel said.

"Besides," Eugene, who was standing near the hearth, said, "Curtis and I have hunting rifles and know how to use them."

"What if one of the babies gets sick in the middle of the night," Cleo said.

"We will send Eugene for the doctor," Isabel said.

"And if someone chokes on food?" Cleo said.

"If someone is still choking after spitting out the food, I will put my finger in that person's mouth and pull the food out."

"What if you cannot reach whatever is causing him to choke? What if Billy swallows a button?"

"He wouldn't get a button," Isabel said, "but if he does, and I cannot reach it, I will hit him on the back. If that does not work, we will turn him upside down, if we have to, but we will get the button out. But there will not be a button to worry about."

"Well, it sounds like you have thought it through," Cleo said. "I would never forgive myself if something happens to you while you are here alone. You know your mama would worry terribly if she knew Papa had left you home alone. I'll tell you what. I will stop by Mrs. Meadows' house and ask her to keep an eye on you while Papa is away. That way, at least there will be some adult supervision only a half a mile away. At least you will not starve." She walked out to her buggy.

"They have already promised to look after us, and the Albrights came by last night, so we're fine," Isabel said.

She breathed a sigh of relief when Cleo left. "All her worrying makes me nervous," she said. She picked up Billy and put him into the high chair.

Fortunately, they had ample supplies on hand, and with the food kind people brought, Isabel merely had to heat up dinner. She had learned to cook under the watchful eyes of her mother, but she never was allowed to build a fire in the stove and cook without supervision. Therefore, Eugene took care of the fire, and Isabel heated up the food. Maggie helped wash the dishes, and Sylvia kept her little brothers occupied by playing school. The older boys took care of the horses and the cow. They all went through the motions, but their hearts were in Roanoke with Mama.

The nights were long and lonely. The howling wind outside the windows often sent the children into Mama's room for comfort from Isabel. The children longed for their mother's good-night kisses and Papa's bedtime stories. Isabel, Eugene, and Curtis tried to fill their shoes, but it just wasn't the same. Therefore, they held each other; dried each other's tears; and prayed until, one by one, they fell into a fitful sleep.

On the third morning without word, Eugene could stand it no longer. "I've got to know how Mama's doing." He took his coat and hat and went to up their most gentle horse to ride to the Meadows' house to ask permission to use their telephone.

Isabel watched out the window as he was preparing, and a horse-drawn buggy pulled into the yard. Eugene looked up in time to see his older sister Lindy stepping out of the driver's seat.

"Morning, Eugene," she said. "Where are you going?"

"Do you have any news for us?"

"No, Eugene, I'm sorry," she said. She lifted a large basket from the back of the buggy. "I came to make sure you are all OK. Besides, I have some clean linen and some fabric we can use for diapers. Has Isabel done any laundry?"

"No," Eugene said, "we didn't even think about it."

"That's what I thought," Lindy said. "I came to do it today. Isabel certainly does not need that responsibility too." Lindy carried her supplies to the door.

Isabel opened the door to her half-sister and welcomed the gesture, for they were running out of diapers and clean clothing, even though people had brought fresh ones. She had not yet tried washing anything, as Mama always boiled them in a large kettle that Isabel couldn't even lift.

Isabel watched Eugene as he rode away on his horse and breathed a quick prayer that he would return with good news.

Isabel was watching from the front window when Eugene rode into the yard. She watched him take a deep breath as he rode up to their small house.

Curtis ran outside and took the reins. Eugene said, "Come inside as soon as you remove the saddle, Curtis. I have news." Isabel thought he looked as if he might crumble to the ground.

Two hours had passed since he left for the Meadows' home, and he was cold. His face was red and chapped, and his eyes were swollen. Isabel knew he had been crying and that the news he carried was not good. He recounted the story for them.

"Eugene, is everything OK?" Mrs. Meadows asked. "You must be frozen, boy." She ushered him into the house.

"I was wondering if I could use your telephone?" he said. He removed his hat and shook snow from his boots before entering her nice, clean house. "I want to check on Mama."

"Of course, you do. First, let me take your coat, and you go over by the fire and warm yourself up. You'll catch cold, and you will be sick too." She led him to the fireplace. "I'll get you a nice cup of hot chocolate, and then you can make your call."

Eugene looked around the well-ordered house for a place to sit down and then decided he might mess up her furniture. So he stood by the fire, with his hands outstretched over the flames. Mrs. Meadows returned with a cup of hot cocoa and a plate of cookies for the boy. He took a sip of the warm liquid to be polite and then asked for the phone.

"I'll just leave you alone while you make your call." She walked toward the kitchen.

He addressed the operator as she stepped into the next room.

"Operator, get me Roanoke Hospital, please."

"Roanoke Hospital. How may I help you?" said a feminine voice over the line.

"My name is Eugene Greene. I'm calling about Elizabeth Greene."

"Let's see. Oh, yes. Here it is. Mrs. Greene expired this morning," she said without any emotion in her voice.

"Expired?" Eugene said as he stared blankly at the telephone.

"Yes," the voice on the phone said. "Mrs. Greene expired this morning."

Eugene silently hung up the phone.

Mrs. Meadows entered the room, carrying a pot of hot cocoa to refill Eugene's cup. She put it on the nearest table and rushed to the boy's side.

"She's gone," he said over and over. "Mama's gone!" He sat down and lowered his face in his hands. His body shook with silent sobs. "What will we do?"

He got up and tried to bolt through the door, but Mrs. Meadows stopped him. She held him in her arms and let him weep until he could cry no more. She prayed for him and the other children. She prayed for Papa too. She knew he needed wisdom and that he must accept help if he were to keep the family together. Mostly, she prayed for the children. "May God's grace be with you," she whispered.

When Eugene was finally calm, she sent him home with a package of food for the others and a hot baked potato in each pocket to keep the boy warm on his trip in the cold.

"Do you want me to go with you?"

He declined.

Eugene did not go directly home. He went to the old barn, where he could be alone to pray and ask for strength.

"Just like that," he told his siblings, "the lady said, 'Mrs. Greene expired.' As if Mama were a library card. Doesn't that woman know that Mama is the most wonderful woman in Virginia?"

"Mama died?" Maggie whispered. Tears ran down her cheeks. It was as if she were afraid to say the words aloud.

"No!" Isabel screamed. "You heard them wrong, or they looked up the wrong person. Mama is not dead—not our Mama." She ran to Mama's room and changed the baby's diapers and tidied the room, but she refused to cry. If she cried, it would make it true.

Two hours later, Aunt Jenny came to the door with the horrible news, and Isabel sat stoically listening—still refusing to accept that her beautiful, gentle, and caring mother had left them in the land of the living to wait for them in heaven. It was unthinkable, unimaginable, horrible.

Aunt Jenny held Billy in her lap as she told him of Mama's "home going."

"Your mama just went to sleep and awoke in the presence of Jesus in heaven. She is with her mama now." Aunt Jenny's voice broke, and she pulled a handkerchief from her sleeve, wiped her eyes, and blew her nose before continuing. "The doctors did everything they could, you know, but your mama was very ill." She took a sip of water and then continued. "Your papa is taking this awfully hard."

Tears welled up in her eyes, and she related the death room events. "Two men had to drag your papa away so they could take care of her body. He is sick with grief. We need to pray for him." She reached out and pulled Jimmy, who was standing near the rocker where she was cradling Billy, close to her. "We must pray for wisdom and strength to go on…"

Jimmy and Billy cried for Mama.

"I want my mama," Jimmy said, and he hit Aunt Jenny as if she had taken his mother away.

Isabel was startled. She didn't realize he was old enough to understand. She ran across the room and took her brother's hands in her own and tried to comfort him; yet she could not find the right words.

"Mama is with Jesus now, Jimmy," Maggie said. "She isn't coughing anymore, and her chest does not hurt now. She is walking on streets of gold and worshipping Jesus with Grandma Isabella.

"But I want her here with me," Jimmy said.

Isabel hugged him. "So do I, Jimmy, so do I."

No one slept much that night. Even the twins cried all night, as though they too realized they would never see Mama on earth again. Isabel felt tears threaten to spill over; yet she refused to allow it. To do so would be to admit that Mama was dead, and Isabel could not, would not do that. So she took a deep breath and told herself to be strong for Maggie, Sylvia, Jimmy, Billy, and the twins.

Papa did not return home until late the next evening, when the children were getting ready for bed. Sylvia heard the automobile and ran to the door to greet him. "Papa's home," she said. The door swung open, a gush of cold air filled the room, and snow floated across the floor.

Isabel gasped when she saw Papa's disheveled appearance. Papa was always conscious of his appearance and had been known to shave twice in one day and always insisted upon a clean, starched, white shirt whenever he went into town. Today, however, he looked as if he had not shaved in days, and his clothing looked slept in.

"Papa has whiskers," Sylvia said. She reached up to touch his face. Papa smiled slightly and patted the child on her head and then proceeded to take off his wrinkled, snow-covered coat.

"Papa, you're finally home," Isabel said. She helped him with his coat and then led him to the warm stove. "I'll make you a nice, warm cup of coffee," she said. "Have you eaten?"

Papa shook his head as he slowly pulled out a kitchen chair and wobbled to it. Eugene rushed to help him, and Isabel returned to making coffee. She prepared a plate of food and sat it before him. He thanked her quietly and bowed his head briefly before picking up his fork.

"Papa," Eugene said, "when did you last eat?"

"I don't remember. Yesterday, maybe."

"Where have you been?" Curtis asked. He sat down at the table, and Eugene followed suit. Isabel decided to make hot chocolate for the children, knowing they would not go to sleep until they had spent some time with Papa.

"I've been with your mama," he said.

"Papa," Eugene said, "Mama is gone. Were you sitting with her body?"

Papa quickly raised his head from his plate and looked at his children. "Then you know?"

"We know," Curtis said. "Eugene called the hospital, and they told him."

"They shouldn't have done that," Papa said. He reached for his eldest son and squeezed his shoulder. "I wanted to tell you myself. I've been walking around downtown Roanoke, trying to figure out how to tell you. I'm so sorry, Son. You should not have been the one to have to carry the news. It must have been a shock to hear it over the phone and all."

Isabel looked at Eugene for his reaction. He was bravely holding back tears. She wondered if he would tell Papa the whole story, but he didn't. He merely nodded his head.

Papa managed to eat a few bites of stew. It seemed as if eating took all of his energy. "Your mama went home peacefully," he said. "She just closed her eyes and went to sleep. Before she did," he took a breath and then continued, "before she died, she said to tell you that she loves you with all her heart and wanted me to encourage you always to trust in the Lord. She said she would wait for us in heaven and that her love for all of us will never grow cold, even though her body will. And then, just like that, she closed her eyes and was gone." Papa's voice broke as he spoke, and Isabel remembered that Aunt Jenny had told them it took two men to pull Papa away from Mama's body. She ran to Papa's side to comfort him. The other children joined them. They held each other and cried again, and yet, Papa did not give in to tears. He patted the children, hugged them all, then put his coat back on, and went outside.

Isabel did not know when he returned. She put the children to bed in their own rooms and then fell into a fitful sleep. She dreamed Mama was back in the kitchen and everything was back to normal. Isabel wanted to stay in her dream and not wake up. However, the sound of a baby's cry pulled her back to reality, and she got up to feed the motherless babies.

Chapter 36

Comfort

THE NEXT FEW days were a blur. People came with more food than the Greene family could possibly eat.

"I've never seen so much food," Eugene said. He placed yet another chocolate cake on the kitchen table. "Miss Catron just brought this by and said not to worry about school for a few days."

"We will never be able to eat all of this food," Curtis said. "Why do people bring food when somebody passes away, anyway?" Curtis expressed Isabel's thoughts perfectly.

"I think," Eugene said, "it's their way of showing how much they care. Since we are sad, they figure we will not eat, so they bring their favorite foods to tempt our tummies. Besides, it won't just be us, you know. After the funeral, people will drop by to visit and remember Mama. The food is for them too."

"It was nice of Miss Catron to bring a cake," Maggie said. She eyed the lovely confectionary. "I'm glad we don't have to go to school tomorrow. I know I couldn't keep my mind on school work; could you, Isabel?"

"I don't think I will be going back," she said. "Papa needs me here."

Visitors also brought well-meaning offers to watch the children until Papa was on his feet again, but he refused to accept them. "No!" he said. "We are staying together!"

And so the people left, slowly shaking their heads, often causing more harm than good. "Perhaps he'll change his mind later, when he has had time to think it through," they said.

"Yes, after the funeral, he will see how hard it is to work and to take care of a large family and will decide it's best for the children to go into other homes," one neighbor replied. The visitors may have been well-intentioned, but their conversation was not.

"Will Papa give us away?" Sylvie asked as one family made their comments on the porch before the front door closed behind them.

"I don't know, Sylvie," Curtis said as he looked to his older brother for help.

"He won't if I have anything to do with it!" Eugene said with conviction. "We have to work together and help Papa. Curtis, Isabel, and I can help with cooking and cleaning. Maggie can help Isabel take care of the twins, and we will all look after Jimmy and Billy."

"I don't need nobody to look after me!" Jimmy announced loudly. "I'm a big boy now."

"Yes. Jimmy, you are a big boy now," Isabel said.

Chapter 37

"PAPA," ISABEL SAID quietly as he shaved at the small kitchen mirror, "who will watch the children while we are at Mama's funeral?"

"Nobody," Papa said with authority. "They're going to show proper respect."

"But, Papa!" Isabel exclaimed. "Jimmy and Billy do not understand about death; they're too young."

"Nonsense," Papa said. "They're going, and that is final!"

"They'll have nightmares if they see Mama in a casket; especially if they see the preacher or the undertaker close the lid," Isabel said as she thought of her nightmares after Grammy Isabella's funeral. "And it will be even worse if they see them lower her in the ground. Couldn't they stay with Sally Anne's mother?"

"Don't argue with me, Gal. I've already said that they are going, and that is final. Besides, children are resilient; they will forget all about it," he said, and Isabel knew the subject was closed. "I'm going outside to take care of the chores before breakfast," he added.

"Eugene," Isabel said as her brother entered the room, "we need to explain to Jimmy and Billy about death and what will happen to Mama's body. Papa said they have to go with us."

"He can't mean that!" Eugene exclaimed as his face flushed and then drained of color. "They won't understand…they'll have nightmares," he stuttered.

"I know," Isabel said sadly. "I tried to tell him this, but he insisted that they must pay proper respect."

"Mama would not want that," Eugene choked. "She would be heartbroken. She always protected us."

"Yes, she always did what she thought was best for us," Isabel said as she listened for Papa's footsteps on the back stoop.

The opportunity to speak to the children presented itself as Isabel dressed the children in their finest church clothes.

"Where are we going, Is'bel?" Jimmy asked, tugging at the small bowtie around his neck.

"We're going to Aunt Jenny's house and then to the cemetery," Isabel explained as the other children gathered around to listen.

"What's a cem-tree?" Jimmy asked. He cast a warning look at his brothers, just in case they snickered. They did not.

"A cemetery is a beautiful meadow where they bury the bodies of people who have died," Isabel said.

"Like the old, gray barn cat?"

"Yes, Jimmy," Isabel said. "Just like the gray barn cat."

"Who are they burying?" Jimmy asked. "An orange cat?"

"No, Jimmy." Isabel prayed silently for the right words and wondered what Mama would say. Then she knew. "You know that Mama went to heaven to live with Jesus, right?" Isabel sat down on the floor, where Jimmy and Billy had plopped down.

"Yes," he said. He balled up his small fists, shoved them into his pockets, wiped his eyes on his white shirtsleeve, and then pulled at his bowtie once more.

"When Jesus called Mama home to be with Him in heaven, the 'real' Mama went with Him," Isabel said. "You know, the inside, invisible part that thinks, that feels happy or sad, that loves us and loves Jesus too. We call the inside part our soul, and we all have one."

"Me too?" Jimmy said. He eyes got big.

"Yes, you too. Boys," Isabel pulled Billy onto her lap and continued talking. "Do you remember last spring when that mama bird built a nest in the tree outside of your window?"

Billy looked at Jimmy, who nodded his head, and mimicked him.

"Well," Isabel said, "what did you see in that nest?"

"Eggs," Jimmy said.

"Eggs," Billy shouted.

"That's right," Isabel said. "And what happened to those eggs?"

"They hatched, and baby birds popped out," Jimmy said.

"That's right," Isabel said. "You see, it was time for them to hatch, and they didn't need their shells anymore, did they?"

"They didn't have any feathers on except for some that stuck straight up on their heads," Jimmy said. "Every day their mama fed them and they got new feathers and then, finally, they learned to fly."

Encouraged by their interest, Isabel continued. "Well, you see, just like the birds no longer needed their shells, Mama no longer needs her body, because her soul is in heaven with Jesus." Tears formed in her eyes. "Her body is now just a beautiful, empty shell. Mama is no longer in her 'shell.' Do you understand?"

"Mama's a birdie?" Billy asked.

Isabel started to speak, but she found it impossible.

"Mama is *like* the bird; she is safe in Jesus' nest," Sylvia said, to everyone's amazement.

"Oh," Jimmy and Billy said together. Isabel was relieved that they almost understood.

"We are on our way to Aunt Jenny's house to see Mama's body-shell one last time," Isabel said. "Her body is in a special bed that looks like a box; we call it a casket." Isabel could hear her sisters crying as she continued to communicate to the little boys. "After we see Mama one last time and say, 'I love you,' we will follow the casket to the cemetery."

"You mean the box drives like the Tin Lizzie?" Jimmy said.

"The men in the family will put the box on the back of the wagon to be pulled to the cemetery," Curtis said, "and then we will bury her and put the cross that Papa and Eugene carved over her grave so that we can come back sometimes to put flowers on her grave."

"Why?" Jimmy asked, his voice beginning to quiver. "Why will we visit and put flowers there?"

"Because it will make us feel better, and it shows everybody who sees Mama's grave that she has a family who loves her very much," Eugene said.

"Isabel," Sylvia said, "it will be dark in the box, and she will get cold, won't she?"

This question took Isabel by surprise, but she tried to answer bravely. However, a lump in her throat prevented her from speaking, so Eugene spoke up.

"Mama will never be in the dark or be cold again because she is in heaven, where it is always light and pleasant. It is perfect there. She is not sick anymore because there is no sickness, dying, or even crying in heaven. There, no one ever has to say 'good-bye.'"

After they arrived at Aunt Jenny's house, Isabel felt butterflies in her stomach as they ascended the porch steps. As they walked through the door, Isabel noticed a strange odor greeted them. A combination of flowers, food, and something she could not identify. Maybe all those ladies paying their respects were wearing strong perfume.

Papa pushed Isabel forward into the parlor, which was filled with fragrant hothouse flowers, and then she saw...her. "Oh," Isabel said, "Mama looks beautiful. She looks almost as if she is smiling."

"Yes, she does, doesn't she?" Aunt Jenny said. She walked over and put her arms around the girl. "I think she would like the new, white dress we bought for her."

Only then did Isabel notice what Mama was wearing. "It looks perfect," Isabel said. "Mama would be so happy. She has needed a new dress for at least two years, but there was never enough money to buy one for her."

"Yes, I know," Aunt Jenny said. She cast a sidelong glance at Papa. "It was a crying shame that Elizabeth sacrificed so much when some people do not sacrifice at all for anyone."

Isabel's stomach began to churn as she looked from Aunt Jenny to Papa, hoping they would not have words. Mama would want them to get along.

After awhile, one by one, the children filed past Mama's casket, each one softly whispering their love and good-byes. Isabel was concerned for Curtis, who was so tenderhearted.

"I will never tell anyone 'good-bye' again," he whispered to Isabel. "It hurts too much."

Isabel nodded and wiped away tears with a handkerchief.

Papa picked up Jimmy so he could see his mother. Isabel noticed he had something in his hand.

Jimmy gently placed a treasure in the casket with Mama. "This is just Mama's body-shell," he said to Papa. "The real Mama is in heaven with Jesus, but she needs something to keep her body from being lonely."

Isabel remembered that he never had liked sleeping in a bed alone. She wondered which of his treasures he had given Mama. A shiny penny, a polished rock maybe. She hoped it wasn't the toad or small turtle that he had often carried in his pockets. His sweet gesture brought tears to everyone's eyes.

The day of the funeral was unusually warm, considering the snowstorm they'd had earlier in the week. Isabel looked around at the sad faces gathered around the grave of her mother. After everyone sang three of Mama's favorite hymns, the pastor read scriptures about heaven. As he read from John 14, about Jesus preparing a place for us, Isabel looked up and saw a beautiful rainbow.

At the end of the rainbow, in the field beyond her mother's grave, Isabel saw a splash of color peeping through the snow. "Daffodils—Mama's favorite spring flower," she whispered to Eugene. They both smiled. It was as if Mama was giving them a little gift.

After the funeral, Isabel picked one of the flowers and pressed it into Mama's Bible. She would keep it always as a reminder to her that Mama would always love them and that she was with Jesus, who loved them enough to die for them. She suddenly felt relief. She knew she and all the children were really in God's hands and that He loved them and would care for them always.

Friends and all but the immediate family silently left grieving man and his children at the graveside and headed to Aunt Jenny's who had invited everyone to help eat the food everyone had so generously provided. After their whispered words of love over their mama's grave, Papa and the children slowly made their way to receive their callers.

Chapter 38

Friends

"I FEEL LIKE the brightest candle in the room has just been extinguished, and we are left in the dim light to wander through the house in the dark."

Isabel turned to see who had just spoken the poignant words about her mother and was surprised to see that it was Mrs. Albright, Sally Anne's mother. The Albright family and their faithful house servants dabbed at their eyes with handkerchiefs and nodded in agreement as they gazed upon the peaceful body in the casket at the end of the room, where Isabel happened to be standing with her back to them. She smiled as she thought about how Mama would have responded to their words of kindness with a beautiful smile and would have given the credit completely to her Lord and Savior, Jesus Christ.

Isabel turned and slowly joined the circle of grieving friends, who welcomed her with open arms and words of comfort that she did not really hear but that she felt deeply. All words were a mere cacophony of sound; indeed, it seemed to Isabel that since Mama's death, life seemed to be a blur. She wondered if she ever would remember the events surrounding Mama's home going or if she would ever wish to. She only wanted to erase the last two weeks and have Mama healthy and happy again, and all would be well.

"You will always be welcome in our home, Isabel," Mr. Albright said. "We hope you know that and will spend some time with Sally Anne. Consider our house your second home, just as our Sally Anne thought of yours."

"Yes," Mrs. Albright said, "you may have your very own room, if you wish. That way, you can stay whenever and as long as you like."

"Isabel will not be staying with anyone." Isabel turned at the sound of Papa's booming voice. It was clear he was not pleased with the conversation he had just overheard.

"Papa, Sally Anne's parents were just inviting me to visit them, not to live with them," Isabel said. Her face turned red from embarrassment. She wanted to plead with Papa not to humiliate her in front of all of these guests, especially since they were getting ready to bury Mama, but experience taught her to keep silent and just to obey Papa, even when she knew he was wrong.

"Mr. Greene, we are so sorry for your terrible loss," Mrs. Albright said. She placed her hand on Papa's arm. "Mrs. Greene was a wonderful woman and will be missed by everyone who knew her. She was so kind to our Sally Anne, and you might say that she saved our family from destruction. We owe our very happiness and stability to your wife and her wisdom. She led us to the Lord, you know."

Isabel reached for Sally Anne's hand as Papa nodded in agreement. Mrs. Albright's words seemed to touch a chord in his heart, and he placed his pride on hold and allowed himself the comfort of sympathetic words from friends. Until now, Isabel had only seen him as stoic, and it worried her; it almost frightened her. Mama was gone, and Papa had not stopped to hear words of sympathy from anyone. Isabel thought perhaps

Papa would not listen because then it would really be true and he did not want it to be true. Isabel reached up with her free hand and wiped a tear with the handkerchief Mama had embroidered for her. Sally Anne put her arm around Isabel, and the two friends wept together as they walked arm in arm outside for fresh air.

"Isabel, I have a gift for you," Sally Anne said as they reached her car.

"You didn't have to get me anything."

"Oh, I know I didn't have to. I did not buy it, anyway. I already had it, but it has always reminded me of you." Sally Anne reached into the car and pulled out a long, white box with a pink, satin bow.

Isabel pulled the bow and held her breath as she opened the box. "Oh, your beautiful dolls. Sally Anne, you shouldn't have. This is your very favorite."

It's my favorite because it reminds me of you and your mama. It always has, which is why I wanted it in the first place. I always wanted that kind of relationship with my mother, and you and your mama have given that to me. Isabel, you and your mama have given me the best gift I could ever have wished for…my parents. I cannot give you your mama back, but I can give you this special reminder of your wonderful relationship you had. It was special, Isabel, very special."

Isabel blinked back tears that threatened to blind her as she looked at the beautiful mother and daughter porcelain dolls. The mother did resemble Mama, and Isabel thought the little girl doll was much more attractive than she was, but they were the most precious gift she had ever received. Her hands trembled as she picked up the mother doll and held it to her breast and sobbed.

The days following Mama's funeral seemed like a blur to Isabel, who seemed to move in a trance, answering when called upon and taking care of her siblings. The twins needed her the most. Their constant crying could only be stilled by the sound of her voice. Someone said it was because she sounded like Mama.

Mrs. Meadows said she thought they associated her with their Mama. In any case, Isabel was the only one in the family who could calm the babies, and Papa depended upon her. Everyone needed her in order to get some much-needed sleep…at least, that is what she told herself as she sat in Mama's rocker with a baby in her arms and tears running down her frail, freckled cheeks.

"I miss Mama too, Ralphy," she whispered. She brushed a kiss on the downy head. "Oh, Ralphy, you and Raymond will probably not remember Mama; you're too young." Isabel's voice cracked, and she wiped tears on her sleeve before continuing. "I'll tell you all about her and teach you about Jesus and many other wonderful things, just as Mama taught us. Eugene and Curtis can teach you how to play musical instruments and to sing just like Mama. Would you like that?"

Baby Ralph kicked his feet and looked at Isabel with his bright blue eyes. He moved his mouth as if to answer her. He cooed sweetly and then poked his small fist into his tiny, heart-shaped mouth.

"Oh, you will miss hearing her sing you to sleep as she rocked you in this chair," Isabel said. Tears slid down her cheek. "When Mama sang, I knew everything would be alright. This was one of Mama's favorites:

"What a friend we have in Jesus,
all our sins and grief to bear.
What a privilege to carry
Everything to God in prayer…"

Chapter 39

Starched Shirts

MONDAY MORNING AFTER the funeral dawned bright and clear. Isabel looked out the window for the tenth time that morning and checked the clock on the shelf.

"It's after 10:00, Eugene," she said. "I don't think she's coming. Are you sure Lindy said she would be here this morning at 8:00 to do the laundry?"

"That's what she said in church yesterday, when you took Raymond outside to change him," Eugene said. "She said she would be here by 8:00 sharp, and we were to be sure to have the water boiling and the washtubs out and ready to go."

"Well, something must have happened because Lindy is never late." Isabel refilled the large teakettle with water and placed it on the stove along with the three large pots of boiling water.

"What are you going to do?" Curtis said as he sauntered into the room and took a cookie from the cookie jar. Isabel pushed his hand away to remind him the cookies were off limits before lunch, just as Mama always had insisted.

"I'm gonna do it myself," Isabel said. She began filling tubs with water on the back porch.

"Do you know how?" Eugene asked.

"Of course I know how. I've helped Mama with the laundry since I was Jimmy's age."

"I know you helped Mama," Eugene said, "but do you know how much soap and starch to use? Remember, Mama was awfully particular."

"Well, no," Isabel said, "but it shouldn't be too hard to figure out."

"Don't forget," Curtis said, "Papa likes his white shirts, collars, and cuffs starched just right."

"I know that," Isabel said. "We just have to be careful, that is all."

Isabel put flakes of soap into the washtub along with the water to make bubbles, and she added the white clothing. She gently rubbed the clothing on the washboard, just as Mama had taught her, and then she swished the clothing around in the water and wrung it out by hand. She placed each clean article into the rinse tub, which contained bluing to make the clothes bright white, and swished it around and dunked it several times to get the suds out. Then she wrung out each piece by hand until she could not squeeze any more water out and placed the items into Mama's large wicker basket.

Next, she washed the diapers and then the color clothes and then, lastly, the items that needed to be starched. Isabel added what she considered a small amount of starch to the water; placed Papa's shirts, collars, and cuffs into the water; and swished them around and around again.

"Did you add enough starch?" Eugene asked as he peered over Isabel's shoulder to inspect his sister's work.

"Of course I did," Isabel said, "at least, I think so."

"Well," Eugene said, "we should add some more for good measure. Remember, he likes them nice and crisp."

"Maybe you're right," Isabel said. She picked up the box to add a little more. Just as she tilted the box over the washtub, Sandy ran up and jumped on Isabel, causing her to spill the entire box into the water.

"Oh no," Isabel said. "Bad dog! Look at Papa's shirts now." She held up Papa's best white shirt in her hand. The shirt was more than crisp. It was stiff. "Oh no!" She reached into the water and pulled out Papa's long johns.

"You forgot to wring out Papa's underwear," Eugene said, "and now look."

Isabel did not know whether to laugh or cry, but the sight of Papa's pink long johns was so funny that she burst out laughing. The rest of the children saw the humor as well and laughed with her. Then, just as suddenly as the laughter began, laughter turned to tears. Seven children stood around the washtub laughing and crying hysterically.

Papa returned home after looking for extra work.

"What's this all about?" he said. Isabel held up his pink, starched drawers. Eugene showed him the stiff shirt. And Papa laughed louder than Isabel had ever heard. "That's a knee-slapper if I ever saw one." He examined the items and surveyed the surprised, emotional faces of his children.

"I'm sorry, Papa," Isabel said. "It was an accident."

"It's the funniest accident I've ever seen," he said. Then his tone grew serious. "Why are you crying? We can probably just wash them again to get them back to normal."

"You're not mad, Papa?" Eugene said.

"Of course not," Papa said. He chuckled. "It was just a funny accident."

Isabel breathed a sigh of relief, and the tears began to flow once more; though, she could not understand why.

"Why are you crying, Belle?" Papa said as he pulled a handkerchief from his pocket and wiped the tears from her face.

"I don't know," Isabel said after blowing her nose loudly on the offered hankie. "I miss Mama."

"So do I, child." Tears gathered in his eyes. "So do I." He reached for Isabel, and they both began crying as he held her tightly.

Jimmy ran up to Papa and tugged on his coat. "I want Mama," he said.

Papa reached for him and waved for the others to join them. Then they all cried together until they could not cry anymore.

Finally, the spell was broken when Sylvia looked up and saw that Papa's long johns, which were lying across the basket, had become stiff as a board.

"Papa," she said, "how will you sit down in those things? Will they break if you do?"

Suddenly, the tears were forgotten as they looked at the silly sight, and the tears turned back to laughter.

"Well," Papa said, "I guess I won't be doing any sitting when I wear those things. Guess they will keep me on the straight and narrow. On second thought, maybe we should rewash them without the starch... I'll tell you what. From now on, why don't you let the boys and me take care of the laundry? You have your hands full with the little ones and the cooking and all."

"Thank you, Papa," Isabel said. Tears welled up in her eyes again. "That will help a lot."

"I'll betcha Curtis can handle an iron too," Papa said.

"Iron?" Curtis said. He looked at his sisters. "OK, but if anybody tells my friends, you're in for it."

"I'll help ya, Curtis," Maggie said. "Mama lets me iron pillowcases and skirts."

"Me too," Sylvia said. "I know how to iron handkerchiefs already, and I have my own ironing board and iron."

"We can do this," Papa said. He picked up the laundry basket. "If we all pitch in and help, I think we'll make it."

"Yoo-hoo, is anybody home?" Isabel cringed as she heard the shrill voice coming from the side yard.

"What's that ol' bag doing here?" Eugene asked. He dumped the wash water and hung the tub on a nail on the side of the house.

"Mr. Greene," said the tall, well-endowed woman as she rounded the corner, "I've brought you something to eat. I know you probably have not had a decent meal since Mrs. Greene died." She smirked as she eyed the faded laundry.

"Thank you, Miz Barker, but that wasn't necessary," Papa said. "Isabel here is a good little cook. Her Mama taught her. Besides, good friends and family members have sent so much food, it will take weeks to eat it all." He might have been exaggerating, but not by much.

"Oh well," she said. She looked at Isabel. "This will keep her from having to cook tonight. Children cannot be depended upon, you know."

"Thank you for your kindness, but as I said before, it wasn't necessary. Isabel has something that smells delicious simmering on the stove. It's all I can do to keep from going into the kitchen to sample it." He turned and grinned at Isabel, putting her at ease.

Isabel felt her heart swell with pride at Papa's praise, especially since he was praising her in front of someone who had made each of the children uncomfortable with her complaints about them most of their young lives. She thought of the times this

woman had made Mama cry with the insinuation that the
Greene children would grow up to be delinquents. Mama later
found out Mrs. Barker had said the same thing about every child
in the neighborhood. Therefore, Mama warned the children to
stay away from the woman if possible, and they had been happy
to comply with Mama's wishes. Isabel's thoughts returned to the
present as the nasal voice began to complain.

"Mr. Greene, I really must insist that the children stop
singing outside; it is very distracting. It seems as if they sing
every time they go outside."

"What's wrong with that? Every one of our children is a
songbird, just like their mama."

"They may be songbirds, but they need to consider other
folks who like their peace and quiet."

"Are they loud and obnoxious?" Papa asked.

"No, I would not say that," Mrs. Barker said. Her eyes
narrowed.

"Do they sing those silly, ridiculous songs they play on the
radio?" Papa looked around at his children and then squarely
at the complaining neighbor.

"No, I don't think so. They sing hymns," she said.

"Well then," Papa said, "I will not ask them to stop singing.
Hymns are comforting to the soul. They help us commune with
God, and they remind us of my Lizzie. As far as I am concerned,
they can sing until the cows come home."

"Well, I've never," Mrs. Barker said. She turned to walk away,
with the platter of food still in her hands.

"Seems to me that you should join them," Papa said. "A little
singing is good for the soul."

The woman stomped away as the children sighed with relief.

"Papa," Isabel said. "She took the dinner she made for you."

"That's alright; it is probably laced with bitterness," he said.
He shook his head in disbelief. "That is what happens when
you don't have any love or music in your life. I doubt she knows

the Lord. Maybe you should sing more quietly from now on. We wouldn't want the wrath of Barker to fall down upon you."

"Papa," Maggie said, "I feel sorry for her. She must be awfully lonely. I think I will pray for her."

"You do that, child," Papa said. He patted Maggie on the head. "Now," Papa said in a lighthearted tone, "let's go taste that delicious supper Isabel made for us."

After supper, they washed the dishes and put them away. They swept the kitchen floor. And Papa gathered the children into the front room, where he sat down in his chair and pointed Isabel toward Mama's rocker. Isabel had Raymond in her arms. He had just awakened from his nap.

"Now," Papa said, "Eugene, go and get me the Good Book, and open it to Genesis 1."

Eugene found the passage and placed the Bible in Papa's outstretched hand.

"'In the beginning God created the heaven and the earth.' God made us, the beautiful heaven, and the earth. He always was and always will be," Papa said. "'And the earth was without form, and void; and darkness was upon the face of the deep. And the Spirit of God moved upon the face of the waters. And God said let there be light and there was light.' The world must have been a terrible and lonely place in the beginning," Papa continued. He looked around the room at his children. "Sometimes it seems dark and lonely to us, but we must always remember that God is here.

"Now, Eugene, will you finish reading the next verses about the first day? I haven't memorized the rest of it very well." He passed the Bible to his eldest son. His hands shook. Eugene read the next two verses and paused as Papa lifted his hand.

"God had a plan from the very beginning. He started by speaking the world into existence. He didn't whisper, He didn't cry, He didn't shout. He *spoke,* and the world was filled with light. We must always remember when things seem the darkest,

God is here to light our way. God is in control." Papa stood and received the Bible from Eugene and placed it on the fireplace mantle.

"Now," he said, "let's go to Him in prayer. We will continue in God's Word every night, just as we did with Mama. If I need to work at night, Eugene will be in charge. Understood?"

Isabel nodded with her brothers and sisters, who were kneeling around Papa. She bowed her head over her baby brother and joined her family in prayer, with tears on her cheeks. Comfort enveloped her like a warm blanket.

 Mama Helped Us

ISABEL FINISHED THE supper dishes and swept the floor. She had fed the children and placed a plate of food in the warming oven for Papa. Eugene and Maggie had tucked the younger siblings into bed and were preparing for bed themselves. Isabel decided to wait for Papa to return home from his second job. He was digging ditches for Roanoke City.

"I can't believe it has been two months since Mama died," Isabel whispered as she walked past the kitchen calendar. "It seems longer and just like yesterday all at the same time."

Isabel looked around to make sure she had finished everything the way Mama had taught her, and then she picked up Mama's Bible and sat down in her comfortable rocker beside the lamp. She had only read a few verses when her eyes began to get heavy.

She drifted into a deep sleep. Suddenly, she felt a soft hand caressing her cheek. "Isabel, wake up. Wake up." She recognized the soft, gentle voice.

"Mama, is that you?"

"Isabel, wake up. Now!"

Isabel opened her eyes. Smoke filled the room.

"Eugene, Curtis, Maggie, wake up!" Isabel yelled. "The house is on fire. Fire!" She ran up the steps to get her brothers and sisters out of danger.

Panic filled the house as quickly as the thick, black smoke. Isabel carried a twin under each arm, along with their blankets. She deposited the babies on the soft, grassy knoll, away from the house and then ran back inside to help the others.

The older children carried the younger ones outside to sit with the babies. Isabel, Eugene, and Curtis then ran back inside to salvage what they could. Smoke was thickening behind the old cook stove as they threw articles of clothing, shoes, Mama's Bible, and a few housewares out the windows. There was neither rhyme nor reason to the articles saved, for the children did not stop to think about what they needed; they merely grabbed from instinct and hoped for the best.

Suddenly, the sickening sound of splintering wood filled the house. Flames began to run along the chimney and spread across the floor, walls, and dry sink.

"Get out of here!" Eugene shouted.

Isabel picked up Mama's floral china gravy boat on her way outside. Isabel heard the sound of the big dinner bell. "Where's Curtis?" She ran to her younger brothers and sisters, who were huddled together. Sylvia was sitting on the ground with baby Ralph in her lap, and Maggie was holding little Raymond. Billy and Jimmy were sobbing uncontrollably, and the girls were trying to calm them.

"I rang the dinner bell for help," Curtis said as he sprinted from the house. "I hope somebody hears and calls for the fire truck."

Eugene ran into the house with a bucket of water.

"Eugene, come back," Isabel said, but he did not listen. He was determined to put out the fire. Isabel started after him, but Curtis pulled her back and then raced to help his brother. She watched Curtis fill up two buckets of water at the outside pump and then haul them into the house. She wanted to help, but she realized the younger children needed her more. "Eugene, Curtis, come back." She called them until she was hoarse, but to no avail. Finally, she sat with the younger children, crooning words of comfort.

The smoke was almost overpowering, and they all coughed until their throats hurt and their eyes burned. They heard a loud crack as flames engulfed the home. "Please, Lord, don't let Eugene and Curtis get hurt," she prayed repeatedly. She did not know if she prayed silently or was speaking aloud.

Finally, after what seemed an eternity, the two soot-covered boys ran out of the house and joined their siblings on the grassy knoll. Isabel realized they were carrying the buckets, with milk for the babies in one and baby bottles and diapers in the other. "I should have thought of that," she said to herself.

A car, followed by a truck and a fire engine, pulled into the yard. The Meadows' had heard the dinner bell and seen the smoke. They'd called for the fire truck.

"Grab the hose, boys," shouted the man who was apparently the captain. Soon, men were working together to extinguish the flames.

Isabel heard a lot of shouting, banging, and the sound of water from the hose, but none of it made sense to her. It was as if she were in a fog and hearing noises but unable to see what was happening. The twins cried, and Isabel fed them a bottle. Sylvia complained that she was cold, and Isabel removed her own sweater and put it around her little sister. She reacted without realizing it. Suddenly, the voices of the firefighters reached her consciousness.

"I can't believe he would leave these children at home alone," one of the firefighters said. "It's a miracle they didn't burn down the house before now."

"It's a miracle no one was hurt," another one said.

"The children didn't cause this fire, Joe," the captain said. "It started in the chimney. When will people realize they must take the time to clean their chimneys? Many of the fires out in the country are chimney fires. This fire could have been prevented."

"What do you think will happen to the children?" the first man said.

"Only God knows." That answer drew Isabel back to reality.

Papa's model T Ford pulled into the yard. He did not stop to turn off the engine or even to shut the door. He ran to his children, making sure everyone was OK. "Thank God you're all OK," he said. He hugged each child close and then took Ralph from Maggie and kissed his forehead. Papa's slender frame shook from emotion as he looked at the burning house. "What happened, Eugene?" he said as he turned to his eldest son. "I left you in charge. You were supposed to look out for your brothers and sisters. Now I don't know what we will do."

Isabel turned to her ashen-faced brother to comfort him, but he was staring into the charred remains of their home, as if he were in a trance.

"Papa," Isabel said, "Eugene did take care of us. The fire was not his fault. It was a chimney fire. I heard the firemen say so. Eugene and Curtis risked their lives to get us out, and they went back inside to get the things we needed for the babies. Don't you dare blame Eugene. It was not his fault." Isabel burst into tears. She turned to her brother. "Tell him, Eugene. Tell him it wasn't your fault. Tell him, the house would have caught on fire if he had been home. Tell him Eugene, tell him." She screamed at her brother to defend himself as the reality of the night reached her consciousness. She wanted to do something to turn back the clock so she could change the events of the last evening and prevent the fire from happening. She wished she would wake up and find it had just been a nightmare. She wished she would wake up in her own bed, in her own room and smell bacon frying in the kitchen as Mama prepared breakfast...

Her thoughts became jumbled memories of Mama and the family around the kitchen table, laughing and talking as they enjoyed their delicious meal. She thought about family altar in the parlor as they sang hymns and Mama read from her Bible—the very Bible Isabel had picked up to read before the fire. She could practically hear Mama playing the squeeze harp and laughing as the children danced around to her music. Her thoughts turned to Maggie and Sylvia playing tea party and Jimmy helping little Billy take his first baby step without Mama or Papa in the room to see the momentous occasion. Then tears streamed down her face as she recalled the ambulance attendants carrying Mama out of the house after the doctor diagnosed her with pneumonia. Mama's last words to her were, "Always be a good girl." Isabel meant to keep that promise.

Suddenly, Isabel wondered if Eugene was thinking about Mama too. She wondered what Mama's last words to him had been. Had she also told him to look after the children? Did he blame himself for the fire? He could not. It was not his fault. She was as sure of this as she was sure of her name. *What will we do now? Where will we live?* Just as she was about to voice her thoughts, Papa's employer and landlord, Mr. Meadows, showed up.

"Mr. Greene," Mr. Meadows said. "Excuse me for the intrusion in your family, but I thought you could bring the children over to the house for the night. Mrs. Meadows is making beds on the floor in the parlor and already has made a pile of sandwiches and a vat of hot chocolate for them. There's a bed for you too."

Papa nodded and opened his mouth to speak, but he could not seem to form words. He turned and handed the baby to Eugene and then walked with Mr. Meadows to assess the damage before they all went to the Mr. Meadows'.

He returned a few minutes later with a large bundle in his hands. Mr. Meadows carried another. "The firefighters found these things on the ground," Papa said. "It looks like you children knew just what to do. I do not think I would have remembered to save anything. I'm proud of you all."

"Isabel got us out," Eugene said. "If it wasn't for Isabel, it would have been too late."

Papa embraced his eldest daughter. Emotion overcame him again, so he could not speak.

"It wasn't anything, Papa," she said. "I didn't even think. Anybody would do the same."

Mama saved us. Isabel knew that, but she thought Papa would not understand. Indeed, she did not quite understand it herself. *Perhaps the Lord used Mama to warn us.*

The children followed Papa to their car and squeezed in. Mr. Meadows offered to take some of them in his truck, but Papa would not hear of it. Understandably, he wanted to drive the children himself. It seemed he did not want to lose sight of them for even a moment.

Papa refused to have his children divided, even for the night. The children bedded down on the Meadows' parlor floor. Snuggled in quilts and blankets, the children tried to fall asleep by the crackling sounds of the fire in a large, stone fireplace.

Mrs. Meadows produced a cradle and an empty dresser drawer for the twins to sleep in. She put a soft pillow in each temporary crib. Isabel watched as Mrs. Meadows bundled each baby in a soft blanket and stroked their faces gently as they closed their eyes in sleep. Isabel missed that. They all did. Each child already missed the warm, loving mother's touch. Mama had only been gone a few weeks, but it seemed like forever. Isabel fluffed her pillow and turned toward the wall so no one would see the tears threatening to spill over her cheeks—still rosy from the heat of the fire.

Papa refused the comfort of the sofa. "I couldn't sleep if I tried, but thank you for your kindness," he said as Mrs. Meadows made up the sofa with a star quilt and placed a fresh pillowcase over the feather pillow she produced from the hall closet. He did, however, accept a cup of hot coffee. Isabel watched as he poured some of the coffee in the saucer to cool, and then she smiled as he sipped the coffee from it.

Mama always fussed at him for his "eccentric" ritual. Even that thought produced a lump in her throat. "Eccentric" was the word Isabel spelled correctly to win the spelling bee the week before Mama died. This was the first time she had used the word in a sentence. She decided never to use it again. Mama made her spell it a hundred times the night before the spelling bee. They tried to see how fast they could spell it without messing up. Mama won. Billy got sick the next day, and Mama stayed up with him for days—and then she got sick.

Isabel wondered why she couldn't stop thinking. So, why not think about her Bible verses she learned in Sunday School? She finally dozed off as she thought of the twenty-third Psalm. "Yea, though I walk through the valley of the shadow of death I shall fear no evil; for thou art with me…"

"Lord, were you with Mama when she passed through the valley?" Isabel fell asleep before she could finish her prayer.

She awoke later with a start. "Something's not right," she whispered to herself.

She sat up and looked around. "Where am I?" Then she remembered the fire. Their house was gone, and they were at the Meadows' house. She glanced around the room. Her brothers were sleeping soundly on the other side, under a blue and gold quilt. Maggie and Sylvia were snuggled together under a pink and yellow gingham square quilt. She noticed that each sister was clutching the rag doll Mama had made for her. Jimmy was sucking his thumb again. Mama finally had gotten him to stop by putting cayenne pepper on his thumb three days in a row. His thumb had been in his mouth continuously since Mama died. Papa did not have the heart to try to break his habit again, and neither did Isabel.

"He needs his thumb for comfort," Papa said when Isabel brought this to his attention after the funeral. "He will outgrow it. Hopefully, he won't have buck teeth."

Isabel wondered if Jimmy would even remember Mama. Billy was probably is too young to remember her, and she knew the twins would not.

She turned her attention to Papa, who was sitting on the edge of the couch, staring into the crackling fire. He did not even notice Isabel as she laid back. Sleep engulfed her.

Isabel awakened to find Mrs. Meadows feeding baby Ralph and Papa feeding Raymond. Isabel started to rise to help, but she was told to go back to sleep.

"All is well for the moment," Papa said.

Another time, she awoke to find Papa and Mr. Meadows in deep discussion.

"We can have the house inhabitable within a few weeks," Mr. Meadows said. Isabel liked the confidence she heard in his voice. "The foundation is strong, and the shell is there. We just need to rebuild the inside. I have been thinking of adding a bathroom for your family. I should have done it long ago."

"There's no need for that," Papa said. "It won't work. I've tried, but it's no use. They need their mama. Why did He have to take her? She was so young and beautiful and so full of life. Why couldn't it have been me? I'm an old man. I cannot take care of nine youngins, especially the babies." His voice broke.

"What about Widow Barker?" Mrs. Meadows said.

"Forget that ol' bag," Papa said.

"You don't need to marry her, Mr. Greene. She could care for your children while you work," Mrs. Meadows said. "The older children will be in school most of the day. She will just be caring for the four youngest. You and the children are welcome to sleep here. I can clean up the attic, and there is the guest room. I know our little Johnny would like to share his room with some of the boys. Actually, I could take care of the children."

However, Papa dashed her plans with stubborn refusal. "We won't impose on you good folks, and that's final. I know you have an invalid mother on Bent Mountain that you help take care of. Your own family needs you. Thank you just the same, though."

Isabel held her breath as the conversation continued. She thought both of Mrs. Meadows' ideas were good, even if they did not like Mrs. Barker.

"You know, Mr. Greene, little Sylvia is the same age as our Johnny," Mrs. Meadows said. "In fact, I remember them playing together in the playpen when they were just babies. They are best friends. Almost like brother and sister, really. We would love to take her off your hands if the time comes for you to find homes for the children."

"No," Papa said in a loud whisper. Isabel had her eyes closed, but she sensed him getting to his feet. She imagined his hands held in tight fists by his side. "I will not split them up. Even if I did, little Sylvia would be the last child I would give away."

Isabel hoped the other children had not heard. She especially hoped Sylvia, who had always been such a happy child, had not heard this terrible discussion. The thought that Papa may give her away was unthinkable. Yet, he was indeed discussing the horrible possibility of separating their family. He was discussing giving his children away. The thought made Isabel shudder, and she felt sick inside. He was refusing to talk about it, but would he eventually do it? *He could not do something that horrible. He just can't.*

Isabel felt resentment rising within herself. *Why did Mama have to die? She never would give us away. Never. She would not even consider it. Oh, Lord, don't let Papa give us away.* She did not finish her prayer. There seemed to be a wall between her and her heavenly Father. She closed her eyes tightly to hold back tears and listened as the adults stepped into the next room to continue their discussion around the dining room table, which was the room closest to the parlor, where the children were sleeping.

"I'm sorry," Mrs. Meadows said. "I did not mean to imply you should give the children away. I did not mean to upset you. It's just that we love Sylvia so, and we want what's best for her. We care for each of your children. They are just like family to us, you know."

"Yes, ma'am. I understand," Papa said. His voice was hoarse.

"Anyway, Avil," Mr. Meadows said, "our offer will stand as long as necessary. You know we would treat her as our own. Please feel free to come to us if things do not work out for you."

"Thank you," Papa said. "I will remember, but I promised my Lizzie before she died that the children will never go into an orphanage and that I will do everything possible to keep our family together. It will be more difficult now that we no longer have a home to live in…"

Mr. Meadows offered to pray with Papa, and the last thing Isabel heard as she finally gave into sleep was an appeal to the Lord for the family to remain together.

Scenes of the night before flashed before her in vivid colors. At times events moved quickly, and the times when Isabel needed to move quickly, she seemed to be stuck in quicksand, unable to move at all. She reached out to pick up her crying brother to carry him away from the burning house, but she could not reach him, and the flames inched nearer the child until she could smell the smoke and hear his hoarse cough. She cried out for help, but her voice was uncooperative. She screamed, but there was no sound. Finally, in urgency, she cried out to the Lord for help.

She felt a hand gently stroke her hair. "It will be alright, child," a voice whispered in her ear.

"Mama, I knew you would help me," Isabel said. "I knew you would come." Tears flowed down her cheeks as she realized she was engulfed in a bear hug.

"No, child, it's not your mama," Papa said. "You were dreaming. You are all right now. Everything will be fine. You will see."

Isabel felt teardrops fall on her arm and did not know if they were hers or if they belonged to Papa. They sobbed together. She did not know how long they grieved together, for time had no meaning that evening.

Finally, Papa broke the spell. "When I woke you up, you thought I was your mama. Were you dreaming about something that happened when she was alive?" Papa asked.

"No, I was dreaming about tonight. Papa, Mama got us out of the house. I put your dinner in the warming oven and fell asleep in Mama's chair. She came to me in a dream and told me to wake up…as she often did when I overslept on school days. If she had not told me to wake up, we would not have gotten out. I just know it, Papa. Mama saved our lives."

"I don't know what to say, Isabel. If God would choose any mother to come back to save the lives of her children, it would be your mother. Maybe He did send her, or perhaps He allowed you to dream about her waking you up just at the very moment you needed to wake up. Who is to say? I think we should both thank Him for saving you all from the fire."

Father and daughter bowed their heads together in prayer for the first time in Isabel's life.

"Now," Papa said, "let me get you a glass of water or some hot milk. Would you like some of that hot chocolate milk? I know that is what your mama always fixed," Papa said. He seemed to realize he had found something he could do to help comfort his child.

Isabel smiled as she envisioned Papa at the stove making hot chocolate. "That's alright, Papa. A glass of water is fine. My mouth is kind of dry." She realized her throat was parched from the smoke earlier in the evening.

"Mine too," Papa said. "My throat's dry as a cotton patch. I'll be right back with a glass of nice, cool water."

Papa returned a few minutes later with a tray containing two glasses of water, milk, a plate of cookies, two apples, and a roast beef sandwich to share.

"Mrs. Meadows offered this sandwich to me earlier, but I wasn't hungry. Then I just heard something growling louder than an old grizzly bear in the kitchen. I looked around the kitchen, thinking some critter was about to pounce on me, and suddenly realized it was just my old belly talking to me."

"Papa, you did eat the lunch I packed for you today, didn't you?" Isabel asked. She sat up quickly, realizing Papa had not eaten a bite of dinner and lunch was almost twelve hours earlier.

"Yes, and that pork chop sandwich you made was the best I ever 'et," he said with a grin.

Isabel gracefully declined a bite of sandwich, but she enjoyed a red delicious apple and some milk. The little picnic with Papa seemed to be just what both father and daughter needed to enable them to forget the horrors of the past evening and the uncertainty of tomorrow.

Chapter 41

A New Dawn

ISABEL FELT THE warmth of sunlight from the window filtering through the partially drawn draperies. She stretched out and yawned before she opened her eyes to look around. It was obviously still early. No one seemed to have awakened.

At least they were still together. She looked around the room. The children were still sleeping, and Papa had finally given in to exhaustion on the sofa. His breathing was heavy and even. He looked very pale and smaller than she had ever realized. She placed her quilt over him and folded the other covers that she had used as a mattress.

She looked at the sleeping twins and smiled at Ralph, whose lips moved as if nursing a bottle and then smiled contentedly in his sleep. Raymond's eyelashes flickered twice, and his little nose twitched like a little bunny's. Isabel covered both babies and hoped they would sleep until she had their morning bottles ready for them. However, she decided to take care of her morning grooming first so that she would not lose her opportunity.

She quietly slipped on shoes and headed for the back door before she remembered that the Meadows family had indoor plumbing, including two water closets. One was upstairs and one downstairs. This fact always had impressed Isabel. They were the only family besides her friend Sally Anne's family with the luxury of two bathrooms.

Isabel tiptoed into the hallway in search of the luxurious necessary room. She was not disappointed. The porcelain "necessary" had a brass toilet paper holder just within reach. There was also a white pedestal sink with hot and cold running water. She ran her hand across the cool, smooth surface of the claw foot tub. "Well, I'll be. Wouldn't it be fun just to soak in a tub like this?" She smiled at the thought. Isabel could not resist the urge to touch the fluffy, white towels hanging on a brass rod over the sink. She breathed in the fresh fragrance of sunshine and then chided herself for messing them up. She noticed a basket of washcloths and a shelf with containers holding toothbrushes and store-bought soap and toothpaste. "They must really be rich," she whispered to the image in the mirror above the sink. That is when she realized her brief attempt to remove soot from her face and neck last night was unsuccessful.

"Oh oh. Hope I didn't mess up Mrs. Meadows' nice, clean blankets and pillow." Isabel reached for the soap and scrubbed in earnest. Then when she reached for the clean, white towel, she changed her mind and pulled a handkerchief from her pocket instead. "I'll mess everything up if I use that towel." She fished her comb from her other apron pocket.

By the time Isabel felt she was presentable, she smelled the wonderful aroma of coffee brewing and bacon frying in the kitchen.

"Good morning, Isabel," Mrs. Meadows said as Isabel entered the blue and white tiled kitchen. She reached for a glass and poured a glass of milk for Isabel. Isabel heard the rattle of bottles and noticed the open door.

"I thought I should double my milk order this morning," Mrs. Meadows said.

The Clover Creamery delivery man stepped through the door. He was carrying a handcart containing milk, a quart of buttermilk, and a pint of cream and butter. The fact that the Meadows family owned a farm but had their milk delivered to their door three times a week always had been a mystery to Isabel, who had often helped her mama skim cream from the top of the milk and churned butter by hand. Of course, this was after one of the boys had milked ol' Bessie, the family's cow. Rumor was that Mrs. Meadows also bought eggs from the family up the street. Sometimes, she even bought eggs from Mama, who was proud of the large, brown eggs her hens produced.

"Oh no," Isabel said. "Bessie hasn't been milked yet, and we need to gather the eggs. None of the animals have been fed either. The poor creatures."

"Don't worry about that. Your half-brothers, Fred and Jim, came by early this morning and did the chores for your papa. They should be back soon with a report on the condition of everything."

"How did they know?" Isabel asked.

"My husband asked me to call them last night. They wanted to come right then, but I told them it was too late and that we would keep you all for the night. Since they had such a long ride from Roanoke, they agreed to wait and come this morning. There is so much to do today, but last night, there was really nothing they could do but stand back and watch with worry. There was no use in having them stay up worrying and talking all night too."

Isabel nodded in agreement. She began slicing and buttering bread to make toast. Soon, breakfast was ready, and Papa offered his thanks to the Lord for His protection of the children and the kindness of his employers. Then he asked a blessing for the delicious food and for the hands that had prepared it.

Fred and Jim knocked on the back door just as the family was sitting down to eat.

"I see we made it just in time, brother," Jim said.

Papa stood as his sons entered the room. "What are you boys doing here?"

"Please, Mr. Greene, sit down and have your breakfast," Mrs. Meadows said. "Jim, Fred, sit down over there, and help yourself." She poured two cups of steaming hot coffee.

Isabel watched with amusement as Fred poured his steaming hot coffee into his saucer and sipped it just like Papa. Isabel looked up to see that Jim was also smiling. He winked as she looked his way. Isabel was not the only one who had noticed this funny ritual.

Just as Papa sopped the gravy from his plate with the last piece of bread, trucks began to drive into the front yard. Isabel followed the family to the large front porch to greet the newcomers. Each person came carrying items of clothing for the children and toys, blankets, books, and food. There were also odd pieces of furniture on the back of an old pickup truck. Isabel looked to Papa for his response; he looked stunned. With a tear on his cheek and a far-off look in his eye, he gazed beyond the crowd into the sky. Isabel stepped closer to hear him utter the words, "He does care."

Just as quickly as the tear came, a look of pride replaced it as the men in the crowd stepped forward to speak with Papa. Most of the families were from church. Others she recognized as neighbors and friends. Isabel followed Papa's gaze, which rested upon Mr. Albright, Sally Anne's father, who walked up the porch steps, took Papa's hand, and shook it.

"Mr. Greene," he said, "we are sorry to hear about the fire and are here to help in any way possible. We heard you had lost everything except the few things the children thought to throw out the window, so we have brought a few things with us that may be useful to you and the children."

"A tricycle," Jimmy said. He ran down the steps toward the offered gift, to the delight of the crowd. He sat down on the red toy and began to ride around the yard, accompanied by a loud squeak.

"We'll fix you right up, boy," said a man in front of the crowd. "It just needs a little oil, and you'll be all set."

"I like it his way, mister," Jimmy said. He rode around the side of the house, squeak and all.

Papa chuckled and shook his head in disbelief. "All this is for us?"

"Yes, sir," Mr. Albright said. "Your family has helped so many people. Mrs. Greene seemed to know when anyone needed help, and she was always generous to everyone. We just want to pay her back; if that is even possible."

Isabel looked around the crowd and recognized a few faces as she remembered how Mama was always ready to help wherever there was a need. Isabel had memories of Mama sending food to the sick and blankets and baby clothes to a poor family that could not afford to buy anything—not even diapers or cloth to make them. She saw the family Curtis and Mama helped. They were bringing a small side table. Tears filled her eyes; she could no longer see individuals, but the group as a whole. She blinked and took a deep breath in order to keep the tears at bay. She stepped forward to thank her wonderful friends and neighbors. She swayed and reached for the railing for support. Sally Anne saw her, ran up the steps, took her hand, and led her to the porch swing, where they sat to watch events as they unfolded.

Papa cleared his throat, started to speak, and coughed again. "Friends, I just don't know what to say…your kindness is too much."

"Nah," said a voice from the crowd, "it's the least we could do, Mr. Greene. Mrs. Green did more for all of us than we could ever repay."

"Did you do this?" Isabel looked to Sally Anne, expecting her answer to be "yes," but was surprised when she shook her head.

"Father and mother organized everyone, but they all planned to bring anything they could. Mr. West came to Father to ask for advice."

"But the fire just happened last night," Isabel said. "How did they all know?"

"Everyone is talking about it, Isabel," Sally Anne said. "They said you are a hero. That you got all of the children out of the house and even saved some important things. I heard you saved your mama's Bible and the gravy boat too."

Isabel nodded and smiled slightly. "It wasn't just me, you know. Eugene and Curtis helped get everyone out, and Eugene went back inside to get milk, bottles, and diapers for the babies. I was so scared, especially when the boys went back inside with a bucket of water to try to put the fire out. It seemed like hours before they both came out carrying buckets with the baby things. I've never been so happy to see someone in my whole life."

"I guess so," Sally Anne said. "I'm thankful you are all alright. It must have been scary."

Isabel nodded and shuddered as she thought about what may had happened if she had not awakened. For a moment, she was tempted to tell her friend that Mama had really gotten them out, but then she changed her mind. Sally Anne would think she was crazy.

"Did you save any clothes?" Sally Anne asked. A woman sat a box of obviously used clothing on the porch steps.

"Yes," Isabel said, "but they smell like smoke. I just hope we can wash the smell out."

"Why don't you let us take them home and wash them in mother's washing machine? It has an agitator that is supposed to get the clothes really clean. Besides, you don't need to do laundry after all you have been through." Sally Anne stood up to get to work immediately, but Isabel motioned her to sit down.

"We can get to it later. It looks like we will have something clean and fresh smelling to wear now." Isabel pushed the swing back with her feet, and the girls sat swinging and watching the kind neighbors bringing their offerings of good will.

Isabel soon felt her eyes closing, and suddenly, everything went black. She felt herself being lifted and carried into the house, but she could not open her eyes to see who had picked her up. She only knew that sleep was upon her.

Chapter 42

Planning

LATER THAT AFTERNOON, Isabel listened carefully as Papa laid out their options.

"We can stay here with Mr. and Miz Meadows while we repair the house and then move back in, but it will be an imposition on the Meadows', and I don't think I can get extra work while we live here—and we need the money now more than ever. Or we could move to Franklin County on Grandpa Greene's property, into the old cabin. Your Uncle Mitt's church offered to help us fix it up. I can drive to Roanoke every day to work, since that's where the opportunities are. Isabel, you will have to take care of the youngins. Boys, I will count on you to plant a garden for our food, and you'll need to hunt for meat. We'll also make barrels to sell, just as your great grandpa did most of his life. The only other option is to farm you out to different families and I promised your mama I would do my best to keep you together and I intend to keep that promise."

"What's the cabin like?" Isabel asked. Her brothers and she looked to Papa for his answer.

"Well," he said as he scratched his head, "it has been a long time since I stepped foot in that ol' cabin, but as far as I can recollect, it has a front room, a big kitchen, and three bedrooms. We'll have to bring water from the well. Mitt has been farming some of the land and drinks from that well, so we know the water is good. The most important thing is that the nosy social worker will not know where we are, so she cannot put you into an orphanage."

"Please, Lord, don't let that ol' social worker find us," Isabel prayed.

Chapter 43

A New Home

"ARE WE THERE yet?" Sylvia asked Papa for the seventh time.

"No, but we'll be there in three shakes of a lamb's tail," Papa said with a hint of aggravation in his voice.

"But you said that last time, and I have counted ninety-five shakes," Sylvia said. She held up a toy lamb that someone donated after the fire.

"Well if that don't beat all." Papa laughed and hit the steering wheel with the palm of his hand. "Gal, you take things too literally."

"Sylvia," Isabel said. She shifted Baby Ralph in her lap. "We should be there soon. Why don't you sing a song for us?"

"OK," Sylvia said with a grin, revealing two more missing teeth. "Here we go round the mulberry bush…"

The automobile rounded a bend in the road and stopped in front of an old log cabin surrounded by trees. Everyone was silent for a full minute and then burst into conversation simultaneously.

"Oh boy," Papa said. He shook his head. "I never thought I would see this place again. It is a wonder that it is still standing. Mitt must be taking care of it."

"Do we have'ta live here?" someone said.

"When is Jim bringing Sandy?" Jimmy asked. He tugged on Papa's coat. "She's lonesome without us, and she does not know Jim very well."

"Where's my room?"

"Whoa," Papa said. "I can only answer one question at a time. Let's see now, yes, we have to live here, and your room is upstairs. You may choose which one. The boys will share one room. Maggie and Sylvia will share the other loft room upstairs. Isabel will take the downstairs bedroom with the twins, and I'll sleep in the summer kitchen at the back of the cabin until we build on another room later. Jimmy, your brother is bringing Sandy this afternoon, and if you try to climb those logs, I'll tan your hide."

"But, Papa," Jimmy said as he jumped up and down—almost stepping on Isabel's feet, "it looks easy. I could do it if you'd just let me…" Jimmy stopped suddenly at Papa's warning glance.

Suddenly, Isabel realized something was missing. Jimmy's pocket looked empty.

"Jimmy," she said, "where's Jay Boy? Did you lose him in the fire? I haven't seen him lately."

"No," Jimmy said. "Jay Boy's with Mama."

Isabel fought the tears threatening to escape and hugged her brother tightly as he struggled to get away. Then she noticed her sisters fidgeting and crossing their feet as they looked around.

"Papa," Isabel said, "where is the necessary?"

"What's left of it is out back at the end of the garden path. Guess we'll have to dig and build a new one." He didn't seem at all concerned.

Maggie and Sylvia turned to Isabel, mirroring her own concerns.

"Where do we go now, Papa?" Isabel asked.

"Out back in the bushes will have to do for now," Papa said. He opened the car door for the children.

"I don't think I like this," Maggie whispered in Isabel's ear.

"Me either, Maggie, me either," Isabel replied.

"Walk around the side of the house with me, and I'll point you in the right direction," Papa said. "Meet us in the cabin. We can go in through the backdoor." Papa kicked a rock out of the path just as Jimmy spied a lizard and ran off to catch him with Billy in tow.

"Leave him," Papa said. Then he herded the boys into the cabin.

The children crept through the dark cabin, pushing cobwebs out of their way as they entered each room.

"Why is it so dark in here?" Isabel wondered, her eyes adjusting to the darkness.

"The shutters are closed," Papa said. "Most of the glass panes are broken." He pulled back the shutters to allow the light to come in. "We'll have to replace them eventually, I suppose."

Isabel looked around the room as she tried to imagine living in such a dirty, dark place that was so far from everyone they knew and loved. Suddenly, her attention was diverted by a puff of dust, followed by the sound of laughter and the honking of horns.

"Who could that be?" Eugene said. He raced for the front door, stepping onto the porch, which gave way under his foot.

"Looks like we'll have to fix the porch," Papa said with a chuckle as he helped Eugene out of his boot, which was firmly stuck.

Chapter 44

ℬ*less the* 𝒞*hildren*

"THE YARD IS full of people, trucks, and wagons," Eugene said. "Not just Jim and Fred with our stuff, but Mr. Meadows, Mr. Albright, and a bunch of strangers with tools and things. Uncle Mitt and Aunt Ida Mae have arrived too. What are they doing here, Papa?"

"I don't know, Son," Papa said. "Your guess is as good as mine. Let's go outside and find out. Watch your step now; we don't want anyone else to fall through."

The children followed Papa outside and into the bright sunshine as family, friends, and strangers greeted them with handshakes and hugs.

"What's going on here, Mitt?" Papa asked. His brother made his way to the front of the crowd.

"I guess you might call this a working party, Avil," Uncle Mitt said. "Your boys, the folks in my congregation, and some of your neighbors wanted to do something to bless the children, who have been through so much. Fixing up the old cabin seemed like the best thing for now." He waved his hand toward the cabin. "Just tell us what needs to be done, and we'll get started."

"I think I will like this place after all," Maggie said. She jumped up and down in excitement.

"Me too," Isabel said. She hid her face behind her hands and cried.

"What's the matter, Dear?" Aunt Ida Mae asked. She pulled the girls close in a motherly hug.

"We're just so happy," Isabel said. "We were so afraid that Papa would have to give us away, and then he told us about the cabin. When we got here, it looked so…"

"Unfriendly?" Aunt Ida Mae said.

"Yes," Isabel said, "dark and dirty."

"I know, Dear," Aunt Ida Mae said. "But we are going to fix that. Now, what color would you like to paint the kitchen?"

"We can paint it?" Isabel said.

"Yes, we certainly can. Your Great Grandmother Lucy insisted on plastering all of the walls inside the cabin. She said, 'It might look like an old log cabin on the outside, but we can brighten it on the inside.' She liked to have everything bright and cheerful. Besides, the plaster helps to keep the cold air out and the warm air in."

Isabel smiled as she imagined Papa in a bonnet. After all, everyone said Papa looked like Grandma Lucy. Isabel started to giggle at the image and then suddenly felt drawn to the old cabin as if it were a member of the family. Her thoughts returned to the present.

"I didn't know we could do that," Isabel said. "We don't have the money for paint."

"It has already been donated," Aunt Ida Mae said. "We have several gallons of white paint for the walls and a gallon of red paint and one of blue paint. I think someone donated their left-over supplies. It sounds patriotic, doesn't it?" She chuckled.

Isabel looked to Maggie, who just smiled without giving a suggestion. Then Isabel spotted a red wagon in the yard. "Could we paint the walls white and have the trim red?"

"Of course, Dear," Aunt Ida Mae said. "That sounds delightful. In fact, I have the perfect fabric for curtains and a tablecloth. Come on inside, and we will talk about what to do with the rest of the cabin to make it feel more like home. We have a few rolls of wallpaper too, and I have a couple of plants that would look perfect sitting on that wide windowsill."

Isabel felt like laughing and crying at the same time, but Raymond's sudden cry turned her attention from herself to the need of the child.

By the time she and Maggie finished feeding the twins their bottles under an old tree, the kitchen was scrubbed from ceiling to floor, two women were stirring the paint, and several men were at work replacing the broken windowpanes. Isabel could not believe how much they had accomplished in such little time.

"Excuse me, miss," said a man wearing overalls. He approached Isabel as she patted the twins to sleep on an old quilt. "We were wondering if you would like a one-hole outhouse or two holes?"

"I beg your pardon?" Isabel said, cheeks flaming.

"Well," he said as he squatted down to her level, "I was thinking we would make a small one for the little children. Would that suit you?"

"Yes, sir," she said. She wondered why he had not asked Papa, but she was thankful he had not. Papa might not have remembered that the younger children feared falling in. "Thank you, that sounds good."

"Yes, ma'am," he said. "I'll put a couple of coats of paint on it too. Makes the wood smoother, you know."

His thoughtfulness brought tears to her eyes. How could all these people care about her and the other children?

About that time, another truck pulled into the yard, and several ladies Isabel didn't recognize began setting up plywood tables and loading them with food from the back of a truck. A bell rang, and the hammering ceased as sounds of conversation and laughter filled the air. Everyone gathered to pray and eat.

"Why don't you go and eat, Dear," said a woman with a kind face. "I'll sit here and watch the babies for you."

Isabel put a protective hand on the twins, not wanting to leave them with a stranger. However, Aunt Ida Mae came to the rescue with a plate of food for Isabel, and the three ladies sat with the twins and chatted.

Baby Raymond started to cry and Isabel gently picked him up, holding him on her lap. "Isabel," Aunt Ida Mae said, "you are such a good little mother to those boys. They're getting to be as big as you are."

Isabel smiled and resisted rolling her eyes at the exaggeration. She picked up her growing brother, hugging him tightly. *Grownups always say that.*

By sundown, the Greene family and Sandy were settled for the night in their freshly painted home, with furniture and everything they needed provided by strangers, friends, and family members who cared. Isabel snuggled down under a down comforter given to her by the Albright family, along with an old four-poster bed, night stands, and a dresser to match.

"I feel rich, don't you, Ralphy?" Isabel whispered to the baby lying in a cradle beside her. "It's not because of all the things, but because all those people care about us."

The next morning, she walked into her bright, clean kitchen and pulled back the red and white gingham check curtains one of the ladies had managed to sew during the lunch break, flooding the room with early morning light. She set the table with mismatched dishes and smiled. "It is just like a flower garden with blooms of every color." Isabel felt like a little girl playing house.

As she stood before the stove, she pondered the generosity of her new neighbors. The pantry was filled with food. The women had given them a "pounding" after the work was done.

"What's a poundin'?" Jimmy had said as he hid behind Papa's long legs.

"A pounding is what we call a generous donation of food by kind people," Papa had said. "They give a pound of this and a pound of that."

"What about a pound cake?" Sylvia asked. She smiled.

"It looks like we have two," Isabel said. The children cheered, which had brought tears to the eyes of the bystanders. She went to the nearest woman to thank her, and the other children followed, rewarding their guardian angels with hugs and smiles.

"Isabel," Maggie had whispered later, before crawling into bed, "do you think Mama sent those people to help us?"

Isabel stopped and thought for a minute, wondering if she should share her dream of Mama waking her up in time to see smoke in the kitchen the night of the fire, but she decided not to. "I think Jesus sent them, but maybe He let Mama watch." Maggie smiled and went to sleep.

"Thank you, Lord, for providing for us," Isabel prayed, "and for allowing Papa to keep us together as a family. Thank you, Lord, for blessing us.

Chapter 45

Feels Like Home

ISABEL DISCOVERED THAT having a daily routine made life much easier and more satisfying. She awoke every morning just before sunrise, made her bed, dressed, and slipped into the kitchen, hoping Papa already had started a fire in the old wood stove. Before preparing breakfast, she opened Mama's Bible, read a psalm, and prayed—just as Mama had done every day.

"Now, let's see," Isabel said. She headed for the kitchen to prepare breakfast. "I set the table last night and laid out the clothes for the twins and for Jimmy and Billy...so that much is done. We are planting the garden, so we will need a good breakfast, or the boys will not have enough energy to plow the land. And I have baking to do, so I will need to keep Jimmy and Billy occupied." Isabel hurried into the kitchen, pumped water into the coffee pot, and reached for the H&C Coffee. Papa liked it strong, so she added another scoop for good measure. By the time the rest of the family joined her, she had breakfast ready and two filled baby bottles waiting in hot water.

"Jimmy," she said, "do you know where your and Billy's pails and shovels are? I thought you might like to dig up a flower garden for me by the back porch. Would you like that?"

"Yes," he said. He ate his breakfast at record speed.

"Whoa, slow down there, boy," Papa said. "That flower garden ain't going anywhere before it's time to dig. We have to get our chores done first. Those chickens are counting on you to give them feed and water, you know."

"Where are you planning to get the flowers, Gal?" Papa turned to Isabel, who was feeding Raymond cereal from a tiny spoon. "I saw some violets and daffodils in the woods the other day. We could dig them up and transplant them."

"That would be wonderful," Isabel said. "Aunt Ida Mae gave me some flower seeds too. Morning Glories, pansies, and I don't know what the others are. They aren't named. She had them in an envelope. She said that she saves seeds from last year's flowers."

"Well," Papa said, "let me have a look at them, and we can decide where to put them. You will need some tall plants like gladiolas in the back, perhaps scarlet sage in front of that, and then smaller plants in front. You may want to stagger them too so off-season flowers will have room to grow. In the fall, we can plant some bulbs so we will have flowers next spring. I will plow up a few feet in front of the cabin so that we can plant there too. You know, Grandma had lilies and Iris plants growing at the corners. She had rose bushes, hydrangeas, lilacs…in fact, I spotted two lilac bushes, which should bloom in a few weeks. They're cutting bushes you know, the more you cut the blooms, the more blooms it produces. We had mountain Laurel at the side of the house and rhododendron bushes too. I don't know what happened to all of Grandma's flowers, but we can look around for some to transplant."

"Mama would have loved that," Isabel said. She blinked back the tears threatening to spill over. "Papa, may we grow some herbs too? Mama always planted parsley, sage, basil, and some mint for tea."

"I'll see what we can do," Papa said. He headed for the back door and picked up his hat from the hat rack. "It's starting to feel like home, yep, it surely is."

A few weeks later, Papa took Isabel into town to buy necessary supplies while he took the plow and the ax to be sharpened. As Isabel entered Mr. Johnson's store, she squinted for her eyes to adjust to the low light after being in the bright sunshine.

"Good morning," said a male voice from behind the counter, "I don't believe we have met. I'm Wesley Johnson. You must be one of the children from the new family in the neighborhood."

"Yes," Isabel said. "I'm Isabel Greene."

"Well, Miss Greene, welcome to the neighborhood."

"Thank you." She handed him her shopping list to fill and walked around the store looking at the merchandise as she waited.

"What kind of sugar does your mama want—granulated, brown, or confectioners?" he said.

"Granulated, please," she said. "I made out the list. My mama died a few months ago."

"Oh," Mr. Johnson said, "I'm sorry to hear that. You have my sympathy."

"Thank you," Isabel said. She wished he would hurry. She didn't want to cry in public.

"Well now, will there be anything else?" he said as he walked behind the cash register.

"Oh, yes," Isabel said, "I almost forgot. I need about three cents worth of fat back."

"What are you making?" he asked. "You do the cooking?"

"Yes, sir," she said. She used her most grownup voice, "Mama taught me how. I take care of the children and the house too, just as Mama did…well, almost. I'm not as good as Mama, you know."

"How many are in your family?"

"Nine children and Papa. The twins don't eat much though…they are just babies."

"That must be tough," he said. He stepped over to the meat case.

"We help each other," Isabel said.

"There you go, Miss Isabel Greene," he said as he laid some bundles wrapped in butcher paper on the counter. "These are for your Sunday dinner. My wife wanted to be at the pounding, but she has been under the weather lately. Consider this our contribution as a welcome to the neighborhood gift."

"Thank you, sir. That is very kind of you, but we can't accept such an expensive gift." That's what Mama always said.

"Nonsense," he said. "We want you to have it. Word is that you are kind of a hero. You saved your family from a fire?"

"I'm not a hero, sir. There was a fire, and I yelled to get everyone out of the house, that's all."

"Sounds like bravery to me," he said. "I have a granddaughter who is about your age, and it scares me to death to think of her in such a situation. However, if she were, I hope she would be able to do what you did."

"Thank you," Isabel said. "Will we see you and your wife in church tomorrow?"

"Well now, I went to church on Christmas Eve and on Easter. Isn't that enough to thank Him for giving me a profitable year?"

"He sent His Son to die on the cross for our sins, Mr. Johnson," Isabel said. "And then He arose on the third day. Doesn't He deserve more than a nod now and then? He loves you and wants you to love Him too." She hoped she hadn't offended him—especially after he just gave them such a generous gift.

"Well, since you put it that way," Mr. Johnson said with a chuckle, "I guess maybe we will be there after all."

All the way home, Isabel chided herself for speaking to the grocer so boldly.

"I just know I said everything all wrong," she said to Maggie as they cleaned up after supper.

"Oh, Isabel," Maggie said. "I think it was the Lord speaking through you. You told him the truth, and if you had told him more today, it would have been more than he wanted to hear. Maybe he will come to church and talk to Uncle Mitt and he can lead Mr. Johnson to the Lord. Did you say that his wife is sick? Maybe we should make a batch of cookies or something for them."

"I was thinking the same thing," Isabel said. She reached for the flour, sugar, and oatmeal. "Do we have any nuts and raisins left? I think oatmeal raisin cookies would be healthier than chocolate."

When Isabel entered the church building the following morning, Mr. Johnson stood up and waved to her to join him. He had saved enough seats for the entire family.

"Hi, Mr. Johnson," she said. "We made these for you and your wife. I thought if she is sick, she probably is not able to bake very often."

"You are right about that," he said. "Gladys will be tickled pink."

"Isabel," Uncle Mitt said at lunch that afternoon, "I don't know how you got Mr. Johnson to come to church, but we have been praying for him and his wife for years, and he has never accepted an invitation to church. He comes every Christmas and Easter, though, like clockwork. He told me after the service that he would like me to tell him about Jesus dying on the cross for him. I told him to expect a visit tomorrow morning, and he said he is looking forward to it."

"Thank you, Lord," Isabel whispered. "Please save him and his Gladys. And thank you for bringing us here. It really feels like home."

Chapter 46

The Letter

ISABEL WALKED THROUGH the rooms of the cottage, straightening up as she went along. She quietly opened the door of her sisters' bedroom and gently covered Sylvia and lowered the window before exiting. She opened the boys' door and gasped as she saw Sandy curled up at the foot of Jimmy and Billy's bed. "You're not supposed to be in here," she whispered as she patted the dog's head. "You can stay tonight; just don't let Papa see you." Convinced her brothers were covered and sleeping soundly, Isabel wandered back downstairs and into the kitchen, where she located a writing tablet and pencil. She had a notion to write to Sally Anne before the twins woke up.

July 28, 1925

Dear Sally Anne,

Everybody in the house is asleep now except me. Papa should be home from sweeping up at the factory soon. Did you know he is working at the Viscose Plant? The twins should wake up for their bottle any minute. They took a late nap. It's almost 11:00 P.M. now. They usually have their bottle at 9:00 P.M. and sleep till 4:00. I'm afraid when they wake up, they'll want to play and not go back to sleep. Doc said to add a little cereal in their bottles at night so that they'll sleep longer. It really works. I've been doing this since they were three and a half months old. Sometimes I feed them cereal from a spoon for breakfast, but they mostly grab for the spoon, and we get cereal everywhere. I can't believe they're over six months old now.

They have been fussy lately because of the heat. They're also getting some teeth. Yesterday, Raymond bit me. He has two teeth on the top and one on the bottom—boy, are they sharp. Papa tells me to put paregoric on their gums where they are red and swollen to numb them, but I don't. That stuff tastes *awful*. Instead, I let them chew on wet washcloths that I keep in the icebox for them, and they love chewing on cold carrots. I give them giant carrots so they can't bite a piece off and get choked. Mama taught me that trick when Billy was a baby. She always said it would "give a taste for vegetables as well as soothe sore gums." They seem to like 'em, but they put *everything* into their mouths...even Sandy's tail. Boy, I've never seen Sandy run so fast. She jumped out of the open window—don't worry, we were in the front room, and it isn't steep at all. Besides, she wasn't supposed to be in the house anyway. Papa is strict about that when he's home.

Papa made a pen to put the twins in whenever we are too busy to chase after them. They roll and scoot everywhere... they are almost crawling. They get up on their hands and knees and rock back and forth, and then they lie down and roll wherever they want to go. It looks so funny. If we sit them down on the floor, they scoot backwards on their bottoms.

It's a good thing they wear diapers, or they might just get some splinters from this old, wood floor. I always put them on the rug or a quilt, but they don't stay there. Maggie and Sylvie chase after them when I'm busy cooking or helping with the laundry. Papa and the boys took over that chore on Mondays, but I have to wash diapers almost every day. I have'ta boil 'em, you know, to get 'em clean enough to put on the babies.

You should see them, Sally Anne, they are so cute and are growing like weeds. I think Raymond will be taller than Ralph. Ralph has cute, little, chubby legs, but he can get around just as fast as his twin.

Now that it's hot, they just wear diapers, unless we have company or are going somewhere. They get too hot with clothes on and get a heat rash. The first time they broke out in red spots, I was afraid they had the measles. Aunt Ida Mae stopped by to check on us, and I'm glad she did. She checked them over and said it was just a heat rash because they got too hot. She said to "take everything off them except their diapers, and they'll be fine." She was right. In twenty minutes, the rash was gone, and the twins were smiling again.

On really hot days, we put a little bit of water from the outside pump into the clean laundry tubs and let the boys splash around in the water. (I sit them on a towel so they will not slip. I hold onto one baby, and Aunt Ida Mae holds the other. They especially like the Ivory Soap boats that Papa carved for them.) I'm glad Auntie lives close by. She comes over every day to help, and she usually brings dinner or dessert with her.

Lots of ladies from the church stop by. They usually bring food too. Papa says they are really spoiling us. Jimmy and Billy especially enjoy the treats and extra attention.

Last week when it rained, everybody got grumpy—even the babies. Maggie had been knitting a baby blanket for winter and was almost finished when little Ralph rolled over to her. She laid her needles down, and Ralphy thought they were toys. He picked them up and pulled the yarn until it completely unraveled. I thought for sure Maggie was gonna cry, but she didn't. You know Maggie, she hardly ever raises her voice—just like Mama.

"Oh no, my knitting," she said.

She reminded me of Mama the day our dog ruined Mama's clean sheets. Remember? I told ya about it. Mama said, "Oh no, my sheet," and then she turned it into a lesson about the gospel. Mama prayed with Maggie and me as we received Christ as our Savior. Later, you told us that you had listened to Mama too and had received Him as your Savior.

I miss Mama so much it hurts, and then I think of Billy and the babies and think how sad it is that they won't remember her at all. I sing them her favorite songs when I rock them to sleep and tell them that Mama will always love them.

I *really* miss Mama on days when the supper burns and the peas boil over onto the stove and it takes me an hour to clean up. I miss her laughter and singing too. She always made cleaning the kitchen after dinner as much fun as playing outside. She always got us to singing, and before we knew it, the kitchen was clean. That doesn't work for us now.

Last week when everyone had to stay inside because of the rain, the babies were teething, Billy caught a cold and wanted me to hold him all the time, and I thought of the day I came home from school and Mama was almost in tears for the same reason. I know how she felt.

Just between us, I think Mama was already sick and didn't want to worry us or Papa. Aunt Jenny said Mama never healed properly after the twins were born and that the doctor didn't do something, but she wouldn't tell me what. She said I have to wait until I'm older to understand.

Mama would be embarrassed because I can't keep the house as clean as she did. Eugene, Curtis, and the girls try to help, but we always have pots and pans on the floor for the twins to bang on. Someone gave Sylvie a tea set, and she hosts tea parties in the front room with her dolls someone gave her after the fire. Eugene carves wood in the evenings while Curtis plays music. Eugene forgets to sweep up the wood shavings or just tosses them into the fireplace. They do make the house smell good, though—like pine or cedar.

I try to clean up the kitchen right after our meals, but sometimes the babies start crying or Jimmy and Billy start fussing and I have to leave the dishes until everyone is happy again. Besides, we need Eugene or Curtis to lift the heavy iron kettle that we heat water in. I'm not strong enough to lift it myself yet.

Aunt Jenny came by yesterday, and she wasn't happy about the mess. She had it clean in no time, but I wish she hadn't. She made me feel like a little kid who can't do anything right. I am trying, Sally Anne, honest I am. She threatened to take Billy and one of the twins home with her, but Papa came in from the field, where he had been picking rocks so they can plow the field for next year.

"We are not separating the children," he told her. "Now you can go home and attend to your own house."

She left in a "huff" as Curtis said. Hope she doesn't stay mad for long. Mama didn't like it when Papa and Aunt Jenny disagreed. I'm glad he said that, though. He made us feel like we are home now.

School starts in September, but I'm not going. The babies and Billy need me. Mama would be sad because she wanted me to finish the eighth grade so we could say I finished school. She wanted all of us to finish school. I'll make sure Maggie, Sylvie, Jimmy, Billy, Ralph, and Raymond finish school. I promised the Lord that they would. Eugene finished, you know, but Curtis couldn't go back for his last year. Papa needs them at home to work the garden, chop the wood, milk the cow Uncle Mitt gave us, and take care of the fire in the stove. They have to lift the cast iron skillets because they are too heavy. This stove is taller than Mama's was, so I have to stand on a box Papa made for me so that I can reach the stove to cook.

You should see our garden; it is almost as big as Mama's, and the food is really good. Of course, I need to can the vegetables and fruit so we will have food for the winter. Aunt Ida Mae and Mrs. Langston from church promised to help me. I thought about you and how Mama had promised to teach us both how to can everything this summer. I hope Cookie will teach you. That way, we can both learn the same thing. Aunt Ida Mae has won ribbons for her pickles and other foods, but it isn't quite the same as having Mama teach us, is it?

I think I just heard the Tin Lizzie pull up into the yard, so I've gotta go for now. Thank you for the beautiful picture you sent me from your trip to Washington, D. C. Did you have a good time? Did you see the president? I can't wait to hear all about it. When are you coming to visit? Soon, I hope.

Your friend,
Isabel

Isabel folded the letter and placed it into a stamped, addressed envelope and sealed it just as Papa entered the house. "I'm glad Sally Anne's mama gave me all of these envelopes with their address and the postage already paid," she said to Papa as he hung his hat on the rack by the door.

"Seems wasteful to me," Papa said. He headed to the kitchen to partake of the meal Isabel had prepared for him. "Yep, mighty wasteful."

"Papa," Isabel said, "didn't you ever want to learn to read and write?"

"Nope," he said, "ain't got time for such nonsense."

Isabel started to reply just as the babies began to cry.

Chapter 47

A Birthday Surprise

ISABEL LOOKED AT the date on the newspaper, and her eyes filled with tears: August 24, 1925. "It's my birthday," she whispered to little Ralph, who lay quietly in her arms as he teetered between sleep and wakefulness. He jumped slightly as he edged closer to slumber, fighting to stay awake. Isabel smiled as she looked down at her eight-month-old brother and thought back in time to last year, when she had been so excited to enter the grownup world of "double digits."

"I wish Mama were here," she whispered. A tear slid down her cheek.

"I wish she were here too, Pumpkin," said a deep voice from the shadows, startling Isabel and the baby.

"Papa, I didn't know you were awake. The rooster hasn't even crowed yet," Isabel said with a hint of teasing in her voice. She rose gently from the rocker.

"No, don't worry about getting breakfast yet; it's too early," Papa said. He took the slumbering baby and laid him in his crib. "Besides, Lena is fixing a breakfast fit for a queen this morning, and she said to be sure to have you and the children at her house there in time to enjoy it while it's hot. Did you get any sleep last night? I think I heard the little ones exercising their lungs a couple of times, but they had stopped before I could get up to see to them."

"They just needed a diaper change and their regular 4:00 a.m. feeding," Isabel said. She stretched and yawned and then walked to the sink to start a pot of coffee."

"Now what did I just tell you?" Papa said with mock consternation in his voice as he watched his eleven-year-old daughter make a strong pot of coffee just the way he liked it—with nutmeg and egg shells to make even the cheapest coffee taste full and rich, just as her Mama had taught her. Isabel looked up just as he was wiping away a tear with his handkerchief.

"Something wrong, Papa?"

"Not today, child. Just had something in my eye, that's all." He wiped at his eye again and then blew his nose before folding his white cotton fabric and putting it back into his pocket.

"Well," Isabel said, "since Lena is fixing our breakfast, I'll just make some muffins to tide us over…and may be the boys will want to eat an apple with their glass of milk since they have to milk the cow and take care of the outside chores before we go. They will really be hungry, and it will take almost an hour to get to Jim and Lena's house."

"That sounds reasonable to me. Just don't tell Lena," Papa said. "She'll skin me alive if she knows I let ya'll eat before we got to her house."

Isabel rushed to get everyone dressed and ready for the trip. No sooner was she ready to step out the door than one twin needed changing and then the next. When everyone was finally squeezed into the seats of the Tin Lizzie and on the road to Roanoke, Isabel breathed a sigh of relief and enjoyed the view. She hoped it would push back the beautiful memories of her last birthday with Mama.

"Happy birthday, Isabel," rang out as Papa's Model T pulled into Jim's yard. Isabel swallowed a lump in her throat as she looked around at her older, married siblings, nieces, nephews, aunts, uncles, cousins, and grandparents waiting at such an early hour to greet her on her eleventh birthday.

"What's everybody doing here?" Isabel asked.

"We are here to celebrate your birthday with you," Grandma Betty said. "You didn't think we would forget your day just because your mother is not here, did you?"

"No, but the other children have had birthdays, and we celebrated quietly at home, with just us."

"That was because they had *you* to make their day special. We knew you would bake a cake and make a big 'to do' for them at home. Also, it was too soon, you know." Grandma Betty held her arms out to baby Raymond and was rewarded with a loud squeal. She lifted him from Isabel's arms.

"It sure is nice to eat a big ol' delicious breakfast and not have to cook it," Isabel said. She fed Ralph his soupy oatmeal, because he had not yet mastered holding a spoon.

"Well, you need not worry about cleaning up either," Lena said. "We have that covered, don't we, Gracie?" Nine-year-old Gracie smiled as she cleared the table, and Maggie jumped up to offer her assistance. Isabel just enjoyed the moment.

"Why don't all of you girls go outside and enjoy yourselves while Grandma Betty and I love on these babies for a while," Lena said. She reached for Raymond as he jumped towards her.

"Play?" Isabel said.

"Yes, play," Lena said. "You know, where you run and act silly and just be a child again."

"I think I have forgotten how."

"Well then," Grandma Betty said, "it is best that you remember while you can. Go outside and enjoy yourself."

Isabel left instructions for the twins and followed her sisters and nieces and young aunts outside to play, feeling somewhat exhilarated and yet strange to be treated as one of the children again.

"Oh, what a shame," Grandma Betty said as Isabel stepped outside the door. "The poor thing has already lost most of her childhood. If only Avil would let go of his pride and allow the children to stay with some of us until he gets back on his feet, I think everything would be OK."

"I know," Lena said, "but he's Papa. What can we do?"

Isabel did not wait to hear the answer; she already knew. There was nothing to do but to obey Papa. She shook dreary thoughts from her head and looked at the smiling faces surrounding her.

"What shall we play?" Isabel looked to Maggie, who looked to Gracie.

"Why don't we play Mother, May I?" Gracie said. She lined everyone up for the game. "Isabel, you can be mother, since it is your birthday."

Isabel stood in front of the group and took a deep breath. "OK," she said, "take one giant step forward."

"Mother, may I?"

"Yes, you may," Isabel said with a giggle. "This is fun, isn't it? I had forgotten."

It didn't take long to finish the game, and Isabel became bored with playing and was ready to go back inside to the babies.

"Oh, Isabel," Gracie said with mock dismay, "you are no fun anymore."

"I know," Isabel said. "But I promise to work on it. Maybe we can play something else later."

When Isabel entered the house, she heard Ralph crying and knew that she had been missed. Her heart swelled with love for her little brothers, who needed her so badly.

"This is the best day we have had in a long time. Thank you so much for making my birthday special," Isabel said as her birthday cake was presented after supper. Not only were there gifts for Isabel, but also there were trinkets for each of the children, including the babies, who were happy just playing with the paper and boxes.

"This is just like Christmas," Jimmy said. He jumped up and down with excitement. "Except without the Christmas tree and the snow." Everyone joined him in laughter.

Before she had time to blow out the candles, a car horn sounded outside. "Who could that be," Jim said as he answered the front door.

"Only your best friend in the world," said a cheerful voice from the foyer.

"Sally Anne!" Isabel ran to greet her friend and found that she was not alone. She had brought her parents, a new baby brother, Cookie, and Arlene Mason.

"Arlene, this is a surprise," Isabel said as she tried to hide her shock. "Thank you for coming."

"You are welcome, Isabel," Arlene said. "I came to apologize for being so mean to you before. I hope you will forgive me."

Isabel sensed that she really meant it. "Of course, Arlene," she said. She hugged her new friend. "This is the best birthday ever. Come inside everyone, and have some cake and ice cream before the boys eat it all."

"Isabel," Mrs. Albright said, "we have something for you from your mother. She wanted you to have this. She made the arrangements months ago, before the twins were born. I hope you like it." Mrs. Albright handed Isabel a large, handsomely wrapped gift box that was tied with a large, satin bow.

Isabel's hands trembled as she pulled the ribbon and opened the box. Inside the tissue paper lay a beautiful drop-waist dress, just as Isabel had seen in the windows at the stores in Roanoke. "How did you know?" Isabel said. She choked back her tears.

"Your mama asked me to buy the fabric and pattern for her several months ago. She did some sewing for me to pay for it, even though I offered to pay the cost myself. She wanted to make it for you, but she fell ill. So I had my dressmaker make it for you. I knew Lizzie would want you to have it for your birthday. No one in the school will have this fabric…it came all the way from New York."

"Oh, thank you, Mrs. Albright!" She ran to her benefactress with a tearful hug. "This is the most beautiful dress I have ever owned. Mama would be so happy if she could see it."

"Well, keep looking, and you will discover a few more surprises from Sally Anne, Mr. Albright, and me."

Isabel lifted the dress and underneath found beautiful gifts to match the dress. "Oh, look at this beautiful shawl. It goes perfectly." Isabel examined the lace wrap. "There is also a handbag and a headband. Thank you so much. You were too generous."

"There are also some under things," Sally Anne said, "but you do not want to show those." Her announcement brought laughter and good-natured teasing from the Greene boys.

"This isn't much, Isabel," Arlene said. She held out a small, white box. "I saw it in the store, and it reminded me of you. I hope you like it."

Isabel opened the box and found a small pin with daffodils hand painted on it.

"Oh, Arlene," Isabel said. "It is lovely. How did you know I like daffodils?"

"Well," Arlene said, "I saw you pick one at your mama's funeral and put it into your Bible. I thought the flower must remind you of her."

"It does," Isabel said with tears in her eyes, "and now they will remind me of you too. Thank you for remembering."

"We miss you, Isabel," Arlene said.

"I miss you too," Isabel said. She realized she had even missed Arlene Mason.

"OK," Aunt Jenny said. She had a box camera in her hands. "Isabel, I want to get a photograph of you with your little friends so you can remember this day. Then we will take photographs of everyone before it gets too dark."

So Isabel stood with her friends for the moment to be captured on film and cherished forever.

Isabel joined her family in Papa's car just as the sun was beginning to set upon the day. "Thank you, Papa, for such a beautiful day. I'll never forget it." Isabel cuddled Raymond in her arms and sat back in her seat to remember her first birthday without Mama, and yet, Mama's presence seemed to permeate the day. She breathed a prayer of thanksgiving for Mama, for Papa, and for a loving family and friends, asking a special blessing upon each person.

Chapter 48

Growing Pains

"BILLY, JUST LOOK at those pants; they are much too short and a little tight too," Isabel said as she got him ready for church. "Maybe I can get Aunt Ida Mae or Aunt Jenny to teach me how to sew some more. You and Jimmy are outgrowing everything."

Isabel fretted all day about the children's clothing. School would start in a few weeks, and everyone needed clothing that would fit and be appropriate for school. It seemed that Sylvia had grown faster than anyone. Isabel let out the hems on all her dresses, and they were still too short. Maggie was not far behind. "I don't need anything new," she said. "Eugene and Curtis will need new coats this year, but the rest of their clothing is fine for now."

However, the rest of the children need everything. What was not too small was worn out. Ralph and Raymond were growing like weeds too. Their dressing gowns were way above their knees. They would need warm clothing when the weather changed.

Isabel smiled at the babies, who were playing on an old quilt. Not only were they sitting up, but also they were practicing getting on their hands and knees and rocking back and forth.

She expected them to crawl any day. Papa also had noticed and warned her that they would soon be into everything.

"We won't have a moment's peace once these two are maneuvering around the cabin," he said. You'd better put away anything that might break and move anything that could fall on them."

Later, when she was alone in the cabin with the twins, she crawled around on the floor, looking for anything that could present a danger to them.

"Don't pull yourself up on this small table, boys. It might topple over with you." She moved the table to the corner of the room and placed Papa's chair in front of it. Her two energetic brothers rewarded her with smiles and baby kisses.

Isabel continued to fret over clothing for the children, but a quick glance at the coffee can bank in the cupboard indicated they were broke.

But my God shall supply all your need according to His riches in glory by Christ Jesus...

Isabel quoted this verse each time she thought of their need. Finally, when Isabel picked up the ash can for Curtis to empty, she had a thought.

"Curtis," she said, "did you and Eugene check the floorboards?"

"What floorboards, Sis?" Curtis said.

"The floorboards in the kitchen at home," she said. "Mama kept a small tin under the kitchen floorboard, where the ash can sits. I saw her put some money in it once."

"Did Papa know about it?" he asked.

"No," Isabel said, "I don't think so. Mama said to tell no one. The money was hers. She had made a tablecloth for Mrs. Albright."

"This is important, Isabel," Curtis said, "when did she put the money under the floorboards? Was it before or after we bought new shoes last year?"

"After," Isabel said. "It was just before the boys were born. I think she may have been saving money for Christmas, but, of course, the twins were born early, and we did not have a regular Christmas. Remember how sad she was because she could not prepare Christmas for us and how she cried when we decorated the small tree that you cut?"

"Yeah," Curtis said, "and you tried to cook a turkey and forgot to clean it out first."

"The potatoes and vegetables were good," Isabel said, smiling at her mistake, "and you did not complain about dessert either."

"Mrs. Meadows came by on Christmas Eve with a large basket of food and a small gift for each of us," Eugene said. He had just entered the kitchen. "Are we planning for Christmas already?"

"No," Curtis said. "Did you know Mama hid money in the old house? Isabel just remembered that Mama put some money in a tin under the floorboards in the kitchen."

"She had a hiding spot in the cellar too," Eugene said. "I cannot believe we did not remember it before now."

"Do you think it is still there?" Isabel asked. She held her breath and crossed her fingers behind her back.

"There's only way to find out. We'll just have to go back and look," Eugene said.

"Should we tell Papa?" Isabel asked. "Mama said she was hiding the money because Papa would use the money for tires or gasoline for the Tin Lizzie, and we needed it for Christmas."

"He would have too," Curtis said. "He bought that automobile with our school clothes money that Mama had saved from her sewing."

"Tomorrow, Curtis and I will take the horses and look for the money," Eugene said. "I'm sure Mama would want you to buy school clothes for the children with it. There's no need to tell Papa until the shopping is done. Besides, he is too busy working two jobs to worry about clothes. We will tell Mr. Meadows and ask his permission to look around."

Early the next morning, the boys left the house after Papa went to work. Isabel prayed for the boys as they traveled and thanked the Lord in advance for providing for their needs.

The boys returned several hours later with smiles on their faces and money in their pockets.

"Mama had several hiding places," Eugene said. "There was two dollars in coins under the kitchen floorboard, ten dollars behind the potato bin, and I dug up the tin in the cellar floor that I knew about. There was twenty dollars in that one. We will be able to clothe the children and put the rest away for emergencies. After we tithe, that is."

"What about the doctor bill?" Isabel said, fearing the worst.

"We went by his house office, and he said the bill had been taken care of."

"Isn't the Lord good?" Curtis said. He brushed away a tear with his sleeve. "He and Mama provided for us a long time ago, and we didn't even know it. Papa will be relieved too."

The following Sunday, Uncle Mitt and Aunt Ida Mae came for a visit after church, bringing a basket filled with fried chicken and potato salad. Isabel had baked a pie, and everyone enjoyed the dinner. After dinner, Papa and Uncle Mitt headed for the front porch while Aunt Ida Mae helped the girls clean the kitchen.

"Thank you for fixing dinner," Isabel said as she passed the last dish to Maggie to dry.

"You're welcome," Aunt Ida Mae said. "We enjoy our little visits. Is that the twins I hear crying? They had a short nap, didn't they?"

Isabel started for the room to get the babies, but Aunt Ida Mae volunteered. "I just love taking care of those adorable boys."

Isabel smiled and rinsed out the dishrag and pulled a pitcher of iced tea out of the icebox. Suddenly, she heard a commotion and turned to see little Ralph crawling toward the hot stove. Aunt Ida Mae, Papa, and Uncle Mitt were chasing him, but they were too far away. To her horror, the baby reached out as he neared the hot oven door. Isabel leaped in front of the stove to catch him. As she did, her foot caught on the rag rug, and she fell. Searing pain engulfed Isabel as she realized that in trying to protect her brother from being burned, she had fallen against the oven door, burning her forehead. She cried out in pain. She felt herself being carried out of the kitchen. She felt sick to her stomach, and voices around her echoed as the room seemed to grow dark.

"Put butter on it," Aunt Ida Mae said.

"No, not butter," Uncle Mitt said. "Put ice water on it."

"Mama put cold tea on burns," Maggie insisted.

Isabel opened her eyes in time to see Papa dunking her clean dishcloth into the pitcher of iced tea. He wrung it out and placed it on Isabel's head. "Hold still, Isabel," Papa said. He held the cool cloth on the burn, causing more pain.

Isabel wanted to scream, but she could hardly breathe. "Ralph," she whispered, "where's Ralph? Did he get burned too?"

"No, Ralph is alright. He's in his crib. You saved him, just like a hero," Curtis said with a hint of admiration.

Papa dipped the cloth into the tea a second time and placed it back on her head. "Just what in tarnation did you think you were doing anyway?"

"I was just trying to keep Ralph away from the stove," Isabel said. Tears began to flow. "I tripped and fell. He didn't get burned, did he?"

"No," Papa said. "But you certainly did. Let's get you to the Doc's before this gets infected or scars."

"You go ahead and take her," Aunt Ida Mae said. "Mitt and I will stay here and watch the youngsters."

Isabel closed her eyes and gave in to the pain. When she opened them, she was on an examination table at the doctor's home office.

"I'm afraid she'll have a scar, Mr. Greene," she heard the doctor say. "How did this happen?"

Papa explained that Aunt Ida Mae had changed one twin and sat him on the floor while she attended his brother. "That little rascal just took off crawling through the house faster than a train. I've never seen him move that fast. Mitt and I were just coming back into the house when we saw the little guy heading straight for the kitchen with Ida Mae running after him. She had Raymond in her arms. Curtis sprinted after him too, but the baby was just too fast. Isabel was in the kitchen and must have seen him coming and tripped on the rug, landing smack dab with her head on the hot oven door. It could have been the baby, but Isabel saved his life."

"I understand the children are often alone, unsupervised," the doctor said. He removed the tea-soaked cloth from Isabel's head.

"I'm home every morning, preparing the fields for the next planting season, and I then go to work at the Viscose plant after lunch. I'm home by midnight. When I am away, Eugene and Curtis are always there, along with relatives and neighbors who come by every day to help. Isabel wasn't taking care of the twins alone when this happened. Three adults, two older boys, and two other little girls were trying to catch that child. It was a terrible accident."

"Indeed," the doctor said. He shook his head. "This accident should not have happened. I'll do what I can, but it will most likely leave a scar that she will have to live with the rest of her life. I want to keep her here overnight to make sure it doesn't get infected. I'll give her something for pain, so she should sleep for several hours."

Isabel saw the doctor's wife, who was a nurse, cross the room with a hypodermic needle in her hand, flinched as she felt a sharp pinch, and then felt as if she were floating. Then sleep engulfed her.

Isabel moaned and tried to open her eyes, but they refused. She didn't know how long she had slept, but she felt the pain on her forehead. Voices from the other room reached her consciousness.

"I'm staying with her, Doc."

"There's no need for that. She should sleep all night."

"That's alright," Papa said. "I'm staying anyway."

"Mr. Greene," the doctor said, "how long have you had that pain in your chest?"

"Just indigestion," Papa said. "A little bicarbonate soda does the trick."

"And just how long have you been having this 'indigestion'?"

"Oh, a few months, I suppose. It comes and goes."

"Let me take a look."

Isabel remembered seeing Papa rubbing his chest and taking a glass of bicarbonate soda almost every night, saying that it was just indigestion. The first time he asked for the soda, she had giggled as he gulped the fizzing water and then sustained a long, loud burp.

"Maybe we should give that to the babies instead of patting their backs," she said at the time.

"Oh no," Papa said. "Don't give this to the babies."

"I'm just joshin' ya, Papa."

Now, as Isabel lay on the bed in the doctor's office, it no longer seemed funny. *Is Papa sick?* She drifted back to sleep.

When she awoke the next morning, Papa was sleeping in a chair beside her bed. He looked pale and gaunt. He must have felt her gaze upon him, for he awoke suddenly, jumped out of his chair, and ran for the doctor.

"How are ya doing, child?" Papa asked as he entered the room with the doctor close behind him.

"I'm OK, Papa," she said. She reached up to touch the bandage on her head.

"You'll need to keep it bandaged a while," the doctor said. "I'll try to get by every afternoon to change the bandage. We don't want it to get infected."

Isabel nodded slightly. "Will it show?"

"Yes," the doctor said. "It will leave a scar. I don't know how prominent it will be, but once it has healed, you can wear bangs to hide it. However, don't think of this as an ugly scar. It's really a beautiful badge of courage. You sacrificed your life for that of your little brother."

"Nah," Isabel said, "I was just trying to keep him from getting hurt, and I tripped and fell. I didn't throw myself against the stove or anything like that."

"Still," the doctor said, "you were injured protecting the baby. That makes you a hero. Remember your little brother whenever you are tempted to feel bad about the scar. It's really a sign of love, and as I said before, it's a badge of courage. Now, after you and your papa eat the breakfast my wife has prepared for you, you may pick out a candy stick for yourself and one for each of your brothers and sisters. Then you are free to go home."

"Go home," Isabel said. "I want to go home."

Chapter 49

Unwelcome Visitor

ISABEL HAD JUST put the twins down for their nap when there was a knock at the door. She pulled back the curtain to see who had come to visit. Most of the neighbors and family members knew the babies napped in the afternoon and never knocked at the door, fearing they would wake them.

"Who's here?" Eugene asked. He took the last bite of lunch and gulped a glass of milk.

"I don't know," Isabel whispered. "I don't recognize the car."

"Well," Eugene said, "let me open the door. It's probably a vacuum cleaner salesman or the Fuller brush man. Just as he opened the door, a woman's voice permeated the peace of the Greene home.

"Is Mr. Greene home?" The woman said. She took a step toward the entrance while Eugene and Curtis blocked the doorway. "May I come in?"

"No, ma'am," Eugene said in his most grown-up voice. "Papa is at work, and we are not allowed to let strangers in."

"Please tell him that Miss Grover from the Virginia Social Services stopped by and that I must see him immediately," she said. She unsuccessfully attempted to pass by the boys and step into the room. "Why aren't you in school?"

"I am fifteen years old, ma'am," he said. "I finished the eighth grade last year."

"What about the other boy and the little girl? And who is taking care of the small children?"

"You will have to talk to my papa, ma'am. Good-bye." Eugene closed the door on the astounded woman and locked it. The children watched her drive away, leaving behind three frightened children.

Papa returned home earlier than usual that evening. Isabel was just putting dinner on the table. "Children," he said, "we can't stay here any longer. The state wants to take you away. Some woman hunted me down when I was digging ditches near the Hotel Roanoke. She tried to get me to put my mark on some paper, but I refused. She said to have you ready to go with her first thing tomorrow morning."

"Papa," Isabel said, "what are we going to do?"

"There's only one thing that I can do," Papa said. His face went ashen. "She said the only way to keep you is to get married so that you will have a mama. You will stay with Widow Barker tomorrow, and we will get married on Wednesday. She has already agreed to it."

"Oh, Papa," Isabel said. "Widow Barker? You would do that for us?"

"A papa will do anything for his youngins," he said with a shaky voice. "After we eat, we will pack only the things you really need. I can come and pick up the rest of our things later."

The children arose and dressed before dawn. No one tasted the breakfast Isabel had made for them. Each one complained of a tummy ache, and Isabel tried her best to console them, yet dreaded the move as much as they did.

"Now, Isabel, you and Curtis must go to school, just like you used to. Mrs. Barker will keep the little ones until you get home.

"Yes, Papa," Isabel said. "It will be nice to see my friends again, but I don't think I can leave the babies and Billy."

"You have to, Belle," Papa said. "Our future depends upon it."

Isabel turned for one last look at the cabin and cried. "We were so happy here. Why can't the state woman just leave us alone? This is the first time we have really felt like we had a home since Mama died."

"We didn't even get to say 'goodbye' to our friends," Maggie said as they turned to look at their cabin home one last time.

Chapter 50

Sad Little Ducklings

AFTER SCHOOL, ISABEL and Curtis literally ran all the way to Widow Barker's house, followed closely by Maggie and Sylvia.

As they stepped into the yard, they heard strange noises coming from the house. Sandy was tied to a tree and was barking and growling at the house. Suddenly, Billy screamed, and then they heard Jimmy crying for help. They ran up the steps and burst through the door in time to see Mrs. Barker beating Billy with a leather strap. Jimmy was trying to take it away from her.

Without thinking, Isabel leaped forward, putting herself between Billy and the strap. She felt her skin tearing and whelps swelling up from the back of her neck to her ankles. It seemed like hours before Curtis was able to wrestle the weapon from her hands, and yet Isabel knew it was only a matter of seconds.

"Billy, Jimmy, run outside," Isabel heard herself say as the angry woman reached out to grab the boys. "Run!" The woman grabbed Jimmy's shirt, but he kicked her, and she let go.

"Brats, that's all you kids are," the irate woman screamed and reached for the fireplace poker.

Just as she raised the poker over Isabel's head, Curtis and Eugene, who had just arrived after running an errand, managed to corner the woman and were trying to take the poker from her as she tried to hit them with it.

"Why are you doing this?" Isabel said. "What did they do?"

"Enough. Take your hands off my children this instant."

"Papa," Isabel said. She ran with Billy into his outstretched arms. He walked her onto the front porch and sat her down on the glider with the other children, who were huddled together crying.

"If you ever lay a finger against any of my children," she heard Papa say to the woman, "you will wish you had never been born. Look in the Bible to see how God deals with people who hurt children. You'll pay for this. You'll see!"

"Children," Papa said, "gather your sacks. We're leaving."

Isabel and Maggie picked up the twins. Curtis picked up Billy. Eugene picked up the burlap sacks containing their things. Sylvia helped Jimmy, who could not seem to be able to move at first. Papa stepped off the porch, and the children followed him down the road in a single line, like ducklings following their mama.

"Papa," Eugene said, "where are we going?"

"We will spend the night at Jim's house tonight, and then only God knows where we will go from there."

Chapter 51

A Dark Day

THE FOLLOWING DAY, Papa, Eugene, Isabel, and the twins were in the Model T returning to Jim's house from a trip to Bent Mountain, where Papa had heard of a job, when the sky opened up. The top was up on the Ford, but rain was coming through anyway. The roads were filling up with water quickly. A tire blew, and Papa used all his muscles to keep the car from slamming into a big oak tree. He pulled to a stop and got out to assess the damage.

"The wheel is ruined, and I don't have a spare," Papa said. He walked around the automobile. "What could possible happen next?"

Suddenly, the door to the house at the end of the road opened, and a man came out carrying an umbrella. "Need some help?"

"Got a flat but no spare," Papa said. "I'm feeling old and foolish. I should have replaced the last one."

"I just happen to have one in the barn," the man said. "Got a newer model now. And forgot to give the spare to the buyer. Why don't we take the children into the house, where it's warm?

Martha will have them dried and fed in no time." He offered a hand to Isabel.

Isabel quietly watched Mrs. Mason as she hurried around the kitchen. She had a meal prepared in no time. She sat so much food on the table that it caused Isabel to look around for the rest of the brood.

"Surely all this food ain't for just us," Eugene whispered.

"I think it is. Don't see signs of anybody else," Isabel said.

Martha turned around as Isabel spoke and rushed over to the table. Eugene had left Ralph on the floor. He didn't notice the child was crawling toward the fireplace. Martha scooped him up in her arms and brushed a kiss against his soft hair. He giggled and showed a small dimple as he did.

"I love babies," Martha said. She sat down with the child and began feeding him mashed carrots with a teaspoon.

Isabel followed her example and began feeding Raymond.

"Mr. Mason and I have always prayed for children, but God hasn't blessed us. Your mama is truly blessed with four beautiful children like yourselves," she continued.

"Our mama's dead," Eugene said. He turned his head to hide his tears.

"Oh, I'm sorry," Martha said. "I didn't know. I wouldn't have said anything to cause you pain." She wiped Ralph's chin with the corner of her napkin.

"That's OK, Mrs. Mason," Isabel said. "You didn't know. Anyway, there are nine of us in all. The rest are at our brother Jim's house. Papa had some things to do today and couldn't fit us all in the car at once."

Mrs. Mason smiled sympathetically and finished feeding the baby. "It feels so good to have a child in my arms. I almost wish the meal would never end. I love having children in my kitchen, around the table."

The door opened, and the men stepped inside. There was rain dripping off their hats.

"Come on in and have some dinner, Mr. Greene," Martha said. She sat two clean plates on the table and poured coffee for the men. She had passed the baby to Eugene, who was trying to keep his little brother from pulling the tablecloth off the table—food, dishes, and all.

The men began eating in silence. Each occupied by his own thoughts. Papa apparently had told Mr. Mason about his situation as they repaired the car.

Eugene watched both men when suddenly, there was a soft thud at the end of the table. Baby Ralph had fallen asleep, and his head hit the edge of the table.

"Why the poor little thing," Martha said. She ran and picked him up, cuddling him close. "They must be plumb worn out." She spoke to no one in particular. "They need to go to sleep." She began swaying back and forth with the child in her arms. He closed his eyes and was soon sound asleep.

"You want 'em?" Papa asked.

The room fell silent. Isabel could not breathe.

"Mr. Greene, what are you saying?" Martha whispered.

"I'm saying that you can have them if you want them. They need a Mama, and you need youngins. Only you have to keep both of them; they're twins and need to stay together. I know you will love them like they are your own. Mr. Mason told me that you have always wanted children, and he has already promised to be good to them," said Papa. He took a sip of coffee as if to close the subject.

"Papa!" Eugene and Isabel cried in unison. They could not believe what had just come out of their father's mouth.

Surely he will not give the babies away! He couldn't! Only a monster could give his children away as if they were puppies or kittens! Mama's *babies, how could he? How can we ever live, knowing our brothers are living with strangers?* It was all too horrible for Isabel to think about.

"Eugene," she whispered with tears running down her cheeks, "please tell me this is just a nightmare. Tell me this isn't happening!" Isabel wanted to wake up and hear Mama singing softly in the kitchen as she fried bacon and scrambled eggs for breakfast. However, it was not a dream; it was real. Papa had just given the twins to the Masons, and Isabel and her other brothers and sisters may never see them again!

"Oh, Mama!" cried Isabel's heart. "How can we go on without you? What are we going to do? I cannot stand it! This is too horrible to happen to anyone!"

Isabel turned to Mrs. Mason with tears in her eyes and asked to hold her brothers one last time. As she did, she whispered words of love into their ears. Pudgy hands reached up to touch the tears on her face.

"Sometimes, they get earaches. If they are crying for no apparent reason and are pulling on their ears, put a drop of warm sweet oil into that ear. Not too hot, though," she warned.

"Thank you, Isabel. I'll remember that," said Mrs. Mason as she gently took the baby from Isabel. Raymond cried and reached for Isabel as Mrs. Mason turned away with the child.

"Ithy," Raymond screamed as Papa ushered Isabel through the door, and Isabel felt as if her heart were breaking. "Did you hear that, Eugene? He said my name; he called me 'sissy,'" she whispered softly, "and I'll never forget it."

Eugene nodded, patted Isabel on the back, and then rushed through the door.

"Don't worry about the twins. We will take good care of them," Mrs. Mason promised as Isabel walked onto the porch and out of the twin's lives with the babies' cries ringing in her ears.

"Eugene," Papa said. "Get behind the wheel while I crank her up."

"I ain't doing anything," Eugene said as he slammed the passenger door. "Do it yourself."

"Don't cross me, boy," Papa said. "You know it takes two people to get this contraption started. Now do as I say."

Eugene continued sitting with his arms crossed, looking out of the window toward the Mason house, refusing to move or even to acknowledge Papa.

"Gal," Papa said to Isabel, "get behind the wheel, and do as I tell you...*now!*"

Isabel slid behind the large wheel and looked at the instruments on the dashboard, trying to remember what Eugene and Curtis pulled in the past while Papa cranked the car to get it started.

"Just do as I say, and we'll get this ol' jalopy going," Papa said.

Soon the car was running, and Isabel breathed a sigh of relief, only to notice the emptiness of her arms and lap without the twins.

The ride home was long and difficult, as memories of Mama and the babies took residence in her mind. She sensed anger brewing in her brother as he continually shifted in his seat and tapped his feet as if he were in a great hurry. As soon the automobile pulled into the yard, Eugene opened the door and dashed to the barn.

Papa opened the door for Isabel, and they silently ascended the steps and entered their home, where music and laughter greeted them. Curtis laid aside his guitar, Maggie pulled the popcorn popper out of the fire, and the room fell silent.

"Where are Eugene and the twins?" Curtis asked. He stepped toward Papa.

"Eugene is in the barn," Papa said. "And the twins are at home with their new family."

Curtis raised his fist in Papa's face and then ran past him into the night.

"It's for the best," Papa said. He strode directly to the room Jim had indicated would be his and the boys' bedroom and shut the door.

The children, Jim, and Lena gathered around Isabel on the front room rug.

"Isabel, what happened?" Maggie asked.

Isabel pulled little Billy onto her lap, with Jimmy leaning against her. She whimpered as she told them what happened.

Sylvia spoke up. "Will Papa give us away too, Sis?"

"I don't know Sylvie. I just don't know."

"Papa did what he thought was best for the boys," Jim said with tears in his eyes. "Maybe we should all get some sleep. It has been a rough day. Tomorrow will seem brighter."

Chapter 52

Changes

THE FOLLOWING MORNING, the children silently piled into Papa's Tin Lizzie for the long ride to Aunt Jenny's house in Roanoke, where they were to spend the day.

"Why are we going to Aunt Jenny's house today?" Sylvia whispered as the car lurched forward.

Papa didn't speak a word during the trip, and upon arrival, he merely opened the door for the children and drove off. Isabel had not slept the night before and suspected no one else had either.

"I reckon your papa didn't want a cup of coffee," Aunt Jenny said as the children walked into the large, white frame house. "Go on into the kitchen, children, and have a glass of milk. I made fresh banana nut muffins just for you."

"Thank you, Aunt Jenny," they said.

"Isabel," Sylvia whispered, "I'm not hungry. My tummy hurts."

"I know," Isabel said, "mine does too, but it will hurt Aunt Jenny's feelings if we don't eat one."

"Alright, Isabel," Sylvia said, "but I don't have to *like it*, do I?"

"No, Sylvie, you don't have to like it, but be pleasant for Aunt Jenny," Isabel said. "Can you do that?

"I think so," Sylvia said.

"Now," Aunt Jenny said, entering the kitchen and picking up Billy to sit him into a high chair, "where are the twins? Did your papa leave them with Jim and Lena?"

"No, Aunt Jenny," Isabel said. "Papa gave them away last night."

"What do you mean, he gave them away? To whom?"

"Papa gave them to a family near Bent Mountain, where our car broke down. They didn't have children, so Papa told them they could have the twins. How could he do it, Aunt Jenny?"

Aunt Jenny walked onto the front porch and sat down as if in a daze. "He just gave them to strangers?" She sat for a long time, apparently fighting for control. "I'm sure he did what he thought was best for the babies." Her voice cracked, and she pulled a hankie out of her pocket, blew her nose, and stood up. "We can't do anything about it now. Let's see if the other children need anything."

Isabel stood glued to the floor. What could they do? Would Papa give them all away? Her stomach churned, and she ran to the nearest bush. It was several minutes before she felt well enough to join the rest in the kitchen. They were making plans to keep busy.

"Curtis and I can help with the farm, Aunt Jenny," Eugene said. He reached for another muffin and asked for another glass of milk. "Have any wood to be split?"

"A whole cord of wood was delivered yesterday," Aunt Jenny said as she refilled his glass.

"Me too," Jimmy said with his chest puffed out. "I can chop wood, can't I, Sis?"

Isabel smiled and pulled her brother close. "You are really good at carrying kindling into the house. Maybe you could help that way."

"Sylvia and I can gather eggs and feed the chickens," Maggie said. Her smile was clearly forced.

"I will help you in the kitchen and take care of Billy," Isabel said as brightly as she could.

"I thought perhaps you would like to play outside or visit Ginny and Tina," Aunt Jenny said. "Pa said they are looking forward to spending the day with you."

"Maybe later," Isabel said without enthusiasm. Normally, she would love to play with her young aunts, but this was a sad day. It seemed that Papa was searching for people to take in the children.

After the children left to do their chores, Isabel finally broached the subject of Ralph and Raymond. "It was horrible, Aunt Jenny," Isabel said. "Papa just gave them to strangers, as if they were just puppies or kittens."

"I know it must have seemed that way, Isabel, but your papa was really showing his love for the babies by finding a home for them with both a mama and a papa who would love them and care for them as if they were their very own."

"But that's just it," Isabel said with irritation edging her voice. "Papa did not know these people. They are strangers to us. The automobile broke down in front of their house. He didn't look for them or spend time with them to see what they are like. They might be mean most of the time and were just acting nice because we were there, like ol' Widow Barker. Why can't they live with you, Aunt Jenny?"

Aunt Jenny dabbed her eyes with the corner of her apron and took a sip of water before speaking. "I would like nothing better than to raise those precious babies, Isabel, but your papa made his choice. Besides, you know how your Uncle Don is around babies…they make him uncomfortable."

"But he likes Billy," Isabel said. She wiped crumbs from Billy's face and washed his hands with a washcloth.

"Yes," Aunt Jenny said as she smiled at the boy, "he loves Billy, and Billy loves him too. As for the Masons, you know, your papa may have known them a long time ago. Just because you do not know them doesn't mean he doesn't. Where did you say they live?"

"At the foot of Bent Mountain...Martin's Creek, I think is what Papa called it."

"What were you doing there?" Aunt Jenny asked.

"Papa said he heard of someone hiring boys to help at their apple orchard and thought maybe they would hire Eugene. You know how much he loves trees." Isabel rolled her eyes. "Papa said they needed to prune the trees or something like that, and then they will need apple pickers in the fall."

"Oh," Aunt Jenny said. "It sounds like your papa has it all planned out."

"Has what planned, Aunt Jenny?" Isabel asked. "I don't like this."

"Isabel, have you stopped to wonder why the automobile broke down at that very house?"

"Well, no," Isabel said. "Why?"

"Perhaps," Aunt Jenny said, "it was God's divine providence. Maybe He planned it that way."

"I never thought of it that way. Do you think He wanted the Masons to be Ralph and Raymond's new family?"

"Yes, that is exactly what I think."

"It is just so hard, Aunt Jenny. Ralph and Raymond are our brothers, and we love them. It feels like Papa has cut out two pieces of my heart and nothing will ever be the same."

Chapter 53

Papa's Solution

"NO!" ISABEL SAID. She watched Papa gather Sylvia's belongings into a satchel, including the doll Mama had made for her. "You cannot give Sylvia to the Meadows; you can't." It was unthinkable that Papa would even consider allowing her sister to live with another family. She looked at Eugene and marveled that he had not lost his temper. His face turned beet red, and his hands were pumping into a fist and flexed out again. Isabel was afraid he might hit Papa, and she knew for his own sake as well as the family's, this must not happen. She slowly stepped in front of her brother to prevent him from doing anything foolish.

"I don't want to do it, Gal. Can't ya see that? If I don't find homes for you all, the state will come, take all of you, and put you in an orphanage, and we may never see any of you again. It won't take long for that woman to figure out where we are. Is that what you want?" Papa turned toward Isabel, his eyes bulging, and the vein on his neck seemed to Isabel as if it were ready to explode. These truths muddled her thinking as he waited for her answer. He massaged his chest. "Well, is it?"

"Of course not, Papa," she said. How could he think she would want that? "What does the state have to do with us? Why can't we just live as we always have, at Grandpa Greene's cabin? I can take care of the children. I will do my best to make sure everyone gets enough to eat, have them ready for school, faces and hands always clean, the house perfect, and…" The gravity of her words filled the room. Her sisters rushed to comfort her, and her young brothers gently patted her head and arms.

Papa rushed to his eldest daughter with lightning speed, as if he were seeing for the first time the pressures he had placed upon her young, tender shoulders. "It's not that simple, child. You were home when that state woman came right to our door, threatening to take you away. Don't you remember? You can't do the impossible. You are a child. You should be in school. You are not your mama, no matter how hard you try, but how we love you for it." Papa wrapped his arms around Isabel as he spoke with muffled emotions.

"We have tried everything in our power to stay together," Papa continued. "I have tried and failed. I have allowed you children to stay home from school to run the household as if you were adults, and I jeopardized your future. That was wrong. Isabel, you tried to raise infant twins on your own when you are only a child, and that was unfair to you and unhealthy as well. You must understand that it broke Papa's heart as much as it did yours to have to find a home for little Ralph and Raymond, but now they have a mama who can properly care for them. I hope this is only temporary for them too. I will never allow them to be adopted. They will always be part of our family. We shall be together again someday.

"Then we tried to find a new mama for you, but well, you remember how that went. I promise you, we will never be with someone who will lay a hand on you. Papa will not permit anyone to harm you in any way. They will have to answer to me."

"We never liked her anyway, Papa," Maggie said.

"I'll say," Curtis said.

"This is the only solution I can find to keep you safe," Papa said. "I will give you some time alone together at your mama's grave to say 'goodbye,' and then I will come to take you to your new homes." Papa left to get the car.

Isabel felt as if her world were crashing around her. She looked around the room and recognized the emotion etched in each face. *This cannot be happening*, but it was. Papa was giving her away. He was giving all of them away, and she trembled with fear of their unknown futures.

"What will happen to us?" Maggie whispered.

"Our heavenly Father will take care of us," Curtis said.

"But who will take care of Papa?" Maggie asked.

Isabel suddenly realized that she did not care what happened to him. "What difference does it make, Maggie? Papa has given up and is getting rid of us, so why should we care about him?" Yet, even as she said the words, she knew that she did care.

"He is our papa, Isabel," Curtis said. "No matter what he does, he will always be our papa and we love him and must give him our respect. Mama would want us to."

Isabel nodded. He was right. Mama would want her to love and respect Papa no matter what. Suddenly, her mind flashed back to the time Mama had told her about Papa's difficult childhood and had asked Isabel to promise to try to understand him.

"I'm sorry," she said. "I shouldn't have said that about Papa. I do love him. I just don't like him very much right now."

"None of us like what he is doing," Eugene said, "but he really thinks this is the only way he can keep his promise to Mama that we will not be put into an orphanage. It looks like we will be apart for a while, so I want you all to know that I am glad you are my brothers and sisters." Then he rushed from the house.

Chapter 54

Arrows of Blessing

"DANDELION SEEDS—THAT IS what we are. We are just like dandelion seeds scattered all over Virginia," Isabel said. "Papa is finding homes for us all over the Roanoke Valley, and we will not be together. We will be scattered, just like old dandelion seeds."

As she spoke, Jimmy pulled away and ran just out of sight, returning with a handful of fluffy dandelions. With tears streaming down his face, he stepped on his mother's grave, blowing seeds gently over the soft, green mound.

"Now Mama will have her dandy lions with her always."

"Yes, Jimmy, Mama will always have her dandelions," Isabel said through her tears.

"Her blessings," Eugene said.

"What?" said the children in unison.

"Mama said we are her blessings. She always wanted us to grow up to bring blessings and not sorrow. Remember? She called us her blessings."

"That's right," Curtis said. "She used to read something about sending out arrows…"

"Yes," Maggie said. "Children are a heritage of the Lord…"

"So we are supposed to be arrows of blessings?" Isabel said.

"I think so," Eugene said. "Maybe God wants us to each go to different places to be a blessing to someone. He wants us to put into practice the things Mama taught us from God's Word. We can be sad and angry with Papa, or we can decide to be blessings to others and allow God to use our circumstances for His glory. I think Mama would want us to choose to be blessings."

Isabel could tell her brother wanted to say more, but he seemed too choked up to speak. Maggie ran over and hugged her brother with all her might. Jimmy pulled at Eugene's coat and was soon sobbing in his brother's arms. Isabel, Sylvia, and Curtis joined the circle.

"I've never told you this before," Eugene said. "When I followed Mama into the ambulance, she told me that she had a dream—a vision in her heart—for each of us; that we would love the Lord and follow Him all the days of our lives. She asked me to help Papa keep us together and to be a good example to you and to help you remember what she has taught us about the Lord."

Chapter 55

Hope Beyond the Sunset

"MAMA WOULD PROBABLY have a song to sing," Isabel said as she wiped a tear with the handkerchief Mama had embroidered for her. "Wouldn't it be great if we could sing with Mama one more time?"

Then almost as if they had practiced, Eugene and Curtis began to sing, harmonizing beautifully:

> God be with you till we meet again,
> By His counsel guide, uphold you,
> With His sheep securely fold you,
> God be with you till we meet again.

Tearfully, the younger children joined them on the refrain:

> Till we meet, till we meet,
> Till we meet at Jesus' feet;
> Till we meet again, till we meet,
> God be with you till we meet again.

The brothers continued singing, with Maggie singing alto. Sylvia joined in as Isabel listened as if enraptured.

God be with you till we meet again,
'Neath His wings securely hide you,
Daily manna still provide you,
God be with you till we meet again.
God be with you till we meet again,
When life's perils thick confound you,
Put His arms unfailing round you,
God be with you till we meet again.

God be with you till we meet again,
Keep love's banner floating o're you,
Smite death's threat'ning wave before you,
God be with you till we meet again. [9]

Just as they were all about to sing the chorus, the wind started to blow through the trees, causing an eerie howling sound, as though it were singing with them. Billy hid his face in Isabel's shoulder, and Jimmy stood closer to her, as if hiding. They moved closer together in a circle at the foot of Mama's grave and continued singing with the wind as their accompaniment.

Till we meet, till we meet,
Till we meet at Jesus' feet;
Till we meet, till we meet,
God be with you till we meet again.

"It's as if Mama were singing with us," Maggie said. Isabel nodded, feeling the same way.

"We should pray before Papa arrives," Eugene said. The children knelt as they dedicated themselves to the Lord and asked for protection for each other and that the entire Greene family would soon be reunited.

At the end of the prayer, they began to sing, in one accord, the refrain once more. But this time, they had an extra voice to help them—a deeper voice. Isabel looked up to see Papa kneeling with them.

"Children," he said at the end of the refrain, "this is not for always. Lord willing, we shall be together again. This is only temporary. You know I love each of you more than life itself and could not bear to lose you forever. It is my hope that one day soon you will look down the road and see Papa coming to take you home." He picked up Billy into his arms and turned toward the gate leading to the road. "The auto is on the other side of the hill."

The children followed Papa up the long country road. As they crested the hill, the sky was aglow with rose, gold, orange, and red as the sun set brilliantly behind the mountain. The family stood breathlessly, as if they were witnessing the hand of God painting a beautiful masterpiece in the sky.

At last, the spell was broken as Jimmy looked up at Papa with eyes full of wonder and whispered, "Papa, what's beyond the sunset?"

Papa stooped down to Jimmy's level, looked deeply into his eyes, and answered with strength and determination: "Hope."

Hand in hand, they walked toward their glowing future together.

Endnotes

1. Isaiah 64:6
2. Ephesians 2:8–9
3. John 14:6
4. 1 Corinthians 15:3–4
5. Isaiah 1:18
6. 2 Corinthians 5:17
7. Romans 6:9–10
8. Psalms 19:1–3
9. "God Be With You"

Made in the USA
Monee, IL
20 September 2022